ROUGH RIDER

BY
B. J. DANIELS

MILLS & BOON

First Published in Great Britain 2017
By Mills & Boon, an imprint of HarperCollins*Publishers*
1 London Bridge Street, London, SE1 9GF

© 2017 Barbara Heinlein

ISBN: 978-0-263-92922-5

46-1017

B.J. Daniels is a *New York Times* and *USA TODAY* bestselling author. She wrote her first book after a career as an award-winning newspaper journalist and author of thirty-seven published short stories. She lives in Montana with her husband, Parker, and three springer spaniels. When not writing, she quilts, boats and plays tennis. Contact her at www.bjdaniels.com, on Facebook or on Twitter, @bjdanielsauthor.

This book is for Anita Green, who opened a quilt shop in our little town. There is nothing like sitting in her shop after a long day writing and dreaming of new projects—both writing and quilting.

Chapter One

Boone McGraw parked the pickup at the edge of the dark, deserted city street and checked the address again. One look around at the boarded-up old buildings in Butte's uptown and he feared his suspicions had been warranted.

Christmas lights glowed in the valley below. But uptown on what had once been known as the richest hill on earth, there was no sign of the approaching holiday. Shoving back his Stetson, he let out a long sigh. He feared the information the family attorney had allegedly received was either wrong or an attempted con job. It wouldn't be the first time someone had tried to cash in on the family's tragedy.

But he'd promised his father, Travers McGraw, that he would follow up on the lead. Not that he believed for a moment that it was going to help him find Jesse Rose, his sister, who'd been kidnapped from her crib twenty-five years ago.

Boone glanced toward the dilapidated building that reportedly housed Knight Investigations. According to the family's former lawyer, Jim Waters, he'd spoken to a private investigator by the name of Hank Knight a few times on the phone. Knight had asked questions that supposedly had Waters suspecting that the PI knew something more than he was saying. But Waters had never met with the man. All he'd had for Boone to go on was a phone number and an address.

The phone had recently been disconnected and the century-old brick building looked completely abandoned with dusty for-lease signs in most of the windows and just dust in others. No lights burned in the building—not that he'd expected anyone to be working this late.

Boone told himself that he might as well get a motel for the night and come back tomorrow. Not that he expected to find anything here. He was convinced this long trip from Whitehorse to Butte had been a wild-goose chase.

His father had been easy prey for twenty-five years. Desperate to find the missing twins who'd been kidnapped, Travers had appealed to every news outlet. Anyone who'd watched the news or picked up a newspaper over the past twenty-five years knew how desperate he was since each year, the amount of the reward for information had grown.

Boone, suspicious by nature, had been skeptical from the get-go. The family attorney had proven he couldn't be trusted. So why trust information he said he'd gotten? His father hadn't trusted the lawyer for some time—with good reason. He swore under his breath. All he could think about was how disappointed his father was going to be—and not for the first time.

But he'd promised he would track down the PI and follow up on the information no matter what it took. And damn if he wouldn't, he thought as he started his pickup. But before he could pull away, he caught movement out of the corner of his eye. A dark figure had just come around the block and was now moving quickly down the sidewalk. The figure slowed at the building that housed Knight Investigations. He watched as the person slipped in through the only door at the front.

Across the street, Boone shut off the truck's engine and waited. He told himself the person he'd seen could be homeless and merely looking for a place to sleep. It was late and the fall night was clear and cold at this high altitude. Butte sat at 5,538 feet above sea level and often had snow on the ground a good portion of the year.

Boone hunkered in the dark, watching the building until he began to lose patience with himself. This was a waste of his time. The cab of the truck was getting cold. What he needed was a warm bed. A warm meal didn't sound bad, either. He could come back in the morning and—

A light flickered on behind one of the windows on the top floor and began to bob around the room. Someone was up there with a flashlight. He squinted, able to finally make out the lettering on the warbled old glass: Knight Investigations.

He felt his pulse thrum under his skin. It appeared he wasn't the only one interested in Hank Knight.

Chapter Two

Climbing out and locking the rig, Boone headed for the door where he'd seen the figure disappear inside. A sliver of moon hung over the mountains that ringed Butte. Stars twinkled like ice crystals in the midnight blue sky overhead. Boone could see his breath as he crossed the street.

The moment he opened the door, he was hit with the musky scent of the old building. He stopped just inside to listen, but heard nothing. Seeing the out-of-order sign on the ancient elevator, he turned to the door marked Stairs, opened it and saw that a naked bulb dangled from the ceiling giving off dim light. He began to climb, taking three steps at a time.

As he neared the top floor, he slowed and quieted the sound of his boot soles as best he could on the wooden stairs. Pushing open the door marked Fifth Floor, he listened for a moment, then stepped out. A single bulb glowed faintly overhead, another halfway down the long empty hallway.

The building was eerily quiet. No lights shone under any of the doors to his right. To his left, toward the front of the building, he saw that there were four doors.

The last door, where he estimated Knight Investigations should be, was ajar. A faint light glowed from within.

As quietly as possible, he moved down the hall, telling himself maybe Hank had come back for something. Or someone else was looking for something in the detective's office.

He was almost to the doorway when he stopped to listen. Someone was in there banging around, opening and closing metal file cabinet drawers. Definitely searching for something.

Boone leaned around the edge of the doorjamb to look into the office. In the ambient light of the intruder's flashlight, he saw nothing but an old large oak desk, a worn leather chair behind it and a couple of equally worn chairs in front of it. Along the wall were a half dozen file cabinets, most of them open. There seemed to be files strewn everywhere.

With Knight Investigations' phone disconnected, he had assumed Hank had closed down the business. Possibly taken off in a hurry. Now, seeing that the man had even left behind his office furniture as well as file cabinets full of cases, that seemed like a viable explanation. Hank Knight was on the lam.

His pulse jumped at the thought. Was it possible he did know something about Jesse Rose and the kidnapping? Is that why he'd taken off like he apparently had?

Boone couldn't see the intruder—only the flashlight beam low on the other side of the desk. He could hear movement. It sounded as if the intruder was rustling through papers on the floor behind the desk. Looking for something in particular? Or a homeless person just piling up papers to make a fire in the chilly office?

Stepping closer, Boone slowly pushed the door open a little wider. The door creaked. The intruder didn't seem to hear it, but he froze for a moment anyway. For all he knew, the person going through papers on the floor behind the desk could be armed and dangerous—if not crazy and drugged up.

Pushing the door all the way open, he carefully stepped in. He took in the crowded office in the ambient light of the intruder's flashlight beam. The office had clearly been ransacked. Files were all over the floor and desk.

He realized that this intruder hadn't had enough time to make this much of a mess. Someone had already been here. Which meant this new intruder was probably too late for whatever he was searching for. If that's what he was doing hidden on the other side of the desk.

The line of old metal file cabinets along the wall all had their drawers hanging open. In the middle of all this mess, the large old oak desk was almost indistinguishable because of piles of papers, dirty coffee cups and stacks of files.

He moved closer, still unable to see the intruder, who appeared to be busy on the floor behind the large worn leather office chair on the other side of the cluttered desk.

The flashlight beam suddenly stilled. Had the intruder heard him?

Boone reached into his pocket, found his cell phone, but stopped short of calling 911. His family had been in the news for years. If the cops came, so would the media. He swore under his breath and withdrew his hand sans the cell phone.

Boone had a bad feeling that anchored itself in the pit of his stomach. He reminded himself that the person behind that desk might be someone more dangerous than he was in the mood to take on tonight.

He looked around for something he could use as a weapon. He had no desire to play hero. He'd always been smart enough to pick and choose his battles. This wasn't one he wanted to lose for a wild-goose chase. Seeing nothing worthy of being a weapon, he took a step back.

The person on the other side of the desk had stopped making a sound. The beam of the flashlight hadn't moved for a full minute.

He took another step back. The floorboards groaned under his weight. He swore under his breath as suddenly the flashlight beam swooped across the ceiling. The figure shot up from behind the office chair. All he caught was a flash of wild copper-colored hair—and the dull shine of a handgun—before the light blinded him.

Instinctively, he took another step backward. One more and he could dive out into the hallway—

"Take another step and you're a dead man."

He froze at the sound of a woman's voice—and the imminent threat in it. Not to mention the laser dot that had appeared over his heart.

C.J. STARED AT the cowboy standing just inside the door. The gun in her hand never wavered. Nor did the red laser dot pointed at his heart move a fraction of an inch.

He was a big man, broad-shouldered, slim-hipped and rugged-looking. He wore Western attire, including a Stetson as if straight off the ranch.

"Easy," he said, his voice deep and soft, but none-theless threatening. "I'm just here looking for Hank Knight."

"Why?"

He frowned, holding up one hand to shield his eyes from the flashlight she also had on him. "That's be-tween him and me. How about I call the cops so they can ask you why you're ransacking his office." He started to reach into his pocket.

She lowered the flashlight so she was no longer blinding him and shook her head. "I wouldn't do that if I were you," she said, motioning with the gun. "Who are you and why do you want to see Hank?"

"Why should I tell *you*?" She could see that he was taking her measure. He could overpower her easily enough given his size—and hers. But then again, there was that "equalizer" in her hand.

"You should tell me because I have a gun pointed at your heart—and I'm Hank's partner. C.J. West."

He seemed to chew on that for a moment before he said, "Boone McGraw."

She took in the name. "Kidnapping case," she said, more to herself than to him. Fraternal twins, six months old, taken from their cribs over twenty-five years ago. A ransom was paid but the twins were never returned. That was the extent of what she knew and even that was vague. The only reason she knew this was because of something she'd recently seen on television. There'd been an update. One of the kidnappers had been found dead.

"Your partner was looking into the case."

"That's not possible."

"Our lawyer spoke with him on two different occasions, so I'm afraid it definitely happened. So how about lowering the gun?"

Frowning, she considered what he'd said, still skeptical. She and Hank talked about all their cases. It wouldn't have been like him to keep a possible case like this from her.

But she did lower the gun, tucking it into the waistband of her jeans—just in case.

"Thanks. Now, if you could please tell me where I can find him…"

"Day after tomorrow he will be in Rosemont Cemetery."

He'd been looking around the office, but now his gaze shot back to her. *"Cemetery?"*

"He was killed by a hit-and-run driver three days ago." Her voice cracked. It still didn't seem real, but it always came with a wave of grief and pain.

"A *hit-and-run?*"

She wondered if he planned to keep echoing everything she said. She really didn't have time for this.

"Clearly you're too late. Not that Hank could have known anything about the kidnapping case." Picking up one of Hank's files, she shone the flashlight on it and then began to thumb through the yellow notebook pages inside.

Not that she didn't watch Boone McGraw—if that

was really his name—out of the corner of her eye. She'd learned never to take anything at face value. Hank had taught her that and a lot more.

The cowboy swore as he looked around the destroyed office. His expression said he wasn't ready to give up. "If you're his partner then why is the Knight Investigations phone disconnected and this office without electricity?"

"Hank was in the process of retiring. I have my own office in my home. I was taking over the business."

"So you hadn't spoken for a while?" He was guessing, but he'd guessed right.

"We were in transition."

"So you can't be sure he didn't know something about the kidnapping case."

She gritted her teeth. This cowboy was impossible. "Hank would have told me if he knew something about the case. I'm sorry you've wasted your time." She just wanted him to leave so she could get back to what she was doing.

Since Hank's so-called accident, she'd been hard-pressed to hold it together. All that kept her going was her anger and determination to find his killer. She was convinced that one of his cases had gotten him murdered. All she had to do was figure out which one.

The cowboy moved, but only to step deeper into the room. "You said he was killed three days ago? Is that when he returned from his trip?"

"His trip?" Now she was starting to sound like him.

He frowned and jammed his hands on his hips as he looked at her. "My father's lawyer talked to him over two weeks ago. Your partner told him that he was going to be away and would get back to us. When we didn't hear from him…"

She shook her head. "He didn't go anywhere."

"Then why did he lie to our lawyer? Unless he had something to hide?"

C.J. threw down the files in her hands with impatience. "Mr. McGraw—"

"Boone."

"Boone, you didn't know Hank, but I did. He wouldn't have lied."

"Then how do you explain what he told our lawyer?"

She couldn't and that bothered her. She studied the cowboy for a minute. Had Hank gone on a trip—just as he'd told the McGraw lawyer? C.J. thought of how distracted Hank had been the last time she'd seen him. He hadn't mentioned talking to anyone connected to the McGraw kidnapping and for a man who loved to talk about his cases, that was more than unusual.

A case like that didn't come along every day, especially given Knight Investigations' clients. But it also wasn't the kind of case Hank would be interested in. If it was true and he'd called the McGraw lawyer, he must have merely out of curiosity.

She said as much and picked up more files.

"It wasn't idle curiosity." Boone stepped closer until only the large cluttered desk stood between them. He loomed over it. His presence alone could have sucked all the air out of the room. Fortunately, all he did was make her too aware of just how male he was. He didn't intimidate her, not even for a moment. At least that's what she told herself.

"I guess we'll never know, will we?" she said, meeting his steely gaze with one of her hard blue ones.

"If there is even a chance that he knew the whereabouts of my sister, Jesse Rose, then I'm not leaving town until I find out the truth. Starting with whether or not Hank Knight recently left town. It should be easy enough to find out. How much?"

C.J. stared at him. "How much what?"

"How much *money*? I want to hire you."

Chapter Three

Boone was surprised by the young woman's reaction.

"Sorry, but I'm not available." She actually sounded offended.

"Because you're too busy going through dusty old files?"

She looked up from where she was leafing through one and slowly put it down. "The reason my partner is dead is in one of these files. I need to find his killer."

"Wait, I thought it was an accident?"

"That's what the police say, but they're wrong."

He shook his head. He'd run into his share of stubborn women, but this one took the cake. "You seem pretty sure of yourself about a lot of things."

She put her hands on her hips and looked like she could chew nails. "Hank was murdered. I'd stake my life on it."

"If you're right, then there is probably a good chance that's what you're doing."

"He would have done the same for me. Hank... Everyone loved him."

Well, not everyone, but he knew now wasn't the time

to point that out. He could see how hard this was on her and told himself to cut her some slack. But if he had any hope of finding out if Hank Knight had known where his kidnapped sister was, then he needed this woman's help.

"I'm sorry. Apparently the two of you were close," he said, which surprised him since Waters had said Hank Knight was elderly. She'd just said the man was in the process of retiring.

Hank's advancing age could be the reason he had such a young partner. In the ambient glow of the flashlight C.J. didn't even look thirty, though given her confidence, she could have been older. Her long curly hair was the deep, rich color of copper, framing a face flecked with freckles. Both made her brown eyes look wider and more innocent. She had her unruly hair pulled back into a ponytail and wore an old Cubs baseball cap. His father had always been a huge Cubs fan. Boone wondered if Hank had been.

C.J. West was a slight woman but one he knew better than to underestimate. He needed her help because the more he thought about it, the more he felt the answers were here in Butte, here in this office.

"I've known Hank since I was a child playing in this building," she said. "My mother had a job on another floor. I used to hang out with him. He taught me everything I know about the investigative business plus much more. He was like a father to me."

Boone nodded. "I can't imagine how hard this is for you. I hate that I have to add to your problems at a time like this, but let's say you're right and your partner was murdered. Why an old case? Why not the McGraw kidnapping? One of the kidnappers is still at large. If your partner knew something and made inquiries that alerted the kidnapper..."

He was winging it, but he saw that at least she was considering it. Of course, there was also the chance that Hank Knight's death was just an accident. That the man had merely been curious about the McGraw kidnapping case. That all of this was a waste of time.

But Boone had always gone on instinct and right now his instincts told him he had to get this woman to help him. If Hank had been telling the truth and he'd left town, then maybe where he'd gone would lead them to Jesse Rose—and her partner's killer.

ACROSS THE STREET from the Knight Investigations office, Cecil Marks slumped down in his vehicle to watch the office of Knight Investigations. He'd been worried when he'd heard that there might be a break in the kidnapping case. That some private investigator in Butte might know not just where Jesse Rose was, but might also know who was the second kidnapper—the one who'd handed the babies out the window to the man on the ladder.

After twenty-five years, he'd thought for sure that the truth would never come out. Now he wasn't so sure. He'd known that Boone McGraw was like a dog with a bone when it came to not letting go of something. The moment he'd heard about Hank Knight and Knight Investigations, he'd known he had to take care of it.

Once he came to Butte and found out that Hank Knight was retiring, he'd told himself that no one would tie the kidnapping to the old PI.

But unfortunately, he hadn't known about the man's partner. It was her up there now with Boone McGraw. He doubted they would find anything. He hadn't when he'd searched the office, and he'd been thorough. He'd left the place in such a mess, even if he had missed something, he doubted it would turn up now.

It was cold in his truck without the motor running, but he didn't want to call attention to himself. As badly as he wanted to go back to the motel where he was staying, he had to be sure they didn't find anything. Once Boone went back to Whitehorse, he figured he wouldn't have to worry anymore.

He told himself that the little gal partner, C.J. West, wouldn't be searching the office if she knew anything. Also if she knew, he would have heard by now.

She suspected the hit-and-run hadn't been an accident. But there was no proof. Nor did he think the cops were even looking all that hard. He'd seen something on the news and only a footnote in the newspaper. Hank Knight had been a two-bit PI nobody. Look at that heap of an office he worked out of.

He tried to reassure himself that he was in the clear. That nothing would come of any of this. He'd done what he'd had to do and he would do it again. His hands began to shake at the thought, though, of being forced to kill yet another person, especially a woman.

But if she and Boone didn't stop, he'd have no choice.

C.J. HATED TO admit that the cowboy might be right. Before Boone McGraw had walked into this office, she'd been sure Hank's death had something to do with one of his older cases. All of his newer cases that he'd told her about were nothing that could get a man killed—at least she didn't think so.

Now she had to adjust her thinking. Could this be about the kidnapping? Her mind balked because Hank loved nothing better than to talk about his cases. He wouldn't have been able *not* to talk about this one un-less... Unless he did know something, something that he thought could put her in danger...

"Why do you think the hit-and-run wasn't an acci-dent?" the cowboy asked.

It took her a moment to get her thoughts together. "This ransacked office for one. Clearly someone was looking for something in the old files."

"You're that sure it involved a case?"

She waved a hand through the air. "Why tear up the office unless the killer is looking for the case file—and whatever incriminating evidence might be in it?"

He nodded as if that made sense to him. "But if it was here, don't you think that whoever did this took the file with him?"

"Actually, I don't. Look at this place. I'd say the per-son got frustrated when he didn't find it. Otherwise, why trash the place?"

"You have a point. But let's say the file you're look-ing for is about the McGraw kidnapping. It wouldn't be an old file since he called only a few weeks ago. When did he turn off his phone and electricity here at the office?"

C.J. hated to admit that she didn't know. "We've both been busy on separate cases. But he would have told me if he knew anything about the case." He wouldn't have kept something like that from her, she kept telling herself. And yet he hadn't mentioned talking to the McGraw lawyer and her instincts told her that Boone McGraw wasn't lying about that.

That Hank now wouldn't have the opportunity to tell her hit her hard. Hank had been like family, her only family, and now he was gone. And she was only starting to realize how much Hank had been keeping from her.

She had to look away, not wanting Boone to see the shine of tears that burned her eyes. She wouldn't break down. Especially in front of this cowboy.

"If Hank did know something about the case, would he have started a file?" the cowboy asked as he picked up a stack of files from the floor, straightened them and then stacked them on the edge of the desk.

"He would have written something down, I suppose."

"But wouldn't have started a file."

C.J. sighed. "No, but you're assuming a twenty-five-year-old kidnapping is what got him killed. It wasn't the kind of case he worked. Not to mention that Butte is miles from Whitehorse, Montana. The chances that Hank knew anything about the kidnapping or the whereabouts of your sister, Jesse Rose—"

"Are slim. I agree. But I can't discount it. He called our attorney. He knew something or he wouldn't have done that. I don't think he was curious and I don't think you do, either."

She wanted to argue. The cowboy brought that out in her. But she couldn't. "Fine, let's say he did know something."

"So where are his notes?"

C.J. shot him a disbelieving glance as she raised her hands to take in the ransacked room. "Let me just grab them for you."

"I'd be happy to help you look."

"I don't need your help," she said. "For all I know, you're the one who tore the place apart."

"And then came back to confront you and pretend to look for my own file? How clever of me. If I couldn't find it when this place wasn't a mess, why would I think you could now?"

She saw the logic, but hated to admit it. "Or maybe you didn't find what you were looking for and hope that I'll find it for you."

He grinned. "I admire the way your mind works, though I find it a little disturbing."

C.J. bristled. Was he flirting with her?

"You really think I'm the killer cozying up to the partner? Pretty darned gutsy of me." He shook his head. "Hit-and-run is a coward's way of killing. Your killer wouldn't have the guts to come waltzing in here and face you." He had a point. "But don't you want to call the cops and report the break-in before you destroy any more evidence?"

"I ALREADY CALLED THEM."

Boone heard the anger in her voice as he noticed the old photographs framed on the walls. "They weren't helpful?" he asked as he got up to inspect them with the flashlight on his cell phone. The snapshots were of the same man, Hank Knight, no doubt, with a variety of prominent men and women and even a couple of celebrities. From the looks of the photos they were old. Which meant Hank Knight had been doing this for years.

"The local cops, helpful?" C.J. let out a laugh. "They don't believe the hit-and-run was murder because we normally don't take those kinds of cases."

"I would think any kind of case could turn violent under the wrong circumstances," he said, turning from the photographs on the wall. "Look, I'm not leaving town until I get some answers. So what do you say? Let me at least help you look through the files. Other than one on the McGraw kidnapping, what are we looking for?"

She glanced up at him and her gaze softened a little toward him as he took off his coat and rolled up the sleeves of his Western shirt. "Fine. While you're looking for something on the kidnapping, keep an eye out for any recent entries, even in the old files." She showed him what to look for on one of the files. "Hank had his own way of doing things."

"I can see that," Boone said as he scooped up more folders.

"We did work closely. Until recently. I did a lot of the legwork. I have to admit, the last few weeks… I hadn't seen much of Hank."

So, just as he'd guessed, she was looking for a needle in a haystack and had no idea what had gotten her partner killed. He dropped the folders on the desk next to the others and began going through them quickly. "I suppose you know from the news. One of the kidnappers was found. Dead, unfortunately, so one is still out there. But it's put the kidnapping back in the news. More information was released. That's why I assume your partner called. Also my brother Oakley's been found, although that information hasn't been released."

She looked up in obvious surprise. "I thought the man who came forward proved to be a fraud?"

Boone nodded. "Vance Elliot was an impostor, but surprisingly he helped flush out my real biological brother. The news media doesn't know about it because he doesn't want the publicity, which I can't blame him for. In fact, he wants nothing to do with my family. Another reason why I need to find Jesse Rose. Hopefully, *she* won't break our father's heart."

THE NEWS TOOK C.J. by surprise. A son who wanted nothing to do with his family? The subject, though, appeared to be closed as he went back to work. Not that she wasn't curious, but right now she had to find out who had wanted Hank dead.

Sometimes she forgot he was gone. She'd spent so many hours in this office with him growing up... She swallowed the sudden lump in her throat. Hank had meant everything to her. The thought of him being gone... She pushed it away, telling herself she owed it to him to find his killer. That's what she had to focus on right now. Later she would have time for grief, for regrets, for the pain that lay just beneath the surface.

She reached for more files from the floor, her fingers trembling. She stopped to squeeze her hands into fists for a moment. If there was one thing C.J. hated to show, it was any kind of weakness. Maybe especially to a man like Boone McGraw. She could look at the set of his jaw or gaze into those frosty blue eyes and she knew what kind of man he was. Stubbornly strong, like a tree that had lived through everything thrown at it for all its years. Just like Hank.

"It's not here," Boone said after an hour had passed. "Unless your partner didn't write it down. Or if he did, whoever tore up this place took the information with him."

With a sigh, C.J. carried a handful of case files over to one of the cabinets and set them inside just to get them out of the way. Files were everywhere. Then again, this was pretty normal for Hank's office. He'd never been organized. It was one reason they'd never been able to share an office.

She took a moment before she turned to look at Boone McGraw. The cowboy took up a lot of space. The broad shoulders, the towering height—all that maleness culminated into one handsome, cocky cowboy. She bet most women swooned at his feet and was glad she wasn't one of them.

"So we're back to square one," she said, sounding as discouraged as she felt. She'd looked through all of the files, including those that Boone had also looked through. Not only hadn't she found anything about the McGraw kidnapping, she hadn't seen any old case that might have gotten Hank killed.

"Not necessarily," Boone said as he put both palms on the desk and leaned toward her. "Your partner knew something about the kidnapping. Hank Knight asked questions about Jesse Rose and an item that was taken from her crib the night she was kidnapped. His questions led our lawyer to believe Hank had knowledge about the crime and possibly where Jesse Rose is now. I think he got too close to the truth. Too close to the kidnapper's accomplice. And if I'm right then you can help me prove it."

Chapter Four

C.J. pulled up Hank's old leather chair and dropped into it. She was too tired, too wrung out, too filled with grief to take on this cowboy. Nor could she see how she would be able to prove anything.

She pushed a stack of old files out of the way and dropped her elbows to the top of the scarred desk to rest her chin in her hands. She watched Boone McGraw pick up files and put them back into the filing cabinets. He was actually cleaning up the office. The sight would have made her laugh, if she'd had the energy.

What she needed was sleep. She hadn't had a good night's sleep since Hank's death. She doubted she would tonight, but sitting here wasn't helping. As she started to get up, she pushed off the desk only to have the worn top shift under her hands.

With a start she remembered something she'd seen Hank do when he was interrupted by a walk-in. Sitting back, she felt into the crack between the old oak desktop and the even older one beneath it. Hank had loved this desk and hadn't been able to part with it even after one of his cigars had burned the original top badly. Rather than replace it, he'd simply covered it up.

She'd seen files disappear from view only to be retrieved later after a client left. Her fingers brushed against something that felt like the edge of a file folder. She worked it out, her heart leaping up into her throat as she saw the name printed on it in Hank's neat script: McGraw.

"Did you find something?" Boone asked, stopping his organizing to step closer.

She looked up, having forgotten about him for a moment. When had Hank shoved this file into the crack? Who would have walked in that he didn't want them to see it? Her heart began to pound. Until that moment, she had refused to believe that Hank would have taken the McGraw kidnapping case—let alone that it could have anything to do with getting him killed.

C.J. tried to remember the last time she'd stopped by Hank's office. The thousands of times all melted together. Had he ever furtively hidden a file when *she'd* walked in? Had he the last time she saw him alive, just hours before he was struck down and killed?

Her fingers were trembling as she opened the file and saw that there was only one sheet of yellow lined notebook paper—the kind Hank always used. There were also only a few words written on it, several phone numbers and some doodling off to one side. She read the words: "Travers McGraw, Sundown Stallion Station, Whitehorse, Montana. Oakley, Jesse Rose, six months old. Stuffed toy horse. Pink ribbon. Pink grosgrain ribbon."

BOONE HAD SEEN her expression when she'd pulled the manila file folder out from what appeared to be a crack between the new desktop and the old warped one. She'd found something that had made her pale.

"May I?" he asked again.

Silently, C.J. handed over the file, crossed her arms and watched as Boone opened it as if she'd known he was going to be disappointed.

"Where's the rest of it?" he said after looking at the words written on the yellow-lined sheet of paper inside.

"That's all there is."

He could see that she was shaken by what she'd found. Not only had Hank started a file, he'd hidden it. That had to mean something given how the color had drained from her face and how shaken she still looked.

She started around the desk, bumped into him as she stumbled into an unstable stack of files. He caught her, his hands going around her slim waist as she clutched at him for a moment before she got her balance and pulled free. She headed toward a small door he hadn't noticed before. As she opened it, he saw it was a compact bathroom.

Boone turned his attention back to the file as she closed the door. So Hank Knight *had* started a file. But if he'd found out anything, there was no indication of it. Maybe the man didn't know anything about Jesse Rose. Maybe he *was* just curious.

Or maybe not, he realized as he stared at the notes the PI had taken. He'd known about the stuffed toy horse. But he'd also known about the pink ribbon around its neck—something that hadn't been released to the press.

He studied the doodling on the side of the page. Hank had drawn a little girl with chin-length hair. His depiction of Jesse Rose from his imagination? Or his memory? Beside the girl, Hank had drawn what looked like a little dog.

A few moments later, he heard the toilet flush. C.J. came out drying her hands on a paper towel. He studied her for a moment. She seemed different somehow. She looked stronger, more assured. He realized she'd probably used the bathroom to get over the shock of finding the hidden file. But what about it had shaken her? The realization that he could be right?

"Did you ever have a dog?"

She blinked. "I beg your pardon?"

He motioned to the file and the doodle on the side.

"You think that means something? Doesn't every little girl have a dog?"

"Did you?" Boone waited patiently for her to answer.

"No, all right? If you must know, we lived in a building much like this one. The landlord didn't allow dogs."

"Hank doodled a dog. A girl with a dog. So there must be more than this," he said, indicating the file.

She shook her head. "Talk about jumping to wild conclusions." She picked up the flashlight from where she'd left it lying on the desk, the beam lighting most of the room, and shone it on the single sheet in the file.

"Hank had his own system. He numbered the pages in each file, keeping a running tally. It was his idea of organization. If you look on the back of the file, it shows how many papers are in each file. That way you can tell if anything is missing."

"Your partner got his office broken into a lot?" Boone quipped.

"It's the nature of the business," she said offhandedly.

He turned the folder over. There was a one on the back. One sheet of paper inside. He looked up to see her headed for the door. "Wait a minute, where are you going?"

"Home to bed," she said, after picking up three file folders from the desk where she'd stacked them earlier.

"That's all you're taking? Aren't you even going to lock the office door?"

"What's the point?" she said over her shoulder. "If there was anything in here worth stealing, it's long gone now."

Taking the McGraw file, he went after her, catching up to her at the stairs. "Look, Ms. West—"

"C.J." She met his gaze. In the dim light of the naked bulb over the stairs, he noticed her eyes were a rich, warm brown, the same color as his favorite horse. "Yes?"

He realized he'd been staring. At least he had the sense not to voice his thoughts. He doubted she would appreciate her eye color being compared to that of his horse's hide even if it was his favorite. "You should at least have my phone number, don't you think?"

He started to reach for his wallet and his business card, but stopped when she smiled, a rather lopsided smile that showed definite amusement. "I already have it." Reaching into her pocket, she brought out his wallet.

"You picked my pocket?" He couldn't help the indignation in his tone. "What kind of private investigator are you?" he demanded, checking his wallet. His money and credit cards were still there. Now he knew what she'd been doing in the bathroom. All she'd apparently taken was his business card.

When he looked up, he saw pride glittering like fireworks in the rich brown of her eyes. "I'm the kind of PI who doesn't take anything at face value. I'm also the kind who doesn't work with amateurs, so this is where we part company. I'll call if I find out anything about your sister or the kidnapping." With that she turned and disappeared down the stairs.

He caught up with her at the street. "I'm not leaving town. If I have to, I'll dog your every footstep."

"As entertaining as that sounds—"

"I'm serious. I'll stay out of your way, but you can't keep me out of this."

She smiled as if she could and would and climbed into an older-model yellow-and-white VW van. The engine revved. He thought about following her to see where she lived. But he wasn't going to sit outside her residence all night to make sure she didn't give him the slip in the morning. He couldn't force her to help him anymore than he could make her keep him in the loop.

The woman was impossible, he thought as he climbed into his pickup and watched C.J. West drive away. A car a few vehicles away started up and left, as well. He glanced at it as it passed but didn't notice the driver. His mind was on C.J. West.

He knew nothing about her. She, he feared, knew everything about him, or would soon. The entire story of his family's lives for the past twenty-five years was on the internet.

Swearing, he reminded himself what was at stake. He couldn't go home without good news for his father. Hank Knight had started a file. He thought of the brief file now lying on the seat next to him. "Pink ribbon. Pink grosgrain ribbon."

It didn't take much of a mental leap to come up with a pink ribbon since Oakley's horse had a blue ribbon on it. If that information had gotten out, then... But pink grosgrain? Had their attorney Jim Waters released that information to the PI? Or had Hank already known about the toy stuffed horse and the key bit of information about the pink ribbon?

Now more than ever, Boone believed that Hank Knight had known something about the kidnapping. Had maybe even known where Jesse Rose was. Or at least suspected. And it might have gotten him killed.

One way or the other, Boone had no choice. He was staying in Butte and throwing in with this woman whether she liked it or not. He just hoped he wouldn't live to regret it.

Chapter Five

C.J. closed her apartment door and leaned against it for a moment. Tonight, being in Hank's office, she'd felt him as if he was there watching her, urging her on.

Tell me who killed you! she'd wanted to scream.

She hadn't been able to shake the feeling that he'd left behind a clue. Some lead for her to follow that even whoever had ransacked the office wouldn't get, but she would because she and Hank had been so close they could almost read each other's mind.

Until recently. Lately he'd been secretive.

But did it have something to do with the McGraw kidnapping? Just because she'd found the file in Hank's hiding place, it didn't mean it was the last case he was working on. While she and Boone had found a couple of recent case files, neither of them had seemed like something that could get Hank killed. Then again, like Boone had said, any case could turn violent.

She'd tossed the three file folders from fairly recent cases of Hank's on the kitchen table as she'd come into the apartment. Now she moved to them. Other than the McGraw file, there was one labeled Mabel Cross.

Inside, she found a quick abbreviated version of Mabel's problem. The woman suspected that her niece had taken an antique brooch of hers. But she also thought her daughter's husband might have taken it. She had wanted Hank to find it and get it back.

The second file folder was labeled Fred Hanson. His pickup had been vandalized. He was pretty sure it was one of his neighbors since they'd been in a disagreement. He wanted to know which one of them was guilty.

The third case, Susan Roth Turner, suspected her husband might be having an affair.

C.J. sighed. None of those seemed likely to have gotten Hank killed. But she knew better than to rule them out since other than the McGraw file, they were his most recent cases and three of his last ones before he was to retire.

Moving to the refrigerator, she poured herself a glass of red wine and headed for the couch. This was the hardest part of her day. As long as she was busy taking care of all the arrangements for Hank's funeral, tying up loose ends with their business dealings and looking for his killer, she could keep the grief away.

But it was moments like this that it hit her like a tidal wave, drowning her in the pain and regret. Hank had taught her everything about the private eye business from the time she was old enough to see over the top of his big desk. Her mother had worked in the building back in those days and C.J. used to wander the halls, always ending up in Hank's office.

He'd pretended that her visits were a bother, but she'd known he hadn't meant it. He'd started bringing her a treat, an apple, a banana or an orange, saying she should have something healthy. He'd always join her, pushing aside a case file to sit down and talk with her. Even extinguishing his cigar so the smoke didn't bother her.

From the time she was little, she loved listening to him talk about the cases he was working on. He never mentioned names. But he loved discussing them with her. She had seen how much he loved his job, how much he loved helping people. He'd hooked her on the PI business. All she'd ever wanted was to be just like him.

Hank had loved it all, especially solving mysteries that seemed impossible to solve. He was good at his job and often worked for little or nothing, depending on how much his clients could afford.

Sometimes we're all a person has, he used to tell her. *They need help and everyone else has turned them down.*

So how was it that he'd gotten himself killed?

Exhausted, still grief stricken and feeling as if she was in over her head, she wandered into the bedroom to drop onto the bed. She desperately needed sleep, but she picked up her laptop because she had a feeling she hadn't seen the last of Boone McGraw.

Within minutes she was caught up on the latest information that had been released to the press about the twenty-five-year-old kidnapping as well as what she could find out about Boone. The more she read about the kidnapping, the more she worried that he was right and Hank had discovered something about the case that had gotten him killed.

She didn't want to believe it. What could he have

found out that had put him in such danger? She recalled something Boone had said and dug her cell phone out of the back pocket of her jeans.

"Can't sleep?" Boone said in answer to her call.

"You said something earlier about this Vance Elliot turning out not to be Oakley McGraw. He must have had some kind of proof to make you think he was the missing son."

"He had my little brother's stuffed horse."

She lay back on the bed. "What made you think it was the same horse?"

"It had a blue ribbon tied around it and some of the stitching was missing. Oakley never slept without it in his crib."

"So how did he just happen to have this horse, if he wasn't the real Oakley McGraw?"

"It's a long story, but basically, someone had picked up the horse as a souvenir at the crime scene and later decided to use it to get money out of my father."

"So you have no idea who in the house helped the kidnapper take the twins? What about the nanny who became your stepmother? She seems the perfect suspect. I just read that she might be released from jail until her trial for attempted murder."

"Suspect, yes. But for trying to kill my father, not for the kidnapping."

Exhaustion pulled at her. She could hardly keep her eyes open. "So they were fraternal twins, right? Six months old." She was thinking of what Hank had written in the file. "I'm assuming your sister also had a stuffed horse toy in her crib that was taken that night? One with a pink ribbon."

"Yes."

She closed her eyes, seeing the yellow lined paper and the words *pink ribbon* written in Hank's even script. *Pink grosgrain ribbon.* "Was there anything about the ribbon around its neck released to the media?"

"No. There was nothing about it being a pink *grosgrain* ribbon."

"That's the kind that has the ridges, right? The lawyer must have mentioned it to Hank—"

"I'm sure he provided information about the kidnapping to Knight Investigations, but not that," Boone said. "Hank knew something before he made the call. Otherwise why would he have contacted our family lawyer with questions about Jesse Rose?"

Good question. Unfortunately, C.J. had no idea. But her gut instinct told her that Boone was right. Hank had already known all about the kidnapping twenty-five years ago. For some reason, he had followed the case closely all these years.

But if he'd kept anything in writing, she hadn't found it. Yet.

"I'm going to the police station in the morning to find out more about Hank's death," Boone said.

"Good luck with that." She hung up and rolled over, too tired to get undressed. And yet her thoughts refused to let her sleep.

Was there more information Hank had hidden somewhere? Why wasn't the information in the file? Because he knew enough to know he was in danger?

If this was about the McGraw kidnapping, had Hank gotten too close to the truth? But wouldn't that mean that he had inside knowledge? Wasn't the fear that Hank had inside information and that was what had her running scared now?

She rolled over on her back and stared up at the ceiling, her mind racing. Had Hank already known about the pink ribbon? Or had the attorney told him? Either way, Hank had written it down. He'd also told the attorney that he had to go out of town. But he hadn't. Or had he?

She thought of Boone McGraw. He'd seen the words *pink grosgrain ribbon* in Hank's scrawl. He'd known then that Hank knew more than he had told the lawyer. Why hadn't the cowboy said something then?

Because he was holding out on her. Just like she was on him.

She felt a shiver and pulled the quilt over her. If Hank had known where to find Jesse Rose, then he would have told the McGraw lawyer, she told herself. Unless…unless he had something to hide.

Her eyes felt as if someone had kicked sand into them. She closed them and dropped like a stone into a bottomless well of dark, troubled sleep.

THE NEXT MORNING, Boone stopped by the police station and after waiting twenty minutes, was led to a Detective Branson's desk. The man sitting behind it could have been a banker. He wore a suit, tie and wire-rimmed glasses. He looked nothing like a cop, let alone a detective.

As Boone took a seat, he said, "I'm Boone—"

"McGraw. Son of Travers McGraw. I know. You told my desk clerk. That's why you're sitting where you are when I'm so busy."

He was used to his father's name opening doors. "I'm inquiring about a private investigator by the name of—"

"Hank Knight. He's dead." He looked back at the stack of papers on his desk, then up again. He seemed surprised Boone was still sitting there.

"Can you tell me under what circumstance—"

"Hit-and-run. Given the time of night, not that surprising, and in front of a bar." The cop shrugged as if it happened all the time.

Boone could see why C.J. hadn't been happy after talking to the cops. "So you think it was an accident?"

Branson leaned back in his chair, his expression one of tired impatience even this early in the morning. "What else?"

"Murder."

The detective laughed. "Obviously you didn't know Hank or you wouldn't even ask that question. Hit-and-run accident. Case closed."

"Surely you're investigating it."

"Of course," Branson said. "Right along with all the other crimes that go on in this city. Why the interest?"

Boone could see that the hit-and-run was low priority. He thought about mentioning the kidnapping case. For twenty-five years anyone who heard the name would instantly tie it to the kidnapping. It had been a noose around his neck from the age of five.

"His partner believes it was murder."

"C.J. West?" He sneered as if that also answered his earlier question. The detective thought this was about him and the private eye?

"She has reason to believe it wasn't an accident," he said.

"PIs," Branson said and shook his head. "They just want to be cops. Trust me, it was an accident. So unless you know different, I have to be in court in twenty minutes…"

The detective went back to his paperwork. Boone rose. On his way out the door, he called C.J. on the number she'd called him from last night. "You were right about the cops."

"You doubted me?"

"My mistake." He could hear traffic sounds in the background on her end of the line.

"Think you can find the Greasy Spoon Café around the corner from the cop shop?" she asked.

Chapter Six

"You call this breakfast?" Boone McGraw said as he looked down at his plate thirty minutes later.

He'd had no trouble finding the small hole-in-the-wall café. This part of uptown Butte hung onto the side of a mountain with steep streets and over hundred-year-old brick buildings, many of them empty. The town's heyday had been in the early 1920s when it was the largest city west of the Mississippi. It had rivaled New York and Chicago. But those days were only a distant memory except for the ornate architecture.

"They're pasties," C.J. said of the meat turnover smothered with gravy congealing on his plate. "Butte is famous for them." She took another bite, chewing with obvious enjoyment. "Back when Butte mining was booming, workers came from around the world. Immigrants from Cornwall needed something easy to eat in the mines." She pointed at the pasty with her fork. "The other delicacy Butte takes credit for is the boneless deep-fat-fried pork chop sandwich."

"Butte residents don't live long, I would imagine," he quipped. "When in Butte, Montana…" He poked at the pasty lying under the gravy. It appeared to have meat and small pieces of potato inside. He took a tentative bite. It wasn't bad. It just wasn't what he considered breakfast.

He watched her put away hers. The woman had a good appetite, not that it showed on her figure. She was slightly built and slim but nicely rounded in all the right places, he couldn't help but notice. She ate with enthusiasm, something he found refreshing.

As he took another bite of his pasty, he studied her, trying to get a handle on who he was dealing with. There was something completely unpretentious about her, from her lack of makeup to the simple jean skirt, leggings, sweater and calf-high boots she wore. Her copper-red hair was pulled back in a loose braid that trailed down her back.

She looked more like an elementary school teacher than a private investigator. Because she was so slight in stature it was almost deceiving. But her confidence and determination would have made any man think twice before taking her on. Not to mention the gun he suspected was weighing down the shoulder bag she had on the chair next to her.

"What does the 'C.J.' stand for?" he asked between bites.

She wrinkled her nose and, for a moment, he thought she wasn't going to tell him. "Calamity Jane," she said with a sigh. "My father was a huge fan of Western history apparently."

"You never knew him?"

With a shake of her head, she said, "He died when I was two."

"Is your mother still…?"

"She passed away years ago."

"I'm sorry."

"Hank was my family." Her voice broke. Eyes shiny with tears, she looked away for a moment before returning to her breakfast. He did the same.

A few minutes later, she scraped the last bite of gravy and crust up, ate it and pushed her plate away. Elbows on the table, she leaned toward him and dropped her voice, even though the café was so noisy, he doubted anyone could hear their conversation where they sat near the doorway.

Her brown eyes, he noticed, were wide and flecked with gold. A faint sprinkling of freckles dotted her nose and her cheekbones. He had the urge to count them for no good reason other than to avoid the intensity of those brown eyes. It was as if she could see into him a lot deeper than he let anyone go, especially a woman.

"Tell me more about the kidnapping case," she said, giving him her full attention. "Don't leave anything out."

He took a drink of his coffee to collect his errant thoughts and carefully set down the mug. Last night she'd been so sure that the kidnapping case couldn't be what had gotten her partner killed. He wondered what had changed her mind—if that was the case.

"We all lived on the Sundown Stallion Station ranch, where my father raised horses. I was five. My older brother, Cull, was seven, Ledger was three. We had a nanny—"

"Patricia Owen, later McGraw after she became your father's second wife and allegedly tried to kill him," she said.

He nodded. "Patty stayed across the hall from the nursery. She heard a noise or something woke her. Anyway, according to her, she went to check on the twins and found them missing. When she saw the window open and a ladder leaning against the outside of the house, she started screaming and woke everyone up. The sheriff was called, then the FBI. A day later there was a ransom demand made. My father sold our prized colt to raise the money."

"Why wasn't the kidnapper caught when the ransom was paid?" she asked.

"The drop was made in a public place, but a fire broke out in a building close by. Suddenly the street was filled with fire trucks. In the confusion, somehow the kidnapper got away with the money without being seen."

She shook her head. "Who made the drop?"

"The family attorney, Jim Waters."

C.J. raised a brow. "Isn't he the one who was also arrested trying to leave the country with a bunch of money and has also been implicated in your father's poisoning?"

Boone nodded, seeing that she knew a lot more than she was letting on. "But so far no charges have been filed against him in the poisoning and there is no proof he was involved in the kidnapping. We now know that

Harold Cline, a boyfriend of our cook, climbed the ladder that night and got away with the twins. The person who hasn't been found is the one who it is believed administered codeine cough syrup to the twins to keep them quiet during the ordeal and passed them out the window to the first kidnapper."

"What about the broken rung on the ladder?" she asked.

"It was speculated that the kidnapper might have fallen or dropped the babies, but we now know that didn't happen. The babies were alive and fine when they were found by our family cook and taken to—"

"The Whitehorse Sewing Circle member Pearl Cavanaugh. Wasn't she or her mother the one who started the illegal adoptions through this quilt group years ago?"

C.J. had definitely done her homework. He figured she must have been up before daylight. Either that or she had known more about the case than she'd led him to believe last night.

"That's right. Unfortunately, they're pretty much all dead, including Pearl."

"So there is no record of what happened to the twins," she said and picked up her coffee mug, holding it in both hands as she slowly took a sip.

"In light of what we learned from our family cook before she died, the babies probably went to parents who couldn't have children and were desperate," he said.

"I can't imagine how they couldn't have known about ... g. So in their desperation, they pretended not to know that the child they were adopting was a McGraw baby? Didn't Oakley's and Jesse Rose's photos run nationally? So no one could have missed seeing them."

He nodded. "It makes sense that whoever got each of the twins knew. We've been led to believe that the adoptive parents were told the twins weren't safe in our house."

She put down her cup, her brown-eyed gaze lifting to his. "Because of your mother's condition."

He thought of his mother in the mental ward, the vacant stare in her green eyes as she rocked with two dolls clutched in her arms. "We now believe that her condition was the result of arsenic poisoning. It causes—"

"Confusion, memory loss, depression... The same symptoms your father was experiencing before his heart attack. Patty's doing is the assumption? So you're saying your mother probably wasn't involved."

He met her gaze and shrugged. "In her state of mind at the time of the kidnapping, who knows? But she definitely didn't run down your partner. She's still in the mental ward. And neither did Patty, who is still behind bars."

C.J. bit at her lower lip for a moment. He couldn't help noticing her mouth, the full bow-shaped lips, the even white teeth, just the teasing tip of her pink tongue before he dragged his gaze away. This snip of a woman could be damned distracting.

"You said Oakley has been found?"

That wasn't information she could have found on the internet. "He has refused to take a DNA test, but my father is convinced that the cowboy is Oakley. He owns a ranch in the area. Apparently he's known the truth for years, but didn't want to get his folks into trouble. They've passed now, but he still isn't interested in coming out as the infamous missing twin. Nor does he have an interest in being a McGraw."

She raised a brow. "That must be both surprising and disappointing if it's true and he's your brother."

"It's harder on my father than the rest of us. He's been through so much. All he wants is his family together."

She said nothing, but her eyes filled before she looked down as the waitress came over to refill their coffee cups.

C.J. STUDIED BOONE while he was distracted with the waitress refilling his cup. She'd known her share of cowboys since this was Montana—Butte to be exact. Cowboys were always wandering in off the range—and usually getting into trouble and needing either a private investigator or a bail bondsman. She and Hank had been both.

But this cowboy seemed different. He'd been through a lot because of the kidnapping. He wasn't the kind of man a person could get close to. Last night she'd noticed that he didn't wear a wedding ring. This morning online, she'd discovered that only one of the McGraw sons, Ledger, the youngest one, had made the walk to the altar.

"You drove a long way yesterday," she said after a few moments. "Seems strange if all you had to go on was Hank asking a few questions about the kidnapping and Jesse Rose."

He pushed away his plate, his pasty only half-eaten. "I quizzed the attorney when he told me about the private investigator calling. Truthfully, I figured this whole trip would turn out to be a wild-goose chase."

"So why are you here?"

"Because my father asked me and because our attorney said that Hank Knight sounded…worried."

Her pulse quickened. *"Worried?"*

Boone met her gaze with his ice-blue one. "I think he knew something. I think that's why he's dead." When she didn't argue the point, he continued. "From what you found last night, we know that he knew more about the ribbon on the stuffed toy horse than has been released."

"Why would he keep that information to himself?" she asked more to herself than to him.

"Good question. He told our attorney that he had to take a trip and would be out of town," Boone reminded her. "Makes sense he'd want to verify what he was worried about, doesn't it?"

It did. "Except I don't think he left town."

"Or maybe he had a good reason not to want me following up on it."

She bristled. "Hank was the most honest man I've ever known. If he knew where Jesse Rose was, he would have told your family."

"Maybe. Unless someone stopped him first."

Chapter Seven

After he paid the bill, they stepped outside the café. The morning air had a bite to it although the sky was a cloudless blue overhead. He was glad he'd grabbed his sheepskin-lined leather coat before he'd left home. Plowed dirty snow melted in the gutters from the last storm. Christmas wasn't that far off. There was no way Butte wouldn't have a white Christmas.

"What do you know about Butte?" C.J. asked as she started to walk up the steep sidewalk.

He shook his head as he followed her, wondering why she'd called him. Was she going to help him find out the truth? Or was she just stringing him along?

"What most Montanans know, I guess. It's an old copper mining boomtown and we're standing on what became known as the Richest Hill on Earth," he said. "It is now home to the Berkeley Pit, the most costly of the largest Superfund sites and a huge hole full of deadly water."

He saw that she didn't like him talking negatively about her hometown and realized he would have taken

exception if she'd said anything negative about Whitehorse, too.

"Why are you asking me about Butte? What does
this have to do with Hank or—"

"Butte was one of the largest and most notorious copper boomtowns in the West with hundreds of saloons
and a famous red-light district."

Butte hadn't lived down its reputation as a rough,
wide-open town. He'd heard stories about the city's famous red-light and saloon district called the Copper
Block on Mercury Street. Many of the buildings that
had once housed the elegant bordellos still stood.

"The first mines here were gold and silver—and underground," she continued. "They say there is a network
of old mine tunnels like a honeycomb under the city."

"Where are you going with this, C.J.?"

"Hank loved this town and he knew it like the back
of his hand."

Boone often wondered how many people actually
knew the back of their hand well, but he didn't say so.
"Your point?"

"He believed in helping people. Often those people
couldn't pay for his services, but that never stopped him.
You've seen his office. He wouldn't have been interested
in your family kidnapping case. It wasn't something he
would have taken on."

"Then how do you explain the fact that he knew
about the ribbon?"

"Maybe the attorney told him. Look, there was only
one sheet of paper in the file. Hank might have been curious given the latest information that's come out about

the kidnapping. But he wouldn't have pursued it. Which means if not an older case, then one of his more recent ones has to be what got him killed. I need to investigate those. I'm sure you have better things to do—"

He didn't believe her. All his instincts told him that she wanted him to believe Hank hadn't known anything about the kidnapping. She was scared that he had. And maybe even more afraid because he hadn't told her.

So she was going to chase a few of Hank's last cases? He'd seen her take three files last night. "Fine, but you aren't getting rid of me, because once you exhaust your theory, we're going to get serious and find out what Hank knew about the McGraw kidnapping and Jesse Rose."

"Fine, suit yourself. I'm going to visit Mabel Cross and see if her brooch has turned up."

Boone shook his head. "Seriously?"

"As Hank used to say, there are no unimportant cases." She headed for her VW van. He cursed under his breath, but followed and climbed in the passenger side. She was wasting her time and his. But he needed her help and antagonizing her wasn't going to get him anywhere, he told himself as he climbed into the passenger seat of her van.

"So we're going to pay a visit to these people?" he asked, picking up the three case files she'd taken from Hank's office last night as she slid behind the wheel. "Tell me we aren't going underground." He didn't want to admit that one of his fears was being trapped underground. The idea of some old mine shaft turned his blood to ice.

She laughed. "I'm afraid we are. So to speak," C.J. said and started the engine.

The buildings they passed were old, most of them made of brick or stone with lots of gingerbread ornamentation. He recalled that German bricklayers had rushed to Butte during its heyday from the late 1800s to the early 1920s.

Nothing about Butte, Montana, let you forget it had been a famous mining town—and still was, he thought as they passed streets with names like Granite, Quartz, Aluminum, Copper—and Caledonia.

As she drove C.J. waved or nodded to people they passed. He couldn't tell if she was just friendly or knew everyone in town. On Iron Street, she pulled to the curb, cut the engine and climbed out. As she headed for an old pink-and-purple Victorian, he decided he might as well go with her.

Glancing around the neighborhood, he took in the historical homes and tried to imagine this city back in 1920. From photos he'd seen, the streets had swarmed with elegantly dressed residents. Quite a contrast to the homeless he'd seen now in doorways.

C.J. was already to the door and had knocked by the time he climbed the steps to the porch. The door opened and he looked up to find an elderly woman leaning on a cane. "Mrs. Cross," C.J. said. "I'm Hank Knight's associate."

"Hank." The woman's free hand went to her mouth. "So tragic. If you're here about his funeral—"

"No, I'm inquiring about your brooch. I wanted to be sure Hank had found it before—"

"Oh yes, dear," she said and touched an ugly lion studded with rhinestones pinned to her sweater. "Silly me. I feel so badly now to have thought my niece or my daughter's husband might have taken it and all the time it was on this sweater in the closet. I told Hank. I suppose he didn't get a chance to tell you before… He was so loved." She sniffed. "You'll be at his funeral, I assume."

"Of course. I'm just glad you found your brooch." C.J. turned and headed for the van.

Boone wanted to point out what a waste of time that had been, but one look at her face when she climbed behind the wheel and he bit his tongue. "When is the funeral?"

"Tomorrow afternoon." She started the van, biting at her lower lip as if to stanch the tears that brimmed in her eyes.

As she pulled out on the street, he saw her glance in the rearview mirror and then make a quick turn down a side street. "So do we check on these other two cases?" he asked picking up the file folders.

"I already called Fred Hanson this morning. Hank got the neighbor to admit he did it and pay restitution."

Boone couldn't help being impressed. Who had this Hank Knight been to have such a devoted following, including C.J. herself?

"I also drove by the Turner house earlier this morning."

"The cheating husband case," he said.

"The husband's clothing was in the yard."

"Another case solved by Hank Knight. So are you

ready to accept that he might have been involved in my family's case?"

She said nothing. On Mercury Street, she stopped in front of a large redbrick building and, cutting the engine, climbed out.

"The Dumas Brothel?" he asked, seeing the visitor sign in the window as he hurried after her.

"One of Hank's best friends works here," she said as she opened the door and stepped in.

He followed, wondering if she wasn't leading him on a wild-goose chase this morning, hoping he'd give up and leave town.

It was cool and dimly lit inside the brothel museum. The older woman who appeared took one look at C.J. and disappeared into the back. Surely C.J. didn't plan on taking him on a tour.

But before he could ask, she turned and went to the front window. He could see her pain just below the surface and reminded himself that her partner had been killed only days ago. He didn't kid himself when it came to her priorities. She was looking for Hank's murderer—not Jesse Rose.

But if he was right, then it would lead them to the same place.

As he studied her, he couldn't help but wonder what she would do when she found the murderer.

An elderly man came into the room and C.J. turned and said, "Can we go out the back?"

Without a word, the man led them through the building and the next thing Boone knew, he was standing in a narrow alley surrounded by tall old brick buildings.

"What was that all about?" he demanded. He had expected her to at least ask the man about her partner or his death.

"Someone's following us," she said as she led him into another building, this one apparently abandoned. A few moments later, they spilled out into a dark narrow alley. "This way."

Boone followed her through the alley between two towering old brick buildings before she dropped down some short stairs and ducked into a doorway. He stopped to look back and saw no one.

"Come on," she called impatiently to him.

He hurried down the steps as she opened a door with a key and he followed her inside another musty building. "Calamity—"

"C.J.," she snapped over her shoulder as she took a set of stairs that led upward. Only a little light filtered through the warbled old dust-coated windows as they climbed.

Four floors up, she stopped. He noticed that she wasn't even breathing hard although she'd scaled the stairs two at a time as if they really were being chased. Now, though, she moved across the landing to a door marked Fourth Floor. Motioning for him to be quiet, she opened it a crack and looked out.

Boone couldn't help but think she was putting him on. All this cloak-and-dagger stuff. Was it really necessary?

She motioned for him to follow her as she finally pushed open the door and headed down the long hallway, stopping short at the last door. From her bag, she pulled out a set of keys, pushed one into the lock and then seemed to hesitate.

"What?" he whispered, even though all the doors along the hallway were closed and he could hear nothing but the beat of his own heart.

C.J. shook her head, turned the key and pushed open the door. It didn't connect until that moment where they were and why she'd been hesitant to enter.

Past her he could see what appeared by the decor to be a man's apartment. There was a photo on one wall of a middle-aged Hank Knight and C.J. when she was about eight and had pigtails. Both Hank and C.J. were smiling at the camera. "You haven't been here since he was killed."

"No." She stepped in and, after a furtive glance down the hall, he followed, closing and locking the door behind them.

Chapter Eight

The first thing that hit her in Hank's apartment was the scent of cigar smoke. It lingered even though he'd quit smoking them some years ago. At work, he had taken up sucking on lemon drops. She'd often wondered if he'd done that for her because of how often she would end up at his office visiting with him about their cases.

Tears stung her eyes. She drew on her strength as she looked around the room. The door opened to a small kitchen and dining room. Past it was the living room, a dark curtain drawn over the only window. Beyond that was the bedroom and bath.

She'd only been here one other time. "I doubt there is anything here to find, but we can look." She hated that she'd brought Boone. But if the McGraw kidnapping had gotten Hank killed…

"I would think this is the logical place for your partner to keep information he possibly didn't want you or anyone else to see," Boone said, stepping past her and deeper into the apartment. "I meant to ask you last night. He didn't use a computer?"

"No." She glanced toward the kitchen sink. One lone

cup sat on the faded porcelain. An old-fashioned brew coffeepot sat on one of the four burners on the stove. A half-eaten loaf of bread perched on an ancient toaster.

She moved to the refrigerator and opened the door to peer inside. A plate with a quarter stick of butter sat next to a half-empty jar of peach jam, Hank's favorite. The jam and butter shared space with two Great Falls Select cans of beer. Other than containers of mustard, ketchup and mayonnaise, there was a jar of dill pickles and one of green olives.

Closing the door, she felt Boone's impatient gaze on her.

"What are you looking for? Don't tell me you're hungry again," he said. Out of the corner of her eye, she saw him reach down to go through some magazines on the coffee table in front of the worn couch.

She didn't answer as she checked the garbage. Empty except for a clean bag. The Hank she knew was far from neat. The other time she'd been here, the garbage had been near full and there'd been toast crumbs on the counter, the butter dish next to them. Was Boone right about Hank either just coming back from somewhere— or getting ready to go somewhere?

"I think you'd better come see this," Boone called from the bedroom.

C.J. headed in that direction, half-afraid of what he'd found. When she looked through the door, she saw a beat-up brown suitcase open on the bed half-full of clothing. Stepping closer, she saw that Hank had packed two pairs of slacks and his best shirts.

She quickly glanced toward the closet, suddenly worried that he had planned to be gone longer than a few days. But most of his clothing was still hanging in the closet.

"What do you make of this?" Boone asked, eyeing her openly.

"He was either leaving or had just come back. His refrigerator is nearly empty and everything is cleaned up."

"So what he told my family lawyer might be true. He'd gone somewhere. To visit family?"

She shook her head. "He didn't have any family that I knew of." On top of that, Hank had hated to travel. In all the time she'd known him he'd left Butte only a couple times a year and always on a case—or so he had led her to believe. That she doubted his honesty now made her feel sick to her stomach.

She stepped to the suitcase to run her fingers along the fabric of one of the shirts. It was a gray-and-white-striped one she'd bought him for Christmas last year. He only wore it for special occasions. So what was the special occasion?

And why had he kept it from her?

BOONE COULD SEE C.J.'s confusion and hurt. Whatever her partner had been up to, he hadn't shared it with her. "I don't see a phone and he'd had the one at his office disconnected. I can see living off the grid, but…"

C.J. seemed to stir. Before that, she'd been staring into the suitcase, her thoughts dark from the frown that marred her girl-next-door-adorable face. "He recently bought a cell phone." Her frown deepened. "It wasn't found on his body."

Boone's pulse kicked up. "Was it possible someone took it off his body?"

Her brown eyes widened. "You mean someone in the crowd that must have gathered outside the bar?"

"We should search the rest of the apartment," Boone said, seeing how hard it was for her to keep her emotions at bay. He looked through drawers in the bedroom while she searched the bathroom and the living room.

"Something else is bothering me," he said when he found her going through a pile of old mail. "How was he planning to travel? I went through the suitcase but there wasn't a plane ticket in there. I suppose it could be an e-ticket on his phone."

She shook her head. "Hank wouldn't have flown. He always said that if God had wanted us to fly, He would have given us wings. He must have driven or been planning to."

"Where's his car?"

C.J. HAD BEEN so upset and busy with funeral arrangements and everything else that she hadn't been thinking clearly. It explained why she hadn't sent this cowboy packing. Like she'd told him last night, she didn't need or want his help. At least the latter was true.

"I hadn't even thought about his car. I just assumed that he'd walked down to the bar from here," she said. "He was hit in front of the bar. Now that I think about it, I didn't see his car parked where he usually leaves it."

"I think we should find it. What does he drive?" Boone asked as they left the apartment via the fire escape and ended up in another alley. The wind had picked up and now blew between the buildings, icy cold. A weak December sun did little to chase away the chill.

"A '77 Olds 88, blue with a white top."

"So where is this bar?"

"Not far." She thought of the bar owner and realized she should have gone to see him before this. Natty would be as upset by all this as her. But then Hank had had so many friends.

A few blocks later, they entered the rear of the bar and she braced herself. This had been Hank's favorite bar. When he'd walk in the door, there would be a roar of greetings. Everyone had wanted to shake his hand and buy him a drink. But, never one to overindulge, he'd merely thank them and say he wasn't staying long.

As she started toward the front of the bar, C.J. half expected to see Hank on one of the stools. She thought of his face lighting up when he saw her and had to swallow back the lump in her throat and surreptitiously wipe her tears.

BOONE CAUGHT THE smell of stale beer and floor cleaner—like every Montana bar he'd ever been in. He'd grown to love the feel of them in college, but had been too busy on the ranch to spend much time on a barstool.

They went down a short hallway that opened into a dark room with a pool table. Ahead of them, he spotted a row of mostly empty stools pulled up to a thick slab of a bar. Only a little light filtered in through a stained-glass window, illuminating a scarred linoleum floor and a half dozen tables with empty chairs pulled up to them.

Following the sound of clinking glasses and the drone of a television, they reached the bar.

"What do you have against front doors?" Boone asked as C.J. headed for the bearlike man washing glasses behind the bar. When the grizzly bartender saw her, he quickly dried his hands and hurried around to draw her into a hug.

"How ya doin', sweetheart?" the man asked in a gravelly voice.

"Okay," C.J. answered. "I do have some questions, though, Natty."

The man called to one of the customers at the bar to hold down the fort and ushered them into an office down the hallway where they'd come in. Natty shot Boone a look, but C.J. didn't introduce either of them. On the wall, though, was a liquor license in the name of Nathaniel Blake.

"Did you see what happened or did anyone else we know?" she asked.

The man shook his head. "We just heard it. A couple of fellas went out to see what was going on." He looked as if he might cry. "I couldn't believe it."

"Did you talk to him before that?" she asked, her voice cracking a little. "I thought he might have mentioned where he was going."

Natty nodded. "I was surprised he was leaving again. He'd just gotten back. But he said he'd be gone for a few days and I knew what to do."

Boone saw her surprise and wondered at the man's words—*and I knew what to do.*

"Natty, he didn't tell me he'd left or that he was leaving again." She sounded close to tears and he wasn't the only one who heard it.

The big man put a hand on her shoulder. "He didn't tell me anything about it. But he hadn't looked happy about either trip. I wish I knew more. Whatever was going on with him, he wasn't saying."

She nodded. "You haven't seen his car, have you?"

"Matter of fact, it was parked across the street. I didn't think anything about it until I saw it being hauled off by the city. I would imagine it's down at the yard. Sorry, I should have called you, but I figured you had your hands full as it was."

She nodded. More sorry than the man could know, Boone thought. Everyone thought Hank's hit-and-run had been an accident. Everyone but his partner.

"I knew it was just a matter of time before you came by." He reached behind him, dug in a drawer for a moment and came out with an envelope. "I've been hanging on to this for you. Hank left it and said if anything should happen to him… I just thought it was because he was flying somewhere. You know how he felt about flying."

So he'd taken a flight. Boone could see that the news had astonished C.J.

"This last time, he said he was leaving town for a while and didn't know when he'd be back, but I got the feeling he didn't think he was coming back. You think he knew?"

Knew that someone might try to kill him? Maybe, since he'd been in so much trouble that he hadn't wanted to share it with his partner, Boone thought.

Natty handed her the envelope. Even from where he

stood, Boone could see that all it seemed to hold was a key. She undid the flap and took out the key. He saw that her fingers were trembling. There was a number printed on the key. 1171. He felt his pulse jump. Was this where Hank had hidden the information Boone desperately needed?

"You have any idea what that key opens?" Boone asked, worried that she might not.

Actually she did know, as it turned out. "It's to one of the lockers at the bus station."

His cell phone rang. He saw it was his brother Cull calling. "I need to take this. You won't—"

"I'll wait for you," she said, clearly upset from the news Natty had given her—and maybe the key, as well?

He stepped out of the office, but stayed where he could watch in case she tried to give him the slip. It wasn't that he didn't trust her... Oh, who was he kidding?

"Hello?"

"I was hoping we'd hear from you by now," his brother Cull said on the other end of the line.

"Afraid I haven't had much to report. It's been...interesting," Boone said.

"I know you didn't think much of Jim Waters's tip—"

"Actually, I'm beginning to think that there was something to it." He quickly told his brother about Hank Knight having been killed by a hit-and-run driver. "I'm hoping he left behind some information. It's why I'm working with Hank's partner to try to find it. What's that noise in the background?"

"Tilly vacuuming," Cull said, raising his voice to be heard. "Let me step into Dad's office."

"*Tilly*? I saw her the other day as I was leaving, but I thought she'd just come by to visit. Didn't she quit when Patty was arrested?"

"Yep," Cull said, the sound of the vacuum dying in the distance as his brother closed the office door. "Dad gave her a nice severance package for all the years she was our housekeeper, but apparently either it didn't last or she missed us."

"More than likely it's the new house," Boone said. "She always thought that the old one was haunted. I'm not surprised Dad took her back, though. I just hope she didn't let her ex get hold of her severance money. He kept her broke all the time. It was one thing after another with that guy."

"I doubt Tilly would want anything to do with him. When she needed him the most he ended up in the hospital after getting drunk and wrecking their car."

"Poor Tilly. I hope you're right about her being back because of the new ghost-less house."

"No ghosts yet anyway," Boone said under his breath.

"So what is this partner like? Does he think Hank's death had something to do with the kidnapping and Jesse Rose?"

"Not exactly. She's been skeptical at best but—"

"*She?*"

Just then C.J. came out of Natty's office saying her goodbyes.

"Is that her? She sounds *young*."

Boone wasn't about to take the bait. "I'll call you as soon as I know something." He disconnected and followed C.J. out the back way of the bar again.

THEY WALKED THE few blocks to the bus station. A cold wind blew between the buildings. They passed a homeless man playing a pink kid's guitar. C.J. dropped a few dollars into the man's worn cowboy hat and he promised to play a song just for her.

After a few chords, they moved on, only to pass other homeless people who C.J. called by name. Each time, she gave them a few dollars and wished them well. Boone found himself enchanted with her generous spirit. Whitehorse didn't have homeless. Sure, a few passed through, spending a night in one of the churches, being fed by locals, but then they were on the road again.

The bus station was empty. Not even any buses in the enclosed cavernous parking area. The lobby had a dozen empty chairs. Past it were the restrooms and finally a hallway filled with old metal lockers.

"Why would Hank leave something here for you?" Boone asked. She had recognized the key so she'd either been here before or—

"When I was a girl, it was a game we played," she said as she pulled the key from her pocket. "He would hide things for me to find and give me clues. He said it was a good way for me to train if I really wanted to be a private investigator like him. I think he did it just to keep me busy and out of his hair and my mother's."

He watched her insert the key and turn it. The locker door groaned open. For a moment, he thought the space was empty. But C.J. reached into the very back and brought out another key, this one to a safety-deposit box.

Boone shook his head. "Are you sure he isn't just keeping you busy again?"

She cupped the key in her hand, her fingers closing over it. "The bank is only a few blocks away," she said, closing the locker and leaving the first key still in the door.

Back out in the fall sunlight, Boone took a breath. He was trying his best not to be irritated by all this cloak-and-dagger secrecy. He kept asking himself, what if Hank Knight's death *had* been nothing more than an accident?

Inside the bank, they were led to the back. C.J. had to sign to get into Hank's safety-deposit box. Apparently her name had always been on the list since they were quickly led into a room full of gold-fronted boxes. The bank clerk put her key into one, then took C.J.'s key and inserted it before she stepped away.

The moment they were alone, C.J. turned her key and pulled out the box. She carried it over to a table and simply stared at it.

"Aren't you going to open it?" he asked.

"I have a bad feeling I don't want to know what's in there."

"Want me to do it?"

She looked up at him with those big brown eyes and nodded.

He stepped closer and slowly lifted the lid, also worried that whatever was in there might devastate C.J. If Hank had been involved in the kidnapping in any way, he feared it would break her heart. Hank Knight was a saint in her eyes. What would happen if she learned he was just a man—a man with a possibly fatal flaw?

Chapter Nine

C.J. wasn't sure how much more she could take. Hank had known he was in trouble. Otherwise he wouldn't have left the keys for her. Why hadn't he let her help him? Maybe he would still be alive if—

She heard Boone open the safety-deposit box, heard him make a surprised sound. Before that, she'd turned away, fighting for the strength she needed to face whatever Hank had left her. A confession? Something he needed her to hide?

"What is it?" she demanded now as she turned to Boone again.

He reached into the box and brought out the contents. He fanned some documents in front of her face.

"What are those?"

"Stocks and bonds, a whole hell of a lot of them. It appears he left you a small fortune."

She shook her head. "How is that possible? He barely made enough money to keep a roof over his head and what he did make, he gave away."

Boone laid the certificates on the table. "C.J., these are pretty impressive. Either he had a good stockbrokcr or he made more money than anyone thought he did or…" His gaze came up to meet hers. He lifted an eyebrow.

"He wasn't into anything illegal." She picked up one of the stock certificates and quickly put it down to look into the safety-deposit box. It was empty. No note. No explanation. Just a whole lot of questions she didn't want to ask herself.

"It appears that you were his sole beneficiary."

BOONE COULD TELL that C.J. was shaken. She put all the stock certificates back into the safety-deposit box and returned it, pocketing the key. He wanted to say something that might make her feel better. Hank Knight had left her a small fortune. She was rich. But clearly she wasn't happy about any of it.

Probably because it brought up the question of where Hank had gotten his money. On the surface, his life made it appear that he didn't care about money.

But the safety-deposit box proved that was a lie. Had Hank Knight been leading a double life? Had he been involved in something illegal? Not the kidnapping, since that money had been found before the first kidnapper had been able to split it with his accomplice. At least that was the theory.

But there still could have been a payoff. It's possible whoever had Jesse Rose had been forced to pay for her. It still didn't explain the amount of money Hank had left C.J., unless selling babies had been an ongoing business.

Boone was half-afraid what else they would find. All

he could hope was that this runaround would eventually lead to Jesse Rose.

He watched C.J. call the city on her cell. She hung up after apparently only reaching a recorded message. "They're closed today. I can't get his car out until tomorrow."

"What now?" Boone asked.

"There's someplace I need to go," she told him. She still looked pale. As strong as she appeared, he could tell that all of this was taking its toll on her.

Again she took to the alleys, working her way through the maze of old buildings overlooking the valley.

He couldn't help thinking of her as a child racing around this tired old city to find the clues Hank had left her. He'd trained her well. So why hadn't he told her what was going on? Wouldn't he know that his holding out on her would hurt her? Clearly he'd been trying to protect her. But protect her from what?

All Boone could figure was if Hank had been half the man C.J. thought he'd been, then he'd been in trouble and didn't want to bring her into it. He felt his heart drop at the thought that Hank had known where Jesse Rose was and had now taken that information to his grave.

Ducking into a tiny café stuck between two old brick buildings, Boone followed C.J. inside. She headed for a table, sitting down with her back to the wall as if wanting to watch the door. Were they really being followed? If so, she hadn't mentioned it again since this morning.

C.J. WATCHED BOONE glance behind him before the door closed. She could tell that he hadn't believed her about someone tailing them earlier. He thought she was putting him on, leading him around just to wear him out. She smiled to herself, thinking that might have been partly true earlier.

"What are we doing?" he demanded.

"*I'm* having lunch," she said glancing past him at the large window that looked out onto the street. She saw movement in the deep shadows next to one of the buildings. But who or whatever it had been was gone now.

"If your plan is just to try my patience or wear me down…"

"You know my plan. It's to find out who killed Hank. If it is because of your kidnapping case…" She didn't need to finish since Boone was smart. He'd hang in as long as he thought she might lead him to his kidnapped sister. Even if it was the last place she hoped Hank's trail would lead them.

Not that she didn't want him to find his sister and reunite his family, but not at the expense of Hank's reputation. If Hank was involved, she wouldn't be able to protect him. Whatever happened now, she had no choice but to do her best to find out the truth. Wasn't that what Hank had taught her?

With obvious reluctance, Boone took a seat across from her. What choice did he have? She was his only hope of finding out why Hank had contacted Jim Waters and they both knew it. Boone had said that he couldn't go home until he had answers. Even if it meant putting up with her. And vice versa.

A waitress appeared and, without even looking at a menu, C.J. ordered "the usual" for them both.

"A little presumptuous," he said. "Tell me we aren't having more of those pasty things."

She ignored him as she looked past his shoulder. He turned to follow her gaze to the street but like her seemed to see nothing of interest.

"Still pretending we're being followed?" he asked, turning back to her.

Her gaze shifted to him. In the light coming through the window, his eyes were a brilliant blue. The cowboy was too handsome for his own good. Not that he seemed to realize it, though. She wondered how many women had flirted with him to no avail.

"Why don't you have a girlfriend?" she asked.

Those blue eyes blinked in surprise. "Who says I don't?"

She chuckled at that.

"I've had girlfriends," he said defensively. "I also have a horse ranch to run with my brothers. My father—"

"Had a heart attack. I understand he's better."

"He is. What about you?"

"I'm fine."

"You know what I mean. You have a steady beau?" He didn't wait for her to answer. "I didn't think so. So what's *your* excuse?"

She shook her head to keep herself from telling him the usual line—too busy, not interested in the men who were interested in her, hadn't met the right one yet and all the other things she'd told Hank when he'd asked the same question.

"I'd think you'd have a string of girlfriends," she said,

knowing she was only trying to distract herself from what they'd found in the safety-deposit box.

"And you'd be wrong."

"Why is that? Some girl break your heart? Make you swear off women?"

"No. Is that what happened to you? The quarterback in high school or some studious young man at college?"

Fortunately she was saved as the waitress came back with two overflowing plates. Fried pork chops hung over the buns next to heaping piles of French fries. "I didn't want you to leave Butte without a pork chop sandwich and this place makes the best ones," she said.

He locked eyes with her. "I'm not leaving until I find out what your partner knew about Jesse Rose and the kidnapping."

C.J. was the first to look away. "Like I think I've mentioned before, I'd have a better chance of finding out the truth without you tagging along."

"Too bad. You're stuck with me."

She glanced out the window again. "Is there any reason someone would be following *you*?"

He laughed. "Seriously? *If* someone really is following us, why would they be after me?"

"I don't know," she said, holding his gaze for a moment before she picked up one of her French fries.

"Well?" He apparently wasn't letting her off the hook.

She took a bite, chewed, swallowed and said, "It's none of your business."

"Aha! There *was* some boy." He laughed again. "I

would think it's hard to find a man willing to date a woman who carries a gun in her purse."

C.J. smiled at that, seeing that he was trying to get a rise out of her. "You know so little about women—and men—it seems." She picked up her pork chop sandwich and took a bite. No simple task given the size of it.

He sighed, picked up his and took a big bite. She saw his expression and hurriedly swallowed before she laughed.

"You like, huh?"

HE LIKED, BOONE thought as their gazes met and held for a long moment. He liked the sandwich. He liked her—a lot. The more he was around her... He looked away first.

They'd just finished their lunch when his cell phone rang. He stepped outside the door to take the call. But he stayed where he could see C.J. He suspected she wanted him around now even less. The things they were finding out about her deceased partner weren't things she wanted anyone else to know—maybe especially him.

"One of those string of women after you?" C.J. asked when he returned to the table after assuring his father he'd call as soon as he knew something.

"My father. After my brother Cull told him about your partner being killed in a hit-and-run, he was worried about me."

"He should be," she said. "Someone has been following us all day."

WHEN THEY LEFT the café, C.J. took them out the back door. Boone's father was worried about him. She was, too. She didn't want to get Travers McGraw's son killed. That's why she knew she should stop this now.

She knew she could get rid of this cowboy without much effort. He didn't know Butte and she did. But she had to admit, there were moments when she didn't want to be alone. Sometimes, she thought, remembering the way he'd devoured his pork chop sandwich, she enjoyed his company. He kept her mind off Hank and the pain of his death.

But the more she learned about Hank, the more worried she was becoming. Where had he gotten all that money for the stocks and bonds? Had he known something about the kidnapping? About Jesse Rose?

She was still shocked and shaken by what she'd discovered at the bank. It was one thing for Hank to be going somewhere without telling her, but all that money... It was as if she'd never known the man. Like the clothes in the suitcase.

Hank hated dressing up. She hadn't even known that he owned a suit. He was as bad as she was when it came to dressing casually for their work. Most of the people they saw couldn't afford to hire a private investigator. They dressed so they fit in with the community since Hank had never been interested in taking what he called highbrow cases.

Let some other PI take care of the rich, he'd always said. *We'll take care of the little guys, the ones who need us the most*. And she'd felt the same way.

It's called giving back to the community, Hank told her the first time she realized he didn't make much money. *People need help. If I can help, I do. This job isn't about the money.*

She'd seen right away how kindhearted the man was. He'd taken her on to raise, hadn't he? The only way C.J. had kept a roof over their heads once she'd become his partner was by taking insurance fraud cases while Hank continued to help those who couldn't help themselves.

That's why she'd been so sure Hank's death couldn't have had anything to do with the McGraws. It wasn't the kind of case that interested him. It was highbrow *and* high-profile. A wealthy horse ranch family. And yet, she'd found the file. She knew that Boone wouldn't lie about Hank talking to his family lawyer. But why?

And did the case have anything to do with Hank's hit-and-run? How about all that loot in the safety-deposit box? It made no sense given the way Hank had lived.

As they came out on the street, she glanced back. She hadn't spotted the tail since before lunch. All she'd caught was a shadowy figure lurking not quite out of sight. Why follow her to start with? Because they were afraid she would find out the truth?

"I should have gone to the restroom back at the café," C.J. said. "I'm going to duck in here."

"I'll wait out here for you," he said after glancing into the Chinese restaurant. He watched her go inside and disappear into a door marked Women. The air was brisk this afternoon, especially in the shade. He stomped his feet to keep them warm as he looked up the street toward the Berkeley Pit. What had once been a large natural bowl sitting high in the Rockies straddling the

Continental Divide was now an open pit that stretched over a mile wide. It had become a tourist attraction, he thought with a shake of his head.

He glanced inside the restaurant. The door to the women's restroom was ajar. There was no sign of C.J. Even before he went inside and saw the rear entrance, he knew she'd given him the slip.

Chapter Ten

C.J. couldn't believe that she felt guilty about losing Boone McGraw. There was someplace she needed to go without him. When she was a girl and Hank was teaching her the PI business from the ground floor up, as he liked to call it, he would leave her messages in an old building uptown. She had looked back on those days, thinking it was charming, the cute things he came up with to keep her busy and out of his hair.

It had been years since he'd left anything for her at this particular place, but after everything that had happened, she felt she needed to check it.

And check it without Boone. He'd already learned too much about her and Hank. She was sure by now that he thought Hank had been dirty—how else could all those stocks and bonds at the bank be explained? That he'd saved that much from his PI practice? Not a chance.

She couldn't stand the thought of an investigation into Hank because of her. Boone swore that all he was interested in was finding his sister. She prayed that was true. Still, she thought as she walked the last block to the old building, she couldn't have Boone tagging along.

Not right now. Hank had been in trouble or he wouldn't be dead right now, no matter what the police thought.

The building was abandoned like so many in Butte. She was just glad to see it still standing. One of these days it would either crumble and fall down or someone would come along and tear it down. Her heart ached at the thought of the memories that would go with it—not to mention the beautiful structure it had once been.

She climbed the steps to the wide double doors, now chained and padlocked, then stepped into the alcove to the right. At one time, there had been a fountain with water sprouting from the mouth of the ancient-looking stone face. But that had been years before C.J. herself. For as long as she could remember, the mouth had been dry like the bowl shape under it.

Today there were leaves and garbage in the bowl that used to catch the fresh water. She wished she'd brought a bag so she could clean it out, then reminded herself why she was there. She couldn't save this place. She wasn't even sure she could save herself if Boone was right and she was Hank's beneficiary. If her partner in business had gotten all that money from something illegal...

Reaching into the mouth, she felt grit and nothing else. Then her fingers brushed something cold. She touched it tentatively before she pulled out the small package. It was wrapped in plastic.

Seeing it, she began to cry. Hank knew her so well and vice versa. With trembling fingers, she saw the thumb drive protected inside the plastic cover and stuffed it into her pocket, her heart in her throat.

AFTER CUSSING AND carrying on for a while, Boone drove down random streets looking for her. Clearly there was someplace she'd wanted to go without him. Or maybe she'd just wanted to be alone.

That thought struck him hard. He'd seen how upset she'd been after finding the stocks and bonds at the bank. Didn't it make more sense to give her some space? He pulled over, parked and spent the next hour learning as much as he could about PI Hank Knight and his partner.

Everywhere he went, he heard nothing but praise about Hank and respect for C.J. The two were well-known around town as do-gooders. People liked them. People had been helped by them.

So where had all that loot come from? Hank had to be into something illegal. Perhaps a baby ring. The thought that Jesse Rose could have been one of the babies set his teeth on edge. C.J. knew more than she was telling him. Once he found her again...

He'd just driven down one of the main streets in uptown Butte, when he spotted her VW van and went roaring after her, riding her bumper. He cursed himself as C.J. whipped across two lanes of traffic on Montana Avenue and came to a tire-screaming stop at the curb. Before he could pull in behind her, she was already out of her van and storming toward him.

"What do you think you're doing?" she demanded.

He wished he knew. He wanted to throttle this woman or kiss her. Right now, he wasn't sure which and that said a lot about his frustration.

"I have no idea what I hope to accomplish by hanging around Butte—let alone tailing a junior PI who can't investigate her way out of a paper bag."

Hands on her hips, she glared at him. "What did you just call me? A junior PI who can't investigate her way out of a paper bag?" she demanded indignantly.

"Prove me wrong. Help me find my sister."

She glared at him for a full minute. "I told you what I'm doing. Trying to find my partner's killer."

"How are you doing on that?"

C.J. narrowed her eyes at him. "There is one more place I need to look. I'm assuming you plan to come along?"

"You're assuming right. We walking or taking my truck?"

She looked as if she could spit nails. "We're taking my van since you don't know where we're going." With that, she spun on her heel and headed for her van. He took a few deep breaths himself before following her.

Once behind the wheel with the van engine revved, she peeled out into the street and roared down the hill. Uptown Butte was a rollercoaster of steep streets. After a few blocks, she swung into a parking spot in front of one of Butte's historic buildings.

He climbed out after her and headed for the front door. C.J., he realized belatedly, was headed down the alley between the two buildings. The alley was just wide enough to walk down. It was cool and dark.

"Where—"

"If you're determined to tag along," she said over her shoulder, "then no questions."

Halfway down the long alley, she stopped at an old

weathered padlocked door. Pulling out a set of keys, she opened the padlock and swung the door open.

Boone peered down a dark narrow concrete hallway, a musty, dank smell wafting out. He didn't like the looks of this.

"Close the door behind you," she ordered and stepped in.

He hesitated but only a moment before following her. Their footsteps echoed on the damp concrete. The smell got much worse as the passage became more tunnel-like.

She made a sharp right, then a left, then another right. He tried to keep track, telling himself he might need directions to get out of here. It crossed his mind that she might be leading him into a trap. If she and her partner were in league…

Boone realized that he'd lost track of the twists and turns. He was screwed if he had to get out of here by himself. If he was that lucky.

C.J. stopped and he almost crashed into her in the dim light. He heard the jingle of keys again. "Hold this," she ordered as she dug a flashlight from her shoulder bag and handed it to him.

He held the light on another padlock and few seconds later, she was entering yet another narrow passage.

"Where the—" He didn't get the rest of the words out as she turned on him.

"Shh," she snapped and was off again.

He had no choice but to go with her. If he thought she'd been leading him on a wild-goose chase earlier, he'd been wrong. But this definitely felt like she was fooling with him.

The next padlock opened into a room filled with file cabinets. She flipped on a light switch and for a moment he was blinded by the overhead bulb.

C.J. had stopped just inside the door.

"What?" he asked.

"Hank didn't leave anything in here."

He stared at her. "You haven't even looked."

"Come on," she said, turning and starting for the door.

"No, wait, we came all this way, why not—"

"The dust."

"What?"

"Didn't you notice the dust on the floor?"

He couldn't say he had.

"Hank hasn't been in that room in months."

"Based on a little dust."

She glared at him in the ambient glow of the flashlight. "I'm just a junior PI who can't investigate my way out of a paper bag, but yes, that's my conclusion. I don't just jump to conclusions without facts."

"Really? And why all this subterfuge? What was it your partner did that he not only had to hide his files, but that he made a ton of money from?"

She gave him an impatient look before turning and heading down a different tunnel than the one they'd come in from. She had the flashlight. He had no choice but to follow her.

They came to a narrow stairway that wound up a couple of stories and the next thing he knew they were standing outside in the sunlight.

He glanced around, trying to get his bearings. The

tall brick buildings that had rivaled New York City now just looked sad, so many of them empty. They had come out not that far from the Berkeley Pit, a huge hole that was now full of bad water. Butte was now the butt of jokes, a decaying relic of better times.

"I don't know where else to look," she said, sounding disheartened. "I need a hot shower. You aren't going to insist on coming along for that, are you?"

It was late afternoon. The sun had sunk behind the mountains to the west. Dark shadows fell across the streets and a cold wind whipped between the buildings. Butte had fallen on hard times, especially the old uptown, and yet there was a quiet elegance to it. He wished he had seen it during its heyday. He was feeling a little nostalgic and disheartened himself.

"I'm sure it is all going to make sense at some point," he said.

Her smile was sad. She looked close to tears. He wanted to take her in his arms. But if he did, he knew he'd kiss her. He realized looking at her now that she had a bow-shaped mouth that just begged to be kissed.

"A hot shower sounds great. Back at my motel," he added, thinking a cold one might even be called for. "If you wouldn't mind dropping me at my truck."

BACK AT HER HOUSE, C.J. closed and locked the door behind her. She kept thinking of Boone. For a moment back there on the sidewalk, the sun slanting down through the buildings, she'd thought he was going to kiss her.

She shook her head now, telling herself she was tired

and discouraged and scared. Boone wanted just one thing from her: answers.

Her hand went to her pocket and closed around the thumb drive Hank had left for her. She feared he'd left her answers—and she wasn't going to like them.

Taking off her jacket, she tossed it aside and picked up her laptop. Popping it open, she slid in the thumb drive, all the time praying she wasn't about to read Hank's confession.

What came up was even more shocking.

The photo was of a beautiful young dark-haired woman with the greenest eyes C.J. had ever seen. She was much prettier than the digitally enhanced photos that had run in the news showing what Jesse Rose Mc-Graw would look like now. The young woman was smiling at the camera, eyes bright, as if whoever was taking the photo had said something funny.

She looked quickly to see what else was on the thumb drive, but there was only the one photo. She stared at Jesse Rose McGraw, her heart pounding. Hank had definitely known something about Jesse Rose.

But did it mean he'd been involved in the kidnapping? Or had he found out about Jesse Rose only recently? That was the question, wasn't it? The fact that he'd inquired with the McGraw family attorney gave her hope that he'd only recently stumbled onto the truth.

So why hadn't he told the attorney? Or at least called Travers McGraw and told him where he could find his daughter? It wasn't like Hank to keep a secret like that. So what had held him back?

It was the thought of what had stopped Hank from

telling the McGraws the truth that had her running scared. Hank had been hiding something, there was no doubt about that. But what had kept him from doing the right thing?

C.J. closed the file, pulled out the thumb drive and pocketed it, her hands shaking. Hank had kept this from her and now she was about to do the same thing with Boone McGraw.

But she couldn't throw Hank under the bus. She had to know how he was involved—if he was. She had to find out where he fit into all of this. And then she would turn over this thumb drive. But until then…

AFTER A HOT SHOWER, followed by a cold one, Boone had gone over everything that had happened that day. None of it made any sense. The only conclusion he'd reached—and one he figured C.J. had, too—was that Hank was dirty.

That made him sad for C.J. Everything he'd learned about the two private investigators, though, was at odds with that conclusion. He'd seen C.J.'s reaction to the stocks and bonds in the safety-deposit box. She'd been dumbfounded. Which meant she had to be devastated by what they'd discovered today.

The question was, though, how did it tie in with the kidnapping and Jesse Rose? If it did at all.

He pulled out his cell phone and called C.J. "I need a drink after a day spent with you. What do you say to joining me?"

"A drink?"

He heard something in her tone. "Look, I don't have

to get you drunk to hit on you, which I'm not, but if I was, I'd just back you up against a wall and—"

"Until you felt my gun in your ribs."

He laughed at the image. "Yes. Just so there is no misunderstanding, let's have dinner. We both have to eat. Or you don't even have to eat. You can just watch me."

She sighed and he thought for sure she was going to turn him down. To his surprise, she said, "There's a steakhouse close to your motel. I'll meet you there. Order me a steak, medium rare."

"Wait, you don't know where I'm stay—" He realized she'd already hung up. Of course she knew where he was staying. He could only guess how she knew. She'd probably followed him last night. He'd been too distracted to notice. He regretted what he'd said to her earlier about not being able to investigate her way out of a paper bag.

BOONE HADN'T BEEN waiting long when C.J entered the steakhouse. She looked a little out of breath as she slid into the opposite side of the booth. She'd told him to order for her and he had.

"I guessed baked potato loaded and salad with ranch dressing," he said.

She cocked a brow as she slid into the booth across from him. "I can live with that. What did you order?"

"The same." There was something different about her, he thought as he studied her. He got the impression that she'd walked here. Which meant she must not live far away. Either that or she'd needed the walk in the cold air.

She'd changed clothes and now wore a blouse and slacks, and her hair was tied at the nape of her neck. It cascaded down her back in a fiery river against the light-colored blouse. Silver earrings dangled from each ear and it appeared she'd applied lip gloss.

Something told him that none of this was about him. She seemed to wear all of it like armor as if she were going to war, reminding him that she was a private investigator first and foremost—and a woman on a mission. That they might not be on the same mission was still a possibility he had to accept.

He studied her, feeling a pull stronger than gravity. "I'm sorry about what I said to you earlier, you know, about the paper bag."

She smiled. "I'm sorry about dumping you earlier."

"It gave me time to do some investigating on my own," he told her, making her raise a brow. "I found out a lot about you and your partner."

"Really?" She seemed intrigued by that—and maybe a little worried. "All bad?"

"Actually, all good. The two of you are considered saints in this town."

She shook her head, almost blushing as she picked up her napkin and dumped her silverware noisily on the table. There was a tenseness to her tonight that he also didn't think had anything to do with him. After what they'd discovered at the bank, he'd seen how thrown she'd been. Had she found out even more to shake her faith in her partner?

"How was your time without me?" he asked.

"Pleasantly quiet." She smiled, though.

"I thought you might have missed me," he said.

She chuckled at that and carefully straightened her silverware. As the waitress brought their salads, C.J. looked eternally grateful for something to do with her hands.

It surprised him to see her so nervous. Was it because she was having dinner with him, almost like a date? Or had something happened this afternoon after she'd dumped him that had her even more upset?

"So you talked to people about Hank?"

"And about you. Both of you are highly respected around town," he said when she didn't ask.

"That's nice. Anything else?"

"No one confessed to killing him, if that's what you're asking."

She nodded and dove into her salad as if she hadn't eaten in a week.

"So what *did* you do without me?" he asked, studying her.

"Just tying up loose ends," she said without looking up.

"You're sure that's all?"

She glanced at him, those warm, honey-brown eyes meeting his. He saw defiance along with something that made his chest ache—fear. C.J. was running scared. He got the feeling that didn't happen often.

"Do we have to talk business?" she asked.

"Is that what I was doing?" He took a bite of his

salad. What the devil had C.J. found out? And why meet him tonight if she wasn't going to tell him?

Their steaks came as they finished their salads. They ate without talking. He was hungry and quickly put away his steak and potato. Considering everything he'd eaten today, it seemed impossible. Must have been the high altitude of Butte that had him so ravenous. Or maybe it was a different kind of hunger that he was making up for.

As he pushed his plate away, he looked at C.J. She put her last piece of steak in her mouth, closed her eyes and chewed slowly.

"I take it you liked your dinner?" he joked, noticing that she'd eaten everything. "You're welcome to lick the plate."

She opened her eyes and swallowed. "I'm sorry you wasted the trip to Butte. There really isn't any reason for you to stick around tomorrow. I can get a friend to take me down to pick up Hank's car. If something else comes up, I know where to contact you."

There wasn't anything to say except, "Dessert?"

As she devoured a large slice of cheesecake, he had to wonder where she put it. She couldn't eat like this all the time. Then again, she probably had the metabolism of a long-distance runner.

"Thanks for dinner," she said after he'd paid and walked her outside. It was dark with a cold breeze coming out of the mountains.

"I'm taking you home," he said, looking down the street to see several homeless men arguing.

"That isn't necessary."

"I'm afraid it is." He opened the passenger side of his truck and waited. He could see her having a private argument with herself, but she finally relented and climbed in.

He went around and climbed behind the wheel. Whatever she'd considered telling him tonight, she'd apparently changed her mind. Why else have dinner with him? Or maybe she'd just been hungry and he was buying.

"Just tell me where to go," he said as he started the pickup.

"Don't tempt me."

He looked over at her. "I'm going to take a wild guess here. This afternoon you found out something even more upsetting about Hank, but you don't want to tell me. In fact, it's why you gave me the slip earlier today. You're running scared that not only am I right about what got Hank killed, but that he is involved somehow in the kidnapping."

She looked out the side window and for a moment, he thought she might get out of the truck. Finally, she turned back to him. "Isn't it possible I'm just exhausted and have enough to deal with without you?"

He nodded. "But you agreed to have dinner with me. I was watching you while you ate. I could see that you were debating telling me something."

C.J. laughed. "You've never been very good at reading people, have you?" She looked out the windshield. "I live up that way."

He put the truck into gear and started in the direction she indicated. "I'm not leaving tomorrow. I'm going with you to the city car lot to get Hank's vehicle. If you don't want to go together, then I'll simply be waiting there for you."

"Turn left up here," she said. "Then right at the light." They were headed up the mountain to an area he'd been told was called Walkerville. The street went straight up through smaller and smaller, less ornate houses until she told him to turn right.

Her house was the last one on a short street that ended in a deep gully.

"Here," she said and the moment he slowed opened her door to get out.

"What time should I pick you up in the morning?" he asked.

In the cab light that came on as she climbed out, he saw her smile. "Are you always this pigheaded?"

"Always."

"Ten."

"I think you mean nine," he said before she could close the door. "That is when the city lot opens and when you're planning to be there, isn't it?"

She smiled. "Nine, then," she said, and slammed the door.

THE NEXT MORNING, he was sitting outside C.J.'s house. Walkerville in the daylight looked even more like an old mining community up on the mountain overlooking the city. As she came out of the house, he climbed out of his pickup and went around to open the passenger-side door for her.

"I was hoping you'd left town," she said, clearly not pleased to see him.

"I almost did."

"What stopped you?" she asked as she climbed in.

"You," he said and shut her door.

As he slid behind the wheel, C.J. asked, "Could we make one stop first on the way? It's uptown. The city yard is down in the valley, so it isn't out of your way."

"Not a problem. I'm all yours. So to speak," he added and started the truck. "Sleep well?" he asked as he drove down the steep narrow streets.

"Fine." He glanced over at her. If she'd gotten any sleep, he would have been surprised. There were dark shadows under her eyes.

"I slept fine, too." Not that she'd asked.

She ignored his sarcasm as she gave directions to where she wanted to go. "Right here," she said and the moment he stopped, she was out of the pickup and heading into another large brick building in the seedier part of town.

He cut the engine, parked and got out to follow her. Today she wasn't getting rid of him as easily as yesterday. But the moment he pushed open the door, he saw her in the arms of a large older woman. The two were hugging. He couldn't hear what was being said—no doubt condolences. He reminded himself of C.J.'s recent loss.

Boone felt a stab of guilt. He'd been so wrapped up in finding out what Hank had known about the kidnapping and Jesse Rose that he hadn't given a lot of thought or compassion to C.J. Maybe she was right and Jesse

Rose and the kidnapping had nothing to do with Hank's death. Given the amount of money in those stocks and bonds, Hank could have been into something more dangerous than kidnapping.

He heard the older woman say, "I'm sorry, but I hadn't seen Hank in a few weeks. He didn't say anything about leaving town. Not to me."

"And he didn't leave anything for me?" C.J. asked, her voice rough with emotion.

The older woman shook her head. "I'm so sorry."

C.J. brushed at her tears and stiffened her back as the woman looked past her to where Boone was standing. Apparently neither had heard him enter. "Thank you," C.J. said. She turned toward him but she didn't look at him as she made a beeline for the door.

He had only a second to get the door open and follow her out before she was on the curb. "I didn't mean to intrude just now."

Before she could answer, he heard the squeal of tires and the roar of an engine. The car came out of the alley at high speed. He didn't have time to catch more than the general shape and color of the car before it headed straight for C.J.

Chapter Eleven

It happened so fast that C.J. didn't have a chance to react. One moment she was standing at the curb, the next she was shoved aside and knocked to the ground with Boone McGraw crushing her with his body and the thick smell of engine exhaust wafting over them.

"Are you all right?"

She groaned as he rolled off her. The sound of the car engine died off in the distance. She became aware of people on the street huddled around them. "Did anyone get a plate number on that car?" she demanded as she tried to get to her feet.

Boone was on his. "Are you sure you're all right?" he asked, sounding a little breathless as he hunkered down beside her.

She nodded, though her knee was scraped and her wrist was hurt, but wasn't broken. She let him help her to her feet. She was more shaken than she'd thought when she was on the ground. One look at the people huddled around them and she could tell how close a call it had been. They were saying the same thing she was thinking. If it hadn't been for the cowboy...

If it hadn't been for Boone, it would have been another hit-and-run. Immediately, she thought of Hank. He hadn't had anyone to throw him out of the way. Could it have been the same car?

"A license plate number," she said to the small crowd around them again. "Anyone get it or a description of the car?" There was a general shaking of heads. Several said it had happened too fast.

"Kids," one woman said. "They could have killed you."

It hadn't been kids. Her every instinct told her that. It was too much of a coincidence that Hank had been run down and now she had almost been killed by a speeding car, as well.

She finally looked at Boone. He appeared even more shaken than she was. She saw that he'd pulled out his phone. "What are you doing?" she asked as the crowd began to disperse.

"Calling the cops."

"To tell them what? Did you see the car?" She saw that he hadn't gotten a look at it, either, before he'd thrown them both out of the way. "Even if they took it seriously, we don't have any information to give them. They'd just say it was another accident."

He hesitated for a moment before he pocketed his phone. "You're sure you're all right?"

She nodded, although still trembling inside. In all the years she'd been around and in the private investigation business, that was the closest she'd come to being killed. She'd been scared a few times, especially when caught tailing a person in a fraud case. But this was something new.

Which was probably why Hank hadn't seen it coming, either.

Boone opened the passenger side of his pickup and helped her in. She knew he was just being a gentleman because he felt guilty for still hanging around, but it made her feel weak and fragile—something she abhorred. She'd always had to be strong, for her mother. Now she had to be strong because otherwise she would fall apart. Hank was gone and she was terrified to find out why.

"You still think Hank's death has nothing to do with Jesse Rose and the kidnapping?" he asked as he started the pickup.

She didn't answer, couldn't. Her heart was lodged in her throat. Someone had just tried to kill her and would have taken Boone with her as she realized how close a call that had been. Worse, after looking at what was on that flash drive, there was no doubt. Hank knew something about Jesse Rose—and possibly her kidnapping.

Last night, she hadn't been able to sleep. She'd moved through her small house, restless and scared. At one point she thought she heard a noise outside. She'd never been afraid before living here. She'd always felt safe.

She'd checked all the doors and windows to make sure they were locked. But looking out into the darkness, she'd thought she'd seen the shape of a man in the trees beside the house. As she started to grab her purse and the gun inside, she saw that it was only shadows.

Her fears, she'd told herself, weren't any she could lock out. Hank had known about Jesse Rose. So why hadn't he told the McGraws?

Boone started the car. "Any other stops?"

She shook her head. "Let's go to the city lot and get Hank's car." With luck, he would have left something in it for her, not that she held out much hope. Hank's car always looked as if he was homeless and living in it. Finding a clue in it would literally be like looking for a needle in a haystack.

A FEW BLOCKS AWAY, Cecil pulled over to the side of the road. His hands were shaking so hard he had to lie over the wheel as he tried to catch his breath.

That had been so close. Just a few seconds later and he would have hit them both. Killed them both. He would have killed Boone McGraw. Killing some old PI was one thing. Even killing his young female partner. But if he had killed a McGraw...

The shaking got worse. He held on to the wheel as if the earth under him would throw him off if he didn't. And yet a part of him felt such desperate disappointment. He had to end this. C.J. West wasn't going to stop. He had to kill her. He had no choice.

When had things gotten so complicated? It had started out so simply and then he'd been forced to kill the PI. Now he would have to kill the PI's partner. As long as he didn't kill a McGraw. Travers McGraw would have every cop in the state looking for him if he did.

He began to settle down a little. He wouldn't get another chance, not with a hit-and-run. She would be expecting it now—and so would Boone. No, he'd have to think of something else. He knew where she lived.

An idea began to gel. Kill her and he should be home free.

Wiping the sweat from his face with his sleeve, he pulled himself together. He was steadier now, feeling better. He could do this. He could make up for his past mistakes. His head ached. He felt confused. There wasn't any other way out of this, was there?

He started to pull out, jumped at the sound of a loud car horn. A truck roared past, the driver flipping him the bird as he continued to lean on the horn.

Heart pounding, he checked his side mirror before slowly pulling out. He'd messed up, but he could fix it. He had no choice. But even as he thought it, he wondered how many more people he would have to kill to keep his secret. In for a penny, in for a pound, he thought.

BOONE DROVE TO the city yard and waited while C.J. went in to get Hank's car released. He still hadn't calmed down after their near miss back uptown. He would have loved to have passed it off as nothing but kids driving crazy fast and out of control—if C.J.'s partner hadn't been killed in a hit-and-run.

He would also love to know what C.J. was thinking now. Was she ready to admit that all this had to be about the kidnapping? Was she finally all in? He still couldn't be sure.

She came out shortly jingling a set of keys. Hank had left his keys in his car? What a trusting soul. It was a miracle the car hadn't been stolen. Not that he ever worried about that in Whitehorse. But this was Butte. He shook his head as he got out and followed her to the blue-and-white Olds.

Unlocking it, she opened the driver's-side door and stopped.

"What is it?" He glanced in expecting to see something awful. But the car looked spotless.

"His car never looks like this. Ever. He cleaned it out." She sounded shocked. And worried.

"So he cleaned his car. Because he was planning to go somewhere in it."

She looked skeptical. "Nowhere I can imagine that he would care."

Boone was disappointed. He'd hoped that they would find something in the car. If the man had cleaned it out, something rare, then he doubted there would be anything to find. "You want me to drive it?"

She shook her head. "I'll take it back to my place. You don't mind following me?"

He'd been following her since he got to town. "Not a problem."

She slid behind the wheel, but before she started the car, she reached up to touch what looked like a new small pine-scented car freshener hanging from the mirror. "This is so not Hank."

Boone went back to his pickup and caught up to her as they headed back to her house. In the distance, he could see the skeletal headframe over one of the old mine shafts, the dark structure silhouetted against the skyline. Another reminder he was in mining country.

Parking, he joined her, looking under the seat to see if Hank had missed anything. The smell of pine was overpowering from the small tree-shaped car freshener hanging from the mirror.

"What do you think he was covering up? A dead body smell?" he asked, only half joking. C.J. hadn't moved from the driver's seat, her hands still on the big steering wheel.

"I don't understand this change in him," she said as if more to herself. "He bought a cell phone, he canceled the landline at his office and had the power turned off. He packed his best clothes and cleaned out his car. It was almost as if…"

"As if he was leaving for good?"

She slowly swung her head around to look at him. There were tears in her eyes. "I need to get ready for the funeral."

"I'm going with you. Everyone knows that the killer always shows up at the funeral."

C.J. looked as if she wanted to put up a fight but didn't have it in her today after what had already happened.

"The problem is I didn't bring funeral attire."

She snorted. "This is Butte. I can promise you that most of the people there will be wearing street clothes because they're street people." She headed toward the house.

He waited until she went inside before he popped open the glove box. C.J. had already looked in it, but he'd noticed something that had caught his eye.

Like the rest of the car, it had been cleaned out, except for the book on the car. He pulled it out, noticing that it looked as if it had never been opened—except to stick two items into it. One was a boarding pass for a flight to Seattle. He looked at the date and saw that it was from last week—a few days before he was run down in the street.

The other was a train schedule. He flipped it over and recognized Hank's handwriting from the McGraw file the man had started. Hank had written dates and times on the back of the schedule—from Seattle to Whitehorse, Montana.

Chapter Twelve

The funeral was held in an old cemetery on the side of the mountain overlooking the city. C.J. used to come up here with Hank when he visited his long-deceased wife, Margaret. She'd asked him once why he never remarried.

When you have the best, it is hard to settle for anything else, he'd told her. *I didn't have her long, but I'm not complaining. I treasure every day we had together. She's all I need, alive or in my memories.*

The wind whipped through the tall dried grass that grew around the almost abandoned cemetery. But as she and Boone neared Margaret Knight's grave, the weeds had been neatly cleared away and there were recently added new silk flowers in the vase at the base of her headstone. Hank must have added them recently, she realized. Next to the grave site, C.J. saw the dirt peeking out from under a tarp and the dark hole beneath the casket.

C.J. had forgone a church service, deciding that here on this mountainside was where Hank would have liked a few words said over him. He didn't go in for fanfare. In fact he preferred to fly under the radar.

Because he'd had something to hide? That was the question, wasn't it?

She pushed all such thoughts from her mind. She couldn't have been wrong about Hank. Just as all these people couldn't have been either, she told herself.

A crowd had already gathered and more were arriving, most of them walking up from town. A few had caught rides. Many were closer to Hank's age, but still the group appeared to be a cross-section of the city's population. All people whose lives had been touched by Hank Knight.

"Are all these people here for Hank?" Boone asked beside her.

She smiled through her tears and nodded. She saw the mourners through Boone's eyes, a straggly bunch of ne'er-do-wells who'd loved Hank. "These people are his family. They're all he had other than his late wife, Margaret." She frowned. "He once mentioned a sister. I got the impression she'd died when they were both fairly young. He'd once mentioned being an orphan." More and more she realized how little she'd really known about Hank.

As the pastor took his place, C.J. smiled at all the people who'd come to say goodbye to Hank. He would have been so touched by this, she thought as the pastor said a few words and several others chimed in before someone burst out in a gravelly rendition of "Amazing Grace."

C.J. felt as if a warm breeze had brushed past her

cheek. Her throat closed with such emotion that she could no longer sing the words. Boone put his arm around her as the coffin was lowered into the ground and she leaned into him, accepting his strength. At least for a little while.

BOONE HAD BEEN to plenty of small-town funerals. Most everyone in town turned up. But he hadn't expected the kind of turnout that Hank Knight got on this cold December day in Butte, Montana. He was impressed and he could see that C.J. was touched by all the people who'd come to pay their respects to her partner. He could tell she was fighting to try to hold it together.

As he listened to the pastor talk, he studied those who were in attendance, wondering if Hank's killer was among them. He spotted one man who'd hung back some. He wore a black baseball cap and kept his head down. Every once in a while, he would sneak a look at C.J.

While the man's face was mostly in shadow, once when he looked up, Boone caught sight of what appeared to be a scar across his right cheek. The scar tissue caught in the sunlight, gleaming white for a moment before the man ducked his head.

Something about the man had caught his eye, but he had to admit there were a dozen others in the crowd who looked suspicious. Hank's clients were a rough-and-tumble bunch, no doubt about it. Anyone of them could have had some kind of grudge against him and done something about it.

But Boone's gaze kept coming back to the man in the

black baseball cap. The moment the pastor finished, the man turned to leave. That's when Boone saw the way the man limped as he disappeared over the hill. Boone kept watching, hoping to see what vehicle the man was driving, but he didn't get a chance to see as the crowd suddenly surrounded C.J. to offer condolences.

She'd stood up well during the funeral, but as the mourners left, some singing hymns as they headed back into town, Boone could see how raw her grief was.

"I'll give you some time alone," he said and walked back toward his pickup. He hadn't gone far when he glanced back to see her, head bowed, body shuddering with sobs. He kept walking, moved by the love and respect Hank Knight had reaped.

When C.J. joined him at the pickup, her eyes were red, but she had that strong, determined set to her shoulders again.

"You must be ready for more food, knowing you," he said. "Where do you suggest we go where we can talk? I found something in Hank's car that I think you need to see."

Just as he suspected, getting back to business was exactly what C.J. needed. He drove to a Chinese food place on the way. It was early enough that the place was nearly empty.

After ordering, he took out the boarding pass and the train schedule. "I found both of these stuck in his vehicle book in a very clean glove box." He pushed the boarding pass across the table. She looked at it and then at him.

"I guess he really did fly to Seattle," she said, sounding sad.

"Who does he know there?"

"I have no idea. He's never mentioned anyone."

"And he's never been before?"

She shook her head, but he could see the wheels turning. "There were a couple times a year when he would take a few days off. I never asked where he went. I just assumed it was for a case. Most of the time he never left Butte. Or at least I thought he hadn't."

Boone nodded. "That's not all." He slid the train schedule across to her. "What do you make of this?"

C.J. studied it for a moment. "This doesn't mean he was planning to take a train," she finally said. "Anyway, no passenger train comes through Butte. The only line is to the north up on the Hi-Line."

He flipped the schedule over. "Look what he had marked. The times for the train from Seattle to Whitehorse, Montana, and the date—day after tomorrow."

Her gaze shot up to his. "I don't understand."

"Your partner was going to meet that train."

She stared at him. "Talk about jumping to conclusions."

"Look at the evidence. He had packed, shut down his office and had this information in the glove box of his car. He flew to Seattle last week. Then he packed and cleaned his car. It seems pretty clear to me that he planned to drive north and meet the train when it came into Whitehorse."

"You're reading a lot into a train schedule and some scribbles."

She wasn't fooling him. He'd seen her expression when she'd recognized Hank's writing, the same way he had. "If you want to find his killer, then I suggest you come with me. Whoever gets off that train is the key."

"Go to Whitehorse?" She raised her eyes to his for a moment. "Let's say you're right. Even if we met this train, how would we know—"

"Whitehorse is just one quick stop for the train. Our depot isn't even manned. Only a few people ever get off there. It shouldn't be that hard to figure out who Hank was meeting. This is about my sister and her kidnapping. Come on, C.J. You aren't going to keep arguing that it's not, are you?"

She met his gaze. He had that urge to gather her up in his arms, kiss her senseless and carry her away. "Whitehorse," she repeated.

He could see she looked scared. "You coming with me?"

BY THE TIME Boone dropped her off at her house to pack for their trip the next day, it was already getting dark. This was why she hated winter hours. Living in Butte, she'd gotten used to the snow and cold. As Hank used to say, *It invigorates a person and makes them really appreciate spring*.

Back in her house, she pulled out her suitcase, but was too antsy to start packing. She made herself a cup of tea and went to sit by the front window. She loved her view of the city below. It had sold her on this house. The view and the small deck off the front. During the warm months, she spent hours sitting out there watching the lights come on. This house had filled her with a contentment—a peace—that she feared she would never feel again.

Hank's death, the revelations he'd left behind, Boone... She thought of the handsome cowboy. Did he really think he was helping her? Just being around him left her feeling...discontent. Certainly no peace. He made her want something she'd told herself she wasn't ready for, didn't need, didn't want.

C.J. shook her head at the memory of being on the street when she'd been so sure he was going to kiss her. He'd been staring at her lips and she'd felt... What had she felt? A tingling in her core. An ache. She'd felt desire.

She groaned. "And now you're really going with him all the way to Whitehorse, Montana, wherever that is? Have you lost your mind?" Her words echoed in the quiet house. She picked up her tea cup and took a sip.

At moments like this she felt the grief over Hank's death more profoundly. She swallowed back a sob as she thought of his funeral and all the people who had shown up. They'd loved him. She'd loved him. He'd saved her when she was a child. Her mother had been struggling just to keep her head above water. Hank had taken up the slack. He'd given C.J. purpose.

So was it possible that he could have been dirty? How else did she explain all that money in those stocks and bonds he'd left her?

Her head ached. None of this made any sense and hadn't since Hank was killed. Exhaustion pulled at her. She'd known the funeral would be hard. She just hadn't realized how hard. But seeing all the people who loved Hank had helped. Just the thought of them brought tears to her eyes again. They couldn't all have been wrong about Hank.

Her mind reeled at the thought of Hank keeping whatever had been going on with him from her. She felt betrayed, adrift. Had he planned to leave town for good and not even mention it to her? Why would he do that?

Because it had something to do with Jesse Rose and her kidnapping. Which meant that Hank either thought it was too dangerous to tell her or... Or he didn't want her to know what he was involved in because he was up to his neck in something illegal.

Either way, there was no more denying it. This was about Jesse Rose and the McGraw kidnapping case. Hank had been to Seattle, and right before he was killed. She had no idea what that might have to do with the second trip he was apparently planning. Seattle was to the west, while Whitehorse, Montana, was up on the Hi-Line in the middle of the state. What did the two places have to do with each other, except for the fact that the McGraw ranch was outside of Whitehorse?

Nor did she have any idea of who he might be planning to meet on the train from Seattle. The same person he'd visited in Seattle in the days before he was killed?

As if all of this wasn't troubling enough, Hank had a whole bunch of money that he'd left to her and she had no idea where it had come from.

Maybe more upsetting than him not telling her about it was the fact that he'd cleaned his car, packed his best clothing and shut down his office as if…as if he wasn't coming back.

Tears filled her eyes. Had he been running away? Then why the train schedule? Was he meeting someone on that train coming from Seattle to Whitehorse? Someone he planned to abscond with?

A shock rattled through her at the thought. Had she known Hank Knight at all?

But that was just it. She *had* known him. He had been a good man and there was a good explanation for all of this. She just had to find it. That meant going to Whitehorse and meeting that train from Seattle—with Boone.

"You should get some rest," Boone had said when he'd dropped her off. "I'll pick you up in the morning. I hope you'll go with me."

"I—"

"Sleep on it," he had said quickly. And for a moment, he'd gotten that look in his eyes.

She shivered now at the memory and touched her upper lip with the tip of her tongue. She almost wished the man would just kiss her and get it over with. That made her smile.

Wiping at her tears, she turned off the light and started out of the dark living room in the direction of her bedroom. She'd only taken a few steps when she heard the noise and stopped. Her gaze shot to the window. She hadn't realized that the wind had come up. It now whipped the branches of the tress outside.

That must be what she'd heard. One of the branches scraping against the side of the house. Only the noise she'd heard… It had sounded like someone trying to pry open a window. Like a lock breaking?

She reminded herself that last night she'd thought she'd seen a man standing out in her yard and it had turned out to be a shadow and nothing more.

A dark shadow swept past the glass. Her breath caught in her throat as her heart began to pound. Someone was out there trying to get in.

She rushed to the table where she'd dropped her purse when she'd come into the house. As she heard another noise down the hallway in her bedroom, much like the first, she managed to fumble her cell phone from her purse. Her fingers brushed her gun as a louder noise came from the back of the house. It had been one of the old cantankerous windows being forced open.

Her heart pounding, she pulled out the pistol, snapped off the safety and laid it on the table as she turned her attention to her phone. She hit 911, all the time estimating how long it would take for the police to get there. Too long. That's if they even came. Once they knew it was her calling, they'd just think she was being a hysterical woman again. Just like she'd been when she'd told them that Hank's hit-and-run had been murder.

BOONE HAD DRIVEN all the way back to his motel but he hadn't pulled in. Something kept nagging at him. He hadn't wanted to leave C.J. alone tonight. After that near so-called accident earlier, he feared she wasn't safe.

Of course, she'd argued that she was fine. She would lock her doors. She had a gun. She could take care of herself.

But still, he didn't like it. He kept thinking about the man he'd seen at the funeral in the black baseball cap. He'd meant to ask C.J. about him. Something still nagged at him about the man. Was it possible he'd been driving the car earlier that had almost run them down?

Reminding himself how exhausted C.J. had looked, he told himself that he could ask her about it tomorrow. She probably wouldn't even know who the man was. Then again, she seemed to know everyone in Butte.

Swearing, he swung the pickup around and went back, knowing it would nag at him until he asked her. Also, it wouldn't hurt to check on her as long as she didn't think that was what he was doing. He told himself that if all the lights were out, he wouldn't bother her. But if she wasn't asleep yet...

As he neared the small house overlooking the city, he saw that the lights were all out. He couldn't help being disappointed. He wasn't good at leaving things undone and for some reason, this seemed too important to wait.

He started to turn around since her house was at the end of dead-end street, a deep gully on one side and an empty lot on the other. Walkerville was even older than uptown Butte since this is where much of the original mining had begun. The houses were small and old, but the view was incredible, he noticed as he swung into her driveway to turn around.

The pickup's headlights caught movement at the back of the house.

IN THE DARK living room, C.J. put down the phone as she heard a loud crash at the back of the house—and picked up the gun. She moved slowly down the hallway toward the back of the house and her bedroom, the gun clutched in both hands in firing position.

She spent hours at the shooting range—but she'd never had to use her weapon as a PI. She hoped she wouldn't tonight.

The cold wind that had chilled her at the funeral earlier had picked up even more. She could feel a stiff breeze winding down the hallway from where someone had opened the window.

Stopping to listen, she heard nothing but the wind and the occasional groan of the old house. She knew most of those groans by heart. What she feared she would hear was the creak of old floorboards as someone moved across them headed her way.

The house was dark, except for the cloud-shrouded moonlight that filtered in through the sheers at the windows. Shadows played across the hallway.

As she neared the bedroom where the noise had come from she could make out the glittered remains of her shattered lamp on the floor. What she couldn't see was her intruder. Snaking her hand around the edge of the doorway, she felt for the light switch. She'd just found it when the curtain at the window suddenly snapped as it billowed out on a gust of wind, making her jump.

She found the light switch again and readied herself. Her intruder had either left. Or he was waiting in the pitch-black corners of her bedroom to jump out at her.

BOONE CUT HIS lights and engine and was out of the pickup in a heartbeat. He ran toward the back of the house, realizing belatedly that he should have grabbed something he could use for a weapon.

The dark shadow he'd seen was gone. He was telling himself that the person had taken off when he'd been caught in the beams of the pickup's lights. Then he saw the open window and the large overturned flowerpot someone had used to step on to climb into the house.

His mind whirled. Had C.J. had time to go to bed? He looked around, not sure what was beyond this open window. The person he'd seen could have dropped off into the ravine next to the house and could be long gone. Or he could have gone into the house and was now inside. He could have C.J.

Boone pulled out his phone and quickly keyed in her number. He waited, listening to the wind and his heart, for the phone to ring. And prayed she hadn't turned hers off.

C.J. JUMPED AS her phone rang in the other room. She glanced back down the hallway, distracted for a split second.

At a sound in the bedroom, she turned back, but too late. A large dark figure came busting out of the bedroom. She raised the gun, got off a wild shot, heard a groan. But then she was hit by the man's large, solid body as he crashed into her. He knocked the breath out of her, slamming her back against the wall before she hit the floor hard, gasping for breath.

Her phone was still ringing as she rolled to her stomach, the weapon still clutched in her hand. All her training took over as her intruder pounded toward the front door. "Stop!" she cried, leveling the laser beam on the man's back.

He was fumbling at the door lock.

C.J. pushed herself up to her knees and tried to hold the gun steady. "Stop!" It happened in slow motion, but only took a few seconds. She raised her weapon, the laser jittering in the middle of his back as her mind raced. Pull the trigger? Shoot him in the back? Or let him leave? She'd seen that he was limping. Had she hit him with the first shot she'd fired?

"Don't make me shoot you!" Her voice broke.

He got the door unlocked, flung it open and stumbled out into the night. As her phone stopped ringing, she leaned back against the wall, still holding the gun, her heart thundering in her chest.

BOONE HEARD THE phone ring inside the house just moments before he heard the gunshot and the pounding of feet headed toward the front of the house. He raced in that direction in time to see a large dark figure come running out of the house, leap the porch railing and disappear over the side of the yard and into the ravine. As he did, Boone saw that the man was limping badly.

"C.J.!" he yelled as he ran up onto the porch. "C.J., it's me, Boone. Are you all right?"

"Boone." Her voice sounded distant and weak.

He rushed into the open doorway and fumbled for the light switch. An overhead fixture blinked on, blinding him for a moment. He saw her cell phone on the table next to her open purse.

"I'm all right."

He turned on the hall light and following her voice, he found her sitting at the end of it, the gun resting between her legs. Bright droplets on the wood floor caught his eye. Blood. He rushed down the hall to drop to his knees next to her. "Were you hit?"

She shook her head. "I fired the only shot. I think I caught him in the leg. He was limping."

"Did you get a look at him?" he asked as he pulled out his phone to call the police.

"Don't do that."

He looked up at her in surprise. "But your neighbors…"

"They've heard gunshots before. They won't call it in."

"But—"

"If we hope to meet that train in Whitehorse, we don't want to get involved with the cops, not now. It wouldn't do any good anyway. Nothing was taken. I didn't get a good look at him. And I don't have the best relationship with the cops in this town right now." There was a pleading in her gaze. "I'll just clean up the blood." She pushed herself to her feet.

Boone wanted to argue but he remembered what the detective had said about PIs. Apparently she was right about their relationship. It wasn't one-sided.

He rose with her. He could tell that she was still shocked and off balance. He knew she wasn't thinking clearly. But he couldn't disagree about what would happen if they called the cops. A shooting would mean a lot of explaining. She was right. They had to meet that train if they hoped to find out who had killed her partner and why—and what it might have to do with Jesse Rose and her kidnapping all those years ago.

But what had this been about tonight?

"I'll take care of the window," he said as he moved to the bedroom. The lock had been broken. "I could pick up a new lock at the hardware store in the morning to fix this."

"I don't think he'll be back."

"So you think it was a robbery gone wrong?"

She shrugged, avoiding his gaze. "What else?"

"How about something to do with Hank's death?"

C.J. finally looked at him. "Why would you say that?"

"Because I saw a man at the funeral. He had a scar on his cheek, wore a dark baseball cap pulled low. Ring any bells? He was limping—like the man who just ran out of here."

She frowned. "He doesn't sound familiar. You said he was limping at the funeral?"

"Yes. He kept his face hidden beneath the brim of his baseball cap except when he was looking at you. He seemed to have a lot of interest in you. And unless I'm mistaken, the man you just chased out of here was wearing a dark baseball cap."

SHE'D SHOT HIM! Cecil couldn't believe it. He drove back to his motel room, parked where he couldn't be seen from the office and limped inside. His leg hurt like hell and it was still bleeding. The blood had soaked into his jean pant leg.

He pulled out the motel room key, opened the door

and slipped inside. In the bathroom, he pulled down his jeans and looked at his leg. It wasn't as bad as he'd thought it was going to be.

The bullet appeared to have cut a narrow trench through the skin. At least the slug hadn't hit bone. Nor was it still in there. That was something, since that leg had already been injured years ago. He still had the scar, a constant reminder of how badly things had gone that night.

Opening the shopping bag he'd picked up at the convenience mart, he pulled out the alcohol bottle, opened it and, gritting his teeth, stepped into the bathtub and poured the icy liquid over his wound.

He had to hold on to the sink to keep from passing out from the pain. What hurt worst was that he'd failed tonight. He pulled the length of cord from his pocket. It should have been around C.J. West's neck.

His cell phone rang. He checked caller ID. His ex-wife. He'd been trying to get back together with her, because he still loved her. Also he needed her more than she could know. He let it ring another time, before he took her call. As he watched his blood stain the white porcelain of the cheap motel room tub, he said cheerfully, "Tilly, I'm so glad you called. I was just thinking about you."

Chapter Thirteen

Boone rubbed his neck and stretched as best he could as he drove.

"You should have taken the bed last night," C.J. said.

"The recliner was fine." He'd had enough trouble convincing her to come to his motel last night. It was that or the two of them staying in her house. He hadn't liked the idea that the man might be the same one who'd tried to run her down and then broken into her house. He wasn't taking the chance that the man might come back.

"At least at my motel, he won't know where you are."

"I can get my own room."

"Could you possibly just let me take care of you for one night? Two brushes with death in one day? Haven't you been through enough today?" She'd given him a look he couldn't read. "Come on, you need sleep. Right now, it appears that the only thing keeping you on your feet is pure stubbornness."

She'd finally relented. But when they'd gotten to the motel, she'd wanted to argue about who was going to take the bed.

"*You're* taking the bed. You want the bathroom first?

Then get in there." When she'd come back out he'd gone right into the bathroom after, giving her a warning look not to argue with him.

Exhaustion had taken her down. When he came out of the bathroom, she was lying on the end of the bed as if she'd been sitting there and had just keeled over for a moment to rest.

Shaking his head, he'd picked her up and carried her around to the side of the bed. He'd never met such a mule-headed woman. She reminded him of... He'd chuckled. She reminded him of himself.

She'd barely stirred but he'd hushed her up as he took off her shoes and tucked her into the bed. Then he'd stood there for a long moment watching her sleep before he'd headed for the recliner.

Not that he'd been able to fall asleep. He kept thinking about C.J. Her loyalty to Hank. Her determination to find his killer at all costs. Her sweet, vulnerable look when she was sleeping. It made him smile.

C.J. West was a complicated young woman who intrigued him more than he wanted to admit.

HIS LEG HURT like hell. Cecil hadn't gotten any sleep. The first thing he'd had to do was put a new bandage on his gunshot wound. Now standing in the bathroom naked, he braced himself for the pain. Pouring more of the rubbing alcohol on the wound, he let out a cry and clutched at the sink.

At least the wound had stopped bleeding, he thought as he covered it with gauze and then a bandage before pulling on his jeans. He hadn't thought to bring more clothing. He hadn't thought out a lot of things, he realized. So many mistakes. And now he couldn't go into a store the way he looked. No, it didn't matter how he was dressed. He needed to finish this.

At the thought of how badly that had gone last night, he wanted to scream. If Boone hadn't come back… Not that he could blame him.

He'd rushed it, just wanting to get it over with instead of waiting until he knew she was asleep. Once inside the house, he'd had a chance to finish it. He'd knocked her down. How much harder would it have been to take the gun away from her, choke the life out of her or use the gun on her?

His first plan had been to wait until she was in bed asleep and then sneak in and put a pillow over her head. He knew he couldn't do it looking at her. But he'd gotten impatient and couldn't wait for her to fall asleep. He had a piece of cord in his pocket. He'd thought that he could get behind her and strangle her as long as he didn't have to see her face.

But things had gone badly. He'd panicked. Isn't that why he hadn't killed her in the hallway last night? It had been so close and personal. Nothing like running someone down in a car.

But he'd even failed at that. His life had been one failure after another. Now if he didn't want to spend the rest of his life in prison…

With a groan, he limped out of the motel bathroom. He had to go back to C.J. West's house. If she wasn't there, maybe he could wait inside for her. Wait and surprise both her and Boone when they came back.

But when he'd gone by her house he'd seen one of her neighbors out in his yard. He'd parked and gotten out, limping over to him.

"I was looking for the woman who lives in that house," Cecil said, and realized he might be able to pass for a delivery boy even at his age. "She placed an order. I was trying to deliver it."

"Must be some mistake," the man said, eyeing him. "I saw her leave this morning with a suitcase. I got the impression she wouldn't be back for a while. Left with some man. What did you do to your leg?"

"Old war injury," he lied.

"Sorry you came all this way. Is it anything I can take off your hands?"

"No, I don't think so, but thanks for the information." He limped to his vehicle and climbed painfully back in. She'd left with a *suitcase*?

He quickly called Boone McGraw's motel only to be told that he'd checked out. Swearing, he tried his ex-wife's number, telling himself that Tilly probably wouldn't know anything if she answered. Since she'd gone back to work, often she was vacuuming the Mc-Graws' big new house and didn't even hear her phone.

She picked up on the second ring. "Hi." She sounded a little breathless. He pictured her with a duster in her hand standing in one of the many bedrooms. She'd been dark-haired when he'd married her all those years go. Now over fifty, she'd gone to a platinum blonde as if thinking it made her look younger.

"Hi," he said. "Busy?"

"These cowboys," she said with a sigh. Tilly usually could find something to complain about. He wondered what she'd found during the years that they had been divorced.

"Well, at least you have less to clean with Boone gone," he said.

"Ha! I just heard not only is he on his way back, but he's bringing some…" she lowered her voice "…woman. I have to get a room ready for her."

"No kidding?" So they were headed back to Whitehorse, back to the ranch. He swore silently. He'd never be able to get to her at the McGraw Ranch. Even though security wasn't as bad out there as it had been following the kidnapping, it would still be impossible to break in without getting caught.

But then again, he had Tilly there, didn't he? No one would suspect anything if she brought her ex—and soon-to-be husband again—out to the ranch where she worked to see the new house.

"How did the job interview go?" she asked now, reminding him of the reason he'd given her for leaving town for a few days.

"I'll tell you all about it when I see you. I'm about to head home. I'd like to take you out to dinner when I get back."

"A date?" He could hear the pleasure in her voice and should have felt guilty for all the lies.

"Why not? You're still my Tilly girl, aren't you?"

C.J. LOOKED OUT at the passing landscape of towering mountains and deep green pines. Boone had told her it was a six-hour drive. She'd wanted to take her own car, but she knew he was right. It made sense to go with him since they were going to the same place, he knew the way and someone was after her. So it was safer being with him, at least according to him.

She hated this feeling of vulnerability and Boone McGraw only made it worse. Being around him left her feeling off balance. Before all this, she'd felt she had control of her life. She'd felt safe knowing what she would be doing the next day and the day after that. She had a plan.

Hank's death had changed all that. She'd lost her biggest supporter. She'd lost her friend and the man who'd filled in all these years as her father. Boone showing up had turned an already confusing time into... Just the freshly showered male scent of him made it hard to think. And she needed desperately to figure this all out. It's what she did for a living. She solved mysteries. She helped people, just as Hank had taught her.

But right now she felt as if she couldn't even help herself. Too many of the pieces were missing and her grief over Hank's death had her too close to tears most of the time.

She rubbed a hand over her face and told herself to quit whining. She was still strong, still determined. She'd gotten through her mother's death. But only because Hank had been there for her. Now she felt...alone. And yet not alone, she thought as she looked over at Boone.

"Thanks for last night."

He shot her a glance. "No problem." His smile warmed an already unbearably handsome face.

She felt her heart do a little tap dance against her ribs and was glad when he turned back to his driving. "I keep going over it in my head. There's no reason anyone would want to harm me."

"You were Hank's partner. Whatever he knew, the killer must assume you knew it, as well. Or realized that you were looking for the truth."

But she knew nothing. The fact that Hank hadn't told her what was going on with him hurt heart-deep. Her head ached from trying to understand what had been going on with him in the days before his death. So many secrets. Not just the stocks and bonds, but Seattle. And maybe Whitehorse as well?

"So tell me about your family," she said and turned to look at Boone, desperately needing to get her mind on something else.

BOONE GLANCED AT her in surprise. "You mean more than what you've already read about my family? I doubt there is much to tell." He knew she'd researched the kidnapping. As she'd said that first night, she didn't leave things to chance.

"I did some research, but it's not the same. You have two brothers you grew up with, Cull and Ledger. So what are they like?"

He could see that she seriously wanted to know. He suspected it was only to keep her mind off the long trip—and what she'd been through the past week—but he was happy to oblige.

"Cull's the oldest, the bossiest." He laughed. "He's great. You'll like him. He's a lot like you, actually," he said and glanced over at her. They'd left Butte behind and now traveled through the mountain pass toward the state capital.

"How so?" she asked suspiciously.

"Stubborn to a fault. Determined to a fault. Independent to a fault. But he's changed since he fell in love." He saw her turn more toward him as if he'd piqued her interest. "He and Nikki St. James, the crime writer, are engaged. She came up to the ranch to do research for a book and her digging around set some things off."

"I heard it also almost got her killed. I suspect I'm going to like her."

He chuckled and nodded. "I suspect you will."

"And Ledger?"

Boone sighed. "Ledger. He fell in love in high school with a girl named Abby. They broke up when he was in college, some misunderstanding perpetrated by her mother, and she married someone else. A bad idea on her part since her husband was abusive."

"Wade Pierce."

"Yep." He grinned. "You probably know all this."

"No, please continue."

He studied the road ahead for a moment, thinking. "But Ledger, also a bit stubborn and determined, hung in there, determined to save her."

"Sounds like someone I know," C.J. joked. "Did he?"

"He did. They're finally together again. This time I don't think anything will tear them apart."

"So you're the last single brother."

Out of the corner of his eye, he could see that she was

smiling. But he wasn't about to take the bait. "Actually, my brother Tough Crandall is still single."

"Right, the one who doesn't want to be a McGraw. Oakley McGraw, the missing twin."

"Yep. Talk about stubborn. I suspect he will always be Tough Crandall. He's made it very clear that he doesn't need the McGraws or want what comes with us—lots of unwanted publicity."

"I guess I can understand that. You don't think he will come around eventually?"

"My dad does. Dad never gave up looking for the twins, never gave up believing they were still alive, just never gave up. Of course, my dad is one of those men who looks at a half-full glass and thinks it is three-quarters full. You'll meet him."

"One of those," she said with a shake of her head and a smile.

"He's never given up on finding the twins, even when we wished he would," Boone said. "For years, the kidnapping has defined us all."

"Probably why you can't get a date," she joked.

He smiled over at her. "I had a date the other night at the steakhouse."

She shook her head. "You call that a date?"

"I would have if I'd gotten up the nerve to kiss you."

C.J laughed and met his gaze. "So why didn't you?"

"I kept thinking about that gun in your purse. I didn't want to feel the barrel poking me in the ribs."

"You're smarter than you look." She turned to glance out the windshield as they passed Helena and began the climb again up another mountain pass. "Strange, the paths our lives take. Not always easy. Was it horrible growing up with the kidnapping hanging over you?"

"Not all the time. My brothers and I love horses so we spent a lot of time on the back of one. We stayed away from the house during the bad times, especially when the anniversary of the kidnapping rolled around. There was always something in the newspaper—thanks to our Dad. That's why I have to help find Jesse Rose if she is still alive. Maybe then Dad can just enjoy his family."

"You're lucky to have such a large family, and with your brothers getting married..."

"Yes, and it's growing. One of the reasons Dad wanted the new house to be so large. He wants plenty of room there for all the family. You'll see."

She shot him a look.

"We're staying out at the ranch." He held up a hand before she could argue. "I'm not letting you out of my sight until this is over. I know you're very capable of taking care of yourself, but if I'm right, the reason someone wants you dead is because of my family tragedy. So let me do this."

She'd opened her mouth to speak, but closed it for a moment. "Fine. Is your stepmother still behind bars?"

He laughed. "Last I heard, thank goodness. Patty, yes. Still locked up so it's safe." He shook his head at thought of her. "I told you that she didn't just try to kill my father by poisoning for months with arsenic—we believe she did the same thing to my mother twenty-five years ago. When Patty wants something... And she wanted my father—until she got him."

"Do you think she was the kidnapper's accomplice?"

"I certainly wouldn't put it past her. But if so, her plan backfired. She didn't get my father—at least not then. She went away for nine years. The only reason she came back when she did was she needed a home for her and her baby."

"Sounds like she had another reason for returning to your ranch and just used the baby to get what she wanted."

He smiled over at her. "It certainly worked. My father raised Kitten all those years only to have Patty send the girl off to some relative. Kitten was a lot like her mother so while it was hard on my father to see her go…"

C.J. nodded. "A lot of drama?"

"Since she was little."

"So what was it like growing up on a horse ranch?" she asked as she made herself comfortable in the passenger seat.

"It was an amazing childhood, actually." He began to tell her about learning to ride at an early age, of horseback rides up into the Little Rockies, of swimming in the creek and racing their horses back to the corral. "Cull usually won, but there was this one time…"

Boone glanced over to see that C.J. had fallen asleep. He smiled and looked to the road ahead. He couldn't shake the feeling that his life had changed in some way he'd never planned. It unsettled him. But soon they would be on the ranch. And once Jesse Rose was found… Well, things would get back to normal. Right, normal—as if that was ever going to happen.

Chapter Fourteen

C.J. felt a hand on her shoulder and sat up quickly, suddenly awake. She couldn't believe she'd fallen asleep. But she'd had trouble sleeping since Hank's death. Last night was the best sleep she'd had in days, but she was still exhausted.

"Where are we?" she asked, looking around. The earlier mountains covered in tall pines had given way to prairie.

"Great Falls. I thought you might be hungry."

Her stomach rumbled in answer, making him smile. She really did like his smile. She wished he smiled more. He was far too serious most of the time, she thought and realized she could say the same about herself.

"Fast food? Or take our chances at that café over there?"

"Given everything that has happened to me recently, I'm up for taking a chance on the café."

"Brave woman. I like that about you," he said as he climbed out of the pickup with her right behind him.

She joined him at the table he'd selected by the window after going to the restroom to freshen up. The café smelled of coffee and bacon and what might have been chili cooking in the back and another scent that made her think of the meals her mother used to fix. Something with burger and macaroni.

As she slid into the booth, she realized she liked the feel of the place. It reminded her of the cafés she loved in Butte. Sun shone in through the window, warming their table, and she felt herself relax for the first time in days.

She had to admit that part of it was her companion. Boone was easy to be around. He made her laugh and he seemed to get her. She thought of some of the men she'd dated and groaned inwardly. Not that she'd thought a cowboy could ever turn her head. Was that what Boone had done?

"Your family knows we're coming?" she asked as she picked up the menu in front of her to chase away that last thought.

"Dad does. Not sure if he told my brothers. We discussed keeping it quiet. Just in case."

She looked up from the menu. "Just in case Hank's killer doesn't know about any of this?"

Boone shrugged. "I can only hope. Based on a train schedule and some of his doodling, I think Hank planned to meet that train tomorrow. But I don't think his killer has this information. Otherwise, why not just meet the train and stop whatever it is from happening? Why try to run you down and later break into your house?"

She shook her head. She had no idea. None of it

made sense. She thought of the thumb drive. More and more she hated keeping it from him. She started to say something when the waitress interrupted.

"Know what you'd like?" the waitress asked suddenly at their table.

"What is your soup today?" C.J. asked.

"Homemade chili with a side of corn bread."

"That's what I thought. I'll have that."

"I'll have the same," Boone said and handed back his menu.

"Anything other than water to drink?"

They ordered colas and were silent as the waitress left. She felt the thumb drive in her pocket, but the moment had passed. She had to wait and see who got off that train. The mystery of who might be arriving on that train had her anxious as well as worried. But she thought that Boone was right, that Hank had planned to meet whoever was coming in from Seattle tomorrow.

"So tell me about growing up in Butte," Boone said. She knew he was asking only to distract her. But he listened as if with interest as she told him about her mother's job in Hank's building at a secondhand store, how back then there were lots of fun junk shops in town and lots of customers.

"But your favorite part was working with Hank," he said when she finished.

She smiled. "On the weekends I was like any other kid. I rode my bike with friends, played in mud puddles, snooped around in abandoned houses and made up stories. I always thought I'd write books one day."

"Really? Then you and Nikki really will hit it off."

Their chili and corn bread arrived and they dove in, both seeming to enjoy the meal as well as the quiet. They had the café to themselves since it wasn't noon yet. Other than the occasional clatter of dishes or pots and pans in the back, the only sounds were the murmurs of enjoyment from them. The chili was good. So was the corn bread, especially with fresh butter and honey.

C.J. finally pushed back her empty plate and bowl.

"How are you feeling?" Boone asked, having finished his.

"Good." The realization surprised her. For the first time in days, she felt as if she might live through this. Which made her laugh. A killer was after her and yet… She smiled over at Boone. "I'm good. Want me to drive for a while?"

THE PAIN IN his leg was worse today. Cecil hoped it hadn't gotten infected. As he drove toward Whitehorse, he tried to think about what to do next.

Tilly hadn't been able to give him much information other than Boone McGraw was returning to the ranch with a woman. That much he'd figured out on his own. The question was why?

Had they found out the truth and were now going to Travers with it? He told himself that they couldn't have. Not yet. But once they found Jesse Rose, once they started putting the pieces together like Hank Knight must have…

He thought about the night of the kidnapping. So many years ago. They'd all changed so much. Tilly had been twenty-five and pretty as a picture. Patty, the nanny, hadn't been much of a looker back then, just a mousy-looking girl. Nor had the older cook been anything to look at.

Things had definitely changed after the kidnapping. The first Mrs. McGraw, Marianne, was now in the loony bin, crazier than a mad hare. Travers McGraw had gone downhill. Now sixty, he'd recently had a heart attack and almost died. Of course, he blamed the nanny who he'd foolishly made his second wife for trying to poison him to death. Patty had most certainly outgrown that mousy look she'd had when she was the nanny.

He shook his head. He could understand why Tilly had liked working out there. She loved minding other people's business and that ranch was a hotbed of gossip.

I'm invisible in that house, she'd once told him. *I can be standing in the same room with my duster and it's as if they don't even see me. They just go on as if I'm not there.*

Smiling in spite of the pain, he recalled how he had loved her stories about what he thought of as the rich and famous. At least in Whitehorse, Montana. Tilly was as much part of that house back then as those walls that he'd often hoped couldn't talk.

It had been on one of his visits to his wife at the old McGraw house that he'd met Harold Cline. Harold had been dating the ranch cook, a stout middle-aged woman named Frieda. He'd wondered at the time about that arrangement since Harold wasn't a bad-looking guy. So when Harold had asked him if he'd like to get a beer, he'd accepted. Actually anyone who was buying back then would get a yes from him.

At a local Whitehorse bar, the two of them had sat in a corner and shot the breeze. After the weather and how work sucked, they talked about what was going on at the ranch.

Like Tilly, Harold's girlfriend had filled Harold in on all the comings and goings. The big topic had been the first Mrs. McGraw, who'd had a set of twins six months before and was now acting strangely. Tilly had been worried about her as well, saying she didn't seem to have any interest in the twins.

"Frieda's worried that Marianne might do something to the babies," Harold had whispered after four beers. "Terrible thing. Apparently, she didn't want any more kids and now she doesn't want anything to do with the twins. Frieda's worried she might hurt them. One night the nanny caught her in the nursery holding a pillow like she was going to smother them."

He'd been shocked to hear this, not that Tilly hadn't expressed concern about Marianne McGraw, saying the woman seemed confused a lot of the time.

I sure hope nothing bad happens to them. Cute little things. Sure would be a shame, Harold had said and bought another round of beer.

Cecil couldn't remember when Harold had mentioned getting the babies out of there before something terrible happened to them.

The plan had seemed so reasonable back then. Harold knew some families who would take care of them until their mother got better. They'd been saving those babies.

But even later when it became clear that they were going to kidnap the McGraw twins for money, Cecil hadn't put up a fight. In fact, by then he'd been out of work for months, Tilly was threatening to leave him and he would have done just about anything to get his hands on some money.

Two hundred thousand dollars? he'd whispered in shock when Harold had told him how much ransom they could get.

It isn't like McGraw doesn't have it. All those fancy horses, that big house, and look at what he pays your wife and my girlfriend, Harold had said.

Actually, Tilly had gotten paid well and been well taken care of out at the ranch. That had been part of the problem. She'd had it so good out there that she'd been thinking she could do better than Cecil, but he'd kept his mouth shut and gone along with the plan. If Tilly had left him like she'd been threatening then he would need the money.

It had crossed his mind that Harold might try to cheat him out of his share. But the man couldn't pull off the kidnapping without him so he'd told himself not to worry.

The night of the kidnapping, Tilly had called to say she was sick and asked if he could bring her some cold medicine. Her timing couldn't have been more perfect.

He'd driven within a mile of the ranch near the Little Rockies. Harold had followed him in his rig. They'd hidden it in the pines, then Cecil had driven on out to the ranch with Harold hunkered down in the back. Tilly had left the side door open for him.

While he'd gone upstairs to take the cold medicine to Tilly, Harold had climbed out and hidden in the pool house. He'd already found a ladder he could use to get to the second floor window of the twins' room.

He'd given his wife a double dose to make sure Tilly was out cold. While he was waiting for her to sleep, he'd noticed a bottle of codeine cough syrup sitting there. Tilly had said Marianne McGraw had given it to her from an older prescription she'd had. Later, Marianne wouldn't remember doing that.

Once Tilly had been asleep along with everyone else in the house, he'd walked down the hall and pretended to leave. Instead, he'd ducked into the twins' room and given each of them some of the codeine cough syrup, hoping he didn't overdo it. Careful not to leave any prints on the bottle other than his wife's and the babies' mother's, he'd left it in the twins' room.

Then he'd waited in a guest room down the hall until it was time. Better to be caught there then in the twins' room. Finally it had been time. He'd checked the hallway. Empty. Not a sound in the house. He'd made his way down to the twins' room, still shocked that he was actually doing this. Both babies had been sleeping soundly.

Cecil had opened the window as Harold climbed up. He'd wrapped up the babies in their blankets with their favorite toys just in case the infants woke up. He'd handed them out and Harold had put them in a burlap bag and then descended the ladder.

He'd been thinking how they'd pulled it off when he'd heard a loud crack and had looked out the window to see that one of the ladder rungs had broken under the big man's weight. He'd thought then that it was all

over, but somehow Harold had managed to hold on—
and not drop the babies.

Then he'd gotten the hell out of there, scared out of
his wits. Back at his vehicle, he'd driven back to where
he'd left Harold's vehicle but it had already been gone.
They'd planned not to meet until the ransom was paid.
Cecil never saw him again, let alone his half of the ransom money.

He'd been so shaken that night that he'd just taken
off, driving too fast, not even knowing where he'd been
going. He'd lost control of his car miles from Whitehorse and spent the next week in the hospital in a coma.

It wasn't until recently that he'd learned what had
happened to Harold and the ransom money. It had given
him little satisfaction to find out from the news that
Harold was dead and the money found with him in his
shallow grave.

The only good news was that no one knew who had
helped Harold from inside the house. But then Tilly
had told him about Hank Knight, convinced that the PI
knew not only what had happened to Jesse Rose, but
who the second kidnapper had been.

Now he looked at the highway ahead, telling himself
he might still be able to get away with it. As long as
Boone and that female private investigator didn't find
Jesse Rose, he should be in the clear. But as he drove,
he couldn't help but worry that they knew something
he didn't. He could be driving back to Whitehorse—
right into a trap.

Chapter Fifteen

C.J. found herself smiling as she drove. She listened to Boone's breathing as he slept. He looked so content, not anxious like he did when he was awake. She felt she'd gotten to glimpse something few people had seen. A peaceful Boone McGraw.

The highway took them from Great Falls up to the Hi-Line and across the top part of the state. They were just outside of Whitehorse when Boone stirred.

He sat up, looking surprised that he'd let himself fall asleep. All semblances of peace and serenity left his handsome face as he glanced out the window and saw where they were.

"You need to turn up here at the next road," he said. "You okay driving? If you pull over I can—"

"I'm fine. Nice nap?"

He looked embarrassed. "I didn't realize that I'd fallen sleep, let alone that I was conked out that long. Thanks for driving. I guess I was more tired than I thought."

She merely smiled and seeing the turnoff ahead, slowed. "We aren't going into town?"

"I thought we'd go straight to the ranch."

"I'd feel better staying at a motel—"

"Not a chance. Since I'm not letting you out of my sight, you'll be much safer on the ranch than in a motel in town." He glanced in his side mirror as if, like her, he wondered if whoever was after her might be somewhere behind them.

"I don't think we've been followed," she said. "I've been watching."

He leveled his gaze at her as she turned onto the dirt road. "I keep forgetting you do this for a living."

She said nothing for a half mile. "What will your family think, me showing up on their doorstep with my suitcase in hand?"

"I'll carry your suitcase," he said.

"You know what I mean."

"They'll think…" For a moment he seemed to consider what they would think. He swore under his breath. "My brothers will give you a hard time. They'll think you and I have more than a professional relationship."

"But you'll make it clear that's all it is, right?"

"Of course. You need to turn up here. See that sign reading No Buffalo? Hang a right there." He glanced straight ahead. "This was all too complicated to explain on the phone. But don't worry. The new house is large with numerous guest rooms. While I've been gone, a designer has been putting the finishing touches on it. My father will be delighted to have you."

"So you all live in the main house?"

"I have a place on the ranch, a cabin, where I usually

stay. But until this is over, I'll be sleeping at the house in a room next to yours."

If he thought that made her feel safe, he was sadly mistaken.

Ahead, the house came into view. She stared, a little awestruck. It was beautiful. Boone had mentioned it was new. She'd read about the explosion and fire that had burned down the original house.

She felt anxious about meeting his family and braced herself. So much felt like it was on the line right now. She thought about the thumb drive in her pocket, feeling guilty for keeping it from Boone, from his family.

But only until tomorrow, she told herself. Whatever happened at the train, she would show it to Boone.

As they pulled into the ranch yard, Cull and Ledger were coming up from the barn. Boone saw their interest in who was driving his pickup and swore again under his breath. The last think he needed was them giving him a hard time about C.J.

Also he'd hoped to talk to his father first. Even better would be to tell everyone at the same time to save repeating himself. But he could tell by the inquisitive looks on his brothers' faces that they were more than curious about the woman behind the wheel of his pickup.

"Looks like you're going to get to meet my brothers right away," he said as she handed him the keys. He opened his door, hopped out and called a hello to them. Not that his brothers noticed him. They were staring at C.J.

Cull lifted a brow as he and Ledger joined them. "Hired yourself a chauffeur?"

"This is C.J. West. She's a private investigator."

Cull shook her hand. "I'm his older smarter, more handsome brother, Cull."

"And this is Ledger," Boone said, wishing his brothers could behave for once.

As C.J. shook his younger brother's hand, Cull said, "I hope you've brought good news."

Just then their father came out on the porch.

"Can we take this inside? I'll tell you everything I know," Boone said with a sigh. "But C.J. and I will be staying at least overnight."

"I'll help you with your bags," Ledger said. "Go on in. I know Dad is anxious to hear what you found out."

"So am I," Cull said.

Boone led C.J. up to the house, introduced her to his father and the three of them entered the new house.

The old one had been huge and quite opulent. This one was more practical. It had a nice big eat-in kitchen, a large dining room and living room, a master suite for their father and a ranch office. The other bedrooms were divided between two wings off the north and south ends of the house on the same level to provide privacy for anyone staying in them.

His father had gotten it into his head that his sons and their wives would be staying over a lot so he would be able to spend even more time with his future grandchildren.

The interior designer his father had hired had been given only one requirement. *Marianne loves sunny col-*

ors, Travers had told her. *We need this house to feel like sunshine.*

Boone had to admit, as he stepped into the house, the designer had done her job well. She'd been finishing when he'd left for Butte. The house looked inviting and at the same time homey. It never had with Patty in command. He was anxious to ask his father what had been going on while he'd been gone, with Patty's upcoming trial, her threat to write a tell-all book and a rumor that more arrests would be made in his father's poisoning case.

"Do you mind if I freshen up while you bring your father up to speed?" C.J. asked as Ledger brought in their bags. He could tell she wanted to give him and his father and brothers time alone and he appreciated that.

"Take the last room on the south wing," his father told her. "And please let us know if there is anything you need or want. Boone—"

"You can put my bag in the room next to hers," Boone said, making his brothers as well as his father lift a brow.

C.J. didn't seem to notice as Ledger steered her toward one of the bedroom wings, leaving the three of them alone.

"Why don't we step into the office?" his father suggested.

They'd barely gotten seated when Ledger joined them. Like the old office, there was a rock fireplace with a blaze going in it and comfortable chairs around it along with a large oak desk.

Boone told them what had happened since he'd last seen them.

"Hank Knight is dead?" Cull said. "And you say C.J. was his partner in the investigation business?"

"She's a licensed private investigator and worked with him. But they were much closer than that. Hank helped her single mother raise her. C.J. and Hank were very close. It's one reason she is determined to find his killer."

Cull was shaking his head.

"What does the C.J. stand for?" Ledger asked.

"Calamity Jane. She said her father was a huge fan of Westerns."

"And he's deceased?"

Boone nodded. "Died when she was two."

"So you think this person who's made attempts on her life—and yours—is somehow connected to the kidnapping and Jesse Rose?" his father asked.

"It seems that way. All we know is that Hank Knight didn't share any of it with C.J., something highly unusual, according to her. And he'd flown to Seattle, also something unusual since he apparently hated to fly. He appeared to be planning another trip before he was killed. That, I believe, was to Whitehorse. We think he planned to meet the train from Seattle tomorrow in Whitehorse at 2:45 p.m."

"Who is coming in on the train?" Travers asked.

Boone shook his head. "We have no idea. But we plan to be there."

"What if no one gets off from Seattle?" Cull asked.

"Then my theory is wrong and then I don't know."

Boone raked a hand through his thick dark hair, his Stetson resting on his knee. "It's possible that none of this has to do with Jesse Rose."

"Then what?" Ledger asked.

He shrugged. "But someone wants to keep C.J. from finding out the truth about her partner's murder. If his inquiries about Jesse Rose and the kidnapping are what got him killed…"

"I want to meet the train with you tomorrow," his father said.

"I'm not sure that's a good idea. I think it would be better if C.J. and I go alone. Whoever is getting off that train is expecting to meet Hank Knight. If there's a crowd," he said, looking pointedly at his brothers, "it might scare them away."

"You're hoping Jesse Rose gets off the train," Cull said. "Would you recognize her?"

"I think so."

"And if it is someone else, someone…dangerous?" Travers asked.

"I can handle myself, and don't forget—I will have a card-carrying, gun-toting private investigator with me."

C.J. PUT HER suitcase on a bench in the last room at the end of the hall where Ledger had led her. The room was lovely, bright and airy with a large sliding glass door that looked out on the mountainside beyond. She could see where it appeared a swimming pool was going in to the right. To the left were corrals and several large barns.

Opening the doors, she stepped out on the patio.

Three horses watched her from a nearby corral. She smiled and walked over to them.

She was stroking one of the horse's neck when she heard someone come up behind her. She didn't turn around, didn't need to. She knew it was Boone. That connection that had been growing between them felt stronger than ever.

"You like horses." He sounded surprised. "We could go for a ride. It's a beautiful afternoon and tomorrow it's supposed to snow. We should take advantage of this weather."

She could tell that he wanted to go for a ride. "Why not?"

"I'll saddle us up a couple of horses. Come on." She followed him into the cool of the barn and watched while he expertly saddled the horses. "I gave you a very gentle one."

"I appreciate that." She smiled as he offered her a foot up. She placed her shoe in his cupped hands and let him lift her. Swinging her leg over, she settled in the saddle. It had been a while since she'd ridden a horse, but it felt good. She took the reins and watched Boone. He looked completely at home in the saddle.

They rode out into the afternoon sunlight. It was so much warmer here than it had been in Butte. She breathed in the fresh air as they rode slowly across a pasture.

"Those are the Little Rockies," Boone said, pointing to the dark line of mountains in the distance. "The story goes that Lewis and Clark originally thought they were the Rocky Mountains. When they realized their mistake, they renamed them the Little Rockies."

C.J. saw some cabins back in a stand of trees. "Is that where you usually stay?"

He nodded. "But see that land on the hillside over there? That's my section. Someday I'm going to build a house on it with a view of the mountains."

"When you get married. Is that what your brothers are doing, building on their land?" She pointed to a spot where some land had been excavated.

"That's my brother Cull's. He and Nikki will start their house in the spring. Ledger and Abby will be building about a half mile farther from there. We all wanted to be close—but not too close."

"So you'll always stay on the ranch," she said, not looking at him.

"That's what I've always planned."

She looked over at him because of something she heard in his tone. "Unless?"

"Unless I fall in love with someone who doesn't want this life."

"You'd go where she wanted?" It surprised her that he thought a woman could get this cowboy off the ranch.

"For the right woman, I would."

They rode in silence as the sun slid farther to the west before they turned back.

BACK AT THE RANCH, Cull came out to say that their father wanted to talk to C.J.

"You go ahead," Boone told her. "I'll take care of the horses and join you in a minute."

"You told them that I don't know anything, right?" she said to him.

He nodded. "But you knew Hank Knight."

"I thought I did."

"It's all right," Boone said. "My father understands."

She followed Cull back into the house. Travers Mc-Graw was waiting for her in his office. He rose to his feet when she entered and she saw that he wasn't alone.

"This is Nikki St. James, the true crime writer who is doing the book on the kidnapping."

C.J. shook hands with Nikki, recalling what Boone had told her about the woman. She'd thought at the time that she would probably like the writer. The woman was pretty with long dark hair and wide blue eyes.

Travers asked C.J. to tell them more about her and her relationship with Hank. She told them about growing up in Butte and the impact Hank had on her life.

"I wish I could tell you more," C.J. said after she'd told them what she knew about Hank's inquiry about Jesse Rose and the kidnapping.

"You said Hank always shared his other cases?" Nikki asked. "Had he ever been involved with adoptions?"

"No."

"Do you know if he knew a woman named Pearl Cavanaugh? She was a member of the Whitehorse Sewing Circle."

She shook her head. She'd thought she'd known everything about Hank. That he could have lived a secret life, or worse, that he was involved in the McGraw kidnapping, seemed inconceivable.

Boone came into the room and took a seat. He gave her a reassuring smile.

"How old are you?" Cull asked. He'd been sitting quietly in a corner, listening. She had almost forgotten he was there. Unlike Boone. Her nerve endings had tingled as he'd walked into the room. She'd never been more aware of a man.

"Twenty-eight," she said, wondering why he was asking.

"So you would have been three at the time of the kidnapping," Boone said and looked at his father. "She would have been too young to know if Hank was involved back then."

"He couldn't have been involved in the kidnapping," C.J. argued. "You didn't know him. He wouldn't…" She felt her eyes burn with tears. "He spent his life *helping* people. He didn't steal babies from their beds."

"I wasn't implying that," Nikki said quickly. "One of the kidnappers who was involved was told that the babies weren't safe. We think that's what gave Harold Cline the idea of kidnapping them. It could also be the reason that someone in that house helped him. At least one of them could have thought they were saving the twins."

C.J. felt her stomach roil. If Hank had thought he was saving the babies… "If he was involved, why would he call your lawyer and ask questions about Jesse Rose and the stuffed toy horse that was taken with her?"

She saw Travers and Boone share a look before Nikki said, "He could have been worried about this new information that was released regarding the kidnapping. If

Jesse Rose still had the stuffed toy horse and she heard about it or her adoptive parents did…"

"Wouldn't they have contacted you?" C.J. asked.

"The parents might be afraid of losing their daughter, getting into trouble with the law… There are a lot of reasons they wouldn't want to come forward, especially if they knew who she was when they received her," Travers said.

"As for Jesse Rose, she might not even know that she was adopted," Nikki said. "Even if she saw the digitally enhanced photos in the newspaper, she might not think anything of it."

"But if she had a toy horse with a pink ribbon tied around its neck, she might start asking questions," Boone said. "If the horse gave the six-month-old baby comfort, the adoptive parents might have kept it."

"Or they might not have known that the stuffed toy horse came from the McGraw house," Nikki said. "They could have thought it was a gift from whoever had taken the baby to save her."

"Once it hit the news, though…" Boone looked to C.J.

She felt sick at the thought of all this. That Hank might have been involved twenty-five years ago… She revolted at the idea. Not the Hank she thought she'd known. She reminded herself that he'd kept whatever was going on from her. Because of shame? Or to protect her because he knew it was dangerous?

That thought gave her a little hope. While it looked bad, there was still the chance that Hank was innocent. After all, he was a PI. He could be working for someone who was neck deep in this and was looking for a way out.

"I guess we'll find out tomorrow, depending on who gets off that train at the Whitehorse depot," Boone said. "Until then all we can do is speculate. You must have seen the digitally enhanced photos in the newspaper and on television. Or looked them up on the internet. Did you ever see anyone who resembled Jesse Rose with Hank?"

"No," she said with a shake of her head and suppressed a shudder at the thought of the thumb drive with the young woman's photo on it. She hated lying and promised herself that after tomorrow, she would show it to Boone and his family. She hated keeping secrets from him. But she also couldn't betray Hank.

If Jesse Rose got off that train, she'd recognize her.

Chapter Sixteen

C.J. said she'd like to lie down for a while. Boone took that opportunity to go into town before dinner. "Don't worry, I'll be back in plenty of time," he told his father.

He drove straight to the sheriff's department and asked to see Patty, his former nanny and stepmother. When she'd been his nanny, she'd had straight brown hair, appeared shy and reserved.

When she'd returned to the ranch nine years later with a baby in her arms, she'd changed in more ways than her bleached hair color, from everything that Boone had heard. All he knew was that she'd certainly conned his father. Travers had married her to help her raise the baby, father unknown. Patty had been hell on wheels for those years as his stepmother. She'd made all their lives miserable.

Boone was just glad to have her out of their lives.

The dispatcher started to explain the visiting hours schedule when Sheriff McCall Crawford came out.

"I need to see Patty," he said, "and I'm not going to be able to make visiting hours for a while."

"Probably just as well since she posted bail and will be released later this evening," the sheriff said.

"What? How?"

McCall shook her head. "She came up with the bail and got a judge to grant it. It's out of my hands."

Boone pulled off his Stetson to rake a hand through his hair. "Then I really need to talk to her before she's released."

The sheriff hesitated for only a moment. "Just keep it short, okay?"

He nodded and let her lead him to the visiting room. He'd barely sat down when Patty slid into the seat on the other side of the glass. She smiled at him before picking up the phone.

The smile was enough to set him off, but he reined it in. He came here hoping for information. Ticking her off wouldn't get him anything except maybe a little satisfaction.

"You're looking good," he said into the phone.

She smiled at that. "You McGraws are such charming liars. Heard you'd been out of town. Go somewhere fun?"

"Butte. Went to see a PI who had information on the kidnapping."

"Really?" Her expression hadn't changed. "So you got it all solved, do you?"

"Not quite. Where is my mother's diary?"

She shook her head. *"Diary?"*

"I know you have it."

"You're wrong. Everyone thinks I'm responsible for

whatever was going on in that house twenty-five years ago. Well, I wasn't the only drama."

"We know about Frieda and her love affair that set off the kidnapping."

Patty smiled. "That was just the tip of the iceberg. Tilly ever confess anything to you?"

Tilly? Their housekeeper?

"I believe Tilly had taken cold medicine the night of the kidnapping and was knocked out and had to be awakened."

Patty just smiled.

"Are you trying to tell me it isn't true?" When she said nothing, he lost his cool. "Dammit, Patty, I know you poisoned my mother twenty-five years ago and then did the same thing with my father over the past year. I know you, remember? I saw how you treat people."

She leaned forward and lowered her voice. "Boone, I'm a bitch, but I'm not a killer. Nor did I poison anyone."

He studied her, surprised that a part of him believed her. Was it possible she might be telling the truth?

"Then who was poisoning my father?"

"Anyone with access to that house. Your former ranch manager, Blake Ryan. Your family attorney, Jim Waters." She shrugged. "They ate at the house all the time."

"What was their motive?"

She looked away for a moment. "Maybe they thought they'd get me and the ranch if Travers was gone."

"Where would they get an idea like that, I wonder?"

Patty swung back around. "Not from me."

"Frieda is dead, thanks to you. Or are you going to tell me that you had nothing to do with that, either?"

"I didn't."

He narrowed his gaze at her. "You had a lot to lose if she talked."

"But not as much as the person who helped with the kidnapping. Yes, I kept Frieda in line with what I knew about her boyfriend. Like I said, I was a bitch but I had nothing to do with killing her."

"Sounds like you're innocent of everything."

"I didn't say that. I've made my share of mistakes. My biggest regret is your father. Believe it or not, I loved him. But I always felt like I was living in your mother's shadow—because I was. He never loved me the way he did her and I knew it."

With Patty in a talkative mood, he had to ask. "Who is Kitten's father?"

She laughed. "Who knows? That's not true. It was nobody. A one-night stand. A handsome guy at a bar when I was feeling vulnerable."

"Not Jim or Blake or my father?"

She shook her head.

"Jim and Blake both think they're her father."

Patty shrugged.

"Again, I wonder where they got that idea?"

She smiled. "Like I said, I'm not innocent of everything." Sighing, she looked him in the eye. "What do you want from me, Boone? I'm about to blow this place and I doubt we'll be talking again for a while, if ever."

"The truth would be nice."

"I guess you'll have to wait for my tell-all book,"

she said with a sad smile and replaced her phone as a deputy came into the room.

C.J. SAT AROUND the big table in the dining room and listened to stories about the boys growing up. It felt good to laugh. She especially liked the stories about Boone.

"He was five when he tried to ride one of the calves," Cull was saying. "He hung on all right. Straight across the pasture. We thought we'd probably never see him again. He was hootin' and hollerin'." They all laughed.

"Came back looking like he'd been dragged through the mud, as I recall," Ledger said. "Told everyone he'd ridden a bull."

C.J. loved the sound of their laughter. It was clear that they all loved each other. She felt the warmth and the camaraderie. And for a while, she forgot what she was doing there with them. Forgot about the thumb drive she kept in her pocket. Forgot that Hank was dead. And worse, that someone might be getting off the train tomorrow who would forever change the way she felt about the man she'd loved as a father.

By the time she'd gone to bed, all she wanted was the oblivion of sleep. She'd thought her thoughts would keep her awake. But the moment her head touched the pillow she was out. In her dreams, though, she kept seeing Jesse Rose's face. The woman was trying to tell her something, something about Hank, but C.J. couldn't hear her because of the noise from the train.

BOONE STAYED UP late talking with his father and brothers. It felt good to be back at the ranch. He'd needed that horseback ride earlier. It was the only place he felt at home.

He couldn't help thinking about C.J.—and what he'd told her on the horseback ride. Would he really leave the ranch for a woman? Not just any woman, but her?

Unable to sleep he went outside. It was a clear, cold night but he needed the fresh air. He loved it here, loved the dark purple of the Little Rockies on the horizon, and the prairie where thousands of buffalo once roamed.

He thought of Butte and C.J. Would she leave it for a man? For him?

Shaking his head, he couldn't believe the path his thoughts had taken. He hadn't even kissed the woman. But at dinner tonight, he also couldn't keep his eyes off her. She was so beautiful. He thought of her with that ragtag bunch of half-homeless people at the funeral. She'd called them her and Hank's family. He doubted he'd ever met anyone with such a big heart.

Or anyone more stubborn.

"I know that look."

He turned to see Cull come outside.

"Something bothering you?"

Boone let out a laugh. "Seriously? I'm terrified that I'm wrong about this whole thing. Who knows if there will even be someone on the train tomorrow and now I've got Dad's hopes up and—"

"What's really got you out here wandering around in the dark?" Cull asked, cutting him off.

"I just told you."

His brother shook his head. "Like I said, I know that look. You think I didn't wander around in the dark after meeting Nikki?" Cull let out a laugh. "I used to go out in the barn and talk to myself. I thought I was losing my mind. How could I fall for a damned true crime writer—one who turned our house upside down for a story?"

Boone chuckled. "You've got it all wrong."

"Just keep telling yourself that. A private investigator from *Butte*? Wondering how you got to this point in your life, aren't you?" He held up his hands. "Don't bother lying. I saw you out here and thought I could dispense some sage advice. Take it from me. I've been there. So just go for it. Seriously. Anyone with eyes can see how crazy you are about her. Stop kidding yourself. You've fallen."

Boone shook his head. "You should get some sleep, big brother. You're talking out your—"

"Yep, just keep telling yourself that," Cull said as he laughed and headed in the direction of his cabin.

Boone watched him go. "Just go for it? Right. So much for sage advice, big brother."

STOPPING JUST OUTSIDE the sheriff's department mid-morning, Patricia "Patty" Owen McGraw breathed in the fresh air and looked toward the deep blue sky overhead. A Chinook had come through and melted all the snow, but she'd heard a couple of deputies talking about a white Christmas. A storm was supposed to blow in by this afternoon.

She'd completely forgotten about Christmas. Her only thought had been freedom. And now here she was. Free. At least for a while.

"Are you all right?" asked the deep male voice next to her in a tone that told her he didn't really care. Probably never had.

"I am now," she said without looking at the former McGraw ranch manager. Blake Ryan wasn't one of her favorite people right now. Hell, no one was.

"You realize it's temporary," he said. "Only until your trial. If you take off, you lose—"

"I know what I lose," she snapped and took another deep breath. Having Blake pick her up from jail had been a mistake. He hadn't wanted to do it. She'd had to almost beg and when that failed, she'd had to resort to blackmail. It seemed no one wanted to get on the wrong side of Travers McGraw.

You betrayed Travers when you slept with his nanny twenty-five years ago—not to mention his wife much more recently, she'd snapped on the phone earlier. *He knows about us, so come pick me up. I need a ride and you need me to keep at least some of the things about you out of my book.*

"This money they advanced you on this tell-all book," Blake said now as he opened the car door.

"What about it?" She couldn't help the irritation in her voice. It was none of his business. She owed him nothing.

"Do you have to give it back if you don't write the book?"

"Why wouldn't I write it?"

He shot her a look and cleared his voice. "Patricia, you can't tell *everything*." She suspected Travers had set up some sort of retirement plan for the ranch manager and still contributed to it. Everyone had their reasons for distancing themselves from her, but they would all pay when the book came out. Or when this went to trial.

She glanced out the side window. "I told the publisher it was a tell-all book that dished the dirt. All the dirt. You wouldn't want me to have lied, would you?" She smiled to herself as she felt his gaze on her before he turned back to his driving.

"It wouldn't be the first time you lied," he finally said.

She burst out laughing as she turned back to him. "I wondered if you'd have the guts to call me on it. And you did. What is it you're afraid of, Blake? How about I write that you were an amazing lover?"

"I don't think that's funny."

"I wasn't trying to be funny. I meant what I said, I'm telling it all. Anyway," she said with a shake of her head as bitterness rose like bile in her stomach. "What do I have to lose? Do I have to mention that I asked for your help and you couldn't be bothered?"

"You know the position I'm in."

"Unlike the one I'm in?"

"Patricia, give me a break. I don't have the kind of money you need to get out of this."

"But I sure found out who my friends and lovers were, didn't I?" She bit at her lower lip as silence filled the truck. "You're in this just as deep as I am."

"Where do you want to go?" he finally asked. "You want a drink? Something to eat? We could swing by Joe's In-n-Out for a quick lunch."

His offer was like a knife to her heart. He didn't want

to be seen with her, hoped to get rid of her as quickly as possible. She studied him for a moment, glad she didn't have a knife because it would be in Blake's chest right now. Why did she always fall in love with weak men?

"Just drop me at the Great Northern Hotel." Had she thought earlier that he would have wanted to take her to his place? Would she have gone if he had asked her?

He drove around the block and pulled up at the entrance to the GN, as it was called locally. As she opened her door to get out, he said, "I wish you wouldn't do this."

She glanced back at him. "Spend a night in a motel room alone?"

"You know what I mean."

She laughed and forced a smile. "You mean what I tell during my trial? Or the book? I'm going to give you a whole chapter, Blake," she said and slammed the door. She didn't look back as she fought the burn of tears.

"How in Hades did Patty make bail?" Boone demanded as he stormed into his father's office. "I just heard. Tell me you didn't—"

"I didn't."

"Did you know?"

His father shook his head. He pushed away the papers in front of him and sat back in his chair. "She must have sold the book she's been threatening to write about the kidnapping. Her tell-all book. She tried to get me to buy her off. I don't care what she writes."

Boone swore. "Well, if anyone knows the truth about

what happened that night, I'm betting it was Patty." He frowned. "But that kind of truth won't set her free."

"Maybe she knows more than she has ever told about someone else being in the house that night," Travers said.

"Is that what you're hoping?" he asked.

"Truthfully? I just want Jesse Rose found. As far as the other kidnapper..."

"You don't want justice?"

"Justice." Travers chuckled. "There can never be justice. Too much was lost." He got a glazed look in his eyes.

Boone studied his boots for a moment. "How *is* Mom?"

"Better. She wants to see Oakley."

He looked up in surprise. "You told her about Tough Crandall?"

"He's her son."

"Are you sure about that?" He ground his teeth at the thought of the arrogant cowboy who'd paid them a visit to set them straight. Tough Crandall had outed the man pretending to be Oakley.

But Tough had refused to take a DNA test to prove that he was the lost twin. In fact, Tough wanted nothing to do with the McGraws—any of them.

"Has Tough agreed to see Mother?"

"Not yet, but he will."

Boone shook his head. His father had lived in a fantasy world for twenty-five years, first believing the twins were alive and would come home one day. And now he thought that cowboy who'd known for years that he was the missing twin—and kept it from his own grieving birth father—would find it in his heart to visit his birth mother?

"Dad—"

"Boone, he just needs time."

He told himself that he didn't want to argue the point with his father. He didn't have time anyway. He and C.J. had to meet the train. He'd had trouble getting to sleep last night and had been anxious all morning. Cull's little talk with him hadn't helped.

Now he tried to concentrate on what had to be done. He just hoped that whoever was on that train knew something about Jesse Rose's whereabouts. That was if she was still alive. That thought was the fear that had dogged him since his father had asked him to talk to PI Hank Knight.

Oakley had been found—kind of—not that it was the happy reunion his father had hoped for. But that didn't mean that Jesse Rose would be found. Twenty-five years was a long time. Anything could have happened.

C.J. FOUGHT TO still her nerves as they drove into Whitehorse. The afternoon wind sent a tumbleweed cartwheeling across the road in front of them as they reached the outskirts of town.

"This is Whitehorse? And you made fun of Butte?" C.J. joked as she took in the small Western town.

"Easy," he said and grinned. "You're in the true heart of Montana."

She scoffed good-naturedly at that as he pulled up to a small building that had Whitehorse printed on the side. She recalled that he'd said it was unmanned. Tickets were bought online. There was only one car parked next to the depot but no sign of anyone.

Across the tracks was apparently the main drag. She saw a hotel called the Great Northern, several bars, a restaurant and a hardware store. Like a lot of towns, Whitehorse had sprung up beside the railroad as tracks were laid across the state.

Looking down the tracks, though, she saw nothing in the distance. They got out into the waning winter sunlight. The air smelled of an impending snowstorm. C.J. shivered although it wasn't that cold as they went to stand on the platform in front of the depot. The train was due to arrive soon, but they were the only ones waiting.

She could tell that Boone was as anxious and worried as she was. Looking down the tracks for the light of the locomotive, she tried to keep her emotions in check. If they were right, Hank had been planning to meet this train.

"What if a dozen people get off the train?" C.J. asked, merely needing to make conversation because she knew exactly what Jesse Rose looked like.

"Not likely,'" he said with a laugh. "This will probably surprise you, but like I told you, not many people get off here."

"That is a surprise," she said.

He smiled over at her. "This area of Montana would grow on you. If you gave it a chance."

She met his gaze. "You think?" She thought about what he'd said the day before. That he'd leave for the right woman. But no woman who'd seen him on his ranch would ever take him from what he loved. No woman who loved him, anyway.

"Ever thought about a change of scenery?"

"Whatever are you suggesting, Mr. McGraw?"

He shrugged as if embarrassed.

What *had* he been suggesting? Whatever it was, he seemed to wish he hadn't brought it up. "You know, if you ever got out this way in the future."

Little chance of that, she thought as snowflakes began to fall. In the distance, she thought she heard the sound of a train.

BOONE COULDN'T BELIEVE what he'd just said to her. What *had* he been suggesting? Whatever it was, it wasn't like him. Like he could take Cull's advice. Like he ever would. And yet he'd realized this morning that no matter who got off that train today, C.J. would be leaving.

He'd take her back to Butte and that would be it. That thought had made him ache. C.J. had gotten to him, no doubt about that. She was funny and smart. He loved the tough exterior she put up. But he could see the vulnerability just below the surface. It made him want to protect her and he knew the kind of trouble that could get him into. Look at his brothers.

But now, as he waited for the train, he couldn't help looking at her as if memorizing everything about her. Her cheeks were flushed from the cold. Her eyes were bright. He watched her stick out her tongue to catch a snowflake as if not even realizing she'd done it.

"We could wait inside," he suggested, seeing her shiver.

Hugging herself, she shook her head. "I think I heard the train."

He could guess what she was hoping. That whoever was on this train would know who might have wanted Hank Knight dead. C.J. wouldn't rest until she found her partner's killer.

He hoped he was around when that happened. C.J. might just find out that she did need someone. Even him. While he loved her independence, he'd learned it was okay to lean on family occasionally. He got the feeling that it had only been her and Hank against the world for too long, and now with her partner gone...

As much as he fought with his brothers and knocked heads with his father, Boone was damned glad he had them in his life. He couldn't imagine how alone C.J. must feel. He felt another stab of that need to protect her.

Not that there was any reaching out to her. She'd rebuffed any attempt to offer comfort. She was determined to go it alone and had only grudgingly put up with him because she had no choice. But she had let him put his arm around her at the funeral. She'd even leaned into him. For a few minutes.

Snowflakes whirled around them. C.J. had her face turned up to the snow, her eyes closed. He saw her shiver again and couldn't help himself. He stepped to her and pulled her close.

She opened her beautiful brown eyes and looked at him. He felt his heart bump against his ribs. He wanted this woman. The thought terrified him. And yet he wrapped her tighter in his arms and drew her into him as the snow spun around them.

Chapter Seventeen

C.J. looked up into Boone's blue eyes as he pulled her against him. She forgot the falling snow, the cold and the worry and pain that had seeped into her bones over the past week. In his arms, she felt warm and safe.

All her instincts told her to pull away, but she didn't move.

Her gaze locked with his and she felt her heart quicken. Slowly, he bent his head until his lips were only a breath away from her own. She couldn't breathe. Didn't dare. She thought she would die if he didn't kiss her.

His lips brushed over hers. She let out a sigh of relief and joy and pleasure. He pulled her tighter against him, taking her mouth with his own. She melted into him and the kiss, heart pounding, desire sparking along her nerve endings like a string of lit dynamite.

The sound of the train whistle on the edge of town made them both jump, bringing them back to reality with a thud. As they stepped apart, C.J. braced herself as the light on the front of the locomotive came into view.

The train puffed into town through the falling, whirling snow. Boone stood next to her as the noisy train slowed and finally came to a stop after numerous cars had gone past. Boone hadn't said a word after the kiss. Nor had she. But she did wonder if he regretted it.

She touched the tip of her tongue to her upper lip and smiled to herself. Not that it would ever happen again, she was sure. Neither of them was ready for…for whatever that had been.

A door opened on one of the coach cars. A conductor put out a yellow footstool and then began to help a passenger off. C.J. held her breath but let it out on a frosty puff as an elderly woman was helped off, followed by an elderly man. They walked toward their vehicle parked beside the depot where they'd apparently left it before their trip.

C.J. felt her heart drop. She shot Boone a look as the locomotive engine started up and the conductor picked up the stool and stepped back on to close the door as the train began to move again.

"Boone?"

The train began to slowly pull away. She wanted to scream. She wanted Boone to take her in his arms again. Tears blurred her eyes.

"It's all right," he said, touching her arm. "They still have to unload the sleeping car."

She blinked. The train hadn't left. She heard it grind to a stop again after going only a short way. This time a door opened on a sleeping compartment car next to the platform. Another conductor stepped off with a stool and reached back in to bring out a suitcase. He set the case on the cold concrete and then reached back in again—this time to help a young woman off the train.

C.J.'s hand went to her mouth as the dark-haired young woman from Hank's thumb drive stepped off and looked in their direction.

Boone made a sound, as if equally startled by the intensity of the woman's green eyes. She was beautiful, slender and graceful-looking in a way that C.J. feared she would never be. Her heart felt as if it might burst. She knew she was looking at Jesse Rose McGraw—and all that it meant.

Oh, Hank, what were you involved in?

She looked over at Boone, gripped by a wave of guilt for withholding the thumb drive. She could see him struggling, as if asking himself if this woman could be the sister he hadn't laid eyes on since she was six months old.

C.J. felt her chest constrict as she touched his shoulder. He looked over at her and she nodded. The train pulled out and was gone as quickly as it had come, leaving the three of them standing in the falling snow.

It was Jesse Rose McGraw all grown up. C.J. stared at the woman through the falling snow, her heart hammering with both relief and fear. She couldn't keep kidding herself. Hank had been involved in all this up to his ears.

"Excuse me," Boone said as they approached the young woman. "Were you expecting to meet Hank Knight here?"

Tears filled the young woman's eyes as she looked

past them for a moment, before settling her gaze on C.J. "Hank…" Her voice broke. "He's gone, isn't he?"

C.J. nodded, not sure how the woman had heard about Hank's death, but glad they weren't going to have to give her the news. "I'm so sorry."

"You must be Calamity Jane," the young woman said through her tears as she stepped to C.J. and threw her arms around her. "Uncle Hank told me so much about you."

Uncle Hank? C.J. shot a surprised look over Jesse Rose's shoulder at Boone. He looked as shocked as she felt.

"But I'm surprised *you're* here," the young woman said as she pulled back to look at C.J. "He said it would either be him or…" Her gaze went to Boone. "Or someone from the McGraw family."

C.J. saw her wipe at her tears as she turned to Boone. Her face lit as she smiled. "You must be one of my brothers?"

"Boone McGraw." He sounded dumbstruck but at the same time overjoyed. "And you're…"

The young woman held out her hand. "Jesse Rose Sanderson."

"Jesse Rose?" he repeated in obvious astonishment as he took her gloved hand in his.

She smiled sadly. "Uncle Hank told me that he tried to talk my mother into changing my name, but I guess when she whispered the name to me the first time she held me, my eyes lit up. She didn't have the heart to change it."

Boone shook his head. "So you know… We definitely need to talk, but we don't have to do it out here in the snowstorm." He ushered them toward the large SUV that he and C.J. had brought into town from the ranch.

C.J. climbed in the back so Jesse Rose could be up front with her brother. As she did, Jesse Rose reached back to clasp her hand.

"Calamity Jane," the young woman said with a laugh. "You're exactly as Uncle Hank described you. But I know you prefer C.J. Sorry. I've always loved your name and wanted to meet the girl who'd stolen my uncle's heart." Jesse Rose's hand was warm in hers. C.J. wondered if she could feel her trembling. Hank had told Jesse Rose all about her?

"I was so hoping Uncle Hank would be meeting the train, but he'd warned me that he might not be able to make it. Was he very sick at the end?"

C.J. shook her head, completely confused. *Sick?*

"I hope he didn't suffer."

"No," she said quickly. Everyone who'd seen the accident said he'd been killed instantly. "He didn't suffer." She felt as if she'd fallen down a rabbit hole.

"Good," Jesse Rose said. "He looked fine when he was out in Seattle but my mother said cancer can do that. She said then that he wouldn't be with us long."

Cancer? C.J. couldn't believe what she was hearing. Was it true? And yet as she sat there staring at the falling snow outside, she knew it was. Hank's sudden decision to retire. It had been so unlike him. He'd loved what he did. She'd tried to talk him out of it but he'd made all kinds of excuses. She'd finally stopped pushing him, seeing that he'd been determined. And yet, she'd also seen how sad he'd been about the decision. Now it made sense.

But why hadn't he told her? She tried to remember if she'd ever seen him looking sick and realized there had been a couple of times when she'd stopped by his office and caught him unaware. She'd just thought he was tired, that the job had taken a toll on him. She'd never dreamed... Cancer.

It explained so much. Why he'd be so set on retiring and closing down his office. Why he'd flown to Seattle without telling her and why he'd warned Jesse Rose than he might not be meeting the train. That one of the McGraw brothers would meet the train. Clearly, he'd planned on going, otherwise he would have let someone at the McGraw ranch know. But then he hadn't planned on getting run down in the street, had he?

Jesse Rose let go of C.J.'s hand as Boone climbed behind the wheel. "I'm just so glad that Uncle Hank told me about my family out here."

"So how long have you known?" Boone asked as he started the SUV. C.J. could tell that he was hoping this wouldn't be another case of a child who didn't want to know her McGraw family like Tough Crandall.

But C.J. suspected the woman wouldn't be here right now if she didn't want to get to know her birth family.

"Known I was adopted? Or known that I had more family?" Jesse Rose asked.

Boone shifted into Reverse. "Both."

"I found out I was adopted when I was seventeen. I was looking for my birth certificate..." She shrugged. "I found it and it said I was born to my parents, but I also found a letter from a woman named Pearl Cavanaugh. Did you know her?"

"I knew who she was," Boone said.

"I only learned recently, though, about the circumstances of my adoption. Uncle Hank told me—over the protests of my mother. He said it was time I met my birth family."

"What about your father?" C.J. had to ask.

"My father died when I was twelve. My mother was apparently the only one who knew that I'd been kidnapped, but according to Uncle Hank, she had wanted a child so much, she would have kidnapped one herself if she hadn't gotten me."

BOONE GLANCED IN the rearview mirror at C.J. as he drove through the underpass and down a block before pulling in front of the Whitehorse Café. He couldn't imagine what was going through her head right now. His was still swimming. But he was more worried about her. This had to have caught her flatfooted.

He'd pictured meeting the train and Jesse Rose stepping off, but he'd never really believed it was going to happen. And then for her to already know about not only Hank's death but her own kidnapping and illegal adoption... It blew his mind. At least Hank had taken care of that.

Why, though, had he kept it all from not only the rest of the world, including the McGraws, but he'd kept it from C.J.? Didn't he realize how much this was going to hurt her? Not to mention Jesse Rose knew all about C.J.

but C.J. knew nothing about Jesse Rose all these years? Clearly Hank was involved in this. How much, though?

As he parked in front of the café, Boone said, "I thought we could have something warm to drink before we go out to the ranch."

Inside, they took at table at the back. Because of the hour, the café was empty. Fortunately, Abby, his brother Ledger's fiancée, wasn't working. The waitress who took their order said hello to Boone and merely smiled at the two women he was with.

"I feel as if I've always known you," Jesse Rose said to C.J. "I've heard so much about you from Uncle Hank for years. He said that he just knew the two of us would hit it off because we are so much alike. He promised that one day we would meet."

"I'm sorry to seem so surprised but Hank never told me anything about you," C.J. said.

Jesse Rose frowned. "I guess I understand under the circumstances. I always wondered why Uncle Hank wouldn't let me come out and visit. I thought it was just my mother's doing. She and Uncle Hank...well, they didn't get along. But I adored him and he... I don't have to tell you how special he was." Tears filled her green eyes. "I'm so sorry he's gone."

"He had cancer," C.J. said as if seeing Boone's confusion. "He'd told her that he might not be able to meet the train. Apparently, he knew he didn't have long."

"Oh, wow, I'm so sorry," Boone said to C.J. Just another thing Hank had kept from her.

"You never suspected you were adopted until you found the letter?" C.J. asked.

Jesse Rose hesitated before she said, "Not really. Don't most kids think they must have been adopted if they aren't that much like their parents or siblings? I didn't have siblings." She shrugged.

"So you aren't like your parents?" Boone asked.

Jesse laughed. "My father was blond and blue-eyed and so is my mother. She always told me that my dark hair came from my father's side of the family." She sobered. "Do you think there is any chance that there's a mistake and I'm not Jesse Rose McGraw?"

"We won't know for sure until we do a DNA test, if you're agreeable, but you look just like our mother when she was your age," Boone said.

Jesse Rose brightened. "How strange and yet wonderful to find out that I might have siblings. I used to dream of having a brother or sister. I was so anxious on the train. That was the longest twenty hours of my life, but I'm like Uncle Hank. I hate to fly. Not that there was any way to fly into Whitehorse except by private plane."

"I'm sure Hank told you, but it isn't just siblings you have, but a twin," Boone said.

She nodded excitedly. "I can't wait to meet him. It's so strange. I've always felt like I was missing a part of myself. I know that sounds crazy."

"Not at all. I've heard that about twins, even fraternal twins."

"Will he be at the ranch when we get there?" When Jesse Rose saw them exchange a look, she asked, "What?"

"No, but he lives around here. His name is Tough Crandall. He ranches in the next county. It's just that he's known he was Oakley McGraw for years but he wants nothing to do with the notoriety that might come from it," Boone said.

"The kidnapping case was fairly well-known," C.J. added. "I hope you aren't worried about that part." Boone couldn't bear for Travers not to at least get to meet his only daughter.

Jesse Rose shook her head. "But if I was kidnapped and my mother knew…" She looked up, those green eyes bright with worry. "My mother wouldn't go to jail, would she?"

"We would do everything possible to keep that from happening. We don't know what your mother was told. Oakley's mother believed she was saving him. Your mother might have, as well."

"Still, I don't understand how my mother could take someone's child," Jesse Rose said.

Chapter Eighteen

All the way out to the ranch, C.J. could see that Jesse Rose was struggling with the news of her uncle's death. It was clear that they were very close even though they hardly saw each other.

She also seemed nervous, not that C.J. could blame her. She was about to meet a family she'd never known, come back to a home she'd only lived in for six months as a baby, face a father who had missed her for twenty-five years.

"Did Hank tell you how you happened to be adopted by your mother?" C.J. finally had to ask.

"No, but he said he would explain everything." Tears welled in her eyes again. "I still can't believe he's gone."

"There's something you should know," C.J. said. "Hank didn't die of cancer. He was killed in a hit-and-run accident," she said. "One of the kidnappers is still at large and we think he might have…" She reached for Jesse Rose's hand and squeezed it. "I didn't know about the cancer. He kept a lot from me."

"I'm so sorry he kept his family from you," Jesse

Rose asked. "He *adored* you. He told us such wonderful stories about you. You were like a daughter to him."

Jesse Rose's words filled C.J.'s heart to near bursting. "How often did he visit you?"

"Just once or twice a year. He said he was too busy to come more than that. I always asked to come visit him but he made excuses. Mother said it was because of the way he lived, like a pauper."

"I'm afraid there might be more to the story," Boone said.

Jesse Rose chuckled. "That Hank was rich." She nodded at her brother's surprise. "His family was very wealthy, but he never wanted anything to do with the money. He wanted to find his own way in life without them telling him what to do. I guess my grandparents almost disowned him when he became a private investigator and moved to Butte, Montana."

"That explains a lot," Boone said and glanced in the rearview mirror back at C.J.

She smiled at him, also glad there was at least one thing she didn't have to worry about. The stocks and bonds Hank had left her hadn't been appropriated by ill-gotten means.

"This is beautiful," Jesse Rose said as she looked out at the country.

It was nothing like Butte, C.J. thought. Butte sat in a bowl surrounded by mountains. This part of Montana was rolling prairie. The only mountains she could see were the Little Rockies on the horizon. She thought about what Boone had said about the country growing on her. Maybe. Look how Boone McGraw had grown on her.

Boone drove up the lane to the ranch house, white wooden fences on each side of the narrow road. Yesterday C.J. had been driving and too anxious to pay much attention. Now she took it all in. The ranch reminded her of every horse movie she'd ever seen as a girl. Miles of pasture fenced in by white-painted wooden fence that made the place look as if it should be in Kentucky—not the backwoods of Montana.

In the front seat, Jesse Rose let out a pleased sound at the sight of a half dozen horses running beside the SUV on the other side of the fence, their tails waving in the wind.

"I love horses. It's one reason I've always wanted to come to Montana. But Uncle Hank…" Tears filled her eyes again. She wiped them. "I always knew he was hiding something from us, but I just assumed it was his lifestyle."

Boone pulled up in front of the large ranch house and cut the engine. "Hope you're ready to meet the family, because they are more than ready to meet you."

The family had come spilling out the door, clearly unable to hold back. C.J. stood back to watch as Travers came down the steps. He took one look at Jesse Rose and pulled her into a hug. It was a beautiful sight, all of the McGraws and future McGraws welcoming Jesse Rose.

And Jesse Rose seemed smitten with all of them as they quickly ushered her inside.

"Hey," Boone said, suddenly next to her. "You all right?"

She wiped at her eyes and nodded, unable to speak.

"I'm sorry about Hank," he said as got Jesse Rose's suitcase from the back and they stepped out of the falling snow and onto the porch.

"Sounds like the killer did him a favor since everyone said he died instantly. I just wish…"

"I know." He put his arm around her and she leaned into his strong, hard body. He smelled good, felt good. She thought she could have stayed right there forever.

But from inside the house, his father called to him. "Champagne!"

JUST OUTSIDE OF WHITEHORSE, Cecil's cell phone rang, making him jump. He saw that it was Tilly. Now what?

"Hey," he said, trying to sound upbeat.

"You can't believe what is happening here," Tilly whispered.

His stomach roiled. Tilly sounded like she might bust if she didn't tell someone.

"Jesse Rose. She's been found. She came in on the train today and Boone and the female private investigator just brought her out to the ranch. Everyone is so excited."

Not everyone. "Must have been a shock to Jesse Rose."

"Didn't sound like it. Apparently she knew—that's why she came out on the train to meet her family. I have no idea how long she's known. Travers is beside himself." He heard her admiration for her boss in her voice and growled under his breath. "Where are you?"

"I'm headed back home," he said as he saw the outskirts of Whitehorse. But he needed time to think.

In fact, he'd asked her not to mention that they were back together. He knew what Travers McGraw thought of him. A lot of people thought he was a loser.

"There is going to be a huge celebration out here tonight," Tilly was saying. "The twins have been found. Bless the Lord."

Yes, he thought, his leg aching.

"When Boone called, did he say who the other kidnapper was?" He held his breath.

"I didn't get to hear all of the conversation," Tilly said, sounding so excited she was breathing hard. "But some letters came today from that private investigator I told you about. And a package from the second Mrs. McGraw."

He heard the distaste in his ex-wife's tone. "A package from Patty? You sure it's not a bomb?"

"Very funny. No, it feels like a book. It's addressed to Mr. McGraw."

A book? He brushed that away. It was the letters that he was worried about. "Who are the letters to?"

"There's one for Jesse Rose, one for that young female private eye, C.J. West, that Boone brought back with him and one for Mr. McGraw."

"Travers?" This was it. His worst fear was coming true. He looked at Whitehorse ahead. He could just keep driving to North Dakota and beyond, but they would eventually find him. Or maybe there was a chance…

"So you haven't given anyone the letters yet?" he asked, praying she hadn't.

"No, everyone is too excited to see Jesse Rose," Tilly said.

"Don't give them the letters! Tilly, are you listening to me?"

"Yes, but why wouldn't I—"

"You can't give them the letters." He racked his brain as to what to do. "Burn them."

"I can't do that!"

"Then hold on to them until I get there. Can you do that?" His mind was whirling. If the McGraws knew the part he'd played in the kidnapping, then he would have heard by now. Tilly would have heard. So the little female PI hadn't found out anything.

Instead, Hank had written letters, letters that would incriminate them both. He swore under his breath. "Tilly, just do as I ask, please."

"I don't understand why you would want me to—"

"Tilly, if you love me, if you've ever loved me, I'm begging you, hide the letters. I'm on my way out there. I will explain everything when I get there."

"SOMETHING WRONG?" BOONE ASKED, making Tilly jump. She had her back to him as she was talking on the phone. She hadn't heard over the commotion in the other room.

He was still in shock. In his wildest dreams, he'd hoped Jesse Rose would get off that train. But he'd never imagined that she would already know about him and the rest of the McGraws—let alone know about C.J.

Uncle Hank? He'd seen C.J.'s expression. She'd been poleaxed by the news. What they didn't know was how Hank's sister had come to have Jesse Rose. Had Hank been involved in the kidnapping?

From everything he'd learned about the man after talking to people in Butte—including C.J.—he found it hard to believe. But the man had known that Jesse Rose had been kidnapped and he hadn't come forward. Until now, Boone thought. Hank had finally come forward after twenty-five years. Because he knew he was dying?

Travers had insisted they have champagne so he'd come into the kitchen hoping to find their new cook, but had found Tilly instead. When he'd heard the shrill rise of her voice on the phone, he'd been worried something might have happened.

But now she quickly stuffed whatever she'd been holding into her large purse along with her phone before she turned. She put on a big smile, making him all the more concerned that she was hiding something.

"If there is anything I can do…" he said seeing that she appeared to be trembling.

"Oh, you are so sweet. You're whole family. I… I feel so fortunate to work here. Your father…he's been so nice to me all these years, and letting me come back to work the way he did…" She sounded close to tears.

"Tilly," he said, stepping to her to take her shoulders in his hands. "You are family to us. That's why you can tell me if something is wrong."

She nodded, tears in her eyes. "It was Cecil on the phone…" She looked at the floor and, taking a deep breath, let it out before she continued. "He doesn't want anyone to know that we're thinking about getting back together."

Boone smiled. "Well, that's good news, isn't it?"

"Yes, of course. Cecil is just worried that people will talk or worse, you know."

He did know. He remembered years ago when Tilly and Cecil had gotten a divorce. Cecil had never been one to work and Tilly had put up with it for years and had finally had enough. Everyone had thought she should have kicked him out a lot sooner. Those same people would probably think she was a fool for taking him back.

"If you're happy, then I'm happy for you," he said. "I just wanted to check and see what room we might put Jesse Rose in."

"Oh, let me show her." Tilly started to head toward the living room, but quickly turned back to grab her purse. "I'll just put this away first."

"I'm sure you all have a lot of questions," Jesse Rose said after glasses of champagne were raised to celebrate her return. "I have a lot myself. But I am so happy to learn about all of you. I always wanted siblings. I can't believe this." She smiled as she looked around the room, her gaze lighting on C.J. for a long moment. "I especially always wanted a sister."

C.J. smiled, happy for Jesse Rose, but feeling like she didn't belong here. Once it came out about Hank… Boone took her barely touched champagne glass and set it aside. His fingers brushed hers as he did, making her start. Their gazes locked for a moment.

"You okay?" he whispered.

She smiled and nodded, but she felt anything but okay and Boone seemed to sense it. He took her hand and led her down a hallway to a sunroom off the south side of the house. "You should be back there with your family," she protested when he let the door close behind them.

"I can see that you're not okay," he said, stepping to her to lift her chin with his warm fingers. "Tell me what's bothering you?"

"I shouldn't be here. This is family—"

"You're with me."

Her pulse leaped at the look in his eyes.

"I want you here. I... I want you."

Before she could move, he pulled her to him. The kiss on the train platform had stirred emotions and desires in her. But it was nothing like this kiss. C.J. couldn't remember ever feeling such swift, powerful emotions course through her. Desire was like a fire inside her that had been banked for too long. Boone deepened the kiss, sending her reeling with needs that she'd kept bottled up. She leaned into him, wanting...

There was a sound outside the door.

He pulled back, his gaze on hers, the promise in those blue eyes fanning the flames.

"Boone!" His brother Cull stuck his head in.

"Oh, there you are." Cull looked embarrassed. "Sorry. Dad needs you."

"Go," C.J. said as she tried to catch her breath. "I'm just going to step outside for a moment. It's hot in here."

Cull was grinning at his brother as they both left.

C.J. grabbed her coat and stepped outside, practically fanning herself with the freezing-cold evening air. Twilight had fallen over the ranch, gilding it and the fresh snow in a pale silver. Cooling down, she pulled on her coat as she looked to the Little Rockies. She thought about what Boone had said about this part of Montana growing on her. It had. Just as Boone McGraw had.

But it was his words just moments ago that still had the fires burning in her. *I want you here. I want you.* She'd heard how hard those words were for him to say.

Her heart was still pounding at the memory of the kiss, to say nothing of the promise she'd seen in his blue eyes, when she heard a noise behind her.

Chapter Nineteen

Before she could turn, C.J. was grabbed from behind. She felt the cold barrel end of a gun pressed to her temple.

"Listen to me," the man whispered against her ear. "Do what I say or you die and so does everyone else in that house. You understand?"

She nodded and he jerked her backward as he half dragged her to the closest barn. She noticed that he was limping badly. This was the man who'd broken into her house. The same one Boone had seen at Hank's funeral. The same one who'd killed Hank and tried to run her and Boone down in Butte?

Once inside the barn, he said, "Call your boyfriend."

"What?" She'd been thinking about her self-defense training. The problem was that the man was large and strong and he'd caught her off guard. And now there was a gun to her temple. Something in the man's tone also warned her that he was deadly serious—and nervous as hell. "I don't have a boyfriend."

"Boone McGraw. I saw the two of you. Call him. Then hand me the phone."

"No." She wasn't going to ask Boone to come out here to face a man with a gun because she'd fallen in love with him. She'd rather die than—

"Listen to me. If you do this, no one will get hurt. If I have to haul you inside the house with this gun to your head, a whole lot of people are going to die. My wife is inside that house and she has some letters I need. Once I have those, you can both go back to your lives. No one gets hurt. Otherwise…"

She thought of Boone's family. She couldn't chance that the man was telling the truth about more people being hurt. Also this would buy time and give her a chance to get out of this.

"You're the one who broke into my house," she said as she got a glimpse of the man with the scar on his face and the black baseball cap covering his graying hair. "You were at Hank's funeral."

He grunted. "Make the call." He held her tighter, the barrel of the gun pressing hard against her temple. She'd had self-defense training for her job. Hank had insisted. But he'd also warned her about acting rash.

Some of these people are all hopped up on God only knows what, he'd told her. *Best to bide your time, try to talk your way out of the situation and if all else fails, use your training.*

She doubted there would be any talking her way out of this. She could feel the man's nerves vibrating through his body. He was too jumpy. In the state he was in, he might pull the trigger accidentally. But that meant there was a good chance of him making a mistake and giving her an opening to escape. She had to count on that. If she got the chance, she would do what she had to do to keep him from killing both her and Boone.

"Okay." Pulling out her phone, she made the call with trembling fingers.

He snatched the phone away from her before she could say a word. "Boone? Just listen if you don't want your girlfriend to die. I have a gun to her head. I need you to find Tilly. She has some letters. Tell her to give them to you and then come outside. Once I see that you have the letters, I will let your girlfriend go."

BOONE LISTENED. SOMEONE had C.J.? Had a gun to her head over some…letters? He recalled earlier when he'd startled Tilly. She said she'd been on the phone with her ex-husband, but had said what he'd overheard had something to do with them getting back together.

He now realized it had been a lie. He excused himself and went looking for Tilly. He thought about taking one of his father's guns, but he didn't want to call attention to himself by going into the gun room where all the guns and ammunition was locked up.

And if anyone in the family knew where he was going, they would want to come with him. He couldn't chance what the man might do. The man on the phone had sounded scared. And maybe unstable. Surely he didn't believe he was going to get away with this, whatever it was.

He found Tilly in one of the bedrooms. "Tilly?"

She'd been pacing and now jumped at the sound of her name. The woman was literally wringing her hands.

"You have some letters?" he said, not having time to find out what was wrong with her right now.

Her eyes widened. "You know about the letters?"

"I was told to get them from you."

She nodded, looking like she might burst into tears. "He told me to keep them. I—"

"It's fine. Just give them to me."

Tilly moved to a table next to the bed where she'd apparently come to clean, picked up her large bag and dug into it, pulling out one business-size envelope after another until there were three on the bed. She handed them to him.

"I just did what he asked me to do," she said.

Boone nodded as he took the letters, noting the names on them and the return address. They were all from Hank Knight. "Who asked you to keep the letters a secret, Tilly?"

"Cecil." She looked confused. "My ex-husband. Isn't he the one who wants the letters?"

C.J. COULD FEEL the man getting more impatient by the moment. He kept looking toward the house and muttering under his breath as he held her tightly, the gun to her head.

"This is about some letters?" she asked.

"As if you don't know. Your PI friend sent them."

"Hank?"

"One to you, one to Jesse Rose, one to Travers Mc-Graw."

"What's in them?" she asked. But she already knew. The answers they all desperately needed.

"Don't you wish you knew? Once they're destroyed, it will finally be over."

She doubted that, but she didn't think telling him would do either of them any good. "The kidnapping," she said with a sigh. "You're afraid there is something in them that incriminates you." She felt her pulse jump. "You think Hank knew who was behind the kidnapping. That's why you killed him." Anger filled her. "And you thought I might discover the truth. Why else would you try to run me down in Butte? You were the kidnapper's accomplice. Now you have a gun to my head? Are you crazy?"

"Crazy like a fox. Without proof there is nothing anyone can do. I got away with it for twenty-five years. If you're partner hadn't stirred things back up…"

She could tell that the man was unhinged. Fear made her heart pound. And now Boone was on his way.

The back door of the house opened and Boone stepped out. He held up what looked like three business-size envelopes.

The man pushed C.J. out of the barn door far enough so Boone could see her. Even from the distance, she could see his jaw tighten as he saw the gun pointed at her head. He started toward them in long strides.

Since hearing of Hank's death, all she'd thought about was finding his killer. Now his killer was right here, but all she could think about was Boone. *I've fallen in love with this man. I can't let this man kill him.*

"Cecil Marks?" Boone called, stopping a few yards short of the barn door. "Let her go and you can have your letters."

"BRING THE LETTERS into the barn," Cecil called back.

Boone shook his head. "Not until you let her go."

"Bring in the letters or I'm going to shoot her and then you!" Cecil was losing it. C.J. could feel him coming apart, his body shaking as if all this had finally gotten to him. "I have nothing to lose at this point. I've already killed two people. You think I won't kill two more? Bring them now or so help me—"

Boone started toward the barn.

C.J. told herself that maybe the man would take the letters and run off. Maybe the best thing was to just hand them over—

"Cecil!"

They all looked toward the house as an older blonde woman came out into the snow. C.J. felt the barrel of the gun move a few inches against her head as Cecil saw her.

"Tilly? Go back. Everything is going to be all right. But you have to go back into the house." Cecil's voice broke.

"I can't let you do this!" Tilly cried and kept coming toward them.

"No, go back!" He was shaking hard now.

C.J. realized she was watching a man come apart at the seams. Boone must have seen it, too.

"Tilly, don't make me do this!" Cecil cried as he dragged C.J. back a step.

She knew there was no longer any time. If she didn't act now...

Preparing herself for the worst, she kicked back at the man's bad leg and let all her weight fall forward, becoming dead weight in the man's single arm holding her. At the same time, she saw Boone rush them.

Cecil let out a scream of pain and began to fall forward with her. He had to let go of her as she fell. She didn't feel the cold barrel of the gun against her temple anymore, she thought, an instant before she heard the deafening sound of the gun's report.

As she dropped to the ground, she saw Boone barrel into the man. The two went flying backward. From the ground, she saw Boone on top of Cecil struggling for the gun. The sound of the gun's first report still ringing in her ears, she started to get up when the gun went off again.

This time it was Tilly who screamed at the entrance to the barn. C.J. turned to see the woman's chest blossom red before she dropped to the ground.

Cecil let out a cry as he saw Tilly fall. Boone wrenched the gun from the man's hand and slammed him down hard to the barn floor. C.J. could hear voices and people running from the house.

The next moment, she was in Boone's arms. Her brothers had Cecil. She'd seen Nikki on the phone to the sheriff and a sobbing Cecil Marks was being restrained as he tried to get to his wife.

From the barn floor, Travers McGraw picked up the three letters Boone had dropped.

Chapter Twenty

"The sheriff just brought these by," Boone said when he found C.J. in the sunroom.

C.J. took the envelope from him and just held it for a long moment. She was still shaken by everything that had happened. Cecil was in jail. She'd heard that he'd completely broken down and confessed everything. Tilly was dead, having died on the way to the hospital.

A minute didn't go by that C.J. wasn't reminded how easily it could have been one of them in the morgue right now. That Boone could have been killed… It gave her waking nightmares.

"If you want to be alone when you open it…" Boone said.

"No." She met his gaze and smiled before patting the cushion on the couch next to her. "I suspect this is about the kidnapping. Has your father opened his letter yet? Or Jesse Rose?"

"They're reading theirs now," he said as he joined her.

Carefully she opened the flap and took out the letter.

Dear C.J.,

If you're reading this, I am no longer with you. I didn't want you to worry about me, that's why I didn't tell you. I'm sorry. I figured you would have enough to deal with once I was gone without knowing that I was dying. I had an amazing life. I don't regret any of it. But you, C.J., you were the light of my life. I can't imagine what it would have been like without you in it from the time you came charging into my office, looked around and said, "What a mess!" You were five.

She laughed as tears welled. Boone, who'd been reading along with her, handed her a tissue. She wiped her eyes and continued reading.

I hope that by the time you read this, you'll have met Jesse Rose. Isn't she wonderful? And that you will see that she makes it home to her birth family, the McGraws.

I've confessed my part in all this to Travers McGraw in the letter I wrote him. But I wanted you to know, as well. Years ago, Pearl Cavanaugh contacted me. She had a child that desperately needed a home. It wasn't the first time I'd helped with adoptions from the women of the Whitehorse Sewing Circle. I never asked where the babies came from. I just trusted that I was helping the infant—and the desperate family that wanted a child.

At the time my sister had been trying to have

a baby and after numerous miscarriages had been told it would never happen. The moment I laid eyes on the little girl who was brought to me, I fell in love with Jesse Rose. I knew who she was. It was in all the news. But I also knew from Pearl that it was felt that the infant wasn't safe in the McGraw house.

I should have done the right thing. But at the time, the right thing felt like not returning her. When I handed Jesse Rose to my sister... Well, I've never felt such emotion. No little girl could have been more loved.

Maybe it was knowing I was dying. Or maybe it was seeing Travers McGraw on television pleading for information about his daughter. I called the lawyer to make sure the baby I'd given my sister really was Jesse Rose McGraw. Then I couldn't keep it from Jesse Rose and the McGraw family any longer. I flew to Seattle and told Jesse Rose and my sister what had to be done.

It was the hardest thing I'd ever done—short of keeping all this from you, C.J. Truthfully, I was a coward. I couldn't bear to see your expression when you heard what I'd done all those years ago. I hope you can forgive me.

I also hope you and Jesse Rose will meet. She's always wanted a sister and you two are the joys of my life.

I will miss you so much.

Hank

Tears were streaming down C.J.'s face as she finished the letter. Boone pulled her into his chest, rubbing her back as she cried.

"I know what he did was wrong, but I miss him," she said between sobs.

"I know."

When she finally pulled herself together, she straightened. "There was nothing in the letter about Cecil Marks. What if Hank knew nothing about his part in the kidnapping? What if—"

"If Cecil was free and clear and would never have been caught if he hadn't panicked?" Boone shook his head. "Apparently Tilly had told him that Hank had called our lawyer and knew something about Jesse Rose and the kidnapping. Cecil had believed it was true."

"So if he hadn't confessed…"

"We would never have known the part he played in the kidnapping."

She nodded, shocked at the irony.

"Maybe there is something in my father's letter," Boone said. "But it doesn't sound like Hank knew who the kidnapper's accomplice inside the house was."

"I need to go find Jesse Rose," C.J. said, getting to her feet. "If her letter is anything like mine…"

BOONE THOUGHT OF his father. Anxious to find out what had been in his letter, he found Travers in his office. The letter he'd received was lying open on the desk. His father looked up as he came in.

"Are you all right?" Boone asked.

"Yes." The older man nodded. There were tears in

his eyes. "It's good to know what happened. Jesse Rose was raised by loving parents. That's all that matters. And now she is home. She wants to stay out here on the ranch. She has a degree in business. I think she can be an asset to the ranch and take some of the load off my shoulders. What do you think?"

Boone chuckled. "I think you're an amazing man. You are so forgiving."

His father shrugged. "If I have learned anything it's that holding a grudge is harder on you than on the person who wronged you. I don't have time for regrets. I just want to spend the rest of my life enjoying my family and it's almost Christmas. The doctors say that your mother can start coming home for visits after the first of year. If those go well... So tell me about C.J."

"What do you want to know?" Boone asked, startled by the change of topic.

"When you're going to ask her to marry you," his father said with a laugh as he leaned back in his chair.

"I barely know the woman."

"I guess you'd better take care of that, then."

C.J. FOUND JESSE ROSE in her room. The door was open so she tapped on it and stepped in to hand her a clean tissue. Jesse Rose laughed, seeing that C.J. was still sniffling, too. They hugged and sat down on the edge of the bed.

"Hank hoped we'd be friends," Jesse Rose said.

"How can we not be?" she said. "We're the only two people who really knew Hank. It's strange, though, the way he brought us together."

"Even stranger the way he brought you and Boone together," Jesse Rose said with a teasing smile.

"You can't think he had a hand in that."

The other woman shrugged and winked. "If Hank could have, he would have. You two are perfect for each other."

"I wouldn't say that exactly." C.J. felt herself blushing. "He's stubborn and bossy and impossible. On top of that, he's a cowboy."

Jesse Rose laughed. "It is so obvious that the two of you are crazy about each other. And every woman wants a cowboy."

"Not every woman," C.J. said with a laugh. "Anyway, I live in Butte and he...he lives here," she said, taking in the ranch with a wave of her hand.

"You don't want to stay on this amazing ranch? I'm going to. I've already talked to Travers...to my dad about it," Jesse Rose said. "It's going to take a little getting used to, calling him Dad and having four grown brothers—one a twin I still have to meet. But I love it here. I know this sounds crazy, but I feel as if this is really where I've always belonged."

C.J. laughed. "It is."

"I know, but after growing up in Seattle..." She shook her head. "I feel like I've come home."

"How is your mom taking it?"

"She's just glad she isn't going to prison."

"You sound angry with her."

Jesse Rose nodded slowly. "I guess I am a little. But Hank knew, too, and I can't be angry with him. I'm just so glad he told me the truth. Maybe my mom will come around. Travers—Dad has asked her to come out for a visit. Maybe she will."

BOONE LOOKED UP to see Jesse Rose and C.J. come into the living room. He was so thankful that C.J. had agreed to at least stay through Christmas.

"We were just discussing everything that has happened," Boone said as the two joined the rest of the family. "Nikki is finishing up her book now that we all know what happened the night of the kidnapping."

C.J. sat down next to Boone. "I still can't believe Cecil Marks thought Hank knew about the part he'd played."

"Apparently Tilly had told him she'd overheard us talking and that Hank knew who the accomplice was," Travers said. "Unfortunately, she got it wrong. Otherwise, we would have never known it was our housekeeper's ex-husband who worked with Howard Cline to kidnap the twins. Finally Marianne will now be cleared of any wrongdoing."

"Tilly was always listening to what was going on with all of us," Cull said. "She really did get caught in the crossfire this time, though."

Nikki elbowed him. "That's awful."

"Well, you know what I mean. It cost her her life."

"At least Cecil confessed to everything," Nikki said. "Now I can finally finish my book."

"So Cecil was never considered a suspect?" C.J. asked.

"Surely he was questioned the night of the kidnapping," Boone said.

"He was—once he regained consciousness," Nikki

said. "He was in a car wreck on the other side of the county and ended up in a coma in the hospital the night of the kidnapping."

"Didn't anyone think that was suspicious?" C.J. asked.

"That was the problem. No one knew exactly what time the twins had been taken," Nikki said. "As it turns out, the twins had been missing for almost an hour before Patty was awakened and went in to check on them. By then, Cecil had stopped at a bar or two and gotten into a wreck. That was a pretty good alibi. Nor was there anything incriminating in his car. No one even knew he'd been out to the ranch that night since apparently Tilly was too doped up to mention it at the time and didn't think it important later I guess."

"Tilly never suspected him?" Cull asked in disbelief.

Nikki shook her head. "She'd taken cold medicine and then he'd given her even more. She was completely out of it."

"At least now we know who put the codeine cough syrup in the twins' room to make our mother look guilty," Ledger said.

"Seems like the perfect crime," Travers said. "But *someone* knew Cecil was in the house that night." Travers had been sitting quietly until then. Everyone turned to look at him. "When the letters came, there was also a package delivered. The sheriff found it in Tilly's purse where she'd apparently put it as Cecil had asked her."

"From Hank?" C.J. asked.

Travers shook his head. "From Patty. It's your mother's diary," he said to his sons. "Marianne saw Cecil coming out of the twins' room that night. That's why she went in. Unfortunately, she failed to tell anyone because of the altered state she was in from being poisoned with arsenic. When the twins were kidnapped, she apparently didn't recall seeing him. But she wrote it in her diary. Because of the poison in her system, it's possible she didn't remember."

"Patty returned the diary?" Boone asked sounding shocked. "Why would she do that?"

"There was only a short note inside. It said, 'Sorry, Patricia.' It seems she's had it this whole time, planning to use it against us."

"Except for that page she put under my door to make Marianne look guilty," Nikki said.

"Yes," Travers agreed.

"But wait," C.J. said. "Who was poisoning your mother?"

The family all looked at one another. It was finally Nikki who spoke. "We don't know. Probably Patty, but there are two other suspects—the former ranch manager, Blake Ryan, and our former family attorney, Jim Waters. Both were in love with Patty and would have done anything for her."

"Let's hope once Patty goes to trial that it all comes out," Cull said. "I suspect all three will be found guilty."

Travers got to his feet. "All I care about is that Cecil's confession clears your mother. Not that I ever believed she was in on the kidnapping. Even if Patty had been poisoning her and making her forgetful and confused, she wouldn't have hurt her babies."

"What will happen to Cecil?" Ledger asked.

"He'll probably get life. Kidnapping and deliberate homicide." Travers shook his head. "For twenty-five years he thought Harold Cline had double-crossed him, when all the time Harold was dead and buried. The man also must have lived being terrified that the truth would come out. So when Nikki began investigating the kidnapping for her book and we released more information…"

"Cecil killed Frieda to keep her from talking, although I doubt she knew anything about who had helped Harold," Nikki said. "Once Tilly told her ex about the call from Hank…"

"Speaking of the upcoming trial, Jim Waters called," Cull said. "He swears he's being framed for the poisonings. He was practically begging for you to help him, Dad."

Travers sighed. "Jim got himself into the mess he's in—he's going to have to get himself out. I would imagine the truth will come out one way or another. Blake Ryan hasn't gotten off free, either. He's being investigated for co-conspiracy with Patty and Jim Waters in the poisonings."

"If all three of them were in on it, one of them will turn on the others," Boone said.

"Jim and Blake both thought they would have Patty and the ranch once you were out of the way, Dad," Cull said.

"So who is the father of Patty's daughter Kitten?" Ledger asked.

"Patty told me it was just some one-night stand," Boone said. "If you can believe Patty." The former nanny, turned second McGraw wife, had always had trouble with the truth, he added.

"You do realize that Patty will probably get off with no more than a few years in prison for what she did to this family," Cull said.

"Probably," Travers agreed. "It's impossible to prove that she was behind the poisoning of your mother all those years ago. But I think a jury will have a hard time believing that she wasn't behind my arsenic poisoning in one way or another."

"Well, it's finally over," Ledger said.

"Except for Patty's tell-all book," Cull said.

"Haven't you heard? Because of the hype around Nikki's book about what really happened, the other publisher decided they weren't interested in Patty's," Travers said and smiled. "Explains why she returned the diary. But apparently she got to keep the advance to pay her lawyer."

A log popped in the fireplace and as darkness descended on the ranch, Boone put his arm around C.J. and looked at the Christmas tree, bright with lights and ornaments.

Ledger's fiancée, Abby, and Jesse Rose came in from the kitchen with plates of sandwiches. They were both laughing about something Jesse Rose had said.

"I don't think I ever believed in happy endings until this moment," Boone said and smiled at his father.

"All that matters is that the twins were found. They've both had good lives. That's all I could have hoped for," Travers said and smiled. "That's all I *did* hope for."

Epilogue

A year later, the family all gathered in the living room on Christmas Eve to celebrate. And they had a lot to celebrate, Travers McGraw thought as he looked at his burgeoning family.

He watched his oldest son, Cull, pour the champagne—and the nonalcoholic sparkling grape juice.

"So much has happened," Travers began, his voice breaking with emotion as he raised his glass in a toast. "I have my family back and so much more." He laughed and looked at the women who'd joined the family in the past year—all of them pregnant. "I never thought I'd live to see my first grandchild born, let alone four."

The room erupted in laughter. Cull and Nikki had started it by getting married and pregnant right after their wedding, then Ledger and Abby, then Boone and C.J.

"We have so much to be thankful for this holiday," he said and looked to his daughter, Jesse Rose. She'd moved in and was now working with the horse business right alongside her father. Travers had extended offers to her adoptive mother to come visit over the past year, but she hadn't come out to the ranch yet.

So much had happened but at least now the kidnapping was behind them. And Marianne would be coming home soon to stay. She'd come for a few visits, but the doctor said they needed to take it slowly. Finding out that she'd had nothing to do with the kidnapping had been huge in her recovery. That and seeing both of her once-lost babies now grown.

"You said Tough has been going by to see mother?" Cull asked.

Travers nodded and smiled. "He said it's gone well. She knew him right away."

"Unlike Vance Elliot," Cull said. "He fooled us for a while. I was starting to believe he really was our brother."

"Vance got his head turned by the idea of cashing in on becoming Oakley," Travers said. "He knew it was wrong."

"I heard that you paid for Vance's lawyer," Cull commented, clearly not approving.

"Yes, I did," his father said. "I saw something in him. In fact, when he gets out of jail, I've offered him a job."

"Dad, do you think that's a good idea?" Ledger asked.

"I do. He's had a rough life. I like to think that showing someone like him kindness can change him."

"Count the silverware," Cull said, but he patted his father's shoulder. "You always see the good in a person. I guess it's something to aspire to."

Boone laughed. "Nothing wrong with being a skeptic. It balances things out." C.J. poked him in the ribs.

Travers laughed. "I'd like to toast Nikki. If it hadn't been for her… Once she started asking questions, the truth started coming out. Thank you," he said, raising his glass. "And congratulations. I heard your book made the *New York Times* bestseller list the first week out."

They all raised their glasses.

"And to Jesse Rose," Travers said. "It is so wonderful to have you home."

BOONE LOOKED AT his beautiful wife. It was true what they said about being pregnant. C.J. glowed. He couldn't believe how quickly this past year had gone. Mostly he couldn't believe that not only had he gotten up the courage to ask C.J. to marry him, but that she'd accepted.

After Christmas last year, he'd driven her back to Butte. They'd talked a lot on the way home, but mostly about the kidnapping and Jesse Rose's return. C.J. had still been dealing with Hank's death and all the secrets he'd kept from her.

Back in Butte, he'd stayed to help C.J. clean out Hank's office and close it for good. When he couldn't think of any other excuse not to return to the ranch, he'd finally realized that he couldn't live without this woman.

He'd asked her out to dinner, gotten down on one knee and proposed.

To his shock, she'd said yes.

He'd been even more shocked when she'd wanted to return to the ranch and give up her PI business in Butte.

It wouldn't be the same without Hank and I've fallen in love with your family, she'd said.

Just my family?

She'd laughed and thrown her arms around him. *I never thought I'd fall in love with a cowboy. But, Boone McGraw, you're the kind of cowboy who grows on a girl. Take me home, cowboy.*

THE LIGHTS ON the Christmas tree twinkled, the air rich with the smell of freshly baked gingerbread cookies and pine. C.J. breathed it all in, feeling as if she needed to pinch herself as she stood looking at this wonderful family scene. She wished Hank could see this. Maybe he could.

She felt Boone come up behind her. He encircled her with his arms. She leaned back against him and closed her eyes as his hands dropped to her swollen stomach, making her smile.

"Happy?" he whispered.

"Very." She opened her eyes and turned in his arms. "I've never had a family like this before."

"Well, you do now. I think Hank would be happy for you."

She nodded. "I was just thinking of him. It's all he ever wanted for me." But it was more than she had ever dreamed possible. When Boone had gotten down on one knee and asked her to marry him it had been the happiest day of her life.

C.J. had thought she couldn't give up her private investigator business. The truth was she wanted a family of her own far more. And now they were expecting. She couldn't wait.

What made it even more fun was that her two sisters-in-law were also expecting and Abby was pregnant with twin girls while she and Nikki were having boys. With all three families building on the ranch and not that far apart, their kids would all grow up together here.

She couldn't imagine anything more wonderful. Jesse Rose was as excited as anyone. All this family and soon all these babies.

Don't worry about me, Jesse Rose had said. *One of these days I'll find me a cowboy and settle down myself. But I'm never leaving Montana.*

"I feel like all of this is a dream," C.J. said now to her husband. "If it is, don't wake me up."

Boone laughed. "Merry Christmas, sweetheart, and many more to come," he said and leaned down to kiss her as the doorbell rang.

"Enough of that!" Cull called from where he and Nikki had gone into the kitchen to check on dinner. "Someone answer the door!"

"I've got it!" Boone gave her another quick kiss before heading to the door.

To Boone's surprise Tough Crandall was standing on the doorstep.

"I was invited," Tough said, taking off his Stetson.

Boone studied his brother. There was no doubt that this cowboy was Oakley McGraw. But he was determined not to be one of them. *Good luck with that*, Boone thought.

"Of course you were invited," he said to his brother. "It's Christmas and like it or not, we're family." Tough didn't have any other family since both his adoptive parents had passed away. Nor did the stubborn cowboy want to be a McGraw, he'd said. But Travers had been visiting him on and off and had obviously somehow talked him into spending Christmas with them.

"Help me with the presents I have out in my truck?"

Boone laughed. "You got it." Together they went out and brought in all the gifts. "Hey, everyone, Tough's here," Boone announced as they came back inside.

His brother actually smiled as he wiped his feet and stepped in.

Say what you will about the McGraws, they were the kind of family that grew on you—whether you liked it or not.

Travers smiled and held out his hand to Tough. "Glad you could make it, son. I don't believe you've met everyone," he said after a moment. He began to introduce each of the family and new additions as he went around the room.

When he got to Jesse Rose, he hesitated. Tough was looking at his twin sister wide-eyed. For the past year, Jesse Rose had been dying to meet her twin, but Tough had been dragging his feet.

"This is…Jesse Rose," their father said.

Tough shook her hand. Their eyes locked and the cowboy seemed to be at a loss for words. "I had no idea," he said, his voice breaking.

She laughed, smiling as she asked, "No idea what?"

"That I would feel…such a connection."

"We're *twins*. Plus we share quite a history, wouldn't you say?"

He nodded. "It's the first time I've really felt like I was a part of this family."

"Well, now that you have," Travers said, "you're just in time for dinner. After that we're going to be opening presents."

"And singing Christmas carols," Jesse Rose said. "It's going to be our new tradition."

"I can see where we're going to have a lot more new traditions," Travers said, putting his arm around Tough and Jesse. "But you might change your mind about the carols when you hear my sons sing."

"Not all of them are tone-deaf," Tough said and grinned.

Boone listened to the good-natured ribbing during dinner. Later Jesse Rose brought out her guitar and began to play "Silent Night." C.J. came to stand by him. He pulled her close, his eyes misting over as he counted his blessings and his family began to sing.

* * * * *

Don't miss the first two books in the
WHITEHORSE, MONTANA:
THE MCGRAW KIDNAPPING *series:*

DARK HORSE
DEAD RINGER

Available now from Mills & Boon!

"I've been away from here for a long time," he said. "I may not be the man you think I am."

"I may not be the woman you think I am," she countered. "If you think about me at all," she added sheepishly.

"Hard to forget someone you meet on top of a bridge."

He saw a shiver go through her as she turned to stare out the windshield. She looked very enticing with her hair all mussed and her lips slightly parted. Another time, another place and Jack might have responded to the subtle invitation in her smile. But a hookup was the last thing he needed. He'd come to town to poke a hornet's nest. Depending on what he found, things could get ugly. Sides might have to be chosen. After all was said and done, he'd return to Houston while Olive would still have to live here.

Jack knew only too well what it was like to be a pariah in Pine Lake.

PINE LAKE

BY
AMANDA STEVENS

MILLS & BOON

First Published in Great Britain 2017
By Mills & Boon, an imprint of HarperCollins*Publishers*
1 London Bridge Street, London, SE1 9GF

© 2017 Marilyn Medlock Amann

ISBN: 978-0-263-92922-5

46-1017

Our policy is to use papers that are natural, renewable and recyclable products and made from wood grown in sustainable forests. The logging and manufacturing processes conform to the legal environmental regulations of the country of origin.

Printed and bound in Spain
by CPI, Barcelona

Amanda Stevens is an award-winning author of over fifty novels, including the modern gothic series, The Graveyard Queen. Her books have been described as eerie and atmospheric, "a new take on the classic ghost story." Born and raised in the rural South, she now resides in Houston, Texas, where she enjoys binge-watching, bike riding and the occasional margarita.

Chapter One

It was an ordinary day. Which made the phone call all the more extraordinary.

Jack King wasn't in the best of moods to begin with. He'd been stuck inside since early morning and boredom had worn down his patience. Even on the rare instances when he found himself in between assignments, he could usually rustle up something that would keep him out of the office. No chore was too tedious so long as it put distance between him and his cluttered desk.

For the past five years, he'd been working for the Blackthorn Agency, a high-profile consultant and security organization headquartered in Houston, Texas. Jack worked in Black Watch, the division tasked with state and municipal government oversight, including police departments. His particular expertise was in exposing corruption in cities large and small where the rot started at the head and worked its way down through the ranks. It wasn't a job for the faint of heart. Cops were notoriously territorial and they knew how to circle the wagons. But Jack enjoyed the challenge and he'd learned a long time ago how to watch his back.

That morning, he'd arrived at headquarters with the expectation of a new briefing. Instead, a mountain of delinquent paperwork and a stern warning from the man upstairs had kept him chained to his desk as his gaze strayed every few minutes to the clock on the wall outside his office. The day had seemed interminable.

Finally at six, he filed his last report, stood, stretched and walked out of his office, wishing the division manager a nice weekend. He was just getting off the elevator when his phone rang. He started to ignore it. Wished a thousand times later that he had. He didn't want to be called back upstairs because he'd dotted the wrong *i* or forgotten to cross a *t*. Whatever technicality needed his attention could damn well wait until Monday.

Still…

He slid the phone out of his pocket and checked the screen. No name, just a number. The area code and prefix pinged his alarm and he told himself again to ignore the call. He couldn't, of course. Curiosity niggled. He'd had no contact with anyone in his hometown in over fifteen years. He'd left Pine Lake the day after his high school graduation and his folks had fled a month later. Only his uncle Leon had remained to tough things out, but he'd passed away last spring. Jack hadn't even gone back for the funeral.

No good could come of that phone call. He knew that. But he pressed the phone to his ear anyway as he strode across the lobby, nodding to the security guard behind the desk on his way out.

"Hello," he said as he pushed open the glass door and stepped through into the early August heat.

"Jack? Jack King, right?"

Unease feathered along his spine. "Yes, this is Jack."

"You don't know who this is, do you? Little wonder. It's been a long time. Fifteen years to be exact."

The caller fell silent. "Damn, this is a lot harder than I thought it would be. It's Nathan, Jack. Nathan Bolt."

Nathan Bolt. Now there was a name from his past. He and Jack and Tommy Driscoll had been best friends all through school. Blood brothers since kindergarten. Thick as thieves, Uncle Leon used to say. Until Nathan and Tommy had turned on Jack during their senior year. They'd given each other alibis for the night of Anna Grayson's murder, leaving Jack alone in the crosshairs of a ruthless sheriff.

With little evidence and zero suspects, the authorities had gone hard after Jack. He was the boyfriend, after all, and unlike Tommy and Nathan, he hadn't been able to produce an alibi. The harassment had continued for months, making him an outcast in the place where he'd lived his whole life. Even after an arrest had finally been made and an ex-con sent back to prison, the community had continued to shun him. In the ensuing years, Jack had done his best to forget about Pine Lake and everyone who lived there, but not a day went by that he didn't think about Anna. Not a day went by that he didn't wish for her the long and happy life she had deserved.

An image flashed through his head. Dark hair, dark eyes. A smile that could light up a stadium.

Sweat beaded on his brow. He wiped it away with the back of his hand.

"Hello? Jack? You there? Did I lose you?"

"I'm here," he said, though his instinct still was to end the call without giving Nathan a chance to explain why he had decided to make contact after so many years of silence. Or how he had gotten Jack's number in the first place. That probably wasn't too hard to figure out. He'd been Uncle Leon's attorney.

"You must be wondering why I'm calling," Nathan said.

"Did Leon give you my number?"

"Yes. We discussed certain things before he died. He said I should give you a call."

"What things?"

Another pause. "Did you get the letter I sent you about his estate?"

"I got it."

"I wondered. I never heard back from you. Things have been left hanging, but that's my fault. I should have followed up. And I should have called when it first happened. I'm sorry I didn't. I'm sorry about a lot of things." He sighed. "I don't imagine that cuts much ice with you."

"If this is about Leon's estate, you should talk to my dad," Jack said brusquely. "He'll give you whatever you need."

"If you read my letter, you know Leon left everything to you. The cabin, the little bit of cash he had in the bank. But this isn't about your uncle."

"Then what's it about?"

"I need to talk to you about Tommy."

It had started to rain, a light drizzle that spiked the humidity and turned the oily streets to glass. As if traffic wasn't bad enough on a Friday afternoon in downtown Houston. Jack pressed against the building to keep dry.

"Why would you need to talk to me about Tommy?"

"He's the Caddo County sheriff. Going on three years now. Leon must have told you about the last election. The accusations of fraud and intimidation. The way that vote went down left a lot of bad blood in this town."

"Leon and I didn't talk politics." They hadn't talked much at all in the past few years and that was on Jack. He'd let himself get too caught up in work because it was easier to focus on the greed and corruption of others than to dwell on his own shortcomings, including a failed marriage. If a day didn't go by without a thought of Anna, his ex-wife hardly ever crossed his mind. That undoubtedly said more about Jack than it did about her. Not her fault he had trust issues. Not for lack of trying that she couldn't breach his walls.

"I've done my research," Nathan was saying. "I know what you do at the Blackthorn Agency. You investigate police departments, right? You expose government corruption."

"Among other things."

"Leon said you were the best at what you do."

"Leon was biased."

"Maybe, but you always were the best at everything you set your mind to."

Was that an edge of the old jealousy rearing its ugly head? Jack and Tommy Driscoll had had a good-natured rivalry on the football field, but the competition with Nathan in the classroom hadn't been so amiable. Nathan needed to be the best and the brightest in order to prove his worth to his father. Jack needed the grades for a scholarship. His early acceptance to a top-tier school had been a bitter pill for Nathan to swallow, but that offer and most of the others had been rescinded when Anna's murder and the subsequent investigation had made the national news. And that had been a bitter pill for Jack to swallow.

"I know I'm catching you off guard," Nathan said. "But I didn't know who else to call. We've got a real problem up here, Jack. Drugs have taken over the whole damn county. Crack, meth, kush. And nobody has a mind to do anything about it. You can't imagine how bad it's gotten."

"I've worked on the border," Jack said. "I don't have to imagine how bad things can get."

"Well, sure. El Paso's one thing, but we're talking about Pine Lake. Last year alone, we had ten murders in Caddo County. *Ten.* Not a lot by big city standards, but you must remember how quiet this place once was."

He remembered, all right.

"Something's going on in our little town. Something bad. Used to be just a few random incidents, but now there's organization. Muscle. And I think Tommy's involved. In it up to his neck, is my guess."

"In what?"

"That's what I need you to find out."

"If you're looking to hire my firm, you'll have to go through the proper channels. I don't solicit work. I go where I'm told."

"I was hoping we could do this off the books. I'll pay you myself. Whatever you want."

"Not interested."

"Even if it could lead you to Anna's murderer?"

Nathan's words were like scissor points gouging a tender wound. "Her killer was sent to prison fifteen years ago."

"What if they pinned it on the wrong man? Have you ever considered that?"

More times than Jack cared to remember. He'd even made a trip to the Texas State Penitentiary a few years back to interview Wayne Foukes for himself. He'd come away more convinced than ever that Foukes belonged behind bars. He was less certain the man had been sent up for the right reason.

"What if I told you Tommy lied about where he was that night?" Nathan said softly. "Would you come then?"

Jack stared out across the street. He could feel a pulse start to pound in his temple. "What you're really saying is that *you* lied about that night."

"I had to. He threatened to hurt someone I cared about if I didn't."

"What are you talking about?"

"Do you remember my cousin Olive? She and my aunt came to live with us after my uncle died."

Jack skimmed his memory, summoning up a hazy image of a slight redhead with glasses. "Vaguely."

"You probably didn't even notice her, but she used to follow me around all the time. I think she just needed someone to pay attention to her. Tommy didn't come right out and say it, but he let me know if I didn't swear to the police he was at my house all night, something bad might happen to Olive."

"I take it he wasn't at your house."

"He slept over just like we said, but I woke up during the night and found him gone."

"And you never once thought about going to the police? Or to your father? He was a big shot in the county. He could have protected you from Tommy Driscoll or anyone else who threatened you."

"I wasn't worried about myself. My only concern was Olive." Nathan's voice dropped. "Poor kid was already a mess. She took her dad's death hard and I wanted to protect her. She was so fragile that even an empty threat could have pushed her over the edge. But I didn't think Tommy's threat was empty. He had a cruel streak, Jack. You never saw it because he kept it hidden from you. But not from me. I was often the brunt of it."

"You never said anything."

"I guess growing up with my old man, I got used to dealing with bullies."

Don't, Jack thought bitterly. *Don't let him get to you. None of this matters anymore.*

So what if Nathan had lied about Tommy's whereabouts? Jack had never been charged. He'd left town a free man and he'd put all that behind him. He was happy here in Houston. Or at least, content. He had friends, a good job. Why go digging up the past now?

Because a man had been sent to prison for a crime he may not have committed. Wayne Foukes was an arsonist, a drug dealer and a serial rapist who'd left a string of ruined lives in his wake. He deserved to be incarcerated, but so did Anna's killer.

"Will you come?" Nathan pressed.

"What is it you expect me to do?"

"What you do in every other place with a corrupt police department. Expose the dirt so we can clean it up."

"You don't think people will question my presence in a town where I haven't set foot in over fifteen years?"

"You have the perfect excuse for coming back. You need to settle your uncle's estate. You can even stay in the cabin while you decide what you want to do with it. I'll have someone go in and give it a good cleaning, stock the refrigerator. You might even enjoy a few days on the lake. All I'm asking is that you keep your eyes and ears open while you're here. Ask a few discreet questions. You'll know how best to handle the situation once you get here."

"I'll think about it," Jack said.

"For how long?"

Irritation flared. "For as long as I need to. I have a job. I can't pick up and leave whenever I want."

"Don't take too long," Nathan warned. "Whatever you decide, I would appreciate you keeping this call between us. My life could depend on it."

He knew how to end the conversation on a dramatic note. Jack would give him that.

Slipping the phone in his pocket, he leaned a shoulder against the building as he mulled over his options. He had vacation time coming. He was between assignments and he'd caught up on all his paperwork. There would never be a better time to take a few days off. Still, he wasn't about to rush into anything. He needed to have a drink, relax, sleep on it. Then he'd talk things over with his boss on Monday.

He deliberately turned his thoughts to more pleasant options, like how to spend the rest of his Friday evening. He could go across the street to Lola's and have a drink with the other Blackthorn employees who would already be congregating in the shadowy back room for happy hour. Like Jack, they were mostly former law enforcement—cops, FBI, DEA. They all got on well except for the military contingent, the ex-Special Forces teams that were often deployed overseas as private security. Mercenaries. Those guys kept to themselves.

He decided he wasn't in the mood for a raucous celebration so he thought about heading over to Ninfa's on Navigation for solo margaritas and fajitas. But it was a popular eatery and on a Friday night with the Astros in town, chances were good he'd need a reservation. He chose a third option. Home.

His apartment was several blocks away, but he didn't mind the rain. Dodging umbrellas, he merged with the pedestrians hurrying toward bus stops and parking garages. The theater crowd would soon converge, tying up traffic for blocks. He was glad to be on foot.

As he strode along the sidewalk, the back of his neck tingled. He could easily chalk up the sensation to imagination or the residue of an unsettling conversation, but Jack had learned a long time ago to listen to his instincts. To pay attention to the signs. He was being followed.

He searched the mirrored facade of the building across the street and turned very casually to observe the traffic. Nothing seemed amiss, but in the chaos of rush hour, a tail could be hard to spot.

OLIVE BELMONT HURRIED along the shadowy streets, suppressing the desire to glance over her shoulder as she rounded the corner toward home. She'd had a funny feeling all day that something was wrong, though she tried to tell herself it was nerves.

School would start in another three weeks and this would be Olive's first term as principal at Pine Lake High School. Just shy of thirty, she was the youngest to ever hold the position and she knew the school board would watch her every move, waiting to pounce on any misstep. With that kind of pressure, she was allowed a few jitters.

Her unease was more than first-day butterflies, though. Pine Lake wasn't the town it once was. Maybe it had never been the idyllic hamlet she'd always thought it, but now the community seemed on the verge of losing itself to the same pandemic of drugs and malaise that affected hundreds of rural towns across the South.

The decline had been gradual in Pine Lake. So slow that only lately had Olive noticed the deterioration. But on a sultry evening like this, one could almost smell the rot. Even the beautiful old Queen Anne homes along Primrose Avenue had fallen into a sorry state and it seemed to Olive that every other week she saw at least one U-Haul heading out of town. She wondered if that was why she'd been offered the job as principal. Maybe no one else had wanted the position.

With all the added stress came the nightmares, those terrifying falling dreams from her early teens. The situation was always the same. She found herself on a bridge clinging to the edge for dear life. She could feel her fingers slip as her legs flailed helplessly. Then she was falling backward into a misty abyss as a shadowy figure peered down at her from the guardrail. Olive could never see a face, but she thought the watcher might be her dad. He'd been killed on a bridge when his car and another had collided head on.

Olive had gone years without having that dream, but for weeks now the recurring nightmare had plagued her sleep. She never hit the water, but on at least two occasions, the sensation of falling had been so real that she'd awakened to find herself on her knees in bed, clutching the headboard. The smell of pine needles and swamp had permeated her tiny bedroom, though she knew the scent was nothing more than a lingering effect from her dream.

She hoped the nightmares would go away once

school started and she settled into her new position. Meanwhile, a chat with Mona Sutton might help. The guidance counselor had been a lifesaver when Olive had been a new student at Pine Lake High School fifteen years ago. Armed with a doctorate in psychology and a fierce determination to save the world, Mona Sutton had taken Olive under her wing, helping her through the pain and loneliness and seemingly insurmountable guilt over her father's tragic death. Olive's mother had been too lost in her own grief to notice that her four-teen-year-old daughter was quietly having a nervous breakdown. Mona had stepped in, then and years later when the pressure of college had caused the dreams to resurface. She would help again if need be, but their re-lationship might be trickier now that Olive was her boss.

Olive's tiny bungalow was just ahead on the corner of Elm and Holly. As she approached the intersection, she finally gave into her premonition and glanced over her shoulder. It was still early, but not a soul stirred. Even the eateries along East Market Street had already closed their doors for the evening.

An abandoned air had settled over the town, deep-ening Olive's unease. For a moment, she had the terri-fying notion that everyone had packed up and left Pine Lake while she'd been working late, readying herself for the coming school year. But she wasn't completely alone. A dog barked from a fenced backyard and she could hear the idling of a car engine somewhere nearby.

As she stepped off the curb, headlights flashed on, catching her in the face. She froze like a deer, staring wide-eyed into the bright beams until she heard the engine rev and then she instinctively retreated to the sidewalk. A split second later, a dark sedan sped past her. She didn't recognize car or driver nor did she get a look at the license plate. The car was going too fast. Reckless driving wasn't unusual in Pine Lake where drag racing down Main Street on a Friday night was still a popular pastime. But she wasn't on Main Street and Olive could have sworn the car had deliberately swerved in her direction as it zoomed past her.

She stood underneath a streetlight, heart thudding as she tried to rationalize the incident. Someone had probably recognized her and decided to have a little fun at the expense of the new principal. She was a small woman and looked years younger than her age so there would be more of the same once school started. No doubt a steady stream of challenges to her authority. She'd better buck up and learn to hide her nerves if she had any hope of making it through the first semester, let alone the whole school year.

Wiping clammy hands down the sides of her pants, she looked both ways and then hurried across the street to her house. She let herself in and then turned the lock behind her. Dragging over a footstool, she shot home a bolt at the top of the door, a precaution she hoped was unnecessary.

It was an unusual place for a lock. Designed to keep someone in rather than a dangerous element out.

JACK HAD DECIDED to stop off at a corner bar where he could watch the street. One drink had somehow turned into three and by the time he left, traffic had thinned and darkness was falling. He headed for the shower as soon as he got home, standing for a long time under the steamy water as he tried to banish the barrage of unwanted memories that had kept him drinking at the bar.

Anna's face swam up out of the back of his mind. He wanted to remember her the way she'd been the summer he fell in love with her, a gorgeous brunette with a killer smile and legs that went on forever. Instead, he kept seeing her dragged from the lake, lips blue, skin gray, eyes glazed and sightless.

Senior year was supposed to have been their time, a long goodbye before college took them in separate directions. Jack had been elected captain of the football team; Anna had been the head cheerleader. They were the all-American cliché. In hindsight, even her death seemed banal, the most beautiful girl in school meeting a violent and untimely demise. The news offered up similar tragedies on a daily basis, but for whatever reason, Anna's story had captivated the national media.

For a while, Jack hadn't been able to leave his house without cameras being shoved in his face. His picture had been splashed across tabloids and gossip-style news programs, making him the most hated seventeen-year-old in the country. And then one night, Wayne Foukes had been pulled over for a broken taillight. Among the cache of drugs in his trunk, the police had discovered Anna's missing class ring.

Once Foukes was charged, the reporters disappeared, but the people Jack had known his whole life continued to avoid him. It was almost as if they needed to believe him guilty in order to justify their behavior. He'd left town vowing never to return, but now Nathan's phone call had changed everything.

Dragging on a pair of jeans, he ambled into the kitchen to scour the refrigerator for dinner. Pickings were slim. He settled on a beer. Later, he'd order in.

Watch a movie, crash on the couch. Assuming he'd be able to sleep.

The night stretched before him, empty and endless. He turned on the Astros game to fill the quiet as he glanced aimlessly around his apartment. The small space, sleek and minimally furnished, boasted a view of the Houston skyline, but it had never felt much like home. Turning up the volume, he took his beer out to the balcony to enjoy the night air. The rain was coming down harder now and he held his hand over the railing to collect a fistful of water.

He could hear his cell ringing inside and he told himself to ignore it even as he flicked the water from his fingers and stepped back through the door. He picked up the phone from the counter and glanced at the screen. It was a Pine Lake prefix but the number wasn't Nathan's. Or at least not the number of the phone he'd called from before.

Jack carried the phone back out to the balcony with him. "Jack King."

"Hello, Jack King. Tommy Driscoll calling." He gave a low chuckle. "Man, oh, man. I wish I could see your face right now. I must be about the last person you expected to hear from tonight."

Pretty damn close. What were the chances he'd hear from his two former best friends on the same night? Jack wasn't a big believer in coincidences. Something was up. He tried to brace himself, but Tommy Driscoll's voice took him aback. He sounded exactly the way Jack remembered—loud, jovial, a man always up for a good time. Except now the jollity sounded forced, but maybe Jack's perception had been tainted by time and Nathan's innuendoes. Or maybe Tommy Driscoll had never been the easygoing guy Jack had thought him.

"What can I do for you, Tommy? Or should I call you Sheriff Driscoll?"

"You heard about that, did you?" He sounded pleased. "Back in our glory days, who would have ever thought a pair of hell-raisers like us would turn out to be cops?"

"I'm not a cop."

"You were, though. Houston PD. See? I've kept up with you through the years." He paused as if expecting Jack to say the same about him. "Now you're with that outfit I see on the news. The Blackthorn Agency. You guys go into some hairy places from what I hear. Must be exciting. Good money, too, I bet. You've done all right for yourself, seems like."

In spite of everything, Jack thought. "Why are you calling, Tommy?"

"I need a favor, buddy. It's about Nathan."

Jack was instantly on alert. "What about him?"

"Have you heard from him lately?"

Something in Tommy's voice prickled Jack's scalp. "Why would you think I'd hear from Nathan? You guys cut me loose a long time ago."

"You sound bitter," Tommy said.

"No, just careful."

"Can't say as I blame you, considering the way you were treated. We were all just scared kids back then. I'm not making excuses, but it was a rough time for everyone."

Sure sounded like he was making excuses. And the half-hearted apology was only now being extended because Tommy needed something from Jack. Just like

Nathan did. He wasn't about to make it easy on either of them.

"This is awkward as hell," Tommy muttered into the loaded silence. "I can't imagine how strange it must be for you."

"No, you can't."

Tommy drew in a sharp breath as if his anger had been goaded. Then he said in a strained voice, "Look, man, I wouldn't even be bothering you except I think Nathan may be in some trouble. Serious trouble. And now that it's all coming home to roost, he's looking for a way out."

"What do you mean?"

Tommy hesitated. "I think he may be trying to set me up."

"For what?"

"I haven't figured that out yet."

Jack stared out into the night, dotted with streetlights spanning the misty cityscape, but his mind had already traveled deep into the piney woods of East Texas. "What is it you expect me to do about it?"

"Nothing, buddy. Not a damn thing. That's the whole point of this call. If Nathan tries to get in touch, I'd appreciate a heads-up. Otherwise, go on about your business."

"You still haven't told me why you think he'd try to get in touch with me."

"He's desperate. And he and your uncle were tight. Maybe he thinks you still have a score to settle and he can somehow use it to his advantage. A word of advice from an old friend." Any hint of joviality disappeared from Tommy Driscoll's voice. "Don't believe a word that comes out of his mouth. Nathan Bolt is a pathological liar. Always has been. Just like his old man."

"What has he lied about?" Jack asked carefully.

Tommy hesitated. "Maybe it doesn't even matter anymore."

"Maybe it does," Jack said. "What did Nathan lie about?"

Another pause. "He wasn't home the night Anna was killed. He left before midnight and didn't come back until nearly sunrise."

Chapter Two

Jack sat on his uncle's boat dock as a fine mist settled over the lake. All around him, the landscape was eerie and primal, a swampy labyrinth of channels and bayous that stretched all the way across the Louisiana border. The town of Pine Lake was less than a quarter of a mile away, but the woods blocked the lights. He could see nothing but the silhouette of trees and a glimpse now and then of the old lake bridge through the curtains of Spanish moss hanging from a dense forest of bald cypress.

Damn, it was dark out here.

Jack had forgotten what it was like to be that deep in the country, without the glow of skyscrapers to create a false daylight. As he stared out at the water, the night came alive. A loon trilled from the woods as a mosquito buzzed his ear. A female alligator grunted nearby, warning predators away from her nest. The nocturnal sounds stirred an uneasy excitement. *You shouldn't have come back here*, a voice in his head taunted. *You're asking for trouble.*

Yeah, maybe he was.

He hadn't told anyone he was coming. Not Nathan, not Tommy. But the cabin had been spotless when he arrived, the cupboards and refrigerator well stocked. Even his uncle's fishing boat had been scrubbed and gassed up. Jack wasn't too pleased by the preparations. Nathan's overconfidence bugged him, but it wasn't misplaced. He was here, wasn't he?

All weekend long he'd brooded about those two phone calls and then come Monday morning, he'd headed upstairs to talk things over with his boss, Ezra Blackthorn. The taciturn head of the agency had listened carefully to Jack's story, but he hadn't offered much in the way of advice. Wading back into the muck of his past had been Jack's decision alone. As much as he dreaded what he might find, he couldn't ignore any chance, no matter how slim, of finally bringing Anna's killer to justice. To resolve once and for all what had really happened on that long-ago Friday night.

But he had no delusions about easy answers. His investigation was likely to get messy. He didn't trust Nathan or Tommy to tell him the truth. Obviously, they were each working an angle. He could well imagine Tommy Driscoll getting involved in something shady. Even as a kid, Tommy's innate charm and athletic prowess had fostered a sense of entitlement. He'd learned early on that he could talk his way out of anything and Jack doubted his attitude had changed now that he wore a badge.

Nathan was a little harder to figure out. He already had money and prestige. Why risk his standing in the community?

Jack really didn't care what either of them was up to. He did care that one or both had lied about their whereabouts on the night of Anna's murder.

He watched the water with a pensive frown, unable

to shake his disquiet. His mind had strayed to such a dark place that when he saw a light flicker on the old lake bridge, he half convinced himself he was being paranoid.

But no, there it was again. Not a flickering light as he'd first thought, but the bobbing beam of a flashlight moving across the wooden deck. The bridge had been abandoned decades ago, but the rotting floorboards and creaking beams had never dissuaded the local daredevils. He watched for a moment, thinking back to his own misadventures on that bridge.

The light was no longer moving, he noted. The beam stayed stationary for so long that he had to conclude someone had set the flashlight down on the deck or perhaps wedged it between the braces. If he concentrated hard enough, he could almost conjure a form standing at the guardrail. He was tempted to start up his uncle's boat and train the spotlight on the bridge, but even so powerful a beam would be swallowed by the misty darkness. Besides which, this was none of his business. He hadn't come to Pine Lake to get sidetracked—

He heard a splash as something heavy hit the water. Then the flashlight beam swept down and over the lake, glimmering sporadically through the trees. Jack was far enough away that he couldn't be spotted, but he instinctively shrank back into the shadows.

For the longest time, the light moved slowly over the water. Then the glow vanished, only to reappear bobbing toward the end of the bridge. A few minutes later, Jack heard the sound of a car engine on the far side of the lake. Not a frantic rev but a stealthy purr as the car slowly drove away on the old dirt road.

He didn't know what to make of the splash or the

light. People had been known to use the lake as a dumping site. If caught, the offense carried a stiff penalty, but back in Jack's day, the area around the bridge had rarely been patrolled. Which was undoubtedly the reason Anna's killer had chosen to dump her body from the deck.

That splash…

What were the chances another body had been thrown from the bridge on the very night he'd returned to Pine Lake? Slim to none, Jack decided, but he knew the sound would niggle at him all night. Might as well take the boat out and have a look.

A FEW MINUTES LATER, Jack maneuvered away from the dock and headed into the channel. It was even darker on the water. He didn't want to turn on his running lights, much less the spotlight in case someone lurked nearby. But it was dangerous to be on the lake blind. Dangerous for others, dangerous for him. If he strayed from the middle of the channel, he had to worry about cypress knees below the surface and those thick mats of aquatic vegetation that could entangle the boat's propeller.

He turned on the spotlight, keeping the beam concentrated on the water ahead of him. As he neared the bridge, he shifted into neutral and drifted as he trained the light along the banks where ground mist thickened. Cypress trees rose from the shallows like bearded sentinels, obscuring both ends of the bridge. Beyond the lake was the pine forest and all along the water's edge, a creeping carpet of lily pads and lotus.

He made a pass underneath the first span of the bridge, once again searching along the banks and in the deeper water of the channel before returning through the second span. Clouds blocked the moon so thoroughly he had to rely solely on the spotlight. Even through the mist, he could pick out turtles and frogs and the red glowing eyes of an alligator, but he saw nothing unusual in the water.

If someone had thrown a body off the bridge, they would have more than likely weighted it. It could take days or even weeks to surface. He was wasting his time and he knew it. All he'd heard was a distant splash. All he'd seen was a bobbing flashlight. He had no reason to believe that anything untoward—

She was there in the shallows, floating on her back among the lily pads.

Jack used the trolling motor to navigate through the strangling vegetation and then a paddle to hold the boat steady as he observed the body. He didn't attempt to drag her from the water. She was dead and had been the moment the bullet passed through the back of her skull and exited between her eyes. During his time as a cop, he'd seen that jagged, X-shaped wound before, usually in drug-related executions. The facial damage was extensive, but the best Jack could tell, she was young, probably no more than early twenties, with long blond hair floating all around her.

He sat for a moment, awash in memories before he took out his phone and called Tommy Driscoll's number.

The phone rang five times before Tommy finally answered. He sounded annoyed and winded. "Driscoll."

"Tommy, it's Jack King."

"Jack? It's a little late, isn't it, buddy?"

"Not for this."

"You heard from Nathan?" he asked anxiously.

"I'm calling about something else."

A long silence. "Where are you?"

"Sitting in my uncle's boat on Pine Lake. I'm about fifty yards south of the old bridge. You'd better get out here. There's a body in the water."

He heard the sharp intake of Tommy's breath. "Do you know who it is?"

"Female Caucasian. Blonde, slim build from what I can tell. She's young. Early twenties, I'm guessing. Looks like someone shot her in the back of the head and then dumped her body off the bridge."

"No need for an ambulance, I take it." Tommy's voice seemed oddly hushed.

"No, but you'd better send for the coroner. I'll stay with her until you get here."

"Jack?"

"Yeah?"

"What are you doing on Pine Lake?"

"I don't think that much matters right now, does it?"

"It might," Tommy said. "I'll see you in a few minutes. We'll talk then."

Jack dropped the phone back in his pocket, his gaze still on the body. He cut the spotlight. The garish brilliance somehow seemed offensive. As darkness slid over him, he had the uncanny feeling that he wasn't alone. He told himself it was just the situation. The similarities to Anna were bound to unnerve him. But he couldn't shake the notion that someone was near. Someone watched him.

Turning on the spotlight, he raked the powerful beam all along the banks and then into the shadowy corners of the bridge. He almost expected to see someone at the guardrail staring down at him. No one was there. He was alone on the water with the dead woman.

He made one more sweep, this time slanting the

beam up in the trees. As he shifted the light, he caught a glimpse of something white through the cypress branches. A barn owl, he thought, or a snowy egret. But as he focused the light, he realized the shimmer of white wasn't in a tree, but at the very top of the bridge. For a moment he could have sworn someone was up in the rafters.

He shook his head and moved the light away. Crazy notion.

He sat in the gently rocking boat and let the night sounds settle over him. Then he angled the beam back to the truss. The white object was still up there.

Pushing off with the paddle he let the boat float back into the center of the channel before he started the motor. The outboard hummed throatily as he navigated toward the bridge. Backing off the throttle he aimed the light up through the Spanish moss. Whatever he expected to find was not what he saw. Never in a million years could he have imagined such a sight.

The floor of the bridge was a good fifteen feet above the water and from the deck, a series of braces and struts climbed another twenty feet to the iron beam that ran the length of the bridge.

On top of that narrow girder, a woman lay curled in the fetal position.

OLIVE'S EYES FLEW OPEN. She had been dreaming again about falling. Down, down, down into that misty abyss. The nightmare had been so real that she still had the smell of the swamp in her nostrils. She could even feel a breeze on her face.

She lay for a moment, breathing deeply as she tried to calm her racing heart.

What was that creaking sound? She couldn't place it. The ceiling fan, maybe?

"Don't move," a male voice said nearby.

That brought her fully awake. She started to sit up, but a hand on her shoulder eased her back down and she realized another hand had clamped around her wrist. Panic exploded. Her instinct was to lash out at the intruder, to fight him off with every ounce of strength she could muster, but she was suddenly aware of her surroundings. That creak didn't come from any ceiling fan. She wasn't even in her bedroom. She was—

"Where am I?" she gasped, as her whole world tilted.

"Don't worry. I've got you." The voice was deep and silky smooth. Olive found it at once soothing and terrifying.

"Got me…where?"

"You know the old bridge over Pine Lake?"

"Yes, I know it…" She trailed away as she tried to peer through the darkness. A light glimmered somewhere below her. She felt compelled to turn and stare into the beam, but the swaying sensation and the hand on her shoulder kept her immobile. "I'm on the bridge?"

"More or less," the voice said.

Terror surged as she pictured the gaping holes in the rotting floorboards and the unstable framework towering over her. The image dizzied her and she had to suppress the urge to flail her arms, searching for a handhold.

Now she understood the creaking and swaying.

"You have to stay calm, okay? I'm not going to let you fall, but you need to do exactly as I say."

"Fall?" She started to tremble.

"We're going to get you down, but it'll take some maneuvering."

"Why can't I just stand up and walk off the bridge?" she asked in a quivering voice.

"You're not exactly on the bridge. You're on top of it."

"On top of it?"

"On top of the truss."

"That's impossible." But even as she protested, she realized the feathery forms all around her were the tops of cypress trees. She could feel the night air on her face and the hardness of the support beneath her. The nightmarish sensation of falling gripped her again and she said in a terrified whisper, "Please don't let go of me."

"I won't," he promised.

Somehow she believed him. "How did I get up here?"

"You tell me."

"Sometimes I sleepwalk. I have these falling dreams—"

"You're not going to fall. If you go, I go and I'm not in the mood for a swim. So here's what I need you to do. Right now, you're lying on your left side facing out toward the water. Take a moment to get your bearings."

"I can see cypress trees. There's a light somewhere below us—"

"Don't look down. Stay focused on the task at hand. Listen to me carefully. I need you to roll to your stomach, but there's not a lot of space to operate. I'd say about a foot, give or take."

She put out a hand and felt nothing but air. "I can't. There isn't enough room."

"If there's room enough for you to curl up and sleep, there's enough room for you to roll over. Besides, you're small. You don't need much space."

"I can't. Please don't make me."

He was silent for a moment. "What's your name?"

"Olive Belmont."

"Olive? As in Nathan Bolt's cousin?" He sounded surprised.

"Yes. You know Nathan?"

"We go back. Listen to me, Olive. We're going to do this together, okay? I'm right here with you. You'll be able to see me in a moment. Put your right hand on the support and clamp your fingers around the edge. Do the same with your left as you slowly position yourself facedown."

Olive clutched the edge, but she didn't roll over. Not for the longest time. Then drawing a breath, she slowly shifted her body. The rafter rocked and the whole frame seemed to shimmy. She froze. "I can't."

"Yes, you can. This bridge isn't going anywhere. Just take your time. That's it. Nice and easy."

Olive tried to ignore the metallic screeches and the disorienting sway of the structure beneath her. Instead, she let that soothing voice guide her as she maneuvered her hands and body until she lay face down on the support, still breathing hard and trembling.

"Good job. Now you're going to get on your hands and knees and slowly crawl toward me. Got it?"

"Yes."

"Don't look down, look at me. Whenever you're ready."

Olive rose on hands and knees, balancing herself on the precarious beam. The light from below provided enough illumination so that she could see the silhouette of the man facing her.

"Follow me, Olive. Nice and slow. We're in no hurry. We have all night."

His voice flowed over her, so honeyed, so comforting in the dark. She could see the gleam of his eyes, the curve of his jaw. He seemed very steady on the rafter. Not the least bit afraid.

She drew a deep breath and released it. "I'm ready."

They began to move slowly, inch by inch toward the end of the bridge. He had the more difficult job because he was maneuvering backward on the unsteady support. He didn't look over his shoulder or down at the water. He kept his eyes trained on Olive. She tried to do the same. She didn't dare look out over the lake. She didn't dare peer down into that misty abyss.

"Almost there. You're doing great, but I need you to stay focused, okay? I need you to stay calm." He came to a halt and she did the same. His eyes gleamed in the dark as he held her gaze. "Now comes the tricky part."

"The tricky part?" she echoed faintly.

"We're going to lower ourselves over the side. The braces form a sort of ladder at the end of the horizontal beam. I imagine that's how you got up here."

"I don't remember."

"It's not as hard as it sounds. I climbed this thing more times than I could count as a kid. Nathan did, too."

"That doesn't sound like Nathan," she said.

"It took a lot of double-dog daring."

She heard a smile in his voice and shivered. "I'm ready."

He went over the side first, finding his footing and then clinging with one hand as he waited for her. Olive counted to ten and then eased into position, lowering her legs and grappling for a foothold. The movement must have put too much pressure on the rusty bolts. She heard a loud snap and then one end of the beam dropped out from under her. For one heart-stopping moment, she found herself in a free fall.

Then a hand clamped around her wrist. "Easy now. I've got you."

"Don't let go!" she pleaded.

"Not a chance," he said as he tightened his grip.

Chapter Three

He pulled her up to the ladder and then his arm came around her, holding her close as she found her footing. Now that one end of the beam had popped free, the integrity of the structure was even more compromised. The struts clanged ominously as Olive and her rescuer began their descent. At deck level, he climbed over the guardrail and helped her through. She clutched his arm, mindful of all those missing planks and the glisten of water far below.

"Let's get off this thing," he said and took her hand, leading her from the bridge. When they were safely on the bank, she stopped and bent double, catching her breath.

"Are you okay?"

She drew in air. "I just need a moment."

"You did great," he said.

She sucked in several more breaths before she straightened. She could see him more clearly now. He was tall and slim with broad shoulders and long legs. Dark hair, dark eyes. Tantalizingly familiar.

She could see him so well, in fact, she wondered if the moon was up, but then she realized the light came from a bobbing boat at the edge of the water.

"I don't know how I can ever thank you. If you hadn't found me when you did…" She trailed off on another shudder. "How did you even know to look for me up there?"

"I didn't. It was just a lucky break." He paused. "You really don't remember how you got up there?"

"I don't even know how I got to the lake. I have no memory of leaving my house." She glanced down at her bare feet, realizing for the first time that she was in her pajamas. The fabric was summer-weight cotton. Sheer if the light hit her just right, but modesty was the least of her worries. She pulled a leaf from her hair and watched it swirl to the ground. "I don't remember anything."

"What about sounds?" he asked. "Did you hear any loud noises? A car engine maybe?"

She shook her head. "I don't think so. But sleepwalking occurs in deep sleep. I never remember anything."

He stared down at her for a moment. "Do you do this often?"

"No, not in years. I had a sleep disorder in my early teens, but I thought I'd outgrown it. Anyway, the point is, it's like having amnesia. I don't even know what awakened me."

"Maybe you sensed my presence up there on the beam or felt my hand on your shoulder. I did my best not to startle you."

"Thank you. That could have been disastrous for both of us." Now that she was on solid ground and the danger was over she found herself growing curious about him. He still seemed familiar and very capable. "You said you and Nathan go back. Did you go to school together?"

"From kindergarten on."

"Wait. I know you," she blurted as recognition dawned. "You're Jack King."

She saw a frown fleet across his face. "My reputation precedes me, I guess."

"It isn't that. I remember you from the year my mother and I moved to Pine Lake. We stayed with Nathan and his dad until we got our own place. You used to come by the house with Tommy Driscoll and some of the other seniors. You'd hang out by the pool. I was invisible to most of Nathan's friends, but you were always nice to me."

"Was I?"

She gave an awkward laugh. "I guess I was invisible to you, too. You don't remember me, do you?"

"I do now, but you've changed. No glasses, no braces." He canted his head, peering down at her in the light. "I think I can still see some freckles, though."

A thrill chased up Olive's spine at his scrutiny. She'd never told anyone—had barely admitted it even to herself—that she'd had a crush on Jack King that year. Nathan's other friends were rude and boisterous, but Jack was different. To a hopelessly romantic fourteen-year-old, he'd seemed deep and introspective. And devastatingly handsome. "You haven't changed a bit," she said.

"I'd wait for better lighting to make that assessment."

"I can see you just fine."

Car engines sounded on the road. Doors slammed and male voices carried in the dark.

"That'll be the sheriff." Jack turned toward the trees and called out to the newcomers. "Down here!"

Olive scanned the woods anxiously. "You called the police? Why didn't you wait for their help to get me down?"

"I didn't think it a good idea to leave you up there any longer than was necessary. Besides, I didn't call the cops because of you." He hesitated, his eyes going past her to the water. "No easy way to say this. I found a body in the lake before I saw you on the bridge."

Olive's hand crept to her throat. "A body?"

"A woman."

"Do you know who she is?"

"No. But if she's local, the sheriff or one of his deputies can likely identify her."

Olive closed her eyes in dread. "If she's local, she's probably someone I know." A former student perhaps or even a friend. "Pine Lake is small. Everyone knows everyone."

"I remember."

She turned to the lake in horror. Someone she knew could be out there in the water at that very moment, dead and drifting. It gave her the oddest feeling. Part fear, part sadness, part relief. If she'd fallen from the rafters, she'd likely be dead and drifting, too.

But she was safe and sound thanks to Jack King and this night was no longer about her.

She wrapped her arms around her middle. "Could you tell how she died? Was it a drowning accident?"

His gaze on her deepened. Olive shivered at the intensity of his stare. The scruff on his lower face made him look dangerously enigmatic. The way he towered over her made him seem just plain dangerous.

"You should wait and ask the sheriff those questions. I wouldn't want to be accused of interfering in his investigation."

"Of course. I understand. It's just…what if it *is* someone I know?"

"You'll find out soon enough," he said with a nod as Tommy Driscoll and two of his deputies came crashing through the underbrush. The subordinates wore uniforms, but Tommy had on jeans, cowboy boots and a white dress shirt with pearl buttons. He looked as if he had been out dancing. Or up to no good.

He stopped dead when he spotted them. Then he said something over his shoulder to one of the deputies before he joined Olive and Jack on the bank.

Olive tried not to show her disdain for the Caddo County sheriff. She respected his position but not so much the man. If Jack King had been her favorite of Nathan's friends, Tommy Driscoll had been her least. Even as a teenager, he'd been arrogant and overbearing and she'd seen no evidence of evolution.

Unlike Jack, the years hadn't been kind to him physically. His muscles had softened as his features had hardened. He was still married to his high school sweetheart, but rumors about affairs had run rampant for years. Beth Driscoll taught science at Pine Lake High School. She was a lovely woman and a dedicated teacher. Olive would never understand why someone who had so much going for her would put up with a man like Tommy.

He and Jack eyed each other warily before Tommy gave a brief nod. "Jack."

"Tommy."

They didn't shake hands, Olive noted.

"Good to see you, buddy. Sorry it has to be under these circumstances. When did you get into town?"

"A few hours ago."

"Helluva homecoming." Tommy's gaze slid to Olive, taking in her pajamas and bare feet. "Olive? What are you doing down here?"

"She just got here," Jack said.

Tommy frowned. "Got here from where?"

"From the road. She said she heard my boat."

It was all Olive could do not to turn and gape at Jack. Somehow she managed to stifle her shock under Tommy's narrow-eyed inspection.

"Let's let Olive answer for herself," he said.

She nodded. "I was out for a walk when I heard the boat. I came down here to see who was out on the lake so late. I thought someone might be dumping trash. You know what an environmental hazard that poses."

"I know you like your causes," Tommy said. "But you're telling me you were out for a walk at this hour? In your pajamas? Without shoes?"

"I didn't expect to end up so far from the house. I've been under a lot of stress lately and I only meant to get a bit of fresh air to clear my head. Next thing I knew, I'd walked all the way to the lake."

Tommy's gaze went from Olive to Jack and then back to Olive. He lowered his voice as he took a step toward her. "Are you sure you're okay?"

His implication couldn't have been plainer and she resented it on Jack's behalf. She told herself it was silly to feel so protective of a stranger, but she found herself pressing closer to him anyway. "Of course, I am," she said coolly. "And I think you've more important things to worry about than me."

He gave her another curious look before turning back to Jack. "Where's the body?"

Jack gestured toward the lake. "I can take you out in the boat and show you."

Tommy nodded. "Yeah, let's go have a look."

The deputies still hovered a few feet away and Tommy went over to confer for a moment.

"What was that all about?" Olive whispered furiously.

"Trust me, I know what I'm doing," Jack said.

"By lying to the police?"

"It'll be okay," he assured her.

Olive wasn't as convinced, but it was a little too late for second thoughts. Not only had she gone along with Jack's fabrication, she'd embellished his account. If she came clean now, it would make both of them look foolish and possibly suspect.

But those lies had flowed just a little too easily, from her and from Jack. Olive had never considered herself the subversive type, although as Tommy had pointed out, she supported causes near and dear to her heart and had never been shy about voicing an opinion. Deliberately misleading the police, though? That was a serious matter and one she shouldn't have undertaken so lightly.

She watched nervously as the two men climbed into the boat and pushed off. When they'd cleared the bank, Jack started the engine and steered them across the channel to the shallow water on the other side. They sat with the motor idling as he angled the spotlight down through the lily pads.

It seemed to Olive they stayed out on the water for an awfully long time. What were they talking about?

Finally, they headed back. Jack tied off and they disembarked.

Tommy climbed up the bank to where Olive and the two deputies waited. "Be easier to get her out from the other side," he said. "Hope you boys brought your waders."

Jack came up the bank, too, and she found herself instinctively gravitating to his side even as she kept her focus on the sheriff. "Who is she, Tommy?"

He hesitated. "I guess you'll find out soon enough. It's Jamie Butaud."

Olive felt sick. "Are you sure?"

"Pretty certain. The physical description matches up. And Jack here spotted a tattoo on her left arm. I remember seeing it on Jamie."

"A mermaid," Olive murmured.

"You knew her?" Jack inquired gently.

"She was in one of my classes a few years ago before she dropped out of school. I always worried about her. She seemed so lost."

"She worked for Nathan, didn't she?" Tommy asked.

Both men peered at Olive in the dark, but it was the fierceness of Jack's sudden concentration that took her by surprise. "Yes, as a receptionist."

"When was the last time you saw her?" Tommy asked.

Olive shrugged. "I don't remember specifically. I rarely go to Nathan's office, but I would see Jamie in town from time to time, usually with her boyfriend."

"She was still seeing the Waller kid?"

"Marc? Yes, as far as I know."

"Bad news, that boy. Comes from a long line of bad news." Tommy ran a hand through his hair. "Look, here, you two. I need you to keep quiet about this, at least until we can notify next of kin. And I'd like the chance to speak with Waller before he tries to skip town."

Olive glanced from Tommy to Jack. "You don't think her death was an accident, do you?"

"That's safe to assume," Tommy said. "We'll know

more after the autopsy, but the first thing we have to do is get her out of the water. You don't need to be here for that. I'll have Hank run you home while we wait for the coroner."

"I can take her," Jack said.

Tommy didn't look too pleased by the offer. "In your boat? How's that going to work? Olive lives in town, last I heard."

"We'll go to my uncle's cabin and get my car. Seems to me you'll need all your manpower here, Sheriff."

Tommy scowled down at her. "You okay with that arrangement, Olive?"

She resisted the urge to inform him that she'd much rather be alone with Jack King than any of the other men present. Instead, she nodded and turned to Jack. "Thanks."

"No problem."

Tommy was still frowning. "I'll need to see each of you in my office first thing in the morning. And remember what I said about keeping this quiet."

Jack took Olive's arm and helped her navigate the slippery bank. Once they'd cast off, she averted her gaze from the spot where he'd taken Tommy to view the body. But she couldn't help glancing back at the bridge. She let her gaze travel up the iron braces to the very top of the truss. If Jack hadn't spotted her…if he hadn't climbed up there beside her…

Something came to Olive as the bridge receded in the distance. Now she understood why Jack had asked her if she'd heard a loud noise or a car engine.

In all likelihood, she'd been asleep on that beam when Jamie Butaud's killer had thrown her body off the bridge.

A LITTLE WHILE later Jack pulled his car into Olive's driveway and parked. She'd been very quiet on the ride into town, staring out the window until she needed to give him directions to her house.

"Are you okay?" he asked.

"Yes, just lost in thought." Her voice had taken on a raspy edge, either from nerves or the night air.

Jack cut the engine and the headlights went out, but the street lamp on the corner cast a hazy glow inside the car. Her skin looked pale in that light, but her face was alive with color—the copper of her freckles and the bright blue of her eyes framed by the deep russet of her hair. She peered at him so steadily he had to shift his gaze to the window, instinctively taking stock of their surroundings.

She lived on a quiet street in the oldest part of town. The houses on her block were small with wide front porches and tidy fenced yards. Jack had grown up only a few blocks over in a sturdy old Craftsman that his mother had loved. It had pained her to leave the house of her dreams, but after everything that had happened to their family, Pine Lake no longer seemed like home.

"What an awful homecoming you've had," Olive murmured, echoing his thoughts. "This night must bring back a lot of bad memories for you."

"This town is nothing but a bad memory." He glanced in the rearview mirror, scanning the street behind them.

"If you really feel that way, why did you come back?"

"My uncle's estate has some loose ends that can't be tied up over the phone or in an email."

"Oh, of course. I was so sorry to hear about his passing. He was a nice man. I always enjoyed his stories." Her regret sounded deep and genuine.

Jack turned in surprise. "His stories?"

"He took classes at the community college where I sometimes teach at night. He was one of my favorite students."

Jack stared at her in astonishment. "Leon went to night school? I never knew him to be interested in anything but fishing."

"Then it may surprise you to learn that your uncle was a very gifted writer."

He cast her a doubtful glance. "Are you sure we're talking about the same Leon King?"

She smiled. "Yes, same man. He always spoke highly of you. He was very proud of the way you'd turned things around after everything you went through." She paused thoughtfully. "For the record, I never believed you did it."

"Why?"

His blunt challenge seemed to catch her off guard, but she recovered quickly. "Because of the way you would look at Anna. Anyone could see you were crazy about her. And why wouldn't you be? She was a beautiful girl, inside and out."

"She was," he said quietly.

"And because it wasn't in you. You weren't capable of hurting anyone. I doubt you are now unless someone backs you into a corner."

"You deduced all that in the space of one car ride?"

"I deduced all that a long time ago. You're a good guy. Just like your uncle. Why else would you have climbed to the top of that bridge to rescue me?"

Her conviction caught *him* off guard. When Jack had decided to come back to Pine Lake, he'd braced himself for the whispers and gossip. The lingering suspicions. But he hadn't prepared himself for Olive Belmont.

"I've been away from here for a long time," he said. "I may not be the man you think I am."

"I may not be the woman you think I am," she countered. "If you think about me at all," she added sheepishly.

"Hard to forget someone you meet on top of a bridge."

He saw a shiver go through her as she turned to stare out the windshield. She looked very enticing with her hair all mussed and her lips slightly parted. Another time, another place and Jack might have responded to the subtle invitation in her smile. But a hookup was the last thing he needed, particularly with Nathan Bolt's cousin. He'd come to town to poke a hornet's nest. Depending on what he found, things could get ugly. Sides might have to be chosen. After all was said and done, he'd return to Houston while Olive would still have to live here. Jack knew only too well what it was like to be a pariah in Pine Lake.

She gave him another tentative smile and he tamped down the urge to tuck back her hair as he studied her face in the dim light.

"I know now why you told the sheriff I had just arrived at the lake," she said. "I figured it out in the boat. You think I was on top of the bridge when the killer dumped Jamie's body in the water."

"Seems a safe bet. It couldn't have taken more than five minutes for me to get to the bridge after I first heard a splash and you were already up there."

"So you wanted to place me on the road rather than the bridge."

He shifted his position, turning toward her as he relaxed his arm across the back of her seat. "I heard that splash and then a few minutes later, a car engine. The vehicle drove away on the other side of the lake. Even if you really had been on the road at the same time the body was dumped from the bridge, you wouldn't have seen anything."

She gave him an anxious look. "That explains why you asked if I'd heard a car engine. But I told you before—I never remember anything when I sleepwalk."

"Jamie's killer wouldn't know that, though. He or she might not want to take the chance that something would eventually come back to you."

That gave her pause. She cast an uneasy glance over her shoulder. "Do you really think I could be in danger?"

He wanted to reassure her that all would be well, but a false sense of security was never a good idea. She needed to watch her back. They weren't out of the woods yet. The story they'd concocted for Tommy Driscoll was only a little more plausible than the actual truth. "As long as we don't give the killer a reason to feel threatened, he'll lay low. As far as anyone knows, I was the first to arrive on the scene. If he gets skittish, he'll come after me."

"That doesn't give me much comfort," she said with a frown.

"It should. I know how to handle myself."

"Leon told me that you'd been a cop. And now you're some sort of security consultant. With all your experience, you must have some idea of how Jamie died."

"Are you sure you want to know?"

She swallowed. "I wasn't. But now I think you have to tell me."

"She has what appears to be a large exit wound between her eyes. I'm guessing she was shot at close range in the back of the head."

"In the back of the head..." Olive repeated numbly.

"Without a closer examination of the body or a look at the autopsy report, I can only speculate. But I've seen the pattern of the wound before in execution-style murders."

"Execution?" She stared at him in shock. "Who would do such a thing to poor Jamie?"

"You never heard talk about her involvement in any illegal activities?"

"She got into some trouble when she was younger. Drugs. Possession, I think. Her mother asked Nathan to represent her, but the family didn't have any money. He agreed to take the case pro bono if Jamie agreed to go to night school and get her GED."

"What about her boyfriend?"

"I don't know him personally, but Tommy was right. Marc Waller is bad news. He was also arrested for possession but with the intent to sell. If convicted, he could have gone to prison for a very long time. But Nathan got the case dismissed because of an unlawful search. Needless to say, that didn't go over well with local law enforcement."

"Nathan Bolt seems to be the go-to attorney for drug charges," Jack observed.

"Well, there aren't a lot of choices in the area and my cousin is very good at what he does." She sighed. "The news about Jamie will devastate him. If it turns out that Marc Waller had anything to do with her death, Nathan will never forgive himself."

These revelations were all very interesting to Jack.

On the night of his return, he'd stumbled across a murder victim who happened to be a young woman that Nathan Bolt had taken under his wing. The timing was a little more than Jack could swallow as happenstance.

"It's late," Olive said. "And we're both expected at the police station first thing in the morning so..."

"Right. I'll walk you to the door."

"You don't need to do that. I'm fine."

Jack reached for the door handle. "For my own peace of mind, I'd like to have a look around before I go."

"To be honest, it's probably best for my peace of mind, too."

They got out of the car and walked up the porch steps together. The front door stood ajar and Olive turned to him with a worried frown.

"I'm sure it's nothing. I probably failed to close it earlier."

Jack brushed past her, glancing over his shoulder to scan the street and all the shadowy corners of the yard before toeing open the door. "Where's the light switch?"

"To your left."

"Wait here." He eased through the quiet house, giving each room a thorough search before returning to the foyer. "All clear."

"Thanks for checking." Olive stepped inside and followed his gaze to the bolt at the top of the door. "A precaution. Not that it did any good tonight."

"You unlocked the deadbolt in your sleep?"

"Apparently."

"You should get a security system, one with a loud enough alarm to wake you if a door or window is opened."

"Yes, my mother had one put in when the episodes

first started. As I said, I thought I'd outgrown them, but after tonight, I won't take any chances. I'll arrange for an installation as soon as possible."

Jack took a last sweep of the small, but comfortable living area. The walls were white and the furniture gray, not unlike the nondescript color scheme in his apartment. But Olive had punctuated the space with pillows and throw rugs in bright shades of red and turquoise. He observed everything, not because her design aesthetic interested him, but because a house could reveal a lot about the person who lived there.

Olive Belmont seemed to be an open book. If her cousin was involved in something as shady as Tommy had implied, Jack doubted she knew anything about it. But then, he had been fooled before.

He stepped out on the porch and scoured the darkness. The breeze had picked up, fluttering through the trees in Olive's front yard and unleashing the scent of jasmine from the bushes that grew up her fence. It was all very lush and homey and familiar and yet Jack felt strangely unmoored as if coming back here to his hometown had caused him to lose his bearings.

He turned back to Olive. "Are you sure you'll be all right for the rest of the night?"

"I'll be fine. If I sleep at all, it won't be deeply enough to leave my bed."

An image of that bed floated through Jack's head—crisp white linens and soft, soft pillows.

"Well, good night, then." He bent impulsively to kiss her cheek. The action took both of them by surprise and she jerked her head just enough so that his mouth brushed hers.

He didn't pull away or offer an apology. Instead, he

tangled his fingers in her hair and brought his mouth to hers, this time on purpose. She responded by parting her lips and kissing him back. When he pulled away, she looked disoriented, as if she had just awakened from another harrowing adventure.

"What a strange night this has been," she murmured.

"Hasn't it, though?" he said over his shoulder as he strode down the steps.

Chapter Four

Olive was just coming out of the local coffee shop the next morning when she spotted Jack on his way in. He held the door for her and she stepped out on the sidewalk to join him, taking a moment to discreetly admire the fit of his faded jeans and the cotton shirt that he wore untucked and rolled up at the sleeves.

His hair was even darker than she remembered, his eyes a deep, rich chocolate. Despite what she'd said the night before, he had most definitely changed since their high school years. The harsh light of day emphasized the fine lines around his eyes, the resolved set of his jaw and a chiseled chin. The changes didn't so much age him as harden him. He was a man in his prime rather than the seventeen-year-old boy who had been driven out of town by both his elders and his peers.

"Good morning," she said in a tone far too bright for the circumstances. "Looks like we had the same idea."

"It would seem so." He stood with one hand still on the door as he gave her a long assessment.

His scrutiny was only fair, she supposed, since she'd done the same to him. Still, she was secretly relieved that she'd taken time with her appearance even though the sleeveless white dress and caged heels were for work and not for Jack King. Normally, she wouldn't have been so formally turned out during summer break, but she had a faculty meeting later that morning, the first of the new school year, and she wanted to make a good impression. That Jack seemed to appreciate her fine-tuning was merely icing on the cake.

"Are you headed over to the sheriff's office?" he asked.

"I've already been in." They moved away from the door to the edge of the street so as not to block customer traffic. "We spoke briefly. I really couldn't add much to my previous statement and Tommy revealed very little about the investigation. Although I gather word has already gotten out about Jamie's death. That's not surprising. Secrets are hard to keep in a town this small."

"That hasn't been my experience." His tone was enigmatic. "You repeated what you'd already told him last night?"

"I stuck to our story if that's what you mean." She shot a quick glance over her shoulder and then leaned in. "Lying to the police before breakfast, let alone my first cup of coffee, is a lot more stressful than I would have imagined. I don't know how career criminals do it."

"If it makes you feel any better, you ad-libbed like a champ last night."

She winced. "That doesn't make me feel better. Worse, in fact. I work with kids. I take my responsibility as a role model very seriously. What does it say about my character that I could so easily withhold the truth in a murder investigation?"

"You have every right to protect yourself. Nothing you could have told him would change the course of his investigation. You didn't see or hear anything. Why put yourself needlessly at risk?"

"I guess."

He glanced back at the shop door. "I should grab my coffee and go. Tommy will be expecting me."

"And I need to get to work. Good luck with your interview." She paused. "Should we get together later to compare notes? I have a meeting at ten, but I'll be in my office all afternoon."

"I'll try to give you a call."

A noncommittal answer if Olive had ever heard one, but she decided not to take it personally. She'd enjoyed their good-night kiss—had been quite stunned by it, in fact—but she didn't attach too much importance to the gesture. Jack had acted on impulse and she'd responded in kind. Blame it on the lingering adrenaline from her rescue. Olive freely acknowledged an attraction to him, but really, wasn't his allure little more than an old memory?

Besides, it was probably for the best to keep some distance. After last night, there would undoubtedly be talk. Olive wasn't one to live her life in fear of gossip, but like it or not, reputation mattered in a small town, especially for someone in her position. The next few weeks were crucial. They could well set the tone for the whole school year, if not the rest of her career. She would be foolish to invite distraction and controversy when everything she'd worked so hard for was at stake.

She murmured a goodbye and then turned to cross the street only to have Jack grab her arm and yank her back to the curb as a black pickup truck roared through the intersection. Her heel caught in a crack and she went down in an ungainly sprawl. The coffee cup flew out of her hand, exploding on impact with the pavement. Mortified, Olive could only stare helplessly at the spreading brown splotches on her white dress.

Jack was instantly at her side. "You okay?"

"I think so." She took his hand and quickly scrambled to her feet. A small group had already started to gather and Olive would have liked nothing more than to sink right through the sidewalk.

"You sure you're okay?"

"Yes, fine." She dusted her hands and tried to salvage her poise. If anything could be more embarrassing than taking a spill in public, it was doing so in the presence of a high school crush. "That's the second time you've had to come to my rescue in as many days. And the second time in less than a week that I almost got hit stepping off a curb. I really should pay more attention."

"That driver was going way too fast. Brazenly speeding right down Main Street." He retrieved the cup and tossed it in a nearby trash bin.

Olive's ankle ached and the heel on her right shoe wobbled. The morning had turned disastrous. Now she would have to go all the way back home and change, leaving little time to prepare for her meeting. She lamented the turn of events until she reminded herself of Jamie Butaud's fate and the kind of morning that awaited her family and friends. Put in the proper perspective, a coffee-stained dress and a battered shoe were hardly worth fretting over.

"Did you get a look at the driver?" Jack asked her.

"It happened too quickly. What about you?"

"I was able to get a partial plate number. I'll give that and a description of the vehicle to the sheriff. Someone is bound to recognize that truck." He scanned the crowd for a moment before zeroing back in on her. "You said this had happened before?"

"Last Friday night. I worked late and it was already dark by the time I left for home. A car came out of nowhere and the headlights blinded me as I stepped off the curb."

His voice sharpened. "Last Friday night?"

"Yes, why?"

He hesitated. "Nothing. I was just thinking back to my own Friday night. Same vehicle?"

"No, it was a car then. A dark sedan, but I couldn't tell the make or model. I really don't think it's anything to worry about. I have a feeling I'm being tested."

"What do you mean, tested?"

The intensity of his focus caught Olive off guard and unease crept over her. Why did she suddenly have the feeling that there was much more to Jack King and his return than he had previously been willing to acknowledge? Despite their history, he was a stranger and now she couldn't help but wonder why he had really come back to Pine Lake. Something was going on, with him and with this town. At that moment, her decision to keep a safe distance seemed like a very good idea.

"In three weeks, I'll be starting my first semester as principal of Pine Lake High School," she explained.

He lifted a brow. "Principal?"

She gave a shaky laugh. "Please don't say I look too young for the job. I've already heard that too many times as it is."

"I was about to say, you're a lot braver than I am."

"We'll soon see, I suppose. Anyway, I think these incidents are challenges to my authority. A way to intimidate me. Neither vehicle came close to hitting me."

Jack's expression sobered. "That's a pretty dangerous way to intimidate. You could have been seriously injured when you fell. Whatever the motive, they shouldn't be allowed to get away with it."

She started to put a restraining hand on his arm, but dropped it to her side instead. "They're just kids. As soon as they accept that I can't be scared off, they'll move on." She glanced around. A few bystanders still huddled nearby as they whispered furiously among themselves. Evidently, Jack had been recognized and Olive's heart sank. Word would spread across town like wildfire now. Jack King had come back to Pine Lake on the same night a young woman had been murdered. And Olive Belmont had been seen with him at the lake and now in front of the coffee shop. No telling what her role would become once the game of telephone took hold.

Jack had noticed the crowd, too. It would be hard to miss the whispers and open stares.

"Ignore them," she said.

He gave a low laugh. "These people mean nothing to me."

His derision sent a chill through her, almost as frigid as the sudden frost in his eyes. "Then why come back here?"

"I told you last night—loose ends."

"But those loose ends don't really have anything to do with your uncle's estate, do they? I saw the way you looked at that crowd just now. *These people.* Why do I have a feeling you've come back for revenge?"

"There's a difference between justice and vengeance."

Olive's heart thudded in trepidation. The disquiet she'd been experiencing for days seemed to culminate in his icy stare. "Your uncle never believed that Wayne Foukes killed Anna. I take it you don't, either."

Even as he hesitated to answer, his gaze on her was relentless. "Wayne Foukes is guilty of a lot of terrible crimes, but he didn't kill Anna."

"How can you be so sure unless—"

His voice grew even colder. "Unless I killed her?"

"Unless you have new evidence. I told you last night I never thought you did it."

"You also told me that you think I'm a good guy. The look on your face right now tells me otherwise."

Olive wasn't quite sure how to respond. It was true, she did feel differently about him this morning. He seemed a little too dark and distant, a little too secretive for her peace of mind. But what if he was right? What if Anna's murderer had gone free all these years and was still living in Pine Lake? Still attending Sunday morning church services and Friday night football games? What if the killer was an acquaintance or a friend or even someone she had dated? What if a cold-blooded murderer had lain low all these years, hidden among the populace of a small, insular town, only to resurface and kill again fifteen years later?

Jack waited patiently for her to respond.

She tried to subdue her agitation as she gave him an honest answer. "I still think you're a good guy. But a good guy on a mission can cause an awful lot of trouble."

"The innocent have nothing to fear from me."

She suspected his was also an honest answer, but it only served to deepen her foreboding. Because in that moment of candor, Olive had glimpsed something in his face that she hadn't witnessed before. Beneath his cool, steady persona was a simmering anger that took her breath away. Despite what he said about justice and vengeance, there was no mistaking his intent. Jack King meant to have his pound of flesh.

She closed her eyes on a shiver. The town wouldn't even see it coming. A few discreet questions and suddenly suspicions would flare and bad feelings would fester. Neighbor would side-eye neighbor. Olive couldn't fault him for wanting justice or even revenge for the way he'd been treated, but she dreaded getting caught in the fallout.

His gaze was still on her, a singular focus that drew another shiver. She tried to look away, but his stare was too hypnotic. Why hadn't she seen this coming? Even on top of the bridge, even in the throes of terror, instinct should have warned her that she was in the presence of a very dangerous man. Her instincts were warning her now. Screaming at her, in fact.

"I…should go," she said.

Before she could step away, he reached out and tucked back an errant strand of hair that had fallen loose from her ponytail. Her pulse jumped at even so slight a touch and Olive knew she was in real trouble.

"Watch where you're going," he said.

"Good advice." *Such* good advice.

JACK GLANCED OVER his shoulder to where Tommy Driscoll sat behind his desk. The Caddo County sheriff was on the phone and had been for a full five minutes.

When he caught Jack's eye, he palmed the mouthpiece. "Sorry about this."

"No problem."

"You need anything? Cup of coffee…bottle of water…"

"I'm good," Jack said as he turned back to the window. "Take your time."

He was glad to have a few minutes to collect his thoughts. With an effort, he unclenched his fists and relaxed his fingers as he tried to rein in his emotions. But even now, he could feel the surge of an unexpected anger.

Jack had been in control for so long he'd forgotten what it was like to give in to those latent resentments. The fury that had defined his behavior all through college had eventually given way to the bitter resignation of his twenties and finally to the jaded disdain that had kept him restless and distrustful at thirty-three. His earlier anger had blindsided him. That the townspeople and their lingering suspicions could still goad him back into that dark place didn't bode well for an objective investigation.

Being back inside the police station didn't help. On the morning he'd first learned of Anna's death, Jack had been ushered into this very office. Despite the passage of time, he still remembered those hours vividly—his mother's tremulous voice waking him from a deep sleep. His grogginess as he dressed and staggered down the back stairs to the kitchen where his father and Sheriff Brannigan sat drinking coffee. His father's somber expression. The lawman's grim tone. *Son, I need you and your folks to come down to the station with me.*

Jack had found out about Anna on the ride downtown. Then later, in the throes of grief and shock and flanked by his parents, he'd sat across the desk from Brannigan for his first interview. The questions had seemed innocuous at first. When had he last seen Anna? What time had he dropped her off? Had they argued that evening?

From there the interrogation had progressed to the most intimate details of their relationship.

Were the two of you sexually active?

Yes, sir.

For how long?

A few months.

Did you have intercourse last night?

Yes, sir.

But didn't you say you took her home because she wasn't feeling well?

Yes. That's true.

But she felt well enough to have sex with you?

I...guess so.

Tell the truth, son. Did you pressure that girl? Use a little force when she wouldn't give in?

No, sir. It was her idea.

Her idea? She asked you to take her home early because she was sick and then she asked you to have sex with her in your car? I find that a little hard to believe. Especially since her folks swear they never heard her come in. Her bed wasn't slept in last night. How do you account for that?

I can't.

Truth is, you didn't take her home, did you, Jack?

I swear I did! I walked her to the door and I waited until she was inside the house before I drove off.

You know what I think? I think you were all hopped up on adrenaline after the football game last night. You guys won, right? You scored the winning touchdown. You must have been in the mood to celebrate. Yeah, you

*were raring to go and things got a little rough, maybe.
Things got out of hand and Anna ended up dead.*

That's a lie! I would never hurt Anna!

*Or maybe she wouldn't give you what you wanted
and so you decided to take it. Hotshot like you always
gets what he wants. You're a real popular guy, aren't
you, Jack? Not used to hearing no, I bet. When Anna
fought back, you bashed her in the head with a rock.*

*No! That's not what happened. You have to believe
me—*

*Then you tore off her clothes and had your way with
her.*

Please—

Made you feel pretty powerful, didn't it?

Please, I'm going to be sick—

*I'm sick, too, Jack. Sick all the way down to my soul
at what you did to that poor girl.*

I didn't do anything. I swear—

*Go ahead and cry if you have to, but those tears
won't help when we match your DNA to the sample we
took from Anna's body.*

Please stop. Please. I can't take this anymore—

*You didn't stop when Anna begged you to, did you?
Afterward you panicked. You had to finish her off and
so you strangled her. You threw her body off the old
Pine Lake Bridge and then you went home, crawled
into your comfortable bed and went to sleep. Did I get
it right, Jack? Tell me where I'm going wrong.*

*You're wrong about everything! I didn't do this.
Mom. Dad. Tell him. Please. I could never do something like this—*

*Your mom and dad can't help you, son. But I can. Tell
me what really happened last night. Tell me the truth*

*and I swear to God I'll do everything in my power to
help you through this.*

Jack's parents had lived in Pine Lake for most of
their lives. Sheriff Brannigan was a friend. They were
of the mind that if Jack cooperated, if he simply told
the truth, everything would be all right. Five hours into
the intense grilling, Jack's father had finally excused
himself to go call a lawyer.

When they were allowed to leave the police station, word had already spread about Anna's murder. A
crowd had gathered in the parking lot. Friends, neighbors, classmates. The open suspicion and outright name
calling had been hard enough to take, but nothing had
gotten to Jack quite like his mother's silent weeping.
She'd taken to her bed as soon as they got home while
his father had gone about the grim business of figuring
out how to pay for the attorney. Throughout the whole
ordeal, they'd stood by him, never for a second letting
on that they doubted his innocence. But after that morning, it seemed to Jack they'd never quite looked at him
in the same way again.

"Jack? You ready, buddy?"

Tommy's drawl pierced through the barrage of memories and Jack turned from the window with a scowl.
"What?"

"The interview. You ready?"

"Yeah, let's get it over with."

Tommy stretched. "Sorry again for the interruption.
The mayor tends to get a little long-winded when he's on
a tear. I don't answer to him, but I try to lend a sympathetic ear now and then. Anyway, before he called, you

were telling me about a black pickup truck that nearly ran Olive over this morning."

"Yeah, it came pretty damn close."

"Black trucks are a dime a dozen around here. Could be hard to track down even with a partial plate. Do you remember any identifying marks? Bumper stickers? A dented fender or a cracked windshield, maybe?"

Jack folded his arms and leaned a shoulder against the window frame. "The paint job was flat black. Custom."

"That'll help." Tommy jotted down a few more notes, tore the sheet from the pad and went out to the squad room where he handed the paper to an officer. He returned a moment later carrying two mugs of black coffee. "You look like you could use a caffeine jolt. I know I can."

Jack had forgone coffee earlier after the incident with Olive. Now, though, he accepted the cup gratefully and took a tentative sip. "Damn."

Tommy chuckled. "Around here, we like it strong enough to put hair on your chest."

"Mission accomplished." Jack went over to the desk and placed his cup on the corner as his gaze traveled across the rows of framed photographs and citations on the walls. "Are all those commendations yours?"

Tommy looked pleased that he had noticed. "I've had a good run."

"It would appear that you have."

He motioned Jack to a seat and then went around the desk and sat down heavily in his creaking chair. "About that black truck." He took a quick sip of his coffee. "Clearly a case of reckless driving, but you're not thinking the driver *deliberately* tried to run Olive down, are you?"

"She said it was the second time she's almost been hit in less than a week. She thinks she's being tested because of her new job."

"Sounds about right. Kids around here drive like bats out of hell. You and I were no different back in the day. And just between us, Olive Belmont isn't the most observant pedestrian. She walks around town with her head in the clouds half the time. Not just her. I've seen people on their cell phones step into the street without ever looking up. Then add in the texting drivers and you start to get a real grim picture."

"Olive wasn't on her phone."

"No, but she was talking to you, right? She was distracted. I'm not saying I won't look into it. I will. But even if I manage to track down the truck, all I can do is give the driver a good talking to. Sometimes that's enough."

"I appreciate your efforts," Jack said. "I wouldn't want anyone to get hurt."

"Nor would I. But right now I've got bigger fish to fry with this murder investigation." Tommy settled back in his chair and clasped his hands behind his head. His casual demeanor didn't fool Jack. Sheriff Brannigan had seemed amiable, too, at first, but he'd quickly revealed himself to be ruthless and obsessed. A simple and single-minded investigator who couldn't be bothered to look for other suspects because Jack had fit his profile. Only months later when he'd failed to come up with anything more than circumstantial evidence had an ex-con in the area pinged his radar. Jack had wondered more than once about the coincidence and convenience of that traffic stop. Wayne Foukes's arrest had taken the pressure off a beleaguered county sheriff. From that day forward, Brannigan had run uncontested every four years until his retirement.

"I need to hear about last night," Tommy was saying. "Start at the beginning and walk me through everything that happened up until the time my deputies and I arrived on the scene."

Jack told him about spotting the flashlight beam on the bridge, hearing a splash and then moments later, the sound of a car driving away.

"So you decided to take the boat out and investigate," Tommy said.

"Don't tell me you wouldn't have done the same."

"Probably," he admitted. "How long did it take you to locate the body?"

"Not long with the spotlight. Five or ten minutes."

"What did you do once you found her?"

"I called it in. Then I tied off the boat and waited on the bank so that I could flag you down when you arrived."

"And that's when Olive came along?"

"Yeah, a few minutes later."

"You didn't think it strange to see her wandering around in the dark in her pajamas?"

"I've seen stranger things."

"Still, the behavior seems peculiar even for Olive."

"You heard what she said. She thought someone might be dumping trash in the lake. I guess she wanted to catch them red-handed."

Tommy gave him a pensive scowl. "Did you know she used to be a sleepwalker?"

Jack shrugged. "She seemed wide awake when I spoke to her."

"That's the thing, though. You can't always tell."

"Have you seen her sleepwalk?" Jack asked.

"Not in years. But when she and her mother were first staying with the Bolts, Nathan and I once found her outside in the middle of the night, sitting cross-legged in the front yard staring out at the street. When I waved my hand in front of her face, she didn't even blink. It was eerie as hell. Another time Nathan said she was out all night before anyone noticed her missing. Next day, she didn't remember a thing. It was like it never happened."

"Okay, so she used to sleepwalk," Jack said. "Like I said, she seemed awake and lucid when I talked to her last night."

Tommy picked up a pencil and examined the eraser. "You didn't get a look at the vehicle that drove off?"

"It was long gone before I arrived at the bridge. And there's no way Olive could have seen it from the road."

"That's pretty much what she said."

Jack shrugged. "Then I guess we're done here."

"Not quite."

Jack had started to rise, but he sat back down as Tommy leaned forward, his gaze narrowed and suddenly hostile.

Jack's guard came up. "What else can I do for you, sheriff?"

"You can tell me what you're doing in Pine Lake."

"I'm here to put my uncle's affairs in order."

Tommy didn't appear convinced. "Let me put it another way. Why have you come back now? Leon passed away months ago. Are you sure there's not another reason for your sudden trip down memory lane? I told you the other night, I've kept up with your career. I know what you do at the Blackthorn Agency. The thought has crossed my mind that someone might have hired you to investigate this office."

"Is there a reason someone would want this office investigated?" Jack countered, taking a perverse satisfaction in Tommy's apparent discomfort.

"Someone's always got a beef. Comes with the territory. But you and me—" Tension crackled as he leveled his gaze across the desk at Jack. "We'll have a real problem if I find out you're working for Nathan Bolt."

"I'm not working for anybody. I'm here of my own accord." Now it was Jack who leaned forward. "But you're right. There is another reason for my trip. Did you really expect I would do nothing about the bombshell you dropped the other night?"

"I was hoping you were smart enough to leave that alone, buddy."

"Then why tell me about it at all if you didn't want me to come to Pine Lake?"

"I wanted to warn you about Nathan. I needed to make you realize how untrustworthy he is."

"See, that's the part I still don't get," Jack said. "What made you think Nathan would contact me in the first place?"

Tommy glanced toward the squad room. The door was closed but he lowered his voice anyway. "One of my informants told me that Nathan's been asking a lot of questions about this office. I was told flat out that he's looking to hire an outside investigator to take me down. And since he and your uncle were so tight, it stood to reason he'd try to get you on his side."

"His side?"

"There's a war going on in this town, Jack. Things have changed since you lived here. Used to be all we had to worry about was a few penny-ante pushers operating out of the old Shady Grove Apartments. The kind of product we're seeing nowadays makes Pine Lake seem like a border town. I've suspected for a long time there's a local kingpin, someone with enough smarts and clout to cover his tracks. Someone who instills the kind of fear or loyalty that keeps his people from cutting deals when they get arrested."

"Are you saying that person is Nathan Bolt?"

Tommy shot another glance toward the squad room. "I'm not prepared to go there yet, but he's involved at some level. We make a bust, nine times out of ten the first person the perp calls is Nathan."

"He's a good attorney from what I hear."

"Yeah, but he's not the only lawyer in the county or even in Pine Lake. And he's sure as hell not the cheapest. You have to wonder who's paying him and why."

"Just because he caters to a certain clientele doesn't make him a criminal." Jack played devil's advocate even though he'd had the same thought about Nathan last night. "He comes from money. Why would he risk his reputation, let alone his freedom, by getting involved in something so potentially dangerous?"

"He has money by Pine Lake standards, but not the kind it takes to finance a political campaign. He's always been ambitious. You know that even better than I do. Remember back in school? His competitiveness bordered on obsessive. He was always looking for an advantage, always looking to come out on top. He's had his eye on Austin for years."

"Even more reason to keep his nose clean," Jack said.

"Not if he's thought this through and Nathan is nothing if not shrewd. You were smarter but he was the more conniving. Think about it. He hires himself out to the drug trade just long enough to salt away the money he needs to launch a respectable state senate campaign. Now he's ready to walk away, but questions are being asked. Dots are being connected. And maybe some of his people aren't quite as loyal as he thought."

"People like Jamie Butaud?"

Tommy's eyes flashed. "What do you know about Jamie?"

"You said last night she worked for Nathan. Wouldn't be the first time a police informant met with a violent end."

"I'm not going to speculate about suspects and motives with you," he said with a pompous edge. "What I will say is that I put very little past Nathan Bolt. If he thought this office was closing in on him, he'd do everything in his power to taint the process. Plant some rumors, plant some evidence and then bring in an outside investigator to put it all together. Masterminding the takedown of a corrupt county sheriff's office would be a pretty effective way to launch a political career."

"Is this office corrupt?" Jack asked bluntly.

"My men and I aren't perfect, but there's not a dirty cop among us."

Jack glanced up at the framed citations. He didn't take the awards or Tommy's declaration at face value. Even as a teenager, Tommy Driscoll had been given to excesses and shortcuts. Now, in his early thirties, the slight paunch and sagging jawline spoke to a lack of discipline. Jack could well believe the man dirty. But had he ever been capable of murder?

"Where were you the night Anna was killed?" he asked suddenly.

Tommy sat in stunned silence before he erupted. "What the *hell*, Jack?"

"It's a simple question. Logical after what you told me on the phone. Why not answer if you've nothing to hide?"

The chair squealed ominously as Tommy shot forward. "Because I don't answer to you. And I sure as hell don't appreciate the implication."

"There's no implication," Jack said with a shrug. "Just a question. You've admitted that you lied about Nathan's whereabouts. So why not tell me where you were?"

"Exactly where I said I was."

"At Nathan's house. All night long."

"Damn straight."

"But now that you've taken Nathan out of the picture, it's just your word."

Tommy was silent for a long moment. "Where are you going with this?"

"Maybe I just want to know why my two best friends lied about their whereabouts on the night my girlfriend was murdered."

"It won't change anything."

Bitterness crept into Jack's voice. "Maybe not, but I think the very least you owe me is the truth."

Tommy's mouth thinned. "What is it you want to know?"

"Where did Nathan claim he went that night?"

"He said he was out looking for Olive. He said she

was sleepwalking again. He noticed that her bed was empty and he went out to find her."

"And you believed him?"

"I had no reason not to at the time. I didn't know then what a liar he was and I'd seen Olive sleepwalk for myself."

"Why didn't you tell any of this to the cops?"

"It didn't seem like a big deal. Who knew the police would come down so hard on you? I wanted to help out a friend, that's all. And as for Olive, she'd already been through hell with her dad dying and having to re-locate to a new town. It seemed best for everyone to just keep quiet."

"Or did you keep quiet because placing Nathan at home all night gave *you* an alibi?"

"Why would I need an alibi? I didn't kill Anna."

"Neither did I, but that didn't keep me from being a suspect."

Tommy hesitated, as if having to hold his temper in check. "You're looking for closure and I get that. But you're never going to find all the answers. Anna left the house after you dropped her off. Maybe she went out to meet someone or maybe she went for a walk. We'll never know. It was nothing more than very bad luck that Wayne Foukes happened to be in the area that night." He paused once more. "You want everything tied up with a nice, neat bow, but that's just not going to happen, buddy."

"Maybe not," Jack said. "But we do know one thing for certain. Wayne Foukes didn't kill Jamie Butaud."

Chapter Five

Olive stood at her second-story office window staring down at the campus. The benches and courtyards were empty but soon enough the common spaces would teem with activity. The classrooms would fill up and the parking lot would overflow onto the empty field across the street. There would be fisticuffs to break up, punishments to dole out and irate parents to soothe. One crisis after another.

Pine Lake had always been a rowdy school, but right now the building seemed eerily silent. Olive had to fight the compulsion to glance over her shoulder. The hollow hallways seemed haunted by the ghosts of Jamie Butaud, Anna Grayson and all the other students that had been lost over the years. Olive had never thought her imagination overactive, but earlier when she'd returned from lunch, she could have sworn she heard phantom footsteps in the stairwell.

The faculty meeting had gone so well that she had no reason for the creeping disquiet. She knew most of the staff, had worked with them for the past six years. If anyone resented her appointment, they'd managed to swallow their pride and conceal their disapproval for the sake of an agreeable work environment. So why did she still feel so anxious? Why the sensation of falling when she was wide awake and on solid footing?

Olive wanted to believe the close call with the truck and the whispering townspeople had rattled her or maybe she was experiencing a sort of PTSD from the terrifying incident on top of the bridge. Not to mention the murder of a young woman who had once been her student and the less-than-forthcoming statement Olive had given to the police. Except for the scare with the dark sedan, all of those events had happened after Jack's return. She didn't blame him for any of them. She certainly didn't think him a killer. But already he'd wreaked havoc on her equilibrium. Already he'd unnerved and jolted her, and now she couldn't shake the notion that she was perched precariously at the edge of a very high cliff.

"Olive?"

She turned from the window with a start. Mona Sutton stood in the doorway, head slightly cocked as she gave Olive a quizzical look. "Are you okay?"

Olive mustered a smile. "Don't I look okay?"

"In my experience, looks can be deceiving. I had to call your name three times before you heard me."

"Sorry. I have a lot on my mind these days. And I thought everyone else had gone home."

Mona hovered in the doorway. "May I?"

"Yes, of course. Come in." Olive motioned her to a chair as she took a seat behind her desk.

"You're making this space your own, I see." Mona's gaze skimmed the artwork on the walls and the framed diplomas and certificates that hung over the credenza.

"Trying to." Olive kept a picture of her dad on her desk and another shot of her and her mother taken last year on a cruise. Other than the photographs and a potted succulent, her work space remained uncluttered. How long that would last was anyone's guess.

Mona gave another of those assessing looks. Olive straightened and tried to present a placid demeanor, but from their first meeting fifteen years ago, the guidance counselor had always been able to read her a little too well for comfort. And yet despite all the intimate details she'd gleaned from Olive's life over the years, Mona Sutton remained a closed book. Beyond her educational and professional credentials, Olive knew very little about the woman's background, though it was obvious she came from money. Her wardrobe alone would cost at least half her yearly salary and then there was the late-model BMW and the restored house on Primrose Avenue.

In her early forties, she was still a very attractive woman—tall, blonde and regal. She could be charming and even funny when she had a mind to be, but she rarely socialized in Pine Lake. As far as Olive could tell, Mona Sutton seemed perfectly content to dedicate herself fully to her career. In addition to her position as guidance counselor, she also had a private practice with a few select clients that she saw in an office in her home.

"I suppose you've heard about Jamie Butaud," she said.

Olive winced. "Such a horrible tragedy. I would have made an announcement at the meeting this morning, but I was instructed by the sheriff not to say anything. Not that it matters. Most everyone in town probably knows more than I do by now."

Mona crossed her legs, displaying the red sole of her

high heel. "Instructed by the sheriff, you say. That explains the talk I heard."

"What talk?"

"That you were the one who discovered her body."

Olive said in shock, "What? No, I wasn't. I arrived at the lake after she'd been found. Actually, it was Jack King who discovered the body. Do you remember him? Tall with dark hair and very good-looking."

Mona lifted a brow. "Interesting that you would choose his physical attributes to jog my memory rather than the more obvious tag."

"You mean his relationship with Anna Grayson?" Olive frowned. "That was a long time ago and what happened to him back then doesn't have anything to do with his finding Jamie's body."

"It's curious, though. On the same night he arrives in town, he discovers a body floating in the same lake where his girlfriend's body was found fifteen years ago. A girlfriend he was accused of murdering."

Irritation prickled. "But he didn't kill her. He was innocent no matter how badly the people in this town wanted to believe otherwise."

"Is that what you think? People wanted to believe him guilty?" Mona was staring at her in that way again.

Olive shrugged. "Maybe not at first. But in their rush to judgment, they treated him so badly the only way to save face was to continue their self-righteous condemnation. They couldn't admit they were wrong because that would have exposed their own character weaknesses. Easier to blame Jack even after another man was tried and convicted."

"Olive Belmont. Champion of the downtrodden."

She pretended to take a bow. "I'll step down off my soapbox now."

Mona was silent for a moment. "You said you arrived after Jamie's body had been discovered. What were you doing at the lake at that hour? And with Jack King, of all people?"

Olive hesitated. Even as a teenager, she'd trusted Mona Sutton with her deepest, darkest misgivings, but the why and how of her lying to the police was a different kind of secret. She'd never before found herself the potential target of a cold-blooded killer.

"I couldn't sleep and went out for a walk. I only meant to take a short stroll to clear my head, but somehow I found myself all the way to the lake."

"Somehow? You don't remember getting there?"

"I just meant that I lost track of time."

"And you happened to run into Jack King?"

"I heard his outboard. I went down to investigate because I thought someone might be dumping trash in the lake. That's when he told me that he'd found a body in the water. He didn't know who she was, of course. It was Tommy Driscoll who identified Jamie from a tattoo."

Mona's voice sharpened. "What tattoo?"

"The mermaid on her arm. It's an unusual design and Jamie was always quite proud of it."

"I remember the tattoo, but I don't understand why he needed it to make—" Mona broke off as realization dawned and her hand crept to her throat. "Oh, no. Was it that bad? I heard she was shot. I just never considered…the damage."

"I don't know if I'm supposed to talk about that," Olive hedged.

"Poor Jamie. She never stood a chance, did she?

Deadbeat father, drug-addicted mother. And that boy-friend of hers."

"Marc Waller."

"I certainly hope Tommy—Sheriff Driscoll—is looking into him."

"No doubt he is. A spouse or boyfriend is always a person of interest if not an outright suspect."

"Which brings us back to Jack King." Mona propped an elbow on the chair arm and crooked a finger beneath her chin. "Why do you suppose he's come back here after all this time?"

"His uncle died a few months ago. I expect he has loose ends to tie up."

"Hmm, maybe."

Olive gave her a curious stare. "Why do you think he's come back?"

"Loose ends of one type or another. I always sus-pected he had issues."

"Anyone would have issues after what he went through." Why did she keep rising to his defense? Olive wondered. Jack King didn't need a champion. He seemed scarily capable of defending himself.

"You're very sympathetic," Mona observed.

"Anyone with a sense of fairness would sympa-thize with an unjust accusation. Especially when the accused was barely seventeen years old. His whole life was changed that summer."

"You had quite a crush on him, as I recall."

Olive was taken aback. "I never told you that."

Mona smiled. "You didn't have to. I saw the way you looked at him when you passed in the hallway. And all those shy glances from your locker."

The conversation had taken an uncomfortable turn,

not because Olive was embarrassed by a typical high school crush, but because it was unsettling to think about being watched from afar. Maybe that was why Mona Sutton was so good at her job. She noticed things no one else did.

"He didn't even know I was alive," Olive said with a self-deprecating smile. "He had eyes only for Anna. They were very much in love."

"*He* certainly was."

A strange little shiver went through Olive at the emphasized pronoun. "You don't think she loved him?" Then she caught herself. "You don't have to answer that. I'm not even sure we should be talking about this."

"I don't see why not. There's no one here but us. Anna worked for me after school a few days a week, but she was never my client. Even if she were still alive, I wouldn't be violating her confidence by noting that she was a very complicated girl."

"Complicated how?" Olive asked reluctantly.

"She was beautiful, popular, came from a good family. She had all the advantages that poor Jamie Butaud lacked, but there was a side of Anna few people ever saw, including those closest to her. Jack most of all, I suspect."

"What do you mean?"

"She once told me that she would like to follow in my footsteps. I was flattered at first, but I developed serious reservations about her intent. Anna wasn't motivated by a desire to help people. She liked knowing things about them. Secrets. I never gave her my password, but I used to wonder if she'd somehow managed to access my files. It was a feeling I had. And then there was a hacking incident. The whole school system was compromised. Grades were changed, scholarships applications deleted. It would have been an explosive scandal if the administration hadn't managed to keep it quiet. They never found out who did it, but I always suspected Anna was somehow involved."

"That's a very serious charge," Olive said.

"I only bring it up as a cautionary tale. These kids are devious and sophisticated and getting more so every year. Which is why I no longer store my files digitally. I've gone back to the old-fashioned method of hanging folders and locked cabinets. A bored kid with a laptop can be inside the system in a matter of minutes. These days, it takes far more effort to drive to the school and break into the building."

"Point taken," Olive said. "I'll be careful."

Mona smiled and rose leisurely. "I've gossiped too much and taken up far too much of your time. An unseemly pastime for someone in my profession."

"Mona—"

She turned at the door.

Olive wavered, not certain she wanted to bring up her sleepwalking. "We've talked about this before and I think I know the answer. Still, I can't help wondering."

"What is it?" Mona came back into the office and perched a hip on the edge of Olive's desk.

"Back when I used to sleepwalk, I never remembered anything when I woke up. You always told me that amnesia was common."

"It is, especially in children and teens. Less so in adults."

"Really? Why is that?"

Mona settled more comfortably against the desk. "I suspect by now you know more about sleep disorders than I do, but to put it in simple terms, non-REM sleep has three stages. Stage one is that drowsy, half-awake, half-asleep sensation. Stage two is light sleep and stage three is deep sleep. Children experience amnesia so completely because they spend more time in deep sleep. As you grow older, sleep is more fragmented. You spend more time in the first two stages when the brain is still somewhat cognitive."

Olive conjured an image of herself on top of the old Pine Lake Bridge and suppressed a shiver. She had been up there when Jamie Butaud's killer had thrown her body off the bridge. If a single bit of her brain had still been awake, what might be hidden in her memory?

"If the brain was partially cognitive during a sleep-walking episode and yet the person can't remember the event upon awakening, would there be a way to trigger those memories? Say, through hypnosis?"

Mona shook her head. "Hypnosis would be unreliable at best. Memory is too prone to suggestion and distortion."

"So you wouldn't recommend it?"

"Never for the situation you just described. But I can't help wondering why you're asking."

"No particular reason. I always found it so disconcerting to wake up somewhere other than my bed and have no recall of how I got there. Even glimmers of memory might have helped."

Mona frowned down at her. "You'd tell me if you were sleepwalking again, wouldn't you?"

"You'd be the first person I'd come to if I needed help," Olive dodged. "But other than a few dreams, my sleep is fine."

"The falling dreams again?"

"It's nothing."

"You know from past experience those dreams won't go away until you find the root cause."

Olive smiled. "I know the root cause. I'm afraid of falling on my face as the new principal."

"Sometimes dreams are just that straightforward," Mona agreed. "And sometimes they're like an intriguing puzzle."

JACK SPENT THE rest of the morning at the cabin sorting through some of his uncle's paperwork and belongings, but he could only take so much of the monotony. Restless and bored, he headed back into town for a late lunch and then afterwards, he drove over to Nathan Bolt's office on Commerce Street.

The law firm was housed in a hundred-year-old building that had once been a button factory. The exterior had been painstakingly restored to the original red brick facade and the interior designed to take advantage of the exposed ductwork, beamed ceilings and polished concrete floors. It was the kind of urban setting one might expect to find in Houston or Austin, but the upscale design seemed out of place in a town like Pine Lake.

A well-dressed young woman at the front desk informed Jack that Nathan was in court and not expected back for at least another hour. Could she take his name and number or perhaps schedule an appointment for later in the week? Her demeanor was polite and professional, but she seemed distracted and Jack couldn't help but notice her reddened eyes. The whole office seemed somber and uneasy. Evidently, word of Jamie Butaud's murder had reached her coworkers.

He departed without leaving his name and as he headed across the parking area at the side of the building, he caught a glimpse of a black truck cruising by on the street. He couldn't be certain it was the same vehicle from that morning, but the flat black paint was unusual.

Instead of another reckless display, the driver coasted along as if he were searching for something, almost coming to a stop in front of the law office. Jack watched the truck for a moment before climbing into his own vehicle. He pulled onto the street, trying to keep enough distance not to be spotted. But the truck was going so slowly he found it difficult to maintain the sedate pace without drawing attention.

A few blocks down, a traffic light stopped Jack. While he waited for a green light, the truck picked up speed and disappeared. When the light changed, Jack drove through the intersection, keeping his eyes peeled as traffic became heavier. Commerce was one of the busiest streets in Pine Lake, with banks, businesses, the post office, the county courthouse and the municipal police department all situated around a crowded square. The Caddo County Sheriff's Office was one street over on Center Avenue and Pine Lake High School a few blocks in the other direction on West Pleasure, an irony that had never been lost on the student body.

As Jack took in the familiar but long forgotten sights, a strange nostalgia settled over him. Before Anna's murder, he and his family had been happy in this town. His parents had been respected members of a close-knit community. His father had owned the local hardware store and his mother had worked at the First National Bank. Jack had once mowed the lawns of the same people who would later look at him with open suspicion and who had gone out of their way to cross the street when they met him on the sidewalk. Just like his one-time friends had avoided him in the school hallways and had refused to sit with him in the cafeteria.

Jack had learned the hard way that a small town could be a cruel, lonely place. By the time graduation had rolled around, Wayne Foukes was behind bars and some of Jack's classmates had begun to make overtures, but it was too late. He wanted nothing to do with any them. He hadn't even gone to his graduation ceremony, preferring instead to pack his belongings and move three hours away to an apartment near Sam Houston State University where he would pursue a major in criminal justice rather than the pre-law degree he'd once dreamed about.

None of that mattered now, of course, and Jack berated himself for his sentimentality. He had come back to Pine Lake for one reason only—to find out why his two best friends had lied about their whereabouts on the night of Anna's murder. Emotion had no place in his investigation. He'd learned that lesson the hard way, too.

At the end of the business district, traffic thinned and the buildings grew seedier as he neared the city limits. Jack figured he'd lost the black truck for good. He started to turn around and head back toward town when he spotted the vehicle parked at the end of an alley that ran between an old tire store and an abandoned building that had once housed the Masonic Lodge. He drove on by, found a place to park and then doubled back on foot.

Two men sat on a bench in front of the tire store watching the street. They spared Jack a glance as he approached, but neither seemed to recognize him. One gave a brief nod while the other looked away quickly as if he didn't want to see too much. Jack understood. Even in a town as small as Pine Lake, there were areas where it was best to turn a blind eye.

Keeping watch on the street behind him, he walked down the alley until he could get a better view of the truck. Then he took out his phone, snapped a shot of the license plate and texted the image to one of his contacts at the Houston Police Department. He heard back in a matter of minutes: *Truck registered to Marc Waller, 212 Locust Avenue, Pine Lake, Texas.*

The name wasn't lost on Jack. The connections were becoming a little too entangled to be coincidental. Strange that Tommy Driscoll hadn't recognized Waller's truck from the description. But to give him the benefit of the doubt, no county sheriff could be aware of every vehicle in his jurisdiction.

Still, Jack had to wonder why Waller had been driving so recklessly through the middle of town on the morning after his girlfriend's body had been discovered and even more curious, why he had seemed hell-bent on frightening Olive. Maybe anyone in that crosswalk would have had the same close call or maybe Olive was right and it was a matter of intimidation. But Waller was no school kid and Jack was starting to have a very bad feeling. Something was going on in Pine Lake. A war, Tommy had called it. Somehow Olive was caught in the middle whether she realized it or not.

Jack put away his phone and approached the truck with caution, checking over his shoulder once again before stepping up to the side window. The cab was empty and the doors locked. His first thought was that the driver had disappeared behind the wooden fence that separated the alley from the rear of another dilap-

idated building. He opened the gate and had a quick
look around, and then as he came back through, he
saw that the side door of the abandoned building stood
slightly ajar.

Flattening himself against the crumbling brick wall,
he pushed open the door just enough to get a glimpse
inside. Lit only by anemic sunbeams that filtered in
through the dusty windows, the interior lay in deep
shadows. He listened for a moment and then slipped
inside, pausing at the threshold to take stock.

At one time, the building must have been a renova-
tion project, but that, too, had been abandoned. He could
see the skeletal outline of a two-story scaffold and the
ragged curtains of poly that had sectioned off the vari-
ous stages of work. Beer bottles, cigarette butts and
pen casings littered the floor. An old mattress had been
shoved up against one wall, a battered sofa against another. The musty scent of time and neglect hung thick
in the air, along with the darker notes of urine and ro-
dent infestation.

Unease trickled down Jack's spine. This was not a
good place. The building had been derelict even when
he'd lived in Pine Lake. It had always been known as a
trouble spot despite its proximity to downtown. He remembered rumors of dark goings-on, everything from
drug-fueled parties to satanic rituals. Once in middle
school, he and Nathan and Tommy had crawled through
a back window to explore, climbing to the roof from
the precarious second-floor access and then descending
all the way down into the basement, a cavernous place
of looming shadows and glowing eyes. They'd been
oblivious to the homeless man who had been living in
the building until he'd rushed from a corner howling

like a dog. Jack could only remember one other time when he'd been so frightened—the first day he'd been subjected to Sheriff Brannigan's vicious style of interrogation.

His senses on high alert, he moved about the dingy space, searching in corners and behind the plastic dividers. When he got to the stairs, he drew up short as his gaze traveled up the steps and through the shadows to the second-floor landing. Someone was up there. He could hear a muted voice—someone on a cell phone perhaps—but he was too far away to pick up the one-sided conversation.

Jack told himself whatever was going on inside that building was none of his business. He should leave now before he was spotted. He hadn't come to Pine Lake to involve himself in an active murder investigation and he sure as hell had no intention of breaking up a drug deal. His only interest in the driver of that black truck was the close call Olive had had with him that morning. Jack wouldn't mind having a long talk with Marc Waller about that incident.

But like it or not, Jack was involved. He'd been involved ever since he'd found Jamie Butaud's body. Maybe even earlier than that, when he'd taken that first call from Nathan Bolt. He'd been lured back to Pine Lake with the bait of the past, but the present-day circumstances had ensnared him because some of the players were the same. He didn't know if there was a connection between the two murders, but he did know that he would always be haunted by the lies surrounding Anna's death if he didn't do everything he could to put those lingering questions and suspicions to rest.

Halfway up the stairs, he froze again. The voice was

getting louder, angrier. He turned an ear to the sound as he searched the shadows on the landing and then pivoted to scour the area below him. He heard nothing else. No misplaced footfalls or creaking doors, but a light breeze drifted up the stairs and feathered along his nape. Someone had come into the building and now Jack had been caught between the newcomer and the person somewhere on the second floor.

He had no choice but to abandon caution, sprint up the stairs and dart into one of the empty rooms. But as he reached the stop step, a door flew open and he found himself face to face with a man he assumed was Marc Waller. Jack assessed him in a glance. He looked just shy of six feet, thin to the point of emaciation with shoulder-length hair and a scraggly beard. More important, he was armed and Jack wasn't.

Footsteps pounded on the stairs and Jack reacted on instinct. He lunged at the man in the doorway, allowing the momentum of the impact to carry them back into the murky room. Waller's gun went flying and as he dove for the weapon, Jack tackled him. They crashed to the floor, rolling and punching and cursing hard.

As Jack straddled his opponent, he seemed to have the upper hand. He was larger and more physically fit, but Waller was a scrapper. He bucked and kicked and thrashed about until it seemed to Jack the scrawny man had superhuman strength. Still, Jack would have eventually prevailed if not for the blow to the back of his head.

Dazed, he slumped to the floor as pain exploded behind his eyeballs. He tried to clear his vision as he lashed out at his new assailant. Before he could shake off a wave of dizziness, he was pinned facedown and a moment later, he felt a prick at the base of his neck.

When he was finally released, he tried to scramble to his feet, but the room spun out of control and he discovered a sudden heaviness in his limbs. The floor pitched and he collapsed, rolling to his back to stare up at the rotating ceiling. After a moment, a strange euphoria seeped through his veins, along with a weighted lethargy. Shadows moved about the dingy room, but they didn't concern him. The voices that came to him were dreamlike and distorted. *We can't kill him. His people will come looking for him and those guys don't mess around.*

Someone knelt and peered down at him. He saw a floating star in the darkness and tried to catch it. Then he drifted away and saw nothing at all.

Chapter Six

"Jack, can you hear me? You need to wake up now. Open your eyes, please."

The brisk voice was annoyingly persuasive, but Jack didn't want to wake up. A jackhammer was going off in his head and he could taste vomit at the back of his throat. Best to just drift back into the darkness. But that voice niggled. Beneath the schoolteacher calm was an edge of fear that nudged him out of his lethargy. He tunneled his way through a thick curtain of cobwebs and opened his eyes to a blurry world.

Someone hovered over him. He struggled to get up but a firm hand on his shoulder pressed him back down. "Take it easy. You'll be okay."

He groaned and put an arm over his eyes. "Where am I?"

"You're home."

"I'm in Houston?"

The voice hesitated. "No, Jack. You're in your uncle's cabin on Pine Lake. You have a bump on the back of your head. Do you remember falling?"

He tried to swallow past all the cotton in his mouth. "No."

"What about the scrapes on your knuckles and the bruise on your cheek? Did you get into a fight?"

"Not that I recall."

Another pause. "Do you know who I am?"

"Olive Belmont."

"Yes, that's right." She sounded relieved.

He blinked to bring her into focus, vectoring in on the freckles across her nose. Her smile was soothing, but her blue eyes looked worried. He wanted to reassure her that he was fine, but the throbbing in his head wouldn't give him any peace.

He pressed fingertips into his temples. "What are you doing here?"

"Nathan called when he found you."

Jack glanced up. "Found me where?"

"Here in the cabin. He drove out to see you and noticed that the front door was open. He thought there might have been a break-in so he came inside to have a look around. He found you here on the couch. When he had trouble rousing you, he called me."

"Why you?"

She shrugged. "Nathan's always been useless in medical crises. He may be older, but I'm the one who had to deal with the blood. Not literally," she quickly added. "You're not bleeding, thank goodness."

"He was always a little squeamish," Jack agreed.

She gave a little chuckle. "See? It's all coming back. Now do you remember how you got all those bumps and bruises?"

"That's still a blank."

"Well, let's take it one step at a time. What's the last thing that you do remember?"

He answered automatically. "I saw you outside the

coffee shop this morning. You had on a white dress and a black truck almost ran you down. Then you left for work and I went to see Tommy Driscoll."

"Jack." She leaned closer, staring deeply into his eyes. "What day is this?"

He frowned at the question. "It's Tuesday. I drove up from Houston late yesterday."

"It's Wednesday," she corrected. "A little after four o'clock in the afternoon. The events you cited happened yesterday morning. Are you telling me you don't remember anything since then?"

A thrill of alarm chased up his spine, along with a dark premonition that something bad had happened during his blackout. He held out his right hand, studying the raw skin on his knuckles. Now he knew how Olive felt after sleepwalking. Losing a chunk of time was terrifying.

He massaged his temples even harder, as if he could somehow resuscitate his memory. "I drove back into town for lunch. I ate at a place on Main Street and then I went by Nathan's office. As I was leaving, I saw the black truck that almost hit you. I followed it, I think."

His revelation seemed to take her aback. "Why would you do that?"

"I wanted to have a word with the driver."

"A word?" She bit her lip in consternation. "Did you?"

"I don't know."

"You don't remember a confrontation?"

"No."

"Where did you go when you followed the truck?"

"I don't know that, either."

Apprehension had slipped back into her voice.

"Think about it for a minute. Do you remember a street name?"

"Commerce."

"Nathan's building is on Commerce. You already said you went by his office. Think harder. Where did you go after you left the law firm?"

"I just remember driving."

Olive looked more anxious by the moment. Jack was getting a little concerned himself. The nausea and memory loss could be symptoms of a concussion, but he didn't think so. The last twenty-four hours had been stolen by something far more insidious than a bump on his head.

She propped an arm on the back of the sofa and the other on the seat as she leaned into him, searching his face. A subtle floral fragrance emanated from her presence. Something lighter than perfume. Shampoo or a body wash, he thought. Odd that he could be so hazy about everything else and yet still be able to focus in on Olive Belmont's scent. Not to mention the vibrant blue of her eyes and the lush copper of her hair, which spilled over her shoulders and curtained her cheeks. He wanted to reach up and tangle his fingers in those thick tresses, pull her down to him for another kiss. If he closed his eyes he could still remember the taste of her on his lips—

"Jack." She touched his shoulder lightly. "You seem to be drifting. Stay with me, okay?"

"Yeah, doing my best." With an effort, he pushed himself up and swung his legs off the couch, sitting for a moment with his head in his hands as the room swam around him.

"We should get you to the emergency room. The

disorientation and memory loss could be signs of concussion."

"I don't think so."

"It's best to let a doctor make that determination. Head injuries shouldn't be ignored," she insisted. "You'll need tests and several hours of monitoring. Can you walk?"

"I don't need to go to the hospital. I'll be fine."

"How can you say that when you were apparently unconscious for over twenty-four hours?"

"More like passed out."

She said in disbelief, "You were drunk?"

"Drugged would be my guess," a voice said from the entrance.

Jack lifted his head from his hands and glanced toward the door where a man stood silhouetted on the threshold. Olive didn't seem at all surprised by her cousin's appearance, leaving Jack to conclude that Nathan Bolt had been hovering right outside the door all along.

As he came inside to join them, Jack gave the attorney a quick appraisal. Unlike Tommy Driscoll, who had softened over the years, Nathan Bolt had lost the extra weight that had stubbornly clung to him all through high school. He was trim and well-dressed with a hairstyle and round glasses that made him look both clever and earnest, especially with his loosened tie and rolled-up shirtsleeves. Jack didn't buy the Boy Scout image. He didn't trust Nathan Bolt any more than he had faith in Tommy Driscoll. Not that he cared all that much, but he couldn't help wondering what had caused their falling out. The lies they'd told after Anna's death? The natural animosity between a cop and a defense attorney? A disagreement over turf?

"Hello, Jack."

"Nathan."

"Drugged?" Olive repeated in disbelief. "Who would do such a thing?"

Nathan sat down in a chair across from the couch. He seemed perfectly at home in Leon's cabin and Jack wondered again about the discussion that had been referenced during their first phone call. According to Nathan, contacting Jack had been Leon's idea. No way to prove that now, of course.

"You said you followed a black truck," Nathan said. "My guess is, you saw something you shouldn't have."

"Like what?" Olive demanded.

"Don't be so naïve, cousin. You know better than anyone what's happening in this town. You see it at school before it filters down to the rest of us."

"You think Jack stumbled onto a drug deal?"

Nathan shrugged. "Wouldn't surprise me."

"That's terrifying! But if they knocked him on the head and drugged him, how did he get home?"

"That's a very good question." Nathan's gaze moved from Olive to Jack. "You still look pretty out of it so I doubt you were in any condition to drive. Someone must have brought you here and dumped you on the couch. Your car is in the driveway."

Jack tried to summon even a glimmer of that trip home. Nothing. His mind was a complete blank.

"Tell me more about this black truck," Nathan said.

"The driver almost ran Olive down this—yesterday morning."

"That's being a little dramatic," she said. "I stepped off the curb and the truck came a little too close for comfort. Luckily, Jack was there to pull me back."

"That is lucky," Nathan agreed. "Are you saying you think it was deliberate?"

"No, of course not. It was probably just a student trying to intimidate me." She glanced at Jack. "We've already been through this."

"Yes, but I'm not as convinced as you," he said.

"Nor should you be," Nathan agreed. "Marc Waller drives a black truck."

Something flashed in Jack's memory, a flickering image of a lanky man that was there one moment and gone the next. He put a hand to the back of his head, locating the knot with a wince. "New with a custom paint job?"

"*Expensive* custom paint job," Nathan said. "He came by the office a few weeks ago to show it off to Jamie. When she wouldn't leave with him, he lost his temper and created a scene. We ended up calling the police."

"What does this guy look like?" Jack asked.

"Thin, twitchy, unkempt. Has kind of a feral look in his eyes."

Olive turned to Jack with an anxious appraisal. "Do you remember seeing him?"

The image flickered again, along with a fleeting memory of muted voices, but Jack shook his head. "I can't place him. Is there any reason he'd want to hurt you?"

"Of course not," she insisted. "I barely know the man."

"Actually," Nathan said slowly, "there might be."

Olive stared at him, dumbfounded. "What do you mean?"

"You're my only family here in Pine Lake since the

old man passed away. Marc knows how close we are. I wouldn't put it past him to use you to get to me."

"What? That's crazy," she said with a frown. "Why would he need to get to you, anyway? You were the one who saved him from serious jail time."

"That was a long time ago. Lately he seems to think I was trying to turn Jamie against him."

"Were you?" Jack asked.

"I helped her go back to school. I gave her a job and encouraged her to continue her education. I opened doors for her, but Marc saw it differently." Nathan paused as he eyed Olive warily. "Would you mind giving us a moment?"

Her scowl deepened. "Yes, I mind. Whatever you have to say to Jack can wait. All of this can wait. He needs to go to the emergency room."

"That's his call, not ours."

She turned back to Jack. "I'll drive you there myself. I don't mean to nag, but you really do need to see a doctor."

"I appreciate your concern," he said. "But I'm already feeling better. A couple of painkillers for the headache and I'll be my old self again."

Olive didn't look at all happy about his decision, but she shrugged in resignation. "I can't force you. I'm going back to the office for a bit and then straight home. If either of you need me, call my cell."

"Thanks for coming, cousin."

"Yes, thank you," Jack said.

She stared down at him for a moment and then with another shrug, picked up her handbag and headed for the door.

Jack had the strongest urge to call her back. She

was right. Whatever Nathan Bolt had to say to him could wait. Right now, he wanted to be alone with Olive. *Needed* to be with her, but he couldn't for the life of him explain his sense of urgency.

She walked out the door and he didn't call her back. Instead, he got up and went into the kitchen on the pretext of needing water and aspirin. He stood at the sink and watched her through the window. Even for a high school principal, the navy dress and beige heels were sedate. Her appearance was understated and professional, and yet Jack felt a dangerous awareness as he took in her slight curves and the graceful sweep of red hair over one eye. She tossed the thick strands aside with a shake of her head, a movement that was unaffected and yet undeniably sensual.

As if intuiting his perusal, she turned to glance back at the house. The sunlight streaming through the window was still so bright, he didn't think she could see him, but her gaze seemed to find his through the glass. She didn't wave or nod to acknowledge his presence, but a smile flitted before she opened the door and climbed behind the wheel.

It was barely a response and yet Jack knew he would have felt the impact of that smile from a mile away.

NATHAN STOOD AT the large window that looked out on the lake. He glanced over his shoulder as Jack entered the room and then turned back to the water.

"I always did say Leon had the best view on the lake."

"Yeah, it's nice." Jack went over to the couch and plopped down on the leather cushions.

"Let me know if you decide to sell," Nathan said.

"I've always wanted a place like this. A little cabin on the water where you can hunker down and get away from civilization."

"It's less than a mile from town," Jack reminded him. "But it *is* a long way from Austin."

Nathan turned with a wry smile. "So you've already tuned into the local gossip, have you?"

"I've heard some things. But you didn't drive out here to talk about politics or real estate."

Nathan shoved his hands in his pockets as he leaned a shoulder against the window frame. "No, you're right. I came to find out why you didn't let me know you were coming to Pine Lake."

"Because I didn't come here to work for you," Jack said bluntly. "I came for my own reasons. And in case you haven't heard, I've been a little busy since I got here."

"Another reason you should think about selling this place. Pine Lake seems to bring you nothing but bad luck."

Jack shrugged. "It's different this time. Unlike you, I don't have a connection to the victim."

"Oh, come on," Nathan said. "You can't think I had anything to do with Jamie's death. I never did anything but try to help that girl."

"I'm sure the sheriff will be sympathetic."

Anger flared behind the round glasses, but Nathan's expression remained composed. "Your attitude about what happened is annoyingly cavalier. Jamie's death may not mean anything to you, but a lot of people have been devastated by the news. She was a good person. Everyone in my office liked and respected her. She did her work without complaint or drama and that's a lot more than I can say for most people."

"I'm sorry for your loss," Jack said sincerely.

Nathan turned back to the water with a brooding frown. "She made mistakes when she was younger, but she learned from them. And she'd been trying ever since to turn her life around. She was even talking about going back to school to become a paralegal. But you know how it is in a place like this. The harder you work to make something of yourself, the harder others will try to tear you down."

"People like Marc Waller, you mean."

"People exactly like Marc Waller. Scum of the earth, that man."

"The one thing everyone around here seems to agree on," Jack muttered. "And yet you were not only his lawyer, you got serious charges against him dropped."

"I don't have to like my clients, but I do have to represent them to the very best of my abilities. Even creeps like Marc Waller."

"It's a dirty job," Jack said.

"It can be." Nathan came back into the room and sat down across from Jack, leaning forward as he draped his elbows over the armrests. "Jamie had been trying to break things off for a long time, but Marc didn't take kindly to rejection. He's a violent, volatile man who seems to have little to no control over his temper. I wouldn't put anything past him if he thought she was seeing someone else."

"Even murder?"

"I think he's certainly capable."

"Was she seeing someone else?"

"I don't know. I suspected but I never saw her with anyone."

"Does Tommy know about the altercation at your office?" Jack asked.

"It's a matter of public record. Jamie filed a complaint with the Pine Lake PD. If Tommy Driscoll wants to talk to me about any of this, he knows where to find me."

"That doesn't sound very cooperative." Jack absently massaged his temples.

"Like I said, he knows where to find me." Nathan's gaze turned shrewd. "I understand you've been in to see him already."

"I'm the one who found the body and the lake area is the county sheriff's jurisdiction. I wouldn't read anything more into it than that."

"I wasn't. But I can't help wondering about suspects. He must have leads," Nathan prompted.

"I can't help you there. Tommy Driscoll isn't likely to talk to me about his investigation."

"I thought he might have let something slip."

Now it was Jack who turned sly. "Your name came up."

A shadow flickered again behind the glasses. "In what context?"

Jack waited a beat before he continued. "He told me that on the night of Anna's murder, you left the house after midnight and didn't return until nearly sunup."

"*Anna's* murder?" Nathan stared at him for a moment as he shifted gears.

"That's the bait you used to get me here. Tommy Driscoll's whereabouts on that night. Seems your movements are also in question."

Emotions flickered across Nathan's face and he grew pensive. Jack wondered if he was thinking back to that night or trying to figure out the best way to squirm out of his lie. Finally he said, "Okay. I did leave the house that night, but there was nothing sinister about my movements. I went out looking for Olive. She had a sleeping disorder back then. She would get up from her bed and wander around at all hours. It got really bad after her dad died. When she and her mother came to live with us, I developed a kind of sixth sense about her sleepwalking. Sometimes I would rouse in the middle of the night and know she was gone. When I woke up that night, Tommy was also missing. At first, I thought they might have left the house together, but Olive despised Tommy. I couldn't see her going off with him so I went out to look for her."

"Where did you find her?"

"It took me half the night, but I finally found her on Lakeside Road not far from the old bridge."

Jack's voice sharpened. "She was sleepwalking?"

"Yes."

"You didn't wake her up?"

"I never did back then. I led her back to the house and she crawled into bed as if nothing had happened."

"Let me get this straight. You're saying Olive was on or near the old bridge on the night Anna was murdered?"

Nathan's gaze burned into Jack's. "Yes. That's exactly what I'm saying. She had a perverse fascination for that bridge. She used to go there a lot. I don't know how much you remember about her circumstances, but her dad was killed in a head-on collision on a similar bridge. He'd been away on a business trip and was rushing back for Olive's birthday. It was raining, the road was slippery. His vehicle went through the guardrail after the crash. Olive blamed herself. She'd begged him to come back that night rather than wait until morning. Her mother was no help. She was so devastated she could barely look after herself let alone deal with Olive's guilt. My old man took charge and moved them in with us. Olive's mother was his baby sister. He was protective of her just the way I've always been of Olive." Nathan's gaze was still on Jack. "Do you see where I'm going with this?"

"I want to hear you say it."

"I didn't go to the police for the same reason you didn't tell Tommy the truth about Monday night." He put up a hand as if expecting Jack to interrupt. "Don't worry. Olive never said a word, but I knew she'd been sleepwalking the moment I heard what happened. She was already at the lake when you found the body, wasn't she?"

Jack said nothing.

"You made up a story because you were afraid she'd seen something. You were worried Jamie's killer would come after her if he found out she'd been there. I understand, Jack. And I can't tell you how much I appreciate your discretion."

"I didn't make up anything. Events happened just the way I reported them."

Nathan smiled. "Of course."

His smugness rankled but Jack let it go. "So you woke up that night and found both Olive and Tommy missing. How did he explain his absence?"

"He told me he'd gone out to meet someone, an older woman that he was seeing. He said there would be serious consequences if anyone ever found out about the affair. Especially for her. She might be fired or even arrested. I assumed he was seeing a teacher."

"He never mentioned a name?"

"No. It's possible he made up the story, but you remember what a horndog he was back then. Still is, from what I hear. I've never understood why Beth puts up with him."

"Maybe she loves him."

"That's even harder to understand. A guy like that? She must have known what was going on behind her back. All those girls in school coming on to him, following him around like a bunch of damn groupies. It was disgusting." Nathan's expression hardened. "You know what he told me once? He said he'd actually talked some of those girls into getting the same tattoo. His mark, he called it. He laughed at their gullibility. He didn't care about their feelings. It was just a game to him. Like cutting notches in a bedpost."

"We all did stupid things back then," Jack said. "I never heard about the tattoos."

"Of course not. Tommy liked to brag to me, but he looked up to you. He always wanted your approval."

"I don't know about that."

"I know," Nathan said. "I saw a side of Tommy Driscoll you never did. He wasn't just mean, he could be downright vicious. A bully in every sense of the word. You asked earlier if I thought Marc Waller killed Jamie. I don't discount the possibility, but he's not the only one with a motive. A few months after Jamie came to work for me, the air conditioner in the office went out. It was sweltering inside the building so I sent everyone home. Jamie volunteered to stay and answer the phones.

She always wore long sleeves in the office to cover her tattoos, but that day she'd taken off her sweater. I saw Tommy's tattoo—his *mark*—on her shoulder."

"You think she was seeing him?"

"I doubt that tattoo was a coincidence. Think about it, Jack. Tommy Driscoll is a married man. That alone gives him a motive, but Jamie was still underage when she first came to work for me. If she and Tommy were seeing each other that far back and if she threatened to expose the affair now, what do you think he'd do? Jack? Are you listening to me?"

Nathan's voice receded to a dull roar. The sudden churning in Jack's stomach had nothing to do with the drug he'd been given. A memory had surfaced, distant and hazy at first, but now the image sharpened as if he'd adjusted a focus ring. He got up and paced to the window, staring down at the water with a brooding frown as his mind tumbled back to a mild fall night on Anna's front porch.

She and some of her girlfriends had gone to Dallas for the weekend. She'd come back with a tattoo of a heart shot through with a lightning bolt, laughing sheepishly when Jack had first discovered it on her hip.

I had a little too much to drink...someone dared me... Do you hate it?

No, I like it. It's sexy. But I'm trying to figure out what the lightning bolt means.

It doesn't mean anything. It was just a whim. A stupid mistake.

Maybe if I could have a closer look...

Stop! My dad could come out here any second. Do you know what he'd do if he found us like this?

I thought you liked to live dangerously.

Maybe I do. Jack?

Hmm?

I love you. You know that, right? You're the best thing that's ever happened to me, but sometimes I wonder... what if I'm not the girl you think I am? Jack? Are you even listening to me?

"Jack?"

He turned. "What did the tattoo look like? The one on Jamie Butaud's shoulder?"

Nathan gave a contemptuous snort. "It was a heart with a lightning bolt rammed through the center. Real subtle. Just like Tommy Driscoll."

Chapter Seven

After a shower and several glasses of cold water, Jack started to feel human again. He grabbed a beer and headed down to the dock to enjoy the last of the sunset. The past twenty-four hours remained a mystery, but the harder he tried to recover those lost memories, the more painful the throbbing in his head became. He told himself to relax. Bit and pieces would come back in due time.

But he still had a nagging worry that something bad had happened during his blackout. Had he found the driver of the black truck? Had he confronted Marc Waller face to face? Had they fought? Jack had no recollection of a conversation, let alone an altercation, but something needled at the back of his mind as he massaged his banged-up knuckles.

Halfway down the steps, he came to an abrupt halt. A woman sat on the edge of the dock, dangling her feet in the water. His first thought was that Olive had come back, but as he descended a few more stairs, he saw that the woman's hair was dark and clipped short.

"Can I help you?" he called out.

She started at the sound of his voice and scrambled to her feet, turning with a wry smile as her gaze traveled up the steps to where he waited. "Hello, stranger!" she called back.

He stared down at her for a moment. "Beth? Beth Driscoll?"

She laughed. "Oh, good! You remember me!"

"Of course, I remember you." He descended the rest of the steps to join her.

Dressed in a simple cotton skirt and sleeveless blouse, she looked young and carefree standing in the afterglow of the sunset—just the way Jack remembered her. Even the short hair was the same. But as he drew closer, he couldn't help noticing the lines around her eyes and at the corners of her mouth. The hardness in her stare and the brittle quality of her smile. His old friend was far from carefree. Marriage to Tommy Driscoll had been no picnic.

"I heard you were back," she said.

"Word always did travel fast around here."

She motioned to the edge of the dock where her sandals had been abandoned. "I hope you don't mind my dropping by like this. It's still so hot out and the water looked inviting. I couldn't resist."

"I don't mind, but you could have just knocked on my door."

A cloud flitted across her expression. "I meant to, but somehow I lost my nerve when I got out here."

"Why would it take nerve to knock on my door? I don't bite," he said as they stood awkwardly facing one another.

Her laugh was self-conscious. "I know that. It's just…" She trailed off. "This is crazy." She closed the distance between them and gave him a quick hug.

He returned the embrace, taking note of her slenderness. She wasn't naturally slight like Olive, and Jack wondered about the weight loss that had stripped away her curves and revealed too much of her collarbone. Her arms and legs looked as fragile and hollow as bird bones.

She said against his shoulder, "It shouldn't be this hard to greet an old friend."

"I wasn't sure I had any friends left in this town."

She pulled away, searching his face. "I know it must have seemed that way back then, but I never stopped being your friend." Her hand came up to flutter against his bruised cheek. "You were always good to me, Jack."

He frowned. "Was I?"

"You don't remember?"

He shrugged as he set the beer on the railing. "I don't dwell too much on those days."

She turned to stare out over the water. "I've always regretted not standing by you when things got so bad. It was never about guilt or innocence. I let you down because I was too wrapped up in my own problems. That's no excuse. And none of this probably means anything to you now. But…" She trailed off on another nervous laugh. "I'm not very good at this."

"You're fine."

"I just need you to know that I always believed in you. That's why I'm here. That's why I came. And ultimately, that's why I couldn't bring myself to knock on your door. Because I'm about fifteen years too late."

"Why now?" he asked without rancor.

"Because you're back and because I've always wanted to say these things to you. The way you were treated. It was disgraceful. *We* were disgraceful." She tilted her head to stare deeply into his eyes. "You were the best part of this town. Nothing has ever been the same since you left."

"I somehow doubt that." Her words touched a nerve. Whether good or bad, Jack wasn't sure.

"It's true." She walked over to the edge of the dock, peering as intently into the water as she had into his eyes. "This place brings back a lot of memories," she said on a shiver. "Remember how we used to come out here at night and swim in the moonlight? You and me and Tommy and Anna. They were such vibrant creatures, weren't they? So full of life. I was a wallflower and you were always so intense. I used to secretly wonder if we'd made the wrong choice. The wrong pairing. Maybe you and I would have been better suited."

"I don't know how well suited I am to anyone," Jack said in a moment of candor. "But you and Tommy have been together for a long time. You seemed to have made a go of it."

"You've been away from Pine Lake for too long. Things around here are rarely as they seem."

Jack thought of that tattoo on Jamie Butaud's shoulder and the one on Anna's hip. A heart with a lightning bolt shot through the center. Tommy Driscoll's mark. A symbol that connected two murders fifteen years apart.

Beth was staring at him over her shoulder, a smile flitting at the corners of her mouth. He had never known her to be coy or sly and yet there was something about that smile that sent a warning up his spine.

You asked if I thought Marc Waller killed Jamie. He's certainly capable. But he isn't the only one with a motive.

"What problems?" he asked abruptly.

"I'm sorry?"

"You said you were caught up in your own problems back then. What was going on in your life?"

The question seemed to catch her off guard. "Oh, you know. The usual stuff. Everything seems a matter of life and death at that age."

Jack wondered about her sudden reticence. He walked over to the edge of the dock, staring into the murky depths just as she'd done. Something plopped in the water and the ripples distorted her reflection. Jack watched, fascinated. Beth Driscoll seemed ephemeral in that moment. Not altogether real. It occurred to him that she had always been like that. Elusive and transitory with no lasting impression.

He saw her shiver as if she were thinking strange thoughts, too.

"Do you remember that trip you and Anna took to Dallas the fall of our senior year? A whole group of you went. She said things got a little crazy."

Beth turned with a wide-eyed stare. "That's what she told you about that trip? Things got a little crazy?"

"Didn't they?"

"That trip was a lot of things, but I would never describe it as crazy. Not the way you seem to mean it."

"How would you describe it?"

She seemed momentarily distracted as she leaned over the water to gaze past him. "I didn't know you could see the bridge from here," she murmured.

"You never could before. I think some trees have gone down. Lightning strikes, most likely." He waited a beat. "Tell me about that trip, Beth."

She sighed as her focus returned to the water. "I haven't let myself think about it for a very long time."

"What happened?"

"We didn't go to Dallas to party. At least, Anna and I didn't. That whole girls' weekend was just a cover. She and I went to an abortion clinic."

The shock was like a physical blow, punching the air from his lungs in a painful rush. "She was pregnant?"

Beth put a soothing hand on his arm. "No, not Anna. We went there for me."

Emotions swept through him. Fifteen years had dulled the pain of Anna's death, but coming back here… finding out all these things about her and the people who had once been his friends had ripped open old wounds. How had he ever thought he could remain aloof from those memories? He hadn't left Pine Lake behind. This town and these people would always be a part of him, of the boy he'd been and the man he'd become. Protective walls could only keep out so much.

The dock swayed beneath his feet and he struggled to regain his footing.

"I'm sorry," Beth said. "You look so distressed. I shouldn't have blurted it out that way. You were bound to think it was Anna."

"Did Tommy know?"

"You're assuming the baby was his."

"I'm sorry. I did assume."

She smiled. "I didn't tell him because I didn't go through with it. I decided to keep the baby no matter what he or anyone else said. Anna brought me home and I holed up in my room for the rest of the weekend. We'd already told everyone we were in Dallas and I didn't want to answer a bunch of questions about why I'd come back early. It was easier to hide out, and I needed time to think anyway."

"What about Anna?"

She shrugged. "I always assumed she drove back to Dallas to be with the others."

But maybe she hadn't rejoined the others that weekend. Maybe she'd been off somewhere getting Tommy Driscoll's mark tattooed on her hip.

Now it was Jack who drew a deep breath as he tried to sort through his feelings. The betrayal didn't matter. Not after all this time. He was too old to harbor grudges or carry torches, but he did care about the consequences. He did care about all the lies. Someone had killed Anna in cold blood. For the longest time, her murder had been considered a motiveless crime that had happened because of a chance encounter with a monster. Jack had never bought into the premise. It had always seemed personal to him, but he'd never had any legitimate suspects. He'd never been able to connect any of those troublesome dots. After a while, it became easier to just let it go. Then two old friends had called out of the blue last Friday night and here he was, back in Pine Lake chasing his past.

"What happened to the baby?" he asked. "If it's not too painful to talk about."

"I had a miscarriage. The stress of the pregnancy and then Anna's death…it was all too much, I guess."

"I'm sorry."

"It was a long time ago. Like you, I don't dwell on it the way I used to. Life goes on." She paused, running fingers through her short tresses. "It's funny. Anna was the only other person who knew about my pregnancy and now here I am telling you about the miscarriage. I don't know why except…" Another pause. "You were always easy to talk to. I could tell you things I could never tell Tommy."

"I don't remember you ever confiding in me before."

"Don't you?" Her smile seemed wistful. "Maybe I told you more than you realized."

"I'm sorry if that's true."

"It doesn't matter anymore. I just wanted you to know why I wasn't around when you were going through all that trouble. It was a dark time and I was pretty far gone myself that year."

"Understandable."

"And now you're back," she said on another sigh.

The sun had dipped below the horizon and already Jack could sense twilight creeping in from the pine forest. The bullfrogs sang with the crickets as nostalgia settled over the landscape. When he was younger, his uncle used to say that the lake had two personalities— one by day and one by night. He wondered about the woman who stood beside him. He could no longer see her reflection in the water, but when he glanced at her profile, she seemed stoic and unassuming. Did more secrets lurk beneath that calm surface?

"I should go," she said as if sensing his scrutiny. "I'm glad you've finally come home. It's been too long."

Would she welcome him back when she learned of his agenda?

"I need to ask you something before you go," he said.

He could sense a sudden tension that made him wonder.

"What is it?"

"How well did you really know Anna?"

A shadow fell across her expression. "That's an odd question. I knew her for most of my life. So did you. We all went to kindergarten together."

"You said she was the only person you told about the pregnancy. Did she confide in you?"

"Of course. That's what girlfriends do."

"Did you know she was seeing someone else?"

The shadow fleeted again. "I don't believe that. Not for a second. Anna would never have cheated on you. She loved you."

"Did she?"

"Yes, of course, she did." Her voice turned ironic. "Besides, it's hard to hide infidelity in a town this small."

"Maybe this town has more secrets than you know." He was still gazing down at her. Her eyes seemed guileless, but who really knew? "That night has always haunted me. I dropped Anna off early. She waited until I was gone and then she slipped back out of her house. It's logical to assume she went out to meet someone."

"Maybe she just went for a walk."

"Alone? At that time of night?"

"It wasn't that late. Anna was a night owl, remember?"

"You didn't talk to her that night? You don't have any idea who she may have gone out to meet?"

"Jack." She placed her hand on his arm. He wondered if she used the same appeasing gesture to calm Tommy's temper. "Why are you letting this get to you now? We've all moved on."

"Have we? Then why did you come out here to talk to me?"

"I told you why. I wanted to apologize, not dredge up all that old pain. Why torment yourself with all those unanswered questions?"

"I'm just looking for the truth, Beth."

She was silent for a moment. "You never believed Wayne Foukes killed her, did you?"

"No."

"Yet you never tried to free him. You never spoke out against his incarceration."

"You don't know what I did," Jack said. "Just because I didn't shout about it from the middle of Main Street doesn't mean I kept those doubts to myself. But the law doesn't put a lot of stock in gut feelings. Especially coming from someone like me."

"Is that why you've come back now?" she asked. "Because of a gut feeling?"

"It's a little more substantial than that."

She frowned. "I don't understand. You have new evidence?"

"Let's just say, I've heard differing accounts of what happened that night. At the very least, lies were told to the police. I intend to find out why."

"No matter who you hurt?"

"What are you afraid of?"

"You misunderstand me." She took a step toward him, so quickly he didn't have time to move away. Her hand fluttered again to his bruised cheek. "I'm not afraid, Jack. I've been waiting fifteen years for the truth to come out."

OLIVE STOOD AT the top of the wooden steps gazing down at the couple on the dock. Jack and Beth Driscoll were old friends and so it came as no surprise to see them together. Yet for some strange reason, Olive felt blindsided. Not because she was jealous or envious or even all that curious about their conversation, but because observing Jack in such an unguarded moment took her breath away.

A panicky tremor shot through her and she could feel a warning prickle all across her scalp. Her intense awareness of him shocked and frightened her, which was crazy. What was there to fear? She was a grown woman and she'd hardly lived her life as a hermit. She'd even been in love once or twice. But the amiable farewells when the relationships ended had only reinforced the necessity of those partings. Breakups shouldn't be so easy. Not if there'd been real passion. Estrangements should be agonizingly tearful with unwise recriminations and long, sleepless nights. Olive had walked away with only a mild sense of regret. Her partners had seemed to feel the same. One had married within six months of their separation, the other had moved out of state. Olive wished them well but not enough to keep up with their lives. If she never saw either of them again, it would be no great loss.

But Jack...

Her trepidation deepened as she watched him in the waning light. Already she dreaded the time when he would pack his bags and leave town, most likely for good this time. In many ways, Olive was still the hopeless romantic she'd been at fourteen and a part of her was irresistibly drawn to the notion of the prodigal son. But this was more than a fantasy or a lingering schoolgirl crush. Somehow in the space of forty-eight hours, she'd developed real feelings for Jack King.

This would not end well, she predicted as she smoothed clammy hands down the sides of her jeans. He'd come to Pine Lake to settle old scores. Getting between a man and his mission was never a good idea. Beth Driscoll would do well to remember that, too.

Olive started toward the dock, letting her sneakers thump against the wooden stairs to alert them of her presence. When Jack turned, she waved and called out a greeting.

"Sorry! I didn't mean to interrupt," she said as she stepped onto the dock. The gentle sway of the platform made her feel light-headed. She put a hand on the rail to steady herself.

"I was just leaving." Beth bent to retrieve her sandals, hooking the heel straps over her index finger. As she straightened, her gaze settled on Olive. "We haven't had a chance to talk all summer, but I've been meaning to call and congratulate you on the promotion. I'm looking forward to the new school year."

Olive studied her in the dusky light. She looked sincere but there was an indefinable edge in her voice. "Thanks, Beth. I'm looking forward to the year, as well."

"I have some suggestions for the science lab. Maybe we can schedule a time to talk in the next week or so."

"Yes, of course. I'll be in my office every day until at least five."

"I'll be sure and stop by." Beth turned back to Jack. "It was really good to see you again. Don't be such a stranger from now on."

"I'll be around for a few days," he said. "Maybe we'll see each other again."

"I hope so. Goodbye for now."

"Goodbye."

Olive glanced up at Jack. His expression was inscrutable as he watched Beth climb the steps. Once she'd disappeared into the shadows, he seemed to shrug off his contemplative mood.

"Sorry again for the interruption," she said.

"You didn't interrupt anything."

"Still, I should have called instead of dropping by this way. I've been worried about that bump on your head. I wanted to make sure you're okay and I didn't trust you to tell me the truth on the phone."

"I feel fine. Headache's almost gone. No dizziness or disorientation."

"How's the memory?"

"Still hazy but I'm hoping it'll come back."

She nodded to the sweating bottle he'd set on the dock rail. "Are you going to drink that?"

"It's probably warm by now. I can go up to the house and get you a cold one," he offered.

"Only if you're having one, too."

He hesitated. "Maybe it's best if I stick to water for now."

"Then I'll take that one off your hands." He gave her the bottle and she took a thirsty drink. "Sorry. I needed that. It's been a long day."

"You don't have to keep apologizing."

"I feel like I do. I keep barging into your life. But I guess I'm not the only one. Word has gotten around about your return and now all your old friends want to see you."

"They want something," he muttered.

"What's that supposed to mean?"

"Don't mind me. I'm being cynical."

"You're entitled. I sensed some antagonism between you and Nathan earlier." When he didn't respond, she plunged on. "I love my cousin, but I'm enough of a realist to know that he usually has an angle for everything he does. Beth, though. She seems like a straight arrow. Were you close in school?"

"I don't know about close. We were friends."

"I can still remember all of you together," Olive said dreamily. "You and Anna and Beth and Tommy. I thought of you as the beautiful people. You were like movie stars to me. Poor Nathan was always the odd man out."

"He didn't seem to mind."

"Of course, he minded. He just never let on." She leaned her forearms against the rail, still cradling the bottle. "He always gave the impression of having it all together, but he was a mess in high school. He just never let anyone see it. I'm sure he still has his moments, but God forbid he should ever let down his guard."

"What do you mean by mess?"

"Don't you remember how competitive he was? How he constantly needed to prove himself?" Olive felt a little disloyal to her cousin for speaking so forthrightly behind his back. "His father was very domineering. He was good to my mother and me and I'll never forget the way he took us in when we were both falling apart. But he was always on Nathan's back, always finding fault, always berating him for some perceived shortcoming. I don't know how Nathan turned out as well-adjusted as he has."

Jack turned to stare at her. "You think he's well-adjusted?"

She laughed. "Relatively speaking. We all have our weaknesses. Mine is sleepwalking and a pathological fear of falling."

"If those are the worst of your weaknesses, I'd say you're in pretty good shape."

"Maybe so." The intensity of his look tingled all along her backbone. She focused on the water to mask her disquiet. "It's nice out here," she said after a moment. "I've always loved this lake. It's so eerie and primal. Listen." She cocked her head. "That was an alligator bellowing."

"The eggs have hatched," Jack said. "And the mothers are protective of their babies. Not a good time to go swimming."

"I'll keep that in mind. Personally, if I owned this place, I would just sit here on the dock all day and night and watch the wildlife. From a safe distance, of course."

"Maybe you'll get your chance," Jack said. "Nathan wants to buy the cabin."

Olive turned in alarm. "You're not going to sell, are you? It's your decision, of course, but I hope you don't. Leon loved this place. He'd be so happy knowing you're here even if you only manage a weekend now and then."

"We'll see," Jack said noncommittally. He motioned to the deck chairs. "Can you stay?"

"For a bit." Olive had nothing on her agenda until the following morning, but she didn't want Jack to think she was settling in for the night.

They sat side by side on the dock, cooled by a soft breeze that blew through the pine trees. The lake grew still and shadowy, a haunted forest of drowned trees and trailing moss. Sinewy bodies glided through the dark shallows. Frogs plopped, herons fished and the water lilies closed up tight, their bloom heads drooping drowsily in the waning light.

Darkness fell swiftly, a moment of complete blackness before the moon rose over the treetops. Olive placed the beer bottle on the dock between the chairs and then tipped her head back to stare up at the sky. Her nerve endings were taut and strumming. Jack was right there beside her, so near she could reach out and stroke a fingertip along his arm. All she had to do was turn her head, part her lips in invitation and she knew that he would kiss her. She wanted him to kiss her. More than anything at that moment. But she kept her gaze focused on the night sky because the last thing she needed was to get in over her head.

Beside her, Jack stirred. She could feel his gaze on her, but she didn't turn. Instead she said softly, "It really is an extraordinary place."

"I'd forgotten what it's like out here. Nothing but moonlight and water and the sound of all that nightlife."

"Not the kind of nightlife you're accustomed to," she teased.

"No."

"Do you like living in the city?"

"I like the anonymity."

She said in surprise, "But you have friends in Houston, don't you? Coworkers, acquaintances. People know who you are."

"They know my name. They know what I do for a living. They don't know me."

Olive swallowed, daring to probe deeper. "There's no one special?"

"No, not anymore."

She waited, wondering if he would elaborate.

"I was married for a time," he said with reluctance. "It didn't take."

"What happened?"

"We decided we were better friends than spouses. We ended things on good terms."

Olive liked the idea of Jack being on good terms with his ex. No tears, no recriminations, no sleepless nights. No unrequited love. No pent-up passion. "I've never married," she said. "I came close a couple of times but they didn't take, either."

He picked up the beer from the dock and lifted the bottle to his lips. The gesture seemed unbearably intimate in the dark.

Olive shivered and searched for a safe topic. "Earlier when Nathan asked for a word alone with you, what did he want? You don't have to tell me, of course. But I can't help thinking it had something to do with me."

"He knows you were sleepwalking Monday night."

"You told him?"

"He guessed. For the record, I didn't confirm. I think it's best we stick to our story even with Nathan."

She glanced at him with a frown. "You don't think he had anything to do with Jamie's death, do you? He was very fond of her. He did a lot to help her."

Jack's gaze met hers in the moonlight. "Did you know that he lied about his whereabouts on the night Anna was murdered?"

"What?"

"He and Tommy swore they were home all night, which gave each of them an alibi. But they lied. Both of them left the house at some point."

"Surely you don't think—" She placed her hand on his arm and then she didn't quite know what to do, jerk it away or leave it there. She slid it back to the arm of her chair. "What motive would either have for killing Anna?"

"I never said they killed her. But they lied and I'd like to know why."

"Did you ask Nathan?"

"He told me that he'd gone out to find you. He said you were sleepwalking that night."

The evening was balmy, but an icy breath blew down her collar. *Had* she gone out that night? She remembered sleeping in the next morning. The sun had been warm and bright in her room when her mother had awakened her to tell her the news. Like everyone else, Olive had been devastated by the tragedy. Anna Grayson's brutal murder had rocked the whole town. To think that Olive may have been out wandering around in the dark when it happened—

"You don't remember?" Jack prodded.

"No. But I rarely recalled anything that happened during an episode. I told you before, amnesia is common in sleepwalking." She'd been gripping the chair arms, but now she made an effort to relax. "Did Nathan say where he found me?"

"On Lakeside Road near the bridge."

"The bridge..." Olive's heart thudded painfully as she stared at Jack in horror. "That's a disturbing coincidence."

"You never knew about any of this?"

She tried to shake off the glacial fingers that gripped her spine. "Nathan never said a word. You...don't think I had anything to do with Anna's death, do you? Or Jamie's?"

"Of course not."

"But you think I saw something."

"It's possible."

"I didn't," she said almost desperately. "My mind is

a complete blank. Just like yours is for the past twenty-four hours. I even asked Mona Sutton about the possibility of recovering memories through hypnosis. She said the procedure would be unreliable at best."

"I imagine that's true. But if you ever want to give it a try, I know someone in Houston who could help you."

Someone he'd worked with? Someone he'd seen professionally? "I'll keep that in mind. Jack?"

"Yes?"

She'd meant to ask him something else regarding Nathan's visit, but instead she sat forward in her chair suddenly, her gaze traveling along the moonlit channel. "There's a light down there. Look. I think someone is on the bridge."

Chapter Eight

Jack swung around, searching the darkness and then rising quickly to stride to the edge of the dock. He stood for a moment tracking the light before he turned back to her. "Wait here. I'm going down there to have a look."

"In the boat?" Of course, in the boat. Did she think he was going to swim to the bridge?

He was already loosening the dock lines. She got up to help. "Let me go with you."

"It's best if you stay here."

"Why? What do you expect to find?"

He glanced back toward the flickering light. "Someone's walking the bridge with a flashlight. The better question is, what do they hope to find?"

"Evidence," she said on a surge of excitement. "Something that got left behind."

"Possibly."

"Even more reason I should go with you. Another pair of eyes." Or another target. She wasn't a particularly brave person. Where was all this sudden pluckiness coming from?

Jack stepped down in the boat and reluctantly offered her a hand. "We'll leave the lights off. He'll hear the outboard, but he may not be able to place the sound until we're already closing in."

Olive was buzzing from head to toe. "Sounds like a plan."

He gave her a warning look. "Running dark is risky in this water. If we hit a stump, we may have to swim ashore."

"Duly noted." She jumped down into the boat and then Jack started the outboard, slowly backing out into the channel. Once he'd cleared the dock, he turned the wheel sharply and hit the throttle. The boat swung around so swiftly, Olive almost lost her balance. She sat down hard and clutched the edge of the seat as the bow lifted out of the water. Jack hit the trim button and they picked up speed, skimming across the dark surface as if the devil himself were behind them. Olive liked the lake and she liked boats, but racing through a dark, perilous channel, possibly toward a murderer, was a thrill like nothing she'd ever experienced.

Behind the wheel, Jack was little more than a silhouette. She watched his profile for a moment and then turned to peer through the flying darkness as the wind buffeted her face and tore at her hair.

He didn't back off the throttle until they approached the bridge and then he shifted into idle speed. The flashlight Olive had spotted earlier was nowhere to be seen. Undoubtedly, the searcher had taken to the woods as soon as he'd heard the outboard. But as Olive scoured the shadowy deck, she could have sworn she saw a dark figure huddled near the guardrail.

"There!" she shouted over the rumble of the motor.

Jack flipped on the spotlight and the powerful beam tunneled through the darkness, leaping out of the water to climb the iron support beams. Olive almost expected to see glowing eyes in a pale face staring back at them. There was nothing but shadows.

Jack turned off the engine and they sat in inky silence as he played the light all along the bridge and up into the truss. Olive traced the beam, shivering as she imagined herself up there asleep but a part of her brain still cognizant.

A car engine sounded in the distance. Jack started the outboard and plowed toward the bank, heedless of the choking green coils clutching at the propeller. As they entered shallow water, he put the throttle in neutral, hopped out and then turned to push the hull back toward the open water. "Can you handle the wheel?"

"Yes, but what about you?"

He was already gone, wading ashore and then running through the woods toward the road. Olive took the wheel, slowly reversing away from the bank and trying her best to avoid those perilous tentacles. Once in deeper water, she turned the boat and headed into the channel, but she felt like a sitting duck in the moonlight. She glided up under the bridge and found a place to tie off.

She sat in the rocking boat and listened to the night. The car engine had long since receded and she heard nothing from Jack. The air was very still. She seemed completely alone on the water and yet she had the strangest feeling that she was being watched. She grew uneasy and fearful. Perhaps hiding out underneath the bridge wasn't such a good idea.

She thought about starting the trolling motor and making a pass along the bank to see if she could find Jack. Surely he would have called out to her if he'd returned, but an awfully long time had passed. What if he'd run into trouble? What if he had caught and confronted Jamie Butaud's murderer? Or worse, been ambushed?

On and on Olive's thoughts churned as she huddled in the boat and waited. After a bit, the feeling came to her again that she was being watched. She scanned the banks and treetops and just as she was about to start the motor and head back into the passage, footsteps sounded overhead. Someone was on the bridge.

She wanted to believe Jack had come back and she had the strongest urge to call out to him. Whoever had been up there earlier with a flashlight would have fled once he or she heard the sound of an approaching boat. That person was probably already in town by now. But what if he wasn't? What if he'd driven down the road, parked and doubled back in order to continue his search?

What if that person had seen Jack disembark and head into the woods, leaving Olive alone on the lake?

What if he knew that she'd been on the bridge the night Jamie Butaud's body had been thrown into the water and had come back to eliminate the only witness?

Olive's imagination exploded as her heart thundered. She kept her gaze trained on the underside of the deck, following the footfalls, and didn't notice that the boat had drifted too close to the support. The scraping sound jolted her. She pushed off and tried to use the paddle to keep free of the pier, but the water lapping against the fiberglass hull sounded as loud as a crashing wave.

A light shone through the floorboards and then almost immediately went out. Olive pictured someone on the deck staring down into the water. At her. She told herself she was hidden in the shadows. No way could she be spotted. But for all she knew, she had been stalked from the moment she'd backed away from the bank.

She felt for the spotlight and then angled the bulb upward. If she flipped the switch, she might be able to catch a glimpse of whoever was up there through the cracks in the floorboards. She gathered her nerve to do exactly that when another sound came to her. A metallic click that might have been the chamber-check of a weapon.

Olive reacted instinctively, casting off as she started the outboard. She pushed away from the support and pressed the throttle forward as she cleared the bridge.

A bullet hit the water in front of her, another beside her. She hunkered behind the wheel until she was out of range and then she brought the boat around to neutral. Water sloshed against the hull, pushing her toward the bank, but she couldn't worry about aquatic entanglements. Someone had just shot at her. Twice.

If not for a powerful surge of adrenaline, she might have collapsed from shock. Instead, she angled the spotlight toward the bridge, playing the beam all along the guardrail and into the shadows on the far side of the deck. No one was there.

For a moment, Olive wondered if she had imagined the footsteps, if she had fantasized the pepper of bullets in the water. Then she saw another form sprinting across the bridge, unmindful of the rotting floorboards and creaking support beams. She was too far away to see his features, but she knew that it was Jack. He had seen something, too. Or else the sound of gunfire had brought him running. Olive kept her gaze on that racing silhouette as she goosed the throttle and the boat shot forward.

He was gone by the time she got back to the bridge. She cruised through the first span, turned and coasted back through the other. After a couple of passes, she heard Jack calling to her from the deck. She eased into the channel until she could see him. He walked back and forth along the guardrail, the beam from his flashlight app trained on the floorboards.

"Pick me up over there," he called down to her. He motioned to the opposite bank where he'd disembarked earlier.

She found an opening in the vegetation and glided through until the bow ran aground. Jack pushed off and climbed aboard.

"Are you okay?" he asked anxiously.

"I'm fine." She took a moment to catch her breath. "Jack, someone shot at me just now. He was on the bridge."

"I heard." Anger edged his voice as his hand came up to tuck back the hair that had blown loose from her ponytail. "Are you sure you're okay."

"I think so." As adrenaline subsided, shock pummeled her. She lifted a trembling hand, observing it almost dispassionately in the moonlight. "Maybe you should take the wheel."

"Okay. But something tells me you could get us out of here just fine," he said as he slid into the bucket seat.

A FEW MINUTES LATER, they floated up to the dock and Jack tied off at the cleats. They climbed the steps in silence and once they were inside the cabin, he went straight to the kitchen and poured them both a healthy shot of whiskey.

"Better not," she said when he handed her the glass. "I still have to drive home."

"Suit yourself." He set the glass on the counter nearby. "But there's no need to drive home. You can stay here tonight. In fact, I think it would be a good idea if you did." Before she could accept or protest, he nodded toward the living room. "I'll take the couch and you can have the bed."

"That's… I appreciate the offer, but I really should go home. I have an early day tomorrow and…" She trailed away, realizing how silly it sounded to worry over mundane things like meetings and budgets when she could have been killed moments earlier. "On second thought…" She picked up the glass and downed the contents in one swallow, gasping out loud at the burn in her throat. "That's potent."

"Leon liked the good stuff." Jack carried his glass with him as he checked the front entrance and then the door to the deck. "Has your alarm been installed yet?"

"They're coming tomorrow," Olive said. "Another reason I should get home."

"Not a good idea to be there alone, at least until your security system is activated."

She turned on the barstool to watch him make his rounds. "You think whoever shot at me from the bridge would come to my house?"

"What makes you think he wouldn't?"

"What makes either of us assume the shooter was male? I never got a good look."

Jack shrugged. "Law of averages. Gut instinct. A

professional guess. The point is, you need to be careful until we figure this thing out."

He made it sound as if they were in this together. Partners in crime, so to speak.

Olive didn't mind that notion at all. "Shouldn't we call the police?"

"That's not a good idea." He gave her a grim look. "I don't trust Tommy Driscoll."

"What about the Pine Lake Police Department?"

"This area is out of their jurisdiction. They'd just refer the call to the County Sheriff's Office."

"Jack?"

"Yes?"

"Is there anyone in this town you do trust?"

"No," he answered frankly. "Although after seeing the way you handled that boat just now, I can think of few people I'd rather have at my back."

"My father and I used to do a lot of fishing and skiing. He made sure I knew how to drive in case anything happened to him. And for the record, you can trust me."

"For the record, I don't *not* trust you. But Nathan Bolt is your cousin and I don't at all trust him."

"Fair enough." Olive followed him into the living room and sat down heavily on the sofa. Folding her arms around her middle, she watched as he restlessly prowled the cabin. "You're nervous," she said.

"Wired. Adrenaline always makes me jittery."

"Who do you think was on the bridge tonight?"

"I can't answer that. Like you, I never got close enough to catch a glimpse. But whatever he—or she— was looking for was important enough to risk detection. He must have taken to the woods as soon as he heard the outboard. Maybe the suspect drove away or maybe his car was just that well hidden. I never saw it. At any rate, the person doubled back to the bridge, maybe to continue the search or maybe because he knew you would be there alone."

"That's a whole lot of maybes," she said.

"Best I can do right now."

"I was under the bridge when he came back. He stood right over me. I heard footsteps. I even heard the click of a weapon. He shot in the water as I headed out to the channel, but he never came close to hitting me. Maybe his intention was to scare me."

"Another maybe."

"Best I can do," she said with a tremulous smile. "All these close calls are curious, though. You would think if someone wanted to hurt me, they could have done so by now. Maybe it really is as simple as Marc Waller wanting to get to Nathan through me."

"Nothing about this is simple," Jack said. "I do know that at first light, we need to get down there and search that bridge."

We again.

"As much as I appreciate you looking out for me, I can't stay here tonight. I don't even have a toothbrush." Her feeble attempt to lighten the mood fell flat as she searched for a more substantial excuse.

Jack's dark gaze took her in. "Lucky for you, my uncle kept plenty of spares."

"That is lucky. Jack?"

"Yes?"

"Do you have a weapon?"

"I do."

"Here in the cabin?"

"Yes."

"Why don't you carry it?"

He paused. "I'm not a big fan of guns. I carry on a need-to basis."

She glanced at him in surprise. "But you were a cop." When he merely shrugged, she said, "Why did you leave the police department?"

"I figured out I was better suited to private security. My superiors would tell you that I didn't play well with others."

"Why do I get the feeling there's more to the story?" she murmured.

"There's always more to every story." He brought the bottle in from the kitchen to replenish their glasses.

"I thought you were going to stick to water," she reminded him.

"Tomorrow I go back to water."

He poured her another drink. She took a sip and set the glass on the coffee table. "What do we do now?"

"I could fix some dinner. Are you hungry?"

"I'm still too shaky to eat."

"If you're going to keep drinking that whiskey, you need something in your stomach," he said. "Just sit there and relax. I'll see what I can rustle up."

"Jack?"

"Yes?"

"Who do you think killed Anna?"

His eyes took on a faraway look as he scrubbed the back of his hand along the scruff on his lower jaw. He appeared as rugged and capable as ever, but somehow vulnerable. Not fragile by any means, but certainly haunted. "I must have asked myself that question a million times in the past fifteen years. The answer is always the same. I don't know."

"No professional guesses or hunches? No gut feeling?"

"Mostly just questions and I have plenty of those." He went to the refrigerator to survey the contents. "I'm a pretty basic cook," he warned as he reached for a carton of eggs.

Somehow Olive doubted he was basic at anything. She moved from the couch back to the bar so that she could watch his preparations. The motion of his hands mesmerized her as he chopped vegetables. Her gaze lingered on his battered knuckles as she imagined his fingers trailing along her backbone. She thought about their kiss that first night and wondered if the impulse would ever be repeated. Jack seemed more than content to keep her at arm's length. If that was a good thing, why did she suddenly feel so bereft?

She picked up her whiskey and sipped.

"Jack?"

"Yes?"

"I need to tell you something."

"I'm listening."

"It's about Anna."

The knife froze as he glanced up. He searched her face for the longest moment. "What about her?"

"I've heard something that you might not know. Maybe you don't want to know," Olive added.

He went back to his chopping. The blade sliced through the vegetables with studied precision. "Tell me."

"She used to work for Mona Sutton after school and sometimes on Saturdays."

"I remember. She wanted to be a psychologist."

"Yes, Mona said she was flattered at first that Anna

wanted to follow in her footsteps, but after a while, she started to worry about Anna's motivation. She said it wasn't so much that Anna wanted to help people. She liked knowing things about them. Secrets."

Jack frowned. "What kind of secrets?"

"Mona wasn't specific, but she wondered if Anna had somehow accessed her files. She also told me about a hacking incident. Evidently, the school's whole system was compromised. Grades were changed. Scholarship applications were deleted. It would have been a real scandal if the district hadn't managed to keep it quiet. Mona thought Anna might have been involved. Did she ever say anything about it to you?"

Jack had gone very still. He seemed to drift away until the sizzle of butter in the frying pan brought him back. He lowered the heat and set the skillet aside. "I don't know anything about a hacking incident, but I did wonder about some of my grades. When I questioned a couple of the teachers, they claimed to have found mistakes. And there was one scholarship in particular that I never heard back from. The others were mostly rescinded after I became a suspect."

"That was so unfair to you."

He shrugged. "I don't know why Anna would have changed my grades, though. Let alone deleted scholarship applications."

"Maybe she didn't want you going away to school."

"She was going away herself." He grew pensive. "The one thing I could never figure out was motive."

"A motive for her murder, you mean? Do you think she found something incriminating in Mona's files? Something she used to blackmail another student? That seems out of character from what I remember of her."

"Anna was complicated."

"That's exactly what Mona said. I don't remember her that way at all, but then, I really didn't know her. I didn't know any of you very well, even my own cousin. But I find it hard to believe that a student could have a secret so dark he or she would be willing to kill to keep it from coming out."

"Who says it was a student?"

"I just assumed…" Olive trailed off as she watched him. "You have someone else in mind?"

"How well do you know Mona Sutton?"

"*Mona?* You can't be serious. What motive could she possibly have?"

"You said she suspected Anna had accessed her files. Maybe Anna found out something about her."

"Like what?"

Jack shrugged. "You tell me."

"This is pointless," Olive said with an irritated sigh. "We could sit here and build a case against anyone. It's easy when nothing more is required than idle speculation."

"Take it easy," Jack said.

"Sorry," she relented. "But Mona's a friend and Nathan is my cousin. I feel guilty talking about them behind their backs."

"We're just trying to find answers."

"Tie up those loose ends," she murmured.

In the ensuing silence, the coffeemaker started to drip, filling the cabin with a delectable aroma that reminded Olive of her mother, a true coffee connoisseur. She could drink cup after cup, but Olive wasn't so immune to caffeine. Coupled with the lingering adrenaline, she wondered if she would sleep a wink that night.

She glanced up from her drink to find Jack watching her. "What is it?"

"I was just wondering if you'd ever heard any rumors about Mona Sutton. An involvement with a student, anything like that?" His expression never altered, but Olive saw a flicker in his eyes that made her wonder.

She answered without hesitation. "No, never. Not so much as a whisper. Mona Sutton's reputation and behavior are exemplary."

"Doesn't it strike you as odd that someone with her credentials and education would choose to remain in a place like Pine Lake as a high school guidance counselor? The pay can't be that great."

Olive bristled. "Her salary is commensurate to mine. Which, you're right, isn't that great. But most of us don't do it for the money. We do it because we love our jobs and because what we do is important."

"I didn't mean to imply otherwise. I'm sorry if I offended you."

"I'm not offended. And, yes, I suppose I have wondered why someone like Mona would remain in Pine Lake. But she also has a private practice in addition to her work at school."

"I didn't know that."

"Now you do." Olive paused. "It's fine for the two of us to toss around conjecture in the privacy of this cabin, but a public accusation of this nature could ruin a career."

"Which is exactly my point," he said.

"Your point being that Anna may have found something on Mona Sutton. Possibly a relationship with a student. And the name of this student?"

"Tommy Driscoll."

Olive gaped. "You know this for a fact?"

"I don't know anything for a fact. As you said, this is nothing more than speculation in the privacy of my uncle's cabin. A conversation that will go no farther than the front door."

"Mona and Tommy." Olive shuddered. "I don't buy it. I just can't see it. She's a beautiful, sophisticated woman. Tommy Driscoll is…well, Tommy Driscoll. I suppose he's attractive in a good-old-boy kind of way and some might consider him charming, but he's always been so full of himself. So cocky."

And yet…

Hadn't she wondered herself why Mona had never married or even socialized in Pine Lake?

"Mona may have killed Anna because her relationship with a student was about to be exposed. That's your theory?"

"That's *a* theory," Jack said.

"I don't buy it."

"So you said."

"But now I'll never get that image out of my head. Thank you for that."

She saw a grin flash as he turned back to the stove.

He dished up the scrambled eggs, poured the coffee and they ate at the bar, choosing to discuss innocuous topics. Olive talked about her plans for the coming school year and her mother's recent marriage. Jack said little about his own life, but from the bits and pieces that she could cobble together, he seemed to lead a solitary existence. His parents had moved to Phoenix years ago and he had no siblings or cousins or anyone in his life he seemed close to. Undoubtedly his choice, but

Olive sensed a restive nature that might always keep him discontent.

The meal concluded, she insisted on cleaning up while Jack went down to the dock to have a look around. She finished putting away the last of the dishes and then went outside to join him.

"You shouldn't be out here," he said. "It may not be safe."

"It may not be safe anywhere," she said with a shrug. "I've been thinking about that person on the bridge earlier. Why do you suppose he or she didn't wait until later to conduct a search? It was barely dark when I spotted the flashlight."

"Maybe he or she was afraid someone else would get there first."

Olive leaned her forearms against the rail, staring out over the water. Moonlight shimmered on the dark surface, reminding her of the fathomless mystery of Jack King's eyes. "First I was nearly run down by a truck that may or may not have been driven by Marc Waller. Then you were drugged and now I've been shot at it. What's going on in Pine Lake? What have we gotten ourselves into, Jack?"

"I don't know," he said in a strange tone. "But I'm sorry you got dragged into it."

"That's hardly your fault. I'm the one who climbed to the top of the bridge in my sleep, remember? I'm the one who was there when Jamie Butaud's body was thrown into the lake."

"I'm talking about tonight. I shouldn't have taken you with me."

She straightened. "If I'd stayed behind, whoever was on the bridge might have come looking for me here."

"No one knew you were at the cabin. Unless you told Nathan."

"I didn't. But aren't you forgetting someone? Beth knew."

"Yes." That odd note in his voice again.

"What if the cabin was being watched? What if I'm being watched? If Nathan figured out I was sleepwalking Monday night, maybe someone else has, too. Maybe the plan all along was to lure you away from the cabin."

"More maybes."

Olive glanced along the glimmering channel toward the bridge. The iron truss loomed dark and forbidding in the moonlight.

Slowly, she traced the shallow water, her gaze traveling the tree line and all along both banks. Nothing stirred. She saw nothing untoward in the darkness. No flickering lights, no furtive searching. The night was still, with the gentlest of breezes blowing across the water. And yet she had that same uncanny feeling she'd had earlier underneath the deck. Someone watched. Maybe from the bridge, maybe from the pine forest on the other side of the lake. Maybe even closer, from a boat hidden by a thick curtain of Spanish moss.

Someone watched.

Chapter Nine

Jack awakened with a start. A noise had roused him, but he couldn't say with any certainty what that sound had been.

He took a moment to orient himself to the darkness. He was in the bedroom of his uncle's cabin on Pine Lake. Olive lay sleeping in the living room, having insisted on taking the couch. Jack pushed himself up on his elbows, listening for a sign that she might be up stirring about, or worse, that an intruder was somewhere on the premises. A faint breeze drifted across the room, rippling the curtains at the window. Somewhere in the cabin, an outside door had been opened.

He rose from the bed and pulled on his jeans. Taking his weapon from the nightstand drawer, he left the room and slipped down the hallway to the living area. He checked the couch first. The covers lay crumpled and abandoned on the floor. The breeze tickled across his bare shoulders, drawing his gaze to the wall of windows that looked out on the deck. One of the glass doors stood slightly ajar.

He didn't think Olive would have left the cabin of her own accord, but she might not be cognizant of her actions. Tucking the gun in the back of his jeans, he went out on the deck. The moon was up, casting an eerie glow over the water as it shimmered down through the cypress trees. Across the lake, the pine forest loomed dark and impenetrable. Night sounds assailed him. The hoot of an owl. The forlorn cry of a loon.

An icy premonition stole down Jack's spine. Olive was somewhere out there alone, wandering the dark in her sleep while a killer lay in wait.

He left the deck and hurried down the steps to the dock. He hoped he might find her sitting in one of the chairs safe and sound, having slipped out of the cabin for a breath of fresh air. No such luck. He started to race back up the steps, but a flutter of movement out of the corner of his eye froze him. He turned slowly toward the water.

Olive was in the boat. Still dressed in the T-shirt he'd laid out for her earlier, she sat behind the wheel staring straight ahead. One hand rested on her bare leg as the other came up to trace along the instrument panel. She paused on the ignition. Then that hand also dropped to her lap and she remained motionless for the longest time until those furtive fingers came back up to search the dash.

Jack took a quick scan of their surroundings. The dock lines had been unfastened. If not for a knot that had caught on one of the cleats, the boat would have drifted away.

"Olive?"

She didn't answer. She didn't acknowledge his presence with so much as a glance. Her fingers were still moving along the panel, pausing yet again on the ignition.

He knelt on the dock and pulled the boat back against

the bumpers. Then he climbed down, steadying the rocking motion as best he could so that the movement didn't startle her awake. With her back to the lake, her face was a pale mask in the filtered moonlight, her eyes glassy and sightless. Gooseflesh prickled at Jack's nape.

"Olive," he called softly.

She gazed up at him and for a moment, Jack thought he must have roused her. But the eyes were blank, the hand moving along the dash unnervingly persistent.

"Can you hear me?" he asked.

"I need to go," she said.

Her expressionless voice sent another chill down his spine. "Go where?"

She stared out over the dock toward the bridge.

"Olive, you need to wake up." He waved a hand in front of her face. No reaction. Not even a blink.

She turned back to the wheel and the movement of her hand on the panel became more frenzied.

"Where do you need to go?" he asked again.

She didn't respond and Jack didn't know what to do. The last thing he wanted was to startle her awake. She could injure herself if she became frantic in such a small space and he might not be able to restrain her. But he certainly couldn't leave her here. It wasn't safe for either of them to be out in the open like this.

"Come on, Olive. Time to wake up." Taking her arm, he tried to gently ease her to her feet. He'd read somewhere that sleepwalkers were somewhat docile. Head them in the right direction and they would often go back to their beds. Olive wouldn't be budged.

He hunkered beside her, lowering his voice soothingly as he studied her profile. "Tell me where you need to go."

Once again she turned to stare out over the water.

"Are you trying to tell me you need to go back to the bridge? Why, Olive? Why the bridge?"

He thought about his earlier conversation with Nathan. The old lake bridge had once been important to Olive, a place she often retreated to after her father's tragic death. Maybe that was why she wanted to go there now. In some strange way, the bridge could still be a comfort to her. Or a punishment.

The frantic movement of her fingers along the panel seemed almost piteous to Jack now. He wanted to help her, calm her, but what he had in mind was risky and not altogether selfless. Olive had been wandering along Lake Side Road on the night of Anna's murder. What if she'd seen something before Nathan found her? What if those buried memories kept pulling her back to the bridge?

"Do you want me to take you there?" he asked.

No answer. She seemed oblivious to his presence, but when he eased her up from the seat, she willingly moved to the other side of the boat. Which seemed strange to Jack, and he wondered if a part of her brain was still cognizant.

He untangled the knot from the cleat and then fished in his pocket for the key. He had no idea if he was doing the right thing. He was in unfamiliar territory. Taking her to the bridge could be extremely dangerous. For all he knew, Jamie Butaud's murderer could still be prowling the darkness. But Jack had a gut feeling the situation could be even more perilous if he were to thwart Olive's compulsion. It was obvious that something important kept luring her back to the bridge.

The outboard rumbled to life, but the sound didn't

faze her and Jack wondered if she'd been subconsciously braced for the roar. He placed one hand on the wheel and the other on the edge of his seat, ready to snatch her from danger if she started to get up, or worse, jump overboard. For now she sat motionless and stared straight ahead as he backed away from the dock and turned down the channel with only the moonlight to guide them.

The cypress trees were feathery against the pale light, the dripping Spanish moss undulant in a soft breeze. To his right, Jack could see the skeletal remains of a tree that had been struck by lightning. To his left, the glowing eyes of a night creature. Beside him, Olive sat silent as a ghost. An eerier trip Jack could hardly have imagined.

He found a place to put in near the bridge and hopped out, allowing the bow to run aground. He started to take Olive's arm but she was already climbing out, unmindful of his assistance. Her bare feet splashed in the water as she moved past him to the bank.

She went straight to the ladderlike support they had used two nights ago and Jack worried that she meant to climb to the top of the truss. He would have to stop her if she tried, but for now he stood nearby and let her take the lead.

For the longest time, Olive remained by the support, her head tilted skyward, as if she couldn't decide what to do. Then she turned and went up the bank to the deck. Jack followed at her side, guiding her away from the guardrail and around the treacherous spots in the floorboards.

Halfway across she paused to gaze out over the water. Then she turned to glance back at the bank as if she feared being followed. Satisfied, she fell to her knees and bent over the planks, trailing her hands all along the rough surface.

Jack knelt in front of her, mesmerized by the motion of her hands as they moved back and forth across the deck. She paused, hands hovering as she lifted her head, attracted by a night sound that only she could hear. Once again she cast a furtive glance over her shoulder before returning her attention to the floorboards.

Removing his phone from his pocket, Jack bent low, angling the flashlight beam along the deck beneath Olive's hands. What was she looking for? Or was she merely acting out some fragment of a long forgotten dream?

He trained the light straight down through the planks, expecting to see nothing but the distant glimmer of water. Instead, the beam sparked off something metallic wedged between the cracks of the floorboards. The tiny gold chain had fallen so deeply into the crevice and had been so thoroughly rooted in dirt and debris that it would never have been noticed if not for Olive's methodical searching.

The only tool Jack had with him was the boat key. He used the bit to dig down into the fissure until he could hook the chain over one of the teeth. Carefully, he fished the necklace up through the crack, catching his breath at the sight of the gold heart that dangled from a link. Despite fifteen years of dirt and grime, the embedded ruby—Anna's birthstone—still flashed with fire as the gemstone caught the moonlight.

Time had rendered the engraving on the back nearly illegible, but no matter. Jack remembered the simple inscription word for word: To Anna, from Jack. Love you always.

He'd given the necklace to her during their senior year and she'd worn it every day until her death. He'd never known her to take it off. In hindsight, he wondered now if his choice of a heart had been his unwitting way of diminishing the significance of the one on her hip—the tattoo that had secretly labeled her as one of Tommy Driscoll's conquests.

Olive sat back on her heels, following the movement of the pendant as though under a hypnotist's spell. Then with a strange little sigh, she lay down on the bridge and closed her eyes, oblivious to her surroundings, oblivious to Jack, oblivious to the significance of her discovery.

OLIVE OPENED HER eyes to sunlight. She lay very still, staring up at the cedar plank ceiling as her heart thudded in panic. For a moment, she had no idea where she was. Had she sleepwalked into an unfamiliar bedroom?

Then bits and pieces of the previous night came back to her. Jack had talked her into staying at the cabin, which, to be truthful, hadn't been all that difficult after the events at the bridge. The last thing she'd wanted was to be alone in her unprotected house. Something sinister was going on in Pine Lake, and like it or not, she and Jack were in the middle of it. His growing list of suspects included Mona Sutton, a colleague and friend, and Nathan Bolt, the only remaining family Olive had left in this town.

For all she knew, she could be on Jack's list, too, although that seemed a reach. He'd given no indication that he was suspicious of her, but she needed to watch her step if for no other reason than to preserve her well-being. Her feelings for Jack King could easily get out of hand. An attraction was one thing, but she couldn't let herself fall in love with him. His stay in Pine Lake was transient and Olive knew from past experiences that she didn't handle loss well. Not real loss, the kind that hollowed out your insides and left you bereft. Three days ago, before Jack's return, she'd been perfectly happy with her life. Why rock the boat now—

Her thoughts splintered as she lifted up on her elbows and glanced around. Wait a minute. Why was she in the cabin's only bedroom? She'd insisted on taking the couch. She distinctly remembered watching the moon through the windows while she waited for sleep.

What had happened during the night? And why couldn't she remember? She hadn't had that much to drink, surely.

Swinging her legs over the side of the bed, she grabbed her clothes—neatly folded on a nearby chair—and padded down the hallway to the bathroom. After washing up and brushing her teeth, she dressed and followed the aroma of freshly brewed coffee out to the living area. Jack was in the kitchen fiddling with the coffeemaker. He turned when she came in and said good morning. Maybe it was Olive's imagination, but his greeting sounded stilted and he seemed to have a hard time meeting her gaze, making her wonder yet again about last night's events.

She went over and sat down on one of the barstools.

"Coffee?" he asked.

"Yes, please. Black and strong."

He poured a cup and set it before her. "How about some breakfast? I've got toast, cereal, fruit."

"No, thanks. I'm not much of a breakfast person. Coffee is fine."

He stood leaning against the counter, observing her as he folded his arms.

She put down her cup. "You're acting very strangely this morning so you may as well tell me what's wrong. Something happened last night, didn't it? I went to sleep on the couch and I woke up in the bedroom. I'd like to know why."

"You were sleepwalking," he said. "After I got you back inside, I thought it best that I take the couch so I'd awaken if you tried to leave the cabin again."

Icy fingers slid up her spine. "I left the cabin?"

He folded his arms as he gazed at her across the kitchen. "You really don't remember anything, do you?"

She frowned. "The last thing I remember is settling down on the couch."

"That's not entirely true," he said slowly.

Her scowl deepened. "What do you mean, it's not true? I would know if I remembered anything else."

"Would you? Are you sure about that?"

She said in exasperation, "Please stop dancing around the issue and tell me what happened last night."

"It's not just about last night, but that's a good place to start." He turned and poured himself a cup of coffee. "Let's go sit on the deck. I could use some air."

She reluctantly followed him outside, dreading what she might learn. If only they could sit in peace and quiet and enjoy the morning. It was early and the lake was lovely and calm. No voices, no cars, no ringtones. Just a fleeting moment of tranquility as the water lilies opened and the songbirds awakened.

Olive hated to shatter the zen-like stillness, but there

was dark business to discuss. She turned to Jack, studying his profile as a breeze drifted across the deck, carrying the scent of the pines.

"I'm waiting," she said.

He took a gold chain from his shirt pocket, dangling it in the light before he closed his fist around it. "I woke up and you were gone," he said. "I found you down at the dock in the boat."

"What was I doing in the boat?"

"You'd tried to untie the lines, but a knot got caught on one of the cleats. Otherwise, you would have drifted away."

"I don't even remember leaving the cabin. What do you think I was doing in the boat?"

"You said you needed to go."

Her eyes widened. "I talked in my sleep?"

"Is that unusual?"

"Not for sleepwalking in general. Mumbles and moans are quite common, and some people have been known to carry on whole conservations without ever rousing. I don't think that's ever happened to me, though."

"How would you know unless someone told you?"

"I suppose that's true. So you found me in the boat…" she prompted.

"You were fiddling with the dash as if trying to start the ignition. And you kept gazing down the channel. It was obvious you meant to go back to the bridge. So I took you."

She stared at him in shock. "You took me back to the bridge? After someone shot at me there?"

"I know how that sounds." He looked momentarily chastised. "But it seemed important to you. Urgent, even. And I was with you the whole time. I never left your side for an instant. You've no reason to believe me, but I wouldn't let anything happen to you. Not then, not now."

Olive's breath quickened. His eyes were dark and deep and so piercing she could feel her armor crumbling. Quickly, she glanced away before he could see the alarm—and the longing—in her own gaze. "You don't owe me anything. You barely know me."

"It doesn't matter. I meant what I said."

Olive merely nodded because she didn't trust herself to speak at that moment. She didn't trust her resolve. It would probably be best for both of them if she got up and walked away. Kept her distance and her peace of mind. Instead, she sat there on Jack's deck, eyes fiercely focused on the water as her heart beat an uneasy rhythm inside her chest.

"To be honest, I had another reason for taking you to the bridge," he said. "I thought you might remember something."

"In my sleep?"

"I don't know how sleepwalking works. It seemed worth a shot. And my hunch paid off. Something did come back to you." He opened his fist, revealing the gold chain he'd taken out of his pocket earlier.

Olive noticed the heart pendant then and the flash of a tiny embedded ruby. She glanced up and found him watching her carefully. "*I* found it? Where?"

"It had fallen between the floorboards on the bridge. Impossible to see unless you knew where to look."

"May I?" She put out her hand. He seemed reluctant to relinquish the necklace at first, but then lifting his gaze to hers, he let the chain slip from his fingers into her palm.

The winking ruby enthralled Olive. The flash of fire awakened something in the deepest recesses of her consciousness. Not a memory. More like a lingering emotion from a forgotten dream.

"Do you recognize it?" Jack asked.

"I don't think so. But... I feel something when I look at it."

"What?"

The sharpness in his voice jolted her and the sensation fled. Her defenses came up as unease tickled across her scalp. "I don't understand. The necklace isn't mine. I don't remember having seen it before. And yet..." Her eyes closed briefly. "How could I have known where to find it on the bridge?"

"Look closely," he said. "Are you certain you don't recognize the charm?"

She held up the chain, allowing the heart to swing gently in the breeze. "From the way you're watching me, I assume you expect me to recognize it, but I don't. If I've seen it before, I can't remember where or when. Besides, a heart pendant is hardly an usual design."

"Turn it over and see if you can read the inscription."

Olive complied, furrowing her brow as she concentrated on the weatherworn engraving. Her hand trembled slightly as she glanced up. "This was Anna's?"

"She had it on the night she died."

Dread descended as Olive's heart started to hammer. "The necklace was wedged between the floorboards. Impossible to see unless one knew where to look, you said. If that's true, then I still don't understand how I happened upon it last night."

Jack leaned in, his gaze hard and relentless. "Because you were there the night Anna was killed. You must have seen the pendant fall from her neck. Or maybe the killer grabbed it from her throat. The point is, you saw where it lodged. You went straight to it last night. There's no way you could have known about Anna's necklace unless you witnessed her murder."

THE COLOR DRAINED from Olive's face. She looked vulnerable and yet somehow dauntless in her jeans and sneakers, with her hair still mussed from sleep and her blue eyes shadowed with fear.

For a moment the impulse to protect her was almost overpowering. Jack wanted nothing so much as to take her hand in his, pull her close and tell her that everything would be okay. He fought the urge to tuck back the strands of hair that curled in the breeze, to soothe away the worry lines that wrinkled her brow.

He wasn't a gallant man. Polite and respectful, yes, because he was still his mother's son, but he hadn't felt particularly chivalrous since his high school days. Olive Belmont had changed all that. From the moment their gazes had connected on top of that bridge, she'd made him feel things. Unexpected things. Unwanted things.

Complications, he reminded himself warily. He didn't need them.

She looked at him quizzically. "I don't suppose you believe in coincidences."

"Not in this case. You knew where to find that necklace, Olive. There's no getting around that."

She flinched. "But why did I only now remember? The pendant was wedged between those floorboards for fifteen years. And more to the point, why was someone else searching for it last night?"

"We don't know what that person was looking for. Something could have gotten left behind from Jamie Butaud's murder. But if the searcher really was looking for Anna's necklace, I can only assume my presence has created some anxiety. Here I am, back after all these years, and I'm asking a lot of unpleasant questions. Memories are stirring. Doubts are surfacing. Maybe that's why you remembered."

She glanced down at the chain pooled in her hand. "What are we going to do? This is evidence. We can't keep it to ourselves."

"That's exactly what we're going to do," Jack said. "This doesn't change anything. We already know Anna was on the bridge the night she died. The killer dumped her body in the water. The discovery of her necklace between the floorboards doesn't tell us anything about her death we didn't already know."

"Then there's no reason for the killer to worry. There's no reason why he would have been on the bridge last night."

"No reason that we know of. But the necklace does tell us something about you. If you saw what happened that night—"

"Don't." Olive turned with shadowed eyes. "I don't want to think about that. I don't want to think that this could have ended years ago if only I'd remembered. Maybe Jamie Butaud would still be alive."

"You can't think like that. For all we know, Jamie's murder is unrelated to Anna's."

"Do you really believe that?"

He thought about everything Nathan had told him

the day before. Two young women murdered fifteen years apart, connected by the same tattoo that linked each of them to Tommy Driscoll. Jack didn't want to jump to conclusions, but at the very least, he needed to find out the county sheriff's whereabouts on the night of Jamie's murder.

"Jack?"

He glanced at Olive. She reached across the table and took his hand, placing the necklace gently in his palm and then closing her fingers around his. "You loved her very much, didn't you?"

"It was a long time ago. We were kids."

"Some things you don't get over."

The haunted look was back in her eyes and Jack thought again about his conversation with Nathan Bolt. Olive's dad had died in a terrible accident for which she blamed herself. Might still blame herself even after all these years. On the surface, she seemed like a happy woman, content and well adjusted. But deep down, she had secrets whether she remembered them or not.

She rose and went over to the railing to stare down at the dock. Jack hesitated for a moment and then got up to join her. The sun was up now, dappling the water lilies. The air was warm and redolent with the loamy scent of the lake.

Jack wished he had nothing more pressing than a day on the water with Olive, but a murderer was out there somewhere getting nervous and more dangerous by the minute.

"I should go," she said as if sensing his disquiet. "The security people are coming this morning and then I have to get to work. There's still so much to be done before school starts…" She trailed away into silence. "About that necklace…"

"What about it?"

She briefly touched the back of his hand. "I really don't remember ever having seen it. I'm not lying about that."

"I never thought you were."

"I know how much you want to solve Anna's murder. I'm sorry I can't be of more help."

He shrugged. "You've nothing to be sorry about. None of this is your fault. Not Anna's murder, not Jamie's, any of it."

"Yes, but what if I do have hidden memories of that night? I can't help but wonder how your life might have been changed if only I'd remembered what happened."

"Maybe I like my life just fine the way it is."

"You almost sound convincing."

He straightened, gazing down at her with a pensive frown. "You carry a lot of guilt on your shoulders, don't you?"

She smiled. "It's kind of my thing. And yours is downplaying your feelings. I know how deeply you loved Anna. I could see it on your face every time you looked at her. I used to wonder what it would be like to have someone look at me like that. Sometimes I still wonder." Her tone was self-deprecating but her smile turned wistful.

That smile did things to Jack. The dreaminess. The open yearning.

He scowled at the sparkling water as his restlessness edged into an unexpected longing. "I'll always grieve for what might have been, but for Anna's sake, not mine. She deserved a long and happy life. But I haven't been carrying a torch for her all these years. I'm not still in love with a dead girl." He turned. "Anna's ghost doesn't haunt me, Olive. And her memory has nothing to do with how I feel about you."

He heard her breath catch. Her eyes were very blue as she stared up at him. Clear and yet somehow unfathomable. Earnest and yet deeply guarded. "How do you feel about me?" she asked on a near whisper.

He didn't answer. Instead he reached out and smoothed back her hair, letting his fingers tangle in the russet strands as their gazes clung. If Jack had sensed even the slightest resistance, he would have let the moment slip away. But Olive didn't contest, just the opposite. She leaned in, her lips slightly parted, her eyes hooded and sultry. He stared down at her for another moment before he cupped her neck and pulled her to him.

The kiss was slow and testing, without the spontaneity and adrenaline of their first. And yet the impact rocked Jack to his core. He drew back, searching her face before he bent and kissed her again, this time wrapping his arms around her waist and lifting her so that they were face to face, mouth to mouth, heartbeat to heartbeat. She weighed nothing. So slight she could have easily slipped from his arms and so he tightened his embrace as he deepened the kiss.

Desire flared. Hot and quick. He wanted her then and there, on the deck, in the open, with the leaves whispering all around them and the songbirds looking down from the treetops. He wanted her writhing and ready as the swamp teemed with a primal awakening. But he held back because there was something else in that kiss, too. Deeper, darker, more complicated emotions.

Whether she sensed his hesitation or had her own reservations, he would never be certain, but she pulled away, staring into his eyes as she slid back to the deck. She lifted her fingers to her lips as if she could somehow capture their kiss.

"That was…unexpected."

"Was it?"

She shivered. "Maybe not. Jack?"

"Yes?"

"You never answered my question."

"I think I did. Eloquently, I would hope."

She laughed softly as she turned to stare out over the lake, squinting as a shaft of sunlight bounced off the water. "This—whatever this is…" She made a gesture between them, connecting them. "It isn't going to end well, is it?"

"Probably not."

"But that's not going to stop us."

"No."

She tracked an egret skimming the water before turning back to him with a nod. "Okay," she said. "But just so you know, my eyes are wide open."

Chapter Ten

Olive propped an elbow on her desk and cradled her chin in her palm. Worry and caffeine had given her a headache and she felt apathetic about the million and one things left to do on her agenda. A week ago, all she could think about was excelling in her new position and proving herself to a seemingly dubious school board, but her priorities had suddenly shifted.

It wasn't just her attraction to Jack King that occupied her thoughts. In fact, she was trying her best *not* to think about those feelings or that kiss. There would be time enough later to overanalyze every nuance. Right now, however, Olive had more pressing problems. In the space of one short night, she'd been shot at by an unknown gunman and had recovered Anna Grayson's long-lost necklace. A necklace Anna had been wearing on the night of her murder.

That Olive had apparently witnessed something didn't bode well for her peace of mind or her physical safety. Jack had promised to do everything in his power to protect her, but could she trust him to have her best interests at heart? He also had an agenda. He had come back to Pine Lake to solve Anna's murder and now that he knew Olive was a material witness, how far would he go to try and recover her memories?

Ever since Jamie Butaud's body had been found, Olive had worried that she might have seen something from the top of the lake bridge, that the identity of Jamie's killer might be hidden somewhere in her subconscious, waiting for a trigger to release it. But she'd never considered the possibility that she had witnessed *Anna Grayson's* murder. In fifteen years, not a single clue had surfaced until last night.

But Jack was right. How else could she have known where to look for that necklace? Why else would she have gone in search of it in her sleep?

What else might be locked in her subconscious?

On the surface, it seemed like too much of a coincidence that she could have been an unwitting witness to two brutal slayings, but her presence on the bridge on the night of Anna's murder hadn't been happenstance. After her family's move to Pine Lake, Olive had gone to the bridge to wallow in her guilt and to grieve for her dad. The place had become a haven for her and eventually a habit. From everything she knew about her disorder, a sleepwalker often repeated everyday behavior. Going to the bathroom. Getting a drink of water. Climbing to the top of the old lake bridge.

Her fixation on the structure could explain her presence fifteen years ago, but what about on Monday night? What had brought back the falling dreams and her sleepwalking trip to that bridge?

At first, Olive had chalked up her restless slumber to the anxiety and uncertainty of a new job, but now she wondered if she had been picking up on subtle clues and vibes from the people around her. The people on Jack's list. Mona and Nathan and Tommy Driscoll.

After all, her first close call had come before Jamie's death, before Jack's arrival in Pine Lake. A dark sedan had come out of nowhere last Friday night to send Olive scrambling for the curb. She'd been certain that one or more malicious students had wanted to intimidate her, but in light of recent events, the intent was undoubtedly darker.

Nathan had suggested that Marc Waller was targeting Olive as a means to get to him, but had Marc really been that resentful of Nathan's relationship with Jamie or was there another reason for the bad blood between them? It didn't make sense to Olive and yet she could think of no other reason why she had ended up in Marc Waller's crosshairs. She barely knew him and had had little contact with Jamie since the troubled girl had dropped out of high school.

It pained Olive to think that the power to bring a killer to justice had been within her grasp all along if only she could remember. She could have ended Jack's misery years ago and given closure to Anna's family. The whole town could have healed. And Jamie Butaud might still be alive.

Pointless to blame herself, of course, but Jack was right about that, too. Olive was a master at taking on irrational guilt. She wasn't culpable for what had happened to Anna Grayson or Jamie Butaud any more than she was responsible for her dad's accident. But that hadn't stopped her from agonizing over what might have been. Olive had begged her dad to drive home that night even though she knew the roads were treacherous. She'd been selfish and thoughtless and petulant, but she had also been a kid. She'd eventually forgiven herself, but every now and then, the what-ifs caught up with her. Like now.

She swiveled her chair around to stare out the window, using the slow drift of cumulous clouds against the vivid blue sky to lull her into a meditative state. It was hot and steamy outside, but Olive sat shivering in her air-conditioned office. Maybe if she could conjure up one memory, the rest would fall like dominos. But was that even a good idea? Anna's killer had gone free all these years and if Olive was the only one who could identify him—

She whirled as a noise outside her office startled her. The school was old and full of strange sounds. She told herself to relax. She was hardly alone. In these final weeks, teachers were in and out of the building as they prepared their classrooms and curriculum. The custodial workers and support staff were also hard at work. There was nothing at all to be concerned about. Except...

The sound had seemed furtive somehow. Clandestine footsteps retreating through the reception area.

Olive rose silently and crossed her office to peer through the glass panel. No one was in the outer office. The administrative assistant had gone out for an early lunch and then a doctor's appointment. She wouldn't be back until midafternoon, but others were surely about. All Olive had to do was step into the hallway and she would undoubtedly find someone working in one of the other offices.

She crossed the reception area and once again paused to stare through the window. Then she opened the door and slipped into the corridor glancing both ways in apprehension. Nothing was amiss. No one stirred. And yet Olive had the discomfiting feeling that something was wrong.

Hugging the wall, she made her way down the hallway, checking for signs of life. The empty classrooms seemed to mock her and more than once, she paused to glance over her shoulder. Olive had spent most of her life in academic settings of one level or another. She found comfort in the musty mingle of textbooks, chalkboards and lockers. But there had always been something spooky about a deserted school building. Lingering emotions seemed to echo through the hallways and down the stairwells.

She'd dressed for comfort that morning in slim black pants and a blue knit top. The soft soles of her ballet flats hushed her footfalls on the tile floor as she approached the stairs and glanced over the railing. She took a deep breath and called out in what she hoped was a nonchalant voice. "Hello? Anyone down there?"

The question bounced off the walls and came right back to her. She waited for a response, hoping to hear a good-natured rejoinder from one of the teachers. Instead she was greeted by a weighty silence.

"Hello?" she called down again. The word ricocheted back to her. *Hello. Hello. Hello.*

She turned and retraced her footsteps down the hallway, pausing to peek inside the teachers' lounge. Empty. As were all the nearby classrooms. This was very unusual. Almost as if it had been planned. Olive didn't want to give in to the crazy notion of a conspiracy, but where was everyone?

Mona Sutton's office was located across the corridor and up a short flight of stairs. Olive had never thought

about it before, but the elevation of the guidance counselor's office had the effect of isolating Mona from the
student body. Olive had an image of the cool blonde
hovering on her private landing, observing the students
from afar, taking in things that no one else would notice.
*I saw the way you looked at him when you passed in the
hallway. And all those shy glances from your locker.*

The door was closed and Olive couldn't see a light
or any movement behind the frosted glass panel. She
started to retreat to her own office when she heard a
metallic clank followed by a muted oath.

Nothing to worry about. Mona was undoubtedly busy
with her own preparations for the coming school year.
Perhaps she was going through her file cabinets, which
would explain the noise. It did not explain the voices,
however, one deep and angry and unmistakably male.

Another teacher, perhaps. Or someone from the
cleaning staff.

Olive tried to remain calm, reminding herself sternly
that there was likely an innocent explanation for the
muffled commotion and yet everything inside her
stilled as her instincts screamed another warning. She
wavered indecisively. She could climb the stairs and
barge through the door to confront whoever was inside. Or she could go in search of a teacher or custo-
dian to accompany her. She could even call the police.
The school was located well within the city limits so
she wouldn't have to deal with Tommy Driscoll. But
if Mona was inside the office and Olive had panicked
for no reason, word would get out about her irrational
behavior. Her credibility—never mind her authority—
would be undermined. If she overreacted at the slightest
noise, how would she handle a real crisis?

To be fair, she had every right to be cautious. Considering the events of the previous evening, she would be crazy not to be careful.

Drawing a breath, she tried to rein in her panic as she moved across the hallway and paused at the bottom of the steps. No sound came to her now, but she had an unnerving premonition that someone was on the other side of the door listening for her approach.

Even a week ago, Olive wouldn't have hesitated to bound up the stairs and knock on the door or even to call out to Mona. But Jack's suspicions had rubbed off on her and she found herself conjuring an unwanted image. Mona's fingers sliding around Anna Grayson's neck, squeezing and squeezing until—

Olive's gaze remained fixed on the frosted glance panel as she moved up the steps. A shadow hovered on the other side of the door. Not her imagination. She put a hand on the latch, still unsure what to do when the door was yanked back and she found herself face to face with Mona Sutton. It was the first time Olive had seen Mona since Jack had sown those seeds of doubt and now Olive found herself jumping at the sudden confrontation, her hand flying to her heart in alarm.

The guidance counselor looked uncharacteristically disheveled with tendrils frizzing from her normally sleek bun and her signature ruby lipstick worn thin. She recovered so quickly Olive almost wondered if she had imagined the high color in the woman's cheeks and the feverish gleam in her eyes.

"Olive? What on earth…?"

"You startled me," she said on a breath. "I wasn't expecting to see you."

"Wasn't expecting to see me? This is my office last

time I checked." In one fluid motion, Mona smoothed back her hair as she planted herself in front of the door, blocking Olive's view inside the office. Again, those insidious seeds took root and Olive found herself trying to catch a glimpse over Mona's shoulder.

"I didn't think you were in today," Olive said lamely. "I heard a noise—voices, actually—and I half convinced myself that someone had broken into your office. I couldn't see a light and so I thought…" She gave an awkward laugh. "I know that sounds crazy."

Mona said in a stilted voice, "I was just doing some housekeeping. As for voices, I had a podcast on in the background." The plausible explanation flowed from her lips as she took in Olive's distressed demeanor. "You really do look shaken. Are you okay?"

"Too much caffeine and not enough sleep," Olive said with a shrug. "But now that I'm here, do you have a minute?"

"Of course." Mona pulled the door closed. "I was just on my way out. Do you mind if we walk and talk?"

"That's…fine."

They went down the steps together. The building was silent except for their footfalls, but Olive could have sworn someone remained in the office. She had to resist the urge to glance over her shoulder.

As if sensing her disquiet, Mona took her arm. "What's wrong? You still seem upset."

"I can't stop thinking about what happened to Jamie Butaud."

Mona sighed. "Nor can I. The whole town is on edge. It's all anyone can talk about."

"Can you blame them?" Olive cast an uneasy glance

down the hallway. "Another murder, another killer out there roaming free." Or inside the school building.

Stop it!

Speculation was one thing, but now she was allowing her imagination to run amok. She and Mona Sutton had been friends and colleagues for years. Nothing had changed between them except for Jack King's innuendos.

But that noise in Mona's office. The male voice. Her flustered demeanor and reluctance to allow Olive a glimpse inside…

"It's very unsettling," Mona said.

"Very." Olive ran a hand up and down her chilled arm. "Speaking of unsettling—have you noticed how quiet the building is today? Where is everyone?"

"People are around. I bumped into Beth Driscoll earlier. She was downstairs in the science lab."

"How did she seem?" Olive asked carefully.

Mona's brows lifted. "That's an odd question. She seemed fine. On edge like the rest of us, but coping. Why would you be concerned about Beth?"

Because Jack planted the outrageous notion in my head that you had an affair with her husband when he was still a student, giving you both a motive for Anna's murder.

Olive cleared her throat. "I'm concerned about all the staff. As you said, everyone is on edge."

Mona lowered her voice as she leaned in. "Just between you and me, you've every right to be concerned about Beth Driscoll. It's hardly a secret that she was hoping to be appointed principal. Being passed over must have been a slap in the face. That kind of resentment doesn't go away overnight."

"I had no idea," Olive said, her stomach churning at the thought of conflict in the ranks even before school started.

"Oh, come on," Mona chided. "You must have heard all the grumbling when the announcement was made. Beth even threatened to tender her resignation."

"I knew there would be hard feelings, but I didn't realize the extent of the dissension. Maybe I didn't want to."

"I wouldn't have brought it up, but you asked about Beth." Mona gave her a brief smile. "Anyway, it's settled business. You're the new principal and it's time for everyone to accept your promotion and move on."

Olive thought that everyone had accepted her. The meeting on Tuesday had gone more smoothly than she could have hoped and when she and Beth had spoken at the dock, the science teacher had seemed eager to discuss the coming school year. Had her magnanimous congratulations disguised a simmering resentment? What else might Beth Driscoll be hiding?

"Olive?"

She jumped as her gaze and attention darted back to Mona.

"You really are jittery today, aren't you?"

She smoothed a hand down her pants leg. "Sorry."

Mona gave her a curious evaluation. "You said you haven't been sleeping well. What else is going on with you?"

Olive paused. "I keep thinking about our last conversation. What you said about Anna Grayson's penchant for secrets and your suspicion that she may have accessed your records."

"It was only a suspicion. I never had any real proof."

"For the sake of argument, let's say she did. Do you think it's possible she found something in your files that led to her death?"

"What do you mean?"

"A secret," Olive said. "One so dire that someone was willing to kill to keep it quiet."

Mona frowned. "You know I can't talk about the content of my files."

"Even if it could help bring a killer to justice?"

"Even then." A moment passed before she continued. "Aren't you forgetting something? A man was tried, convicted and is now serving life in prison for Anna Grayson's murder."

"What if they got the wrong man?"

Mona's tone turned mildly reproachful. "You think Wayne Foukes is innocent? Despite his criminal record? Despite his lack of an alibi? Despite Anna's ring being found in his possession?"

"Yes, despite all that. I've always had my doubts."

"Really? Because it seems to me those doubts only surfaced when Jack King came back to town."

"That's not true," Olive defended. "I do have a mind of my own, you know."

Mona's expression grew troubled. "A word to the wise?"

"Of course."

"Watch yourself, Olive. You've got a lot at stake and this year will be difficult enough without all these outside distractions. I know you have a tendency to jump into causes with both feet, but you need to be careful with Jack King. He's been gone from Pine Lake for a very long time. How much do any of us really know about him anymore?"

"How much do we really know about each other?" Olive countered.

That seemed to give Mona pause. She looked as if she wanted to argue, but then she acquiesced with a shrug. "You have a point. But I can't help worrying about his influence on you, especially considering his background. Do you know anything about his life in Houston? About the outfit he works for?"

Very little, Olive realized. "He's in private security."

"The Blackthorn Agency is more than a private security firm. It's a worldwide operation with a reputation that's questionable at best. The owner, Ezra Blackthorn, is rumored to be ex-CIA. His employees, including Jack, are former military and law enforcement officers with seemingly one thing in common—they're all basically misfits and malcontents."

Olive stared at her in shock. "How can you possibly know that?"

Another pause. "I saw Tommy Driscoll earlier. He seems to know quite a lot about the Blackthorn Agency."

"As if I would trust his word about anything," Olive said coolly. She couldn't resist turning to glance behind her. They were out of sight of Mona's office, but she wondered again about that male voice, angry and muted. About Mona's unkempt appearance. "Where did you see him?"

"He was here looking for Beth."

Olive searched her face for a telltale twitch or flinch. Nothing in Mona's deportment gave her away and yet Olive could have sworn she saw something dark swirling in the woman's eyes. "I thought you said Beth is downstairs working in the science lab."

"She was there earlier, but she must have skipped out

after I bumped into her. Tommy couldn't find her. She wasn't answering her phone and with everything that's happened, I guess he got worried. Anyway, we talked for a bit and Jack's name came up. Apparently, the sheriff's office has been looking into his background."

"Why?"

"*Why?* Because a young woman was murdered on the night of his return."

Olive was outraged. "But Jack didn't even know Jamie Butaud. And he's the one who discovered the body, for crying out loud."

"I'm sure the background check is just routine," Mona said with a placating smile.

But Olive was far from pacified. "What else did Tommy say? Tell me the truth. Is Jack a suspect? Is that the reason for your concern?"

Mona looked offended by the question. "Our friendship is the reason for my concern. And I don't need Tommy Driscoll or anyone else to tell me that Jack King is a dangerous man."

BETH DRISCOLL STOOD on the old lake bridge staring down into the water. Sunlight shimmered in her dark hair as a mild breeze billowed the skirt of her yellow dress. On first glance, her stance seemed casual, but as Jack closed the distance between them, he was struck by the intensity of her focus and the way her hands gripped the iron railing so tightly her knuckles had whitened. She seemed a million miles away, completely unaware of his presence. The day was already hot and humid, but he couldn't dispel a sudden chill as he moved up beside her.

"Beth?"

She turned slowly as if taking her time to come back from wherever her mind had wandered. "Jack?" She dropped her hands from the guardrail, tucking them into the pockets of her dress as she gave him a tentative smile. "What are you doing here?"

"I was about to ask you the same thing." He couldn't help but notice the dark circles beneath her eyes and the deep furrows in her brow—physical manifestations of a deeply distressed woman. "Are you okay?"

A veil dropped over her expression. "Yes, why?"

He shrugged. "You seemed pretty tense when I came up just now."

"Oh, I was just daydreaming. Don't tell anyone you saw me, okay? I'm playing hooky." Her tone was light, but something hard glinted in her eyes.

"Your secret is safe with me." The breeze stirred her perfume, a light, floral fragrance with a darker trace of musk. The dichotomy of the notes seemed symbolic of two disparate personalities, and Jack was struck once again by the notion of a night and day Beth Driscoll.

"I always liked coming to this bridge." She swept her gaze along the railing where the remnant of a crime scene tape fluttered in the breeze. "I know that must sound a little insensitive considering everything that's happened, but my memories of this place aren't all bad. We had some good times here, didn't we? All those parties. The midnight swims."

"We had some good times," he agreed.

She tucked back her hair as she gave him a curious appraisal. "So what brings you here this morning?"

He lowered his gaze to the deck as an image came back to him—Olive with glazed eyes and a blank expression kneeling on the floorboards, searching and searching along the planks.

"I thought I'd have a look around," he said. "Someone was on the bridge last night. I spotted a flashlight beam moving around in the dark. I think whoever was up here was looking for something."

Beth glanced at him in alarm. "Did you see who it was?"

"No, I never got a good look."

Was that relief that flashed in her eyes?

"What do you think they were looking for?" she asked worriedly.

"That's what I'm trying to figure out."

She put a hand on the guardrail as if steadying herself against the subtle sway of the truss. Did she know who had been here the night before? Or did she at least suspect?

Jack studied her features, taking note of those shadowed eyes and the wasted lines of her body beneath the thin cotton of her dress. As if all too aware of his scrutiny, she folded her arms and shivered. "Whatever they were looking for, do you think it had something to do with Jamie Butaud's murder?"

"I don't know," he said truthfully. "But it's been my experience that even with the best-laid plans, something always gets overlooked. Something always gets left behind."

She shook her head. "You really don't give up, do you?"

"To the contrary, some might say I have a habit of giving up too easily."

A frown flitted. "I find that hard to believe. You seem dedicated to a fault."

"To a fault, huh?" He rested his forearms on the guardrail as he gazed down into the water. The sun was hot on his back, but an indefinable chill still gripped him. Beth Driscoll had triggered an alarm, but Jack didn't yet know why. "If I were as committed as you seem to think, I wouldn't have left town the way I did. I would have stayed and fought to clear my name. I would have done everything in my power to make sure justice was served."

"You're too hard on yourself. No one can fault you for leaving Pine Lake. Some days I wonder why any of us stayed."

Jack straightened. "Why *did* you stay?"

"The obvious reason. I was in love. Or thought I was. Back then, Tommy Driscoll was my whole world."

"And now?"

She was silent for a long moment. "Let's just say, Jamie's death has brought back a lot of painful memories. For all of us, I suspect. And now here you are in Pine Lake and it's a little too easy to dwell on what might have been."

What caused that glint in her eyes? Jack wondered. What secrets lurked behind her reluctant smile? "You're young," he said. "Why dwell on what might have been when you have your whole life ahead of you? You can still leave Pine Lake. You can do whatever you want."

Her smile turned wan. "You make it sound so easy, but I'm not brave enough to start over. It's easier to accept what I have and pretend it's enough."

The fatalistic note might have stirred Jack's sympathy if not for that strange gleam in her eyes. He still couldn't dismiss the notion that there was more to Beth Driscoll than he'd ever considered. She seemed both deeper and darker than the girl he remembered from high school. He was starting to wonder if his devotion to Anna had blinded him to the complicated nature of those around him. Including Anna.

"Beth?"

She turned.

"I need to ask you something." He watched her carefully as she nodded. "Where were you the night Anna was murdered?"

She looked stunned. "What? *Jack*. You can't be serious."

"We all left the stadium together after the game. I took Anna home early because she said she didn't feel well. Tommy ended up at Nathan's house, but where were you? Why weren't the two of you together that night?"

She ran a finger along the railing. "We had a fight. I don't remember what it was about. Probably a girl. There were a lot of those fights." She glanced at him coyly. "There were a lot of those girls."

"And yet you stayed with him."

"He always came back to me."

"Did you ever fight about Anna?"

Her voice sharpened. "Why would we fight about Anna?"

"You knew about them, didn't you?"

She looked on the verge of denial. Emotions warred in her eyes before her lips thinned and she turned away with a sigh. "I didn't know, but I suspected."

"What aroused your suspicion?" Jack asked.

"I could always tell." Her eyes closed briefly. "With Anna, it was the little things. The way he looked at her. The way she wouldn't look at him."

"You didn't confront them?"

"No." She shrugged. "I guess I didn't want my worst fears confirmed. I thought Tommy was the love of my life and Anna was my best friend. My *best* friend. I confided in her about the pregnancy, about my decision to keep the baby, *everything*." Her hands clenched into fists at her sides. "I was angry with her. You've no idea. I felt betrayed. So helpless and *small*. I just wanted to curl up somewhere and die. I wanted her to die, too, but I didn't kill her. I swear it." She drew a shaky breath. "God, Jack. Say something. *Please*. Don't just stand there staring at me like that."

"I'm still trying to put it all together," he said slowly.

She ran fingers through her ruffled hair. "Put what together? I told you everything. But now you doubt me. I can see it in your eyes."

Jack took a moment before he answered. "Why did you try so hard to convince me of Anna's faithfulness when we spoke on the dock yesterday? Why didn't you just tell me the truth?"

She flung out her hands in supplication. "I didn't want to hurt you. What purpose would that truth serve after all these years? And maybe a part of me still wanted to deny it."

"You should have told me, Beth. This was information I needed a long time ago."

Her eyes flashed with subtle defiance. "Why? Because their betrayal gave me a motive for Anna's murder? It gave you one, too, Jack. Did you consider that?"

"Are you saying you kept silent to protect *me*?"

"Think about it for a minute. In all those months of persecution, the sheriff could never come up with a reason you'd wanted Anna dead. You had means and opportunity, but no motive."

"Your silence didn't just protect me, though, did it, Beth? Or you, for that matter. It kept hidden a link between Tommy and Anna."

She said nothing to that.

"Did he ever tell you where he was that night?" Jack pressed.

"You said yourself he was at Nathan's."

"According to Nathan, Tommy left at some point, supposedly to meet a woman, possibly a teacher. Did you suspect that relationship, too?"

She didn't rise to his bait. She remained cool and almost unnaturally calm. "I wouldn't put too much stock in what Nathan Bolt says. He and Tommy had a falling out years ago and Nathan has been vindictive ever since. Even before that really. Remember how obnoxious and competitive he was in school? Especially with you. He couldn't stand that you had it all—looks, brains, athleticism. He had to trade exclusively on his intellect, and his grades didn't always reflect how smart he claimed to be."

"Are you suggesting he killed Anna to get back at me?"

"You lost all those scholarships, didn't you? You became the town pariah. You think Nathan didn't secretly enjoy every minute of your misery? He wasn't a good person. Not then, not now. Anna couldn't stand him."

"She never told me she had a problem with Nathan."

Beth gave him a sidelong glance. "It seems she didn't tell you a lot of things."

Now it was Jack who refused to rise to the bait.

She smiled at his silence. "Isn't it funny the way

things turned out? You and Anna were the golden couple. Everyone thought you had this grand, fairy-tale romance. Yet Tommy and I are the ones who stayed together."

Was that something she really wanted to throw in his face? Jack wondered.

She cocked her head, giving him a long assessment. "Can I ask *you* something? What's going on between you and Olive Belmont?"

Another alarm sounded, but Jack merely shrugged. "What makes you think something is going on?"

"I'm not blind. I've seen you together and I'm still very adept at reading people. The way you looked at her—the way she looked at you. There was a lot of tension on that dock yesterday. I just can't help wondering why *her*, of all people?"

Of all people? The question grated and Jack frowned. "Do you have a problem with Olive?"

"A problem? No. I just never would have pegged her as your type."

He didn't at all like the direction of this conversation. He didn't trust Beth Driscoll and he braced himself for what she might be up to. "How would you know my type?"

"I know Olive. We've worked together for several years now and I've always found her to be more than a little eccentric."

"Is that a bad thing?"

"Not necessarily but when you put it together with her behavior in high school…" She shrugged. "Don't you remember the way she followed us around all the time? The way she *watched* us."

"She was just a shy kid," Jack said. "I don't remember her ever saying two words to any of us."

"She was only three years younger than we were. Old enough to have a serious crush on you, Jack. It couldn't have been more obvious."

"Why are you telling me this?"

She lifted a thin shoulder as she turned back to the water. "I don't know. I guess I thought you'd want to know. Maybe I thought you needed to know."

Her pensive profile brought back a memory—not of Olive—but of Beth standing at that very rail in a shooter's stance firing at a row of tin cans that Tommy had lined up on a log. Then another image danced into focus, the X-shaped exit wound in Jamie Butaud's forehead.

As if sensing the direction of his thoughts, Beth said abruptly, "I should be getting back before Tommy sends out a search party." She placed a hand on Jack's arm. His first extinct was to shrink away from her touch. "You take care while you're in town, Jack. This is not a good place."

Was that a subtle warning he heard in her voice?

He watched her walk away, hands at her sides, head slightly bowed. When she got to the end of the bridge, she paused and glanced over her shoulder. She held his gaze for the longest moment and then she was gone, swallowed up by the deep shadows cast by the piney woods.

But a chill lingered and an omen niggled as Jack pondered the mystery of Beth Driscoll.

Chapter Eleven

"I had a disturbing encounter this morning," Olive said as she and Jack stood on the dock enjoying a late afternoon drink.

"I had a pretty strange morning myself," he said.

"Oh?"

"You go first."

Olive nodded, but her mind had already started to wander. She'd never considered herself the flighty type—if anything, she was usually a little too rigid and structured—but Jack's proximity threw her. She couldn't organize her thoughts. She couldn't concentrate on anything but the ruffle of his hair in the breeze and the sexy scruff that shadowed his jaw and chin.

Olive had gone straight home after work to shower and change, and her plan had been to settle in with her latest budget projections. But she'd soon grown restless and had gone out for a short stroll. A call from Jack had brought her all the way down to the lake. With every step she took, she'd told herself to turn back, to take this thing between them no farther. But here she was. Here *he* was.

They were both dressed casually for a relaxed evening on the water, but Olive was far from calm and collected. She was too acutely aware of the man beside her, too intensely aware of their last conversation.

She sipped her drink as she gave him a stealthy perusal. He had on sunglasses, which hid his expression so she fixated instead on his mouth. The tiny crease in the center of his bottom lip fascinated her. She studied the anomaly for a moment before trailing her gaze along his jawline, across his shoulders and all the way down his tanned arms to his hands, one of which was wrapped tightly with gauze and tape. The stark evidence of his memory loss gave her only a moment's hesitation as she imagined those long fingers slipping down the small of her back, easing over her hips, gliding along the inside of her thighs…

Drawing a quick breath, she forced her attention back to the lake. The shadows cast by the pine forest crept slowly across the water, but the dock was still bathed in sunlight. Olive lifted her ponytail, allowing the breeze to cool the back of her neck as she watched a heron step daintily into the shallow water.

"Are you going to finish that story?" Jack prompted. "You had a disturbing encounter…?"

"Oh, right. I was working in my office on the second floor. The building was very quiet. My assistant had gone out for lunch and I had the whole place to myself. I don't know if you've ever been in an old school building alone, but it has a strange vibe. More so at night, but even in broad daylight, it can be unsettling with all those odd sounds and old memories that seem to echo through the hallways." She hesitated. "Does that sound crazy?"

"No, I'm with you. Odd sounds, old memories…"

"Yes, well, it started to get to me. A feeling came

over me that I was being watched. The sensation was so strong, in fact, that I left my office to investigate."

Jack's voice sharpened. "Why didn't you call me?"

"Because I hoped it was just my imagination. But I've been experiencing that same sensation for a few days now. I chalked it up to being nervous about my new job and the coming school year. I tend to be a worrywart and I'm sometimes prone to panic."

"You were steady as a rock behind the wheel of the boat," he commented.

She smiled. "On the surface, maybe. Anyway, everything seemed fine at first. Then I heard a noise coming from Mona Sutton's office. The sound was metallic, like someone banging into a desk or closing a file drawer. And I heard voices, one of them male. They were arguing."

"Did you recognize the voices?"

"No, and by that time, my imagination really had gotten the better of me. I became convinced that someone had broken into Mona's office to search through her files. Maybe even to destroy evidence."

"Of what?"

Olive gave him a wide-eyed stare. "Murder, of course."

He lifted a brow. "So you thought it a good idea to check things out on your own?"

"Well...yes. When I got to the top of the stairs, the door burst open and there was Mona, looking all flushed and disheveled. I don't know how well you remember her, but Mona Sutton never looks anything other than perfect. And the way she so abruptly threw open the door made me wonder if she'd heard my footsteps on the stairs and wanted to head me off. She even stepped in front of the doorway to make certain I couldn't see into her office. I kept picturing Tommy Driscoll inside, the two of them *in flagrante delicto*. You put that image in my head," she accused. "You've made me very suspicious."

"You say that like it's a bad thing."

"It is," she insisted. "It's one thing to be cautious, but I hate thinking the worst of my friends and colleagues. I saw it coming, though. That morning in front of the coffee shop…the way you said *these people*… I knew things would get ugly once you started asking questions. Suspicions would flare. People would start to doubt one another. It's already started. I experienced it firsthand this morning with Mona. She tried very hard to convince me that you're a dangerous man, Jack."

His lowered voice raised goose bumps along her arms. "What do you think?"

Olive's heart thudded as she gazed into those dark glasses. She couldn't see his expression, but she could feel the intensity of his stare. It made her feel anxious and excited and wary. She gripped the railing. "I think we need to be careful we don't let anyone turn us against each other."

"Agreed."

"We're in this together, right? That's what you said."

"We're in this together."

"Jack?"

"Yes?"

"Are you dangerous?"

"When I need to be."

Olive swallowed. She knew only too well there could be many kinds of danger.

Jack reached up and removed his sunglasses, folding them and then tucking them into his pocket. All the while, his gaze never left hers. His eyes were as deep and dark as the lake and just as mysterious, just as perilous. Olive could feel the tentacles of their attraction weaving a sensuous trail along her spine, heating her blood and prickling her nerve endings. All she had to do was reach over and put her hand on top of his and the conversation would be over. They would go back up the steps to the cabin, disappear into the shadowy cocoon of his bedroom and live out the fantasy that had been teasing her ever since he'd rescued her from the top of the bridge.

Her fingers tightened around the railing so that she wouldn't be tempted to touch him.

"It's good to be cautious." His words seemed to have a double meaning and Olive shivered. "With Mona Sutton, with Beth Driscoll, with everyone in this town."

"Beth Driscoll?" Olive stared at him in surprise. "What does she have to do with anything?"

"I saw her on bridge this morning. I went back to have a look around and she was at the guardrail staring down into the water. She seemed distracted. So much so that she didn't even notice my arrival. I get the distinct feeling she's a very unhappy woman."

Olive's tone turned derisive. "She's married to Tommy Driscoll. Of course, she's unhappy."

"Have you ever had any problems with Beth?"

The question stopped Olive cold. "How strange that you would ask me that now. A day ago I would have said no. We've always gotten on well. But Mona told me this morning that Beth was very upset by my appointment. She even threatened to resign. I knew there would be hard feelings, but I had no idea anyone wanted to quit, least of all Beth."

"Maybe that explains the tension I sensed when your name came up," Jack said.

"What did she say?" Olive demanded. "What did *you* say?"

The corners of his mouth twitched. "She said you had a crush on me back in the day."

Had everyone in town known about her feelings for Jack? "She actually said that?"

His eyes gleamed. "Not true?"

"Yes, it's true," Olive admitted with a shrug. "But it was just a silly schoolgirl infatuation. It didn't mean anything."

"I never thought it did."

"I was lonely and heartbroken when we first moved to Pine Lake. I'd just lost my dad. I didn't have friends or anyone I could talk to. And I felt so horribly guilty. I'm the one who begged him to drive home that night in the middle of a terrible storm. For a long time, I blamed myself for the accident. And even though my mother would never admit it, I think she did, too. It was a very bad time and you were nice to me."

"I'm glad."

Her voice turned ironic. "I know how pathetic that must sound considering you barely remembered me that first night at the bridge. But your kindness meant a lot to me. It gave me something to focus on instead of my misery. So, yes, I had a crush on you for a while, but it didn't mean anything."

"So you said."

Olive lifted her gaze to his. "How I felt then has nothing to do with the way I feel about you now."

Jack straightened from the rail, placing his bandaged hand on her shoulder. "How do you feel about me now?"

She stood on tiptoes, taking his face in her hands as she drew his mouth to hers. It was a slow, lingering kiss. Languid and easy with the breeze rippling through her hair and the sun still warm on her skin. She slipped her hands to the back of his neck as his arms came around her waist. Their tongues touched and mingled as he pulled her into him.

The dock swayed beneath them and Olive drew away, shaking her head as if to clear her senses. "Jack?"

"Yes?"

"Let's go up the cabin."

His gaze deepened with awareness. "Are you sure?"

"Unless you'd rather do it here on the dock."

"The cabin will be good."

THE LATE AFTERNOON sunlight shone through the long windows in the living room, but the bedroom was cool and shadowy. They were both barefoot and shirtless, having left a trail of discarded clothing down the hallway. Jack pressed Olive against the wall, cupping her breasts through the lace of her bra as he kissed her again and again. She arched into him, wrapping her arms around his neck and running her fingers through the hair at his nape. His lips skimmed downward, tracing her jawline, tickling her lobe, finding the pulse point in her throat. Shivering, she fumbled with the button on his jeans and then the zipper and they laughed softly at her struggles.

"I can't seem to make my fingers work."

"They're working for me," he murmured and Olive's laugh grew breathless and throaty. There was no awkwardness between then, not even a momentary reluctance as they finished undressing.

He lifted her and she wrapped her legs around him, tunneling her fingers through his hair with a deep sigh. They fell back against the bed, Olive on top and they laughed some more as a feather floated up from the pillows and clung to her lashes. Jack tenderly plucked it away and then their expressions sobered as their gazes collided.

He rolled them, so smoothly Olive was barely aware of the motion until he was suddenly staring down at her, smiling and knowing. Her heart pounded, her every nerve ending tingled as he lowered his mouth to her breasts and then trailed his lips down her abdomen, lower and lower until she felt his tongue skim along her inner thigh.

He lingered there, kissing and teasing, until he felt her tremble and then he moved up and over her and she cupped his face, drawing his mouth to hers as she rolled him, not as smoothly, but just as eagerly. She slid down his body, her lips whispering over his abdomen, her hands stroking, her tongue exploring.

The sun had set by this time and the room had grown dim. Jack was little more than a silhouette as Olive moved back up, positioning herself over him, taking him in with a gasp. She smiled down at him as she began to move, and then losing control all too soon, she fell forward, hands splayed against the headboard as Jack grasped her hips. The sensations intensified as their soft moans mingled. He pulled her to him, wrapping his arms around her, holding her close as they both began to shudder.

He didn't release her when it was over. If anything,

his hold on her tightened. Olive buried her head in his shoulder, drinking in the scent of him, luxuriating in the intimate bond that still kept them joined.

"Jack?"

He stirred. "Yes?"

"Don't let go, okay?"

"Not a chance."

DARKNESS HAD FALLEN by the time Jack drove Olive home. He parked in her driveway and cut the lights, but kept the engine and air conditioner running as he took a quick survey of their surroundings. It was still early, just after ten, but the neighborhood already slumbered. Curtains were drawn, blinds were closed and there wasn't another car on the street. The town seemed deserted and haunted.

Olive, face scrubbed clean of makeup, hair still slightly mussed, sat watching him. In the glow of the streetlight, her freckles stood out starkly on her pale skin. Jack had never seen anything so sensuous. He wanted to trail his knuckles along her cheek, to trace her slightly parted lips with his thumb. He could still feel her against him, warm and pliant and quivering.

He draped his arm along the back of her seat, teasing the hair until he felt her shiver.

"Sure you don't want to change your mind?" he said. "You could stay with me at the lake tonight."

"You've no idea how tempted I am. But I've still got work to do and I think a little distance and perspective might be good for both of us."

"You're probably right." But his fingers continued to tease.

She sighed. "Which is why I'm not going to invite you in for a drink."

"That's a shame."

"But in case you couldn't tell, I had a really good time tonight." Her expression suddenly sobered. "Jack?"

"Yes?"

"Can I ask you a question?"

"Ask away."

"Why did you really leave the police department? You don't have to answer if you don't want to. Your past is none of my business and I know I shouldn't pry. It's just... I'd like to get to know you better. Is that wrong?"

His fingers stilled in her hair. "It's not wrong, but the answer may shock you."

Her eyes widened. "Now you have to tell me."

"I shot and killed my partner," he said with stark brevity.

She was silent for a moment. He could tell she was trying very hard to keep her expression neutral. "What happened?"

He dropped his hand to the seat. "I don't talk about it much. I can't even remember the last time the subject came up. I've always thought some things are best left in the past."

"That's an odd sentiment coming from you," she said.

He smiled. "It's a little inconsistent, I guess."

"A little inconsistent? Says the man who came back to his hometown to solve a fifteen-year-old murder."

"Long story short, we were working undercover and he set me up."

"He was dirty?"

"For years, as it turned out. The worst part was that

I never saw it coming. He operated right under my nose and I didn't have a clue." He trailed his fingertip along the steering wheel. "His behavior was hard for me to reconcile. We weren't just partners, we were friends. We went through the academy together. He was the best man at my wedding and I'm godfather to one of his kids. But it came down to him or me and so I took the shot."

"No wonder you don't trust anyone," Olive said. "Were you charged?"

"No. I was exonerated and cleared for active duty, but everything changed after the shooting. I didn't feel the same way about the department so I left."

"I get it," she said softly. "You must have wondered who else might betray you. So how did you end up in private security?"

"An acquaintance introduced me to a man named Ezra Blackthorn. He offered me a job at the Blackthorn Agency and I've been there ever since."

"Is he really ex-CIA? This Ezra Blackthorn?"

Jack turned in surprise. "Where did you hear that?"

"From Mona by way of Tommy Driscoll. She said the Caddo County Sheriff's Office has been looking into your background. Jack…" Olive placed her hand on his arm. "She didn't come right out and say it, but I got the impression that Tommy considers you a suspect."

"For what?"

"Jamie Butaud's murder."

"That's absurd," he said. "I never even met the woman."

"I know that, but if Tommy's looking for a scapegoat, your arrival in Pine Lake couldn't have been timelier."

"A scapegoat? You think he had something to do with Jamie's murder?"

Olive paused. "I never said that. I only meant he's under pressure to make an arrest just like Sheriff Brannigan was fifteen years ago. But that's not what you meant, is it?"

"Nathan thinks Tommy may have been romantically involved with Jamie going all the way back to her first arrest."

"But she was just a kid back then," Olive said. "She couldn't have been more than sixteen."

"Which would give him a powerful motive if she threatened to expose him."

Olive grew pensive. "Does Nathan have any proof of this relationship?"

"He claims he never saw them together, but Jamie supposedly has a tattoo on her shoulder that was once considered Tommy Driscoll's mark. According to Nathan, a lot of girls who had been with Tommy in high school had that tattoo—a heart with a lightning bolt through the center. I didn't say anything to Nathan, but Anna came back from a weekend trip with a similar tattoo on her hip."

Olive gasped. "You're saying that Anna and Tommy Driscoll—"

"It's possible. I don't know for certain."

She sat back against the seat. "This changes everything. If Tommy was involved with Anna, then he could have had a motive for her murder, too."

"So could I, for that matter."

"But you're innocent," she said without pause. "We don't know about Tommy. I've never liked him so I may be biased. Do you think he's capable of cold-blooded murder?"

"I wouldn't rule it out because he wears a badge."

"No, I guess you wouldn't."

"Look," Jack said. "This isn't your fight. You should go inside, lock your door and forget we had this conversation."

Olive dismissed the suggestion with a careless wave of her hand. "Don't worry about me. I know what I'm doing, too. Eyes wide open, remember?"

"Olive—"

She folded her arms. "We're in this together. That's what you said."

He sighed. "I don't want you to get hurt."

"I don't want you to get hurt, either… Jack?"

"Yes?"

"I don't care what Nathan said about tattoos and marks and Tommy Driscoll's conquests. Anna really loved you. I know she did."

He reached out and tucked back a strand of her hair. "That was all a long time ago. You don't need to worry about my feelings."

"I know."

"But I like that you do." He leaned across the console, brushing his lips against hers and then deepening the kiss the moment he felt her respond.

"It's getting late," she said when they finally broke apart. "I should go in."

"I'll walk you to the door."

"You don't have to. I set the security system before I left."

"I'd feel better if I have a look around before I go."

"Jack?"

"Yes?"

"You can come in for a nightcap if you want."

Chapter Twelve

Jack had only been gone a few minutes when a soft knock sounded on Olive's door. She was still up working on the reports she'd neglected earlier. Wondering if he'd forgotten something, she hurried to answer, taking a glance through the peephole before disarming the alarm and opening the door to her cousin.

"What are you doing here so late?" she asked in surprise.

"I'm sorry for dropping in like this," Nathan said. "I thought about calling but I didn't want to disturb you in case you'd already gone to bed. So I drove by, saw your lights on and decided to take a chance you were still up." He glanced past her into the foyer. "You alone? Can we talk for a minute?"

"Sure, come on in." She stood back so that he could enter. "What's this about?"

He shoved his hands in his pockets as if unsure where to start. "Is that fresh coffee I smell? At this hour?"

"I'm working and it's going to be a long night. You want some?"

"I was about to suggest something stronger, but coffee will do."

He followed her into the kitchen and she motioned

him to the table as she got down another mug from the cupboard. "You want something to eat?" She poured his coffee and topped off her own, then turned back to the counter. "I've got cheese and crackers, some fruit."

"I'm fine."

She went back over to the table and sat down across from him. He took a drink of the coffee and grimaced. "Bitter."

"Is it? I hadn't noticed." Olive took a tentative taste. "I guess it is a little. But you didn't come over here to critique my coffee, did you?"

"Have you talked to Jack tonight? I was hoping I'd find him here."

"He left a little while ago. Why are you looking for him?" She sipped her coffee as she studied her cousin's demeanor. "What's going on, Nathan? You seem agitated."

"I don't mean to worry you, but I'm a little concerned about his whereabouts."

"Why?" she asked in alarm.

Nathan took off his glasses and wiped the lenses. His eyes looked bleary and unfocused until he put them back on. "Has he said anything to you about his blackout? Has he remembered anything about those missing hours?"

"Not that I know of. Nathan..."

"I'm getting to the point, I promise. He said the last thing he remembered was following Marc Waller's truck down Commerce. Then he remembered nothing else until the next day when I found him unconscious in the cabin with bumps and bruises that he couldn't explain."

"Yes, I know," Olive said impatiently. "I was there, remember?"

He lowered his voice. "I have contacts all over town. You know that, too, right? Nothing happens in Pine Lake that I don't hear about."

"Nathan, please—"

"Marc Waller was found murdered in the old Masonic Lodge on Commerce."

She gasped. "When?"

"The body was found earlier tonight, but he'd been dead for at least a day or two. Someone beat him up and then shot him in the back of the head."

Olive's heart thudded so hard she felt light-headed. "You're not suggesting Jack had anything to do with Marc's murder, are you?"

Nathan hesitated. "I don't know what to think. Especially in light of what the police found at the crime scene."

"What are you talking about?"

"Jack's fingerprints were all over that place."

IT WAS LATE by the time Jack got back to the cabin. His hair was still damp from Olive's shower as he climbed out of the car and took the porch steps two at a time. Then he paused at the top, attracted by a light reflected in one of the front windows. He thought at first the glow emanated from somewhere in the woods, but then he turned and realized the flash of red and blue came from a light bar atop the police car easing down the road.

The cruiser pulled into his driveway and parked. When the door opened and the red dome light came on, he recognized Tommy Driscoll.

Jack could hear the intermittent static of the radio

as the Caddo County sheriff communicated with his dispatcher. Then he climbed out of the car, closed the door and stood with one hand on the hilt of his gun as he surveyed his surroundings.

His gaze lit on the porch and he drew his weapon. "Who's up there?"

"It's me." Jack moved out of the shadows to the edge of the porch. "What brings you out to the lake at this hour?" He nodded toward the gun. "I gather this isn't a social call."

"We've serious business to discuss, Jack. Come down the steps slowly and keep your hands where I can see them."

Déjà vu niggled as he descended the steps. "What's going on?"

"You armed, Jack?"

He felt the cold metal of his weapon at his back. "Yeah."

"Put it on the ground and kick it over here."

Jack did as he was told.

Tommy picked up the gun and tucked it into his waistband. "I need you to come down to the station and answer a few questions."

"About?"

"Marc Waller was found murdered earlier this evening. Someone worked him over good and then put a bullet in the back of his head. Could be a drug deal gone wrong, could be something else. He got crossways with the wrong guy, that's for damn sure."

Jack drew a steadying breath and reminded himself to remain calm. He wasn't seventeen anymore. He could handle Tommy Driscoll. "What's that got to do with me?"

"We found your fingerprints at the crime scene."

An image flashed behind Jack's eyes. He didn't remember meeting Marc Waller and yet he somehow knew what the man looked like. Tall and lanky with scraggly brown hair and a bad disposition. Jack's scraped knuckles tingled a warning as memories started to nudge him.

"You think I killed him?"

"I just need you to answer a few questions."

"If I refuse?"

Any hint of the old Tommy was obscured by the grim set of his mouth and the steely gleam in his eyes. "You don't want to do that, Jack. I could shoot you where you stand and no one would fault me. A lot of people in this town still think you killed Anna."

"Is that so?"

"You know it is. That's why you came back, isn't it? To clear your name? Instead, you've ended up in a real jam. You've already lied to me once. You and Olive both. If you refuse to cooperate, I'll have no choice but to drag her down to the station and I promise you things won't end well for her. What do you think the school board would do if they found out their new principal gave a false statement to the police in a murder investigation? She'll be canned within a week and I doubt another school district will touch her. That what you want, Jack? You want to take Olive Belmont down with you?"

Jack's hands flexed at his sides. He took another deep breath. "I'll cooperate."

"Glad to hear it. Now turn around and put your hands behind your back."

"Am I under arrest?"

"No, but I don't trust you not to try something stupid."

Jack turned and held out his arms, wincing when he heard the snap of the locks.

"You never should have come back here," Tommy said, a split second before pain exploded at the base of Jack's skull. He staggered forward, trying to stay on his feet, but the blow felled him. He crashed to the ground as shadows swirled all around him.

"I'm SORRY TO spring this on you, but I have to find Jack," Nathan said as he finished his coffee. "I wouldn't be surprised if Tommy Driscoll is already tracking him down and I need to make sure things don't get out of hand."

"Out of hand?" Olive felt sick and dazed and she couldn't seem to focus. "Jack was here earlier…"

"So you said."

"I don't—" She tried to rise and then dropped back down to her seat as a wave of dizziness washed over her.

Nathan rose and knelt in front of her. "What's wrong? You don't look so good."

"I feel light-headed. The room is spinning…" She put a hand on the table to steady her balance and knocked over her cup. She stared at the spilled coffee and then slowly brought her gaze back to Nathan. "What did you…"

"I'm sorry it had to come to this, Olive. Truly I am. You're the only person in this town I ever cared about. I tried to protect you, but once you found Anna's necklace you became another loose end."

"How did…?"

"I saw you last night. I saw you every other night that you went to the bridge, too. I've been watching you, Olive. Following you for weeks. I couldn't put my finger on it exactly, but little things you said…the way you looked at me at times… I had a bad feeling you were starting to remember."

Olive tried to swallow past the bile in her throat, tried to form a coherent thought. She could barely focus, could barely utter a sound. But inside she was screaming. *Someone* was screaming…

On some level, Olive knew she was dreaming. The screams weren't real and yet she found herself reluctantly moving toward the sound, controlled by that strange mix of urgency and inertia that only a nightmare could produce. The bridge loomed over her. She could see the truss silhouetted against the night sky, a monstrous manifestation of all her deepest fears and her darkest guilt. She didn't want to go there. She didn't want to follow those screams. Something bad was happening on that bridge. Something she didn't want to see.

Wake up, Olive! Wake up now!

But the lethargy of sleep lured her back under even as those screams pulled her toward consciousness. She floated in and out of her dream, watching figures, hearing voices…

Let her go! We can't do this, Nathan!

What do you think will happen if I let her go? She'll go straight to the cops, you idiot. Your football career will be over and no decent school will let me in. Our lives will be ruined. Don't you get that?

You said it was just a prank. A way to teach her a lesson. That's what you said. If we scared her enough, she'd leave us alone. That's what you said!

She knows all about you and that Sutton bitch. She

talks and your girlfriend goes straight to prison. That'll be on you, Tommy. Is that what you want?

Don't pretend this is about me. You're the one who planned this whole thing. You're the one who'd be in big trouble if the school ever found out you hacked into their system and changed your grades. Your old man is just looking for an excuse to disown you. Everyone in this town knows you'd be nothing but a loser without his name and money.

And you're nothing but a sniveling coward. You don't have the brains or the balls to do anything on your own. I'm the one who has to think of everything. Where do you think you're going?

Home. I've had enough of this—

Get back here! You're not going anywhere. You think you can just walk away from this? We're in this together whether you like it or not. You're the one who called Anna, remember? You're the one who convinced her that Beth was in trouble. You lured her out of her house and into your car under false pretenses. That's kidnapping, Tommy. And now you're an accomplice to murder.

She's not dead yet.

Then shut your stupid mouth and help me end this. She's coming around.

I'm not committing murder. Not for you, not for anyone. I swear to God, if I have to—

What? What will you do? Kill me, too? This isn't even about Anna, is it? You did all this just so you could get back at Jack King...

The voices faded, replaced by an echo within Olive's dream. Please help me, please help me, please help me.

A part of her wanted to wake up from the nightmare even as she felt compelled to sink deeper into oblivion.

Where she floated now was dark and silent, but she knew she wasn't alone. She could still see those distant silhouettes. Every now and then she heard a grunt of exertion. And then the voices came back, one hushed with fear, the other quivering with excitement.

Is she...?

Yeah. You should have seen the way her eyes bulged—

Stop it! I'm gonna be sick.

I'd hold it if I were you. You don't want your DNA spewed all over this bridge.

I need to get out of here, Nathan. Please. It's done. Can't we just go home now?

Help me get her clothes off first.

What?

Relax, I'm not a perv. We need to make it look like a sexual assault. She was with Jack earlier. They did it in his car.

How do you know that?

Because I saw them, dummy. If we get lucky, maybe there'll be some of his DNA left when the cops find the body.

Jesus, Nathan.

What? The boyfriend is always the number one suspect. Especially if they find her broken necklace in his vehicle. It'll look like they struggled.

You hate him that much?

Let's just say, wiping that smug look off his face will be almost as much fun as—

Stop talking. Please. Let's just get this over with.

THE MEMORY FLEETED as Nathan knelt in front of Olive to check the dilation of her pupils. She wanted to shove him away, but she couldn't lift her hands from the chair seat. "Almost there," he murmured.

He rose and grabbed some paper towels from the counter to clean up the spilled coffee. Olive tried to scream, but her tongue felt thick and heavy and she couldn't open her lips. She clutched the edge of her chair as the room spun faster and faster. Her mind clouded, but she used every ounce of her strength to keep the shadows at bay. The moment she succumbed, it would be over. The way it had been for poor Anna.

THE VOICES HAD gone silent again as Olive stepped onto the bridge. She could feel the night wind on her face, could hear the distant hoot of an owl. Consciousness was within arm's reach, but something—someone— kept pulling her back under.

Hang on, Olive. Just a little while longer. Sleep is your friend right now.

Daddy?

Shush. Sleep...

One of the silhouettes came toward her. Something dangled from his fingers. A necklace or a charm. The sparkle of the gold mesmerized her, but when he spotted her in the shadows, the chain slipped from his fingers and disappeared through a crack in the floorboards. He barely seemed to notice. He came to her slowly, calling her name.

That you, Olive? What are you doing out here? Answer me!

Shush. Sleep...

He waved a hand in front of her face. Olive? You awake? Olive!

Sleep...sleep...

OLIVE FOUGHT OFF the shadows even as lethargy lulled her. She wanted nothing so much as to close her eyes and let the darkness take her, but she could hear a voice in her head—Jack's voice now—urging her to fight. *Don't let go, Olive. Don't ever let go.*

Nathan stood over her with mounting impatience.

"Give it up, Olive. Just close your eyes and go to sleep."

She blinked rapidly to let him know she was still cognizant and defiant.

He sighed. "I should have ended it when I saw you on the bridge that night. I should never have taken a chance that you would one day remember, but I was still on such a high after Anna. I felt invincible. Like nothing could touch me. And I liked you, Olive. I liked having you around. The old man was almost decent to me with you in the house. So I took you back home, put you to bed and in all this time, your memories have stayed buried. Maybe they would never have surfaced if I'd left you well enough alone.

"But I got restless. Father was content to be a big fish in a small pond, but not me. I want more. You can understand that, can't you? I don't want to forever be known as *his* son. I want to make my own mark. Achieve what he never had the guts to do. But Tommy was always going to be a problem. So long as we were both in Pine Lake, I could keep him in line, but the higher I climbed, the lower he sank. He would always be there with his threats and bribes, needing me to clean up his messes. So I started making plans, figuring out the best way to eliminate the problem without incriminating myself. And one day, the solution fell right into my lap."

Nathan finished mopping up the coffee and threw away the paper towels.

"I had lunch with Jack's old attorney about another case. Jack's name came up. Imagine my surprise when he told me that they still kept in touch and that neither of them had ever believed Wayne Foukes was guilty. He said Jack would never rest until the truth came out. Right then and there, I decided that Jack King would have to come back to Pine Lake and kill Tommy Driscoll."

JACK FOUGHT HIS way up out of the darkness. He could hear voices nearby, but the pounding in his head muted the sound. He knew at once where he was. The floorboards swayed beneath him as the truss creaked and rattled above him. His right wrist had been handcuffed to the guardrail of the old Pine Lake Bridge.

A few feet away, someone lay motionless near the edge. It took Jack a moment to put it together—the slight body, the copper-colored hair.

"Olive!" He whispered her name. "Olive, can you hear me?"

She didn't answer.

"Olive!"

He yanked at the cuffs and then forced himself to remain still as he concentrated on the voices.

"I did as you wanted," Tommy Driscoll said angrily. "I got him out here, didn't I? The rest is up to you. I don't want any part of it."

"Tommy, Tommy." Nathan's voice was deceptively soft, dangerously persuasive. "How many times do I have to remind you that we're in this together? Just like old times. It's in both our best interests that Jack not be allowed to leave Pine Lake alive."

"Jack is one thing. What about Olive?"

"She's become too much of a liability, I'm afraid."

"For God's sake, Nathan, you can't keep killing people. First Jamie and then Marc Waller. And now *this*. Even I can't whitewash four bodies."

"You can do anything you want. That's why I helped get you elected. Despite our clashes and your back-stabbing, we've both benefitted from our arrangement. We've each turned a blind eye when we needed to. All that would have ended if Jamie had made your affair public. You should be thanking me for cleaning up another of your messes."

"Thanking you? For murdering someone I cared about?"

"You'll get over it. And as for Marc Waller, what were you thinking, paying him to terrorize Olive? You thought you could manipulate me by threatening my cousin, but when has that ever worked out for you, Tommy? All you accomplished was to open yourself up to blackmail. And once again I had to clean up after you. Marc Waller's blood is on your hands, too, so get off your high horse and let's end this once and for all."

"What do you want me to do?"

"You brought Jack's gun?"

A moment of silence while Jack imagined his weapon changing hands.

"I still say you should have left well enough alone," Tommy said sullenly. "Everything was fine until you brought him back here."

"Everything was *not* fine. He was never going to rest until he solved Anna's murder."

"You say that, but he hadn't been back in fifteen years."

"He would have come back eventually. Wouldn't you, Jack?" Nathan turned to peer at Jack through the darkness. "It was always going to come to this."

Jack didn't answer.

"Look at it this way." He came over and hunkered on the bridge just out of Jack's reach. "Now you get to go out the hero."

Jack slowly lifted his head. "There's only one way that can happen."

Nathan grinned. "You've figured it out, haven't you?"

"It's your plan so not exactly rocket science."

The smile vanished as Nathan stood, aiming the gun at Jack's head. "You're the one who's going to expose Anna's killer after all these years. Like I said, you'll get to be the hero. Unfortunately, a dead hero, but your name will finally be cleared. That must give you some satisfaction."

"What the hell are you talking about?" Tommy stalked into Jack's periphery.

"You need to have a little talk with your partner. Nathan's gone to a lot of trouble to set you up, Tommy."

"Set *me* up? You're the one handcuffed to the bridge."

"No, he's right." Nathan turned. "You're just too dumb to figure it out. First you killed Anna and now you've gone and killed Jamie Butaud and Marc Waller."

Tommy tried to draw his weapon, but Nathan was quicker. He spun and fired two rounds straight at Tommy's heart. He dropped with barely a sound.

Jack shifted so that he could keep Olive in his line of

sight. She didn't make a sound, hadn't moved a muscle. Either she was out cold or—

Nathan said with chilling aplomb, "You'll notice that I shot him with your gun, Jack. You found out he killed Anna and confronted him. He drew his weapon and it was either him or you. Just like with your old partner. Photographs of Jamie will be found in his possession, along with Anna's necklace. Thank you for finding that, by the way."

"You haven't missed a trick, have you?"

"I've always been a lot smarter than you, Jack. This just proves it. You want to know the real beauty of my plan? Nothing will touch me. I checked into a Dallas hotel this morning. I had lunch with old friends and pre-dinner drinks with a colleague before attending a fundraiser. Now I'm fast asleep in my room where the police will likely awaken me in the morning to tell me about poor Olive."

He moved away from Jack. His focus now was on retrieving Tommy's weapon. He turned his back on Olive and her hand shot out to snake around his ankle. He lost his balance and crashed to the floor but not before he'd kicked Olive aside. She rolled beneath the guardrail, clutching the floorboards with a gasp.

Jack's left hand shot out helplessly. "Hang on. Hang on. Hang on," he said under his breath as Olive clung to the edge of the bridge.

Nathan was picking himself up, reaching for the gun…

As Jack tore at his restraint, a movement to his right caught his eye. Something glinted in Tommy Driscoll's outstretched hand…the handcuff key…

Jack strained toward the key even as his wrist

screamed in protest. He had the key between his fingers. *Don't drop it, don't drop it, don't drop it...*

He was free, lunging for Olive with one hand as he grabbed Tommy's weapon with the other. "I've got you," he said as he turned and fired.

Chapter Thirteen

The next two days passed in a blur of police interrogations. Olive barely saw Jack. When the dust finally settled, she drove out to the cabin late one afternoon and they had drinks on the dock as they watched the sunset.

The last thing she wanted to do was rehash what had happened. What more could be said? Nathan and Tommy had killed Anna and then given each other an alibi. The secret had eventually destroyed their friendship even as it had kept them dependent on one another until Nathan had decided to break free.

A breeze picked up as twilight moved in from the pinewoods. Out on the lake, a loon trilled a warning. Olive shivered as she searched Jack's profile.

"I was allowed to see Nathan today," she told him.

He turned. "How did that go?"

"As you might expect. He shows no remorse. Quite the opposite, in fact. He seems rather proud of the way he's manipulated people in this town for years, especially those closest to him. Tommy, Mona, Beth Driscoll. Me most of all, I think. I can't believe I never saw the real Nathan. I trusted him. I always thought he had my back."

"He fooled a lot of people," Jack said. "He knew as

soon as he made that call to me, I'd come back here
to search for Anna's killer. He played me, too, Olive."

"He did say one thing that I think you should know.
Jack…" She put her hand on his arm. "Anna never
cheated on you with Tommy. Nathan saw her tattoo
that night on the bridge when he tore off her clothes.
He made up the story about Tommy's 'mark' so that
you would go after him even harder."

"What about Jamie Butaud's tattoo? He didn't make
that up. I saw the autopsy report."

"No, but he manipulated her into getting a similar
tattoo. Even then, he was laying the groundwork to
frame Tommy. The heart tattoos connected the vic-
tims. Or maybe Nathan just got a sick thrill out of seeing Anna's tattoo on Jamie Butaud. I don't know. But
Tommy wasn't innocent. He could have stopped Anna's
murder. He could have been faithful to Beth instead of
having an affair with Mona Sutton and then later going
after a troubled young woman like Jamie. He made it
too easy for Nathan. I guess we all did." Olive paused,
tucking a strand of hair behind her ear. "I just wanted
you to know about Anna."

Jack touched his knuckles to her cheek.

"Jack?"

"Yes?"

"Nathan said that Tommy hired Marc Waller to come
after me."

"He thought he could somehow control Nathan by
threatening you."

"That explains the incident in front of the coffee
shop, but who was in the dark sedan that almost ran
me down before you got to town?"

"Could have been Waller, then, too, or Beth Driscoll.

She drives a dark sedan and she had an ax to grind. She'll deny it, of course, but I wouldn't be surprised if she's always known the truth about Anna. Or at least suspected."

"Mona must have suspected, too. I have to wonder if it was Tommy in her office the other day trying to coerce her into remaining silent."

"Maybe it was the other way around," Jack said.

"Another maybe," Olive said with a faint smile. "Will we ever know the whole truth?"

"One can hope. Nathan's trial should prove interesting."

"What happens in the meantime?"

"He'll be incarcerated once he's released from the hospital. After everything he's done, he won't get bail."

"That's not what I meant." Olive paused. "I mean what happens to us? You and me. School will be starting soon and you'll be heading back to Houston. After everything we've been through, do we just say goodbye?"

His gaze deepened. "What do you want to happen, Olive?"

"I don't know," she answered truthfully. "I know I don't want you to leave town."

"Even if I plan to come back?"

"For the trial, you mean."

"Before that." Jack stared out over the water for a moment. "I've decided to hang on to the cabin. I'll need a place to stay when the trial starts, and in the meantime, I can drive up on weekends and holidays. Maybe you can come down to Houston now and then."

"Are you suggesting a long-distance relationship?"

"For now. Until we can sort things out. I care about

you, Olive. I may even be falling in love with you." He brought her hand to his lips. "I don't want to lose you."

"I don't want to lose you, either." She entwined her fingers with his and squeezed his hand.

"Olive?"

"Yes?"

"Don't let go, okay?"

She smiled. "Not a chance."

* * * * *

MILLS & BOON®

INTRIGUE
Romantic Suspense

A SEDUCTIVE COMBINATION OF DANGER AND DESIRE

A sneak peek at next month's titles...

In stores from 19th October 2017: